ALSO BY L. C. CHU, WRITING AS LILY CHU

The Stand-In
The Comeback
The Takedown
Drop Dead

LIBRARY

FLOWERS

L. C. CHU

Published by Sourcebooks Landmark, an imprint of Sourcebooks
1935 Brookdale RD, Naperville, IL 60563-2773
(630) 961-3900
sourcebooks.com

Cataloging-in-Publication Data is on file with the Library of Congress.

Printed and bound in the United States of America.
LSC 10 9 8 7 6 5 4 3 2 1

For my mother, Mui Lan

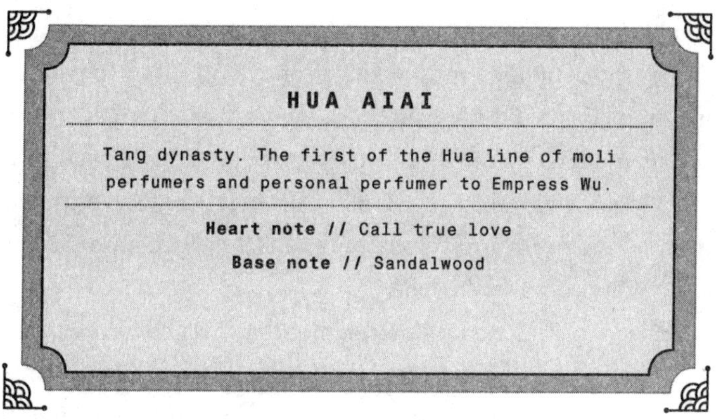

used to like being alone. I adored solitude when it meant long walks or curling up on the sofa reading under a faded quilt with a cup of lemon tea.

But over time, solitude built to loneliness, and loneliness? Loneliness sucks.

Toronto is the seventh city I've lived in since leaving Vancouver more than a decade ago. The longest I've stayed in one place was three years. That was Montreal, with its fashionable citizens and cobblestone streets so beloved by tourists looking for an authentic steak frites experience without the hassle of going overseas.

My shortest stay was Winnipeg, where the snow and I arrived

within two days of each other in mid-October. Through November, the dusty white layers climbed higher on my windowsill until they achieved the crenulated aspect of a geographic formation. In December, my nose froze shut. The barista at the coffee shop, who was the person I spoke to most, assured me it was a dry cold and I'd get used to it. I nodded politely but knew I wouldn't.

Call me a weakling, but I packed my bags and, a day and a half later, emerged, cramped and blinking, from the VIA train into the dim grandeur of Toronto's Union Station. Granite-faced commuters gripping coffee and overstuffed bags rushed around me as though I were a pillar, looking as if they could only bear to let themselves think of their pasts and futures, never their presents. I fetched my own coffee and thought I could stay awhile.

I've been in Toronto for thirteen months now and have a routine I like—and probably need more than I admit. Today, for example, I'm doing the same thing I do every two weeks, which is arrange the window display at my little perfume shop, Ile de Grasse. Well, half a perfume shop, since I share space with Auntie's Closet Vintage.

On the counter are nine fresh rosebuds, ivory petals barely exposing their crimson centers. It's a number I may have chosen unconsciously for good luck, because despite trying to slough off most of my mother's superstitious dictates, the habits and rituals of childhood remain hardwired.

As I'm about to play ikebana master, I notice a small chip on the edge of the Blue Mountain Pottery vase I'd snatched up in a thrift store, and run my finger over the rough brick-red interior. Unacceptable. Into the garbage it goes, replaced by a modern blue amphora after I confirm that it's flawless.

Once the flowers have the exact symmetrical effect I want, I carry the arrangement to the bay window. A teenage couple is making out on the sidewalk, her hands clutching his jacket and their heads bent at such unnatural angles—his down and hers up—that my own neck twinges. I restrain myself from banging on the window to startle them into fleeing like stray cats and turn my attention to organizing.

After a few moments of fussing, the display is perfect. I can depend on Ana, who owns Auntie's Closet, to leave it alone once I set it up. It had been a lucky day for me last year when I'd passed by just as Ana was placing her sign looking for a pop-up partner to share rent and help bring in more customers. The flexibility of subletting suits me much better than the legal chains of leasing my own space. Although our tastes aren't aligned—she sells exquisitely curated modern and vintage clothes and accessories, the louder the better—Ana's place suits me and, strangely, complements my more austere displays.

We have a good thing going, at least on the financial front. I make fragrances, and since Kensington Market is a tourist destination as well as a local shopping district, the people who come are ready to be seduced by a new perfume and, feeling luxurious, splurge on want-don't-need items like one of Ana's pretty scarves. And vice versa.

I'm testing a silver heart-shaped clutch in the display when the door bangs open to reveal Ana, accompanied by gusts of cold wind and the contradictory smell of a sunny beach afternoon. She stomps her boots on the brown coir welcome mat, careful to remove the gray-ish slush that blankets the ground outside. We mop at least four times a day in the winter to stop the industrial road salt from eating through our floors, swabbing with a huge janitorial mop that's as stringy as a bad witch's wig. The floors were painted in the fall, a turquoise Ana adores that reminds me of a 1950s swimming pool. I'd wanted a nice chestnut stain to bring out the natural wood but lost the coin toss.

"Hi, Ana." I test the soil of my gardenia plant. My counter is painted the same off-white as the rest of Ana's fixtures, and the var-iegated green of my plants looks influencer-good against the neutral background. They're accompanied by rows of my fragrances in their slim obsidian bottles, lined up with the precision of a championship marching band.

"Hi, yourself." Satisfied with the state of her boots, Ana adjusts the mat, which inexplicably bears the image of a chinchilla and reads "Just chinchillin.'"

"I changed the display," I say.

"I noticed. It screams, 'Valentine's Day is a capitalist venture that encourages the consumption of material goods as a proxy for affection, but since you have to do it, better buy something cool.'"

"That's what I was going for."

"Then achievement unlocked." She strides across the room and leans over to shove her neck close enough for my nose to squish tight against her chilled skin. "Smell me."

"Tempting, but I'll pass." I step back to rub my face. "Remember we talked about those pesky things called boundaries?" It had been a necessary conversation because Ana's love languages are extremely touchy touch and open, honest communication. My love language is evasion.

Ana adjusts the fluffy brown bangs that peek out from her hot-pink beret, which she insists on calling raspberry. "I have a new perfume. You make perfume. I want your opinion."

"I can't smell it when you suffocate me like that. Also, shouldn't you ask before you spend a hundred and thirty-seven dollars plus tax for thirty milliliters, and not after?"

"That was a fearsomely accurate price guess." Ana's huge hazel eyes widen enough for me to see the whites. "How did you know?"

"Because this is my job, and you are very obviously wearing Plage by Lafayette. Which, by the way, is unseasonable. It's a summer marine fragrance, designed to evoke the scent of ocean water and sand." I finish dusting the leaves of my jasmine. I love white flowers with distinctive scents. Give me a powerful tuberose or sweet orange blossom any day. "On you, there's also a hint of draft beer that I don't recall being part of its fragrance profile."

"The Molson Export is bottled, not draft, and it's all me. So's the sweat."

"Wow."

"Jayne's bar sells twenty-dollar cocktails," she says earnestly. "I'd go broke if I drank them every day, and Molson is the least fancy beer she has. She'll think I'm cheap if I don't get anything."

Ana's gold tooth glints when she speaks. Compared to my standard black V-neck sweater and dark jeans, her look is as eclectic as her part of the store. Today she's decked out in mustard crushed-velvet leggings with an oversize green hoodie that comes to her knees and reads "Fred's Gas 'n Go." Always on brand, she's wound a gold-sequined cord around her waist for a belt and puffed out the bottom of the sweatshirt like a mushroom. Little disco balls hang off the ends of the cord and bounce when she moves.

"That wouldn't be a problem if you were girlfriends. Like you want to be." I'm not psychic; Ana has no filter when it comes to talking about her life. I don't mind, so long as she lets me be quiet about mine. "It's nice you have a crush."

"Crush, smush. This is love, I'm telling you." She looks distant. "I remember my first crush."

"Yeah?" Sometimes conversations with Ana are only a matter of adding in the occasional word.

"His name was Marcus. He had brown hair and was good at soccer," she reminisces. "Then Kimmy moved to our town, and *she* had brown hair and was good at soccer. It's also when I realized I liked boys and girls."

I look over. "What happened?"

"My personal epiphany aside, Marcus and Kimmy got together at the grade 8 dance. Let me just say, they did not leave room for the Holy Spirit."

"What did you do?"

"To drown my sorrows, I chugged so much McDonald's orange drink that I threw up neon sludge all over the girls' bathroom. How about your past mistakes?"

"I haven't had a crush since I was a teenager." I suppose my voice says more than I want it to, because Ana looks at me, her blue-lined eyes troubled.

"Oops, I didn't mean to pry."

It's been a long time since I thought of Rafe, but as always, the memories shove past my mental barriers.

It was a classic storybook crush. I fell for him when we were thirteen and had been shooed out of the house where our parents were talking, under the assumption that all kids the same age must be friends. He trailed after me to the beach and showed me a sea star, looking at it with a gentle, unabashed wonder that made me realize boys didn't have to be mean to be cool.

That was all it took. I was in love. I was in love for years. We hung out and read books and watched movies, and each moment was special because we were together and he was my best friend.

Then, when I was twenty, it was all over.

I laugh and pack thoughts of Rafe back into the mental suitcase I use to drag my emotional baggage to each new home. One day I'll have the courage to forget it in a closet. "I'm only upset you're wearing a summer scent in the winter."

As expected, this derails her from exploring my love life. "You're such a stick-in-the-mud, with your rules about seasons and what's appropriate when."

"I don't make the rules."

"Au contraire, you love rules. But a free spirit comme moiself—"

"That's the worst French I've ever heard."

"—*moiself* knows there's no better time for a beach scent than days when it gets dark at five in the evening. C'mon, Lucy. Tell me what you think."

This time, when she leans in as if offering her jugular to a vampire, I close my eyes to lose myself in the fragrance. I'd smelled it in the store on one of my regular surveys of new scents. It's always good to track trends. Although I hadn't been impressed at the time, on Ana,

Plage melts into a charming softness. A hit of tiare adds depth to the creamy coconut, conjuring up the scent of freshly applied sunscreen, which is layered with marine and shot through with the sea spray of calone.

"It suits you," I say. "Good choice."

"Correct answer." Ana shakes out her shoulder-length curls from her hat.

"Why did you ask if you were already sure?"

"I'm psychologically weak and crave validation." On her way to hang up her coat in the back, she lights one of my candles, which will eventually fill the space with lush ripe fig and black currant touched with cedar. "By the way, those Duran Duran 'Reflex'–era lace gloves you hate? I sold four pairs today."

"I don't hate them," I say, noting a small blemish in my ballet-pink nail polish. I hide my hands behind my back. "I said they were retro monstrosities that I wouldn't be caught dead in."

"Which reminds me: A package came for you before I left. Sorry, I totally forgot."

"What about the gloves reminded you of a package?"

Ana ignores me as she shoves aside a pile of neon corsets to put the box on a display table. "It's from Vancouver."

My mood plummets as I regard it warily. The box has been wrapped and double-taped along every seam with the same fastidiousness a drug mule would use to hide a brick of cocaine from sniffer dogs. Except...that name. Written over the original recipient of the battered packing box, the shaky black script reads *Hua Luling, Jle de Grasse Perfumery.*

Not "Lucy Hua."

Ana joins me. "Luling. Pretty. Is that your real name?"

A cold sweat breaks out over my back. I keep my answer safe and my voice polite but distant. "I prefer Lucy."

"The return address is to Hua Yulan."

"My grandmother." Waipo never uses my chosen English name.

Ana gives me a sharp look. "That's from your family? You don't talk about them much."

"No." I have a lengthy list of topics I don't consider anyone's business, and my family is the undisputed holder of position number two.

Not the number one spot, though. That's reserved for the secret that is 49 percent of the reason why I'm currently shivering in the Toronto snow instead of the Vancouver rain.

My mother is the other 51 percent.

I contemplate the box. Waipo has rarely contacted me since I left, and isn't the type for care packages, so chances are good it's not warm socks or homemade brownies. What could she possibly need to send? I hover in the liminal zone between curious and concerned, the two intersecting waves forcing each other higher as they drag my growing unease along for the ride.

I extend my hand and Ana slaps a box cutter in my palm with a flourish, her ragged but glittery nails tapping against my damp skin.

Two slashes of the blade later, I realize impatience has consequences. I should have taken the package home to open because Ana will have questions I'll have to answer or risk damaging the pleasant rhythm of our business relationship. It's too late now. Ana bends over from the other side of the table, wafting the languid afternoon of Plage in my direction as I pull apart the meticulously folded white tissue.

Ana whistles. "That's old. Is it a first edition? No wonder I had to sign for it."

It's a book not meant for any eyes other than a Hua woman's, and I instinctively cover it up again. Ana's right: The book is old—from the 1920s—but what's older is the information it contains. In that box is my family's precious register, a list of fragrance formulae, notes, and personal histories, handed down to each eldest daughter and kept in the possession of the oldest Hua woman in the direct line.

Since that's Waipo, not me, it should be safe across the country, instead of here in Toronto. My heart already knows what my head refuses to accept, and my breath shallows out as it catapults me into the cold chill of truth.

I stare at the box and do my best not to hyperventilate as Ana's worried questions drift over me. My phone rings, piercing through the rush in my ears. It's my mother, and for the first time since I left Vancouver, I answer without hesitation.

"Luling?" Mom's voice wavers through the phone. "Luling."

"I'm here." I think I say it, but I'm not sure.

"Luling," she says again. "I have bad news. It's your grandmother."

Despite Ana's gaze, I pull back the tissue again to float my shaking fingers over the book. The brown leather corners have worn and faded to a pale sand. A few scratches score the front cover, embossed with a golden stylized peony, and the leather is patterned with darker blots from the fingers of busy women who gripped it with the loving, casual carelessness of familiarity.

It's as fat as a sleeping cat on a rainbow pile of Ana's chiffon scarves, and it's my birthright and my curse.

"I know," I say to the book, my mother eavesdropping on the phone. "Waipo's gone."

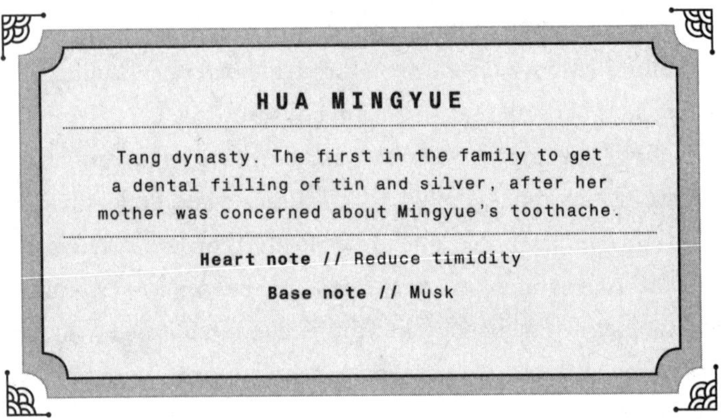

've been in Vancouver for twenty-three hours and seven minutes—I know because I'm counting every second—and it's become clear that if there was a national championship for "most awful person," I would be a worthy contender. Forget regional or national; I could make the grade on the global stage.

The competition would start with Selfish and Neglectful Daughter. I can hear the commentators now:

Commentator 1: Lucy Hua has been a strong fan favorite in this event, ever since she deserted her family to live her own life without considering the impact this would have on anyone else.

Commentator 2: You know, Jennifer, we thought Lucy—and I'll add here that her mother hates that she doesn't use her given name of Luling—

Jennifer: That's a few more points on the board, Martin.

Martin: Absolutely. Going back to what I was saying, we thought Lucy had her title sewn up during the Lunar New Year visit from several years ago.

Jennifer: That's right, when she stomped out of a crowded dim sum restaurant because her mother had the nerve to ask what her plans were. Note the strategic use of a public setting to maximize impact.

Martin: Her brother, Eric, was not impressed, although the judges were mesmerized—especially when she kicked over her grandmother's cane on the way out.

Jennifer: Apparently an "accident," but the entire meal was classic Lucy. This is something we've come to expect from a competitor of this caliber.

Martin: It's all the more impressive since Hua Meilin was a devoted daughter to her own mother. Not a lot of role-modeling was available for Lucy, who was forced to go out and learn to be an absolute ass all on her own.

Jennifer: Now, with the death of her mother, Meilin is clearly worried about the family legacy.

Martin: Yet Lucy's expertly setting her up for a Big Disappointment, one of the compulsory elements in this competition, of course, along with Taking Everything Personally and Avoiding Hard Conversations.

Jennifer: Where Lucy has a major advantage is in our current event, Horrible Granddaughter.

Martin: I agree. Lucy had a disappointing performance at the actual funeral ceremony, where she made the unusual error of showing affection to her mother.

Jennifer: Only nonverbally, however, and through a stiff one-armed hug, thus limiting the damage.

Martin: The judges will hopefully take that into consideration. She'll have a chance to make up ground here at the reception.

Jennifer: Oh, look! This is it, Martin, the Lucy we know and despise. Here she is, at her own grandmother's funeral, and she's not thinking about her waipo at all. Not sparing a single thought for all the times Hua Yulan brushed her hair and dressed it in the same braids she herself wore as a child. She's forgetting those happy moments as a little girl when Yulan let her sit to calm herself by watching her work.

Martin: She's not sparing a single regret for the heartbreak she caused her grandmother when she left.

Jennifer: Not contemplating the fragility of life and the preciousness of family.

Martin: Or noticing the lines on her mother's face and wondering how much more time they'll have together. Instead, she's thinking about...

Jennifer: A man. There we have it, Martin! Lucy is back in fighting fashion. Watch out, competitors!

I'm on my third circuit of the room, black pants dragging on the industrial carpet since I brought flats instead of heels, when I realize, to my absolute disgust, that my heart leaps every time I glimpse a tall man. It infuriates me that I'm thinking about Rafe. But the grief for my grandmother burned fast and bright before settling into an emptiness I'm not sure how to deal with and am doing my best to ignore.

My mother comes up to halt my progress, tidy in her black suit, her short salt-and-pepper hair tucked behind her ears. Her eyes are clear, because if she cries, it's never in front of me. We both smell of lemon, Waipo's favored scent. Mom's is mixed with vanilla for a comforting, warm aura, while mine is sharp and spiky thanks to black peppercorn. I know without asking that, like me, Mom formulated her perfume specifically for today, and neither of us will wear them again. She glances at my too-long pants. She already asked twice why I didn't bring appropriate shoes to my own grandmother's funeral.

Before I can say anything, she moves aside to reveal the woman behind her.

"Luling, I'm sure you remember Ms. Kang."

In a blink, I'm twenty years old again because I remember Ms. Kang perfectly. She was my first client and witness to my immediate failure as a Hua perfumer.

I had done my best to not think about who was in this room to honor my grandmother. Among her remaining friends and our business contacts are trusted patrons who know the Huas as more than just the family who run Yixiang Parfums. These are people whose ancestral memories include our glory days.

They remember that we're witches.

That's not a direct English translation for what we are, but it's close enough. For a thousand years, Hua women have been able to control emotions with our magical moli fragrances. My mother, for instance, has the power to lift moods. Not much, but enough to make the days of those who wear her perfumes about 10 percent happier. It's a nice little boost, like catching the bus when it's about to pull away in the rain or receiving an unexpected compliment. My grandmother's moli perfume kept bad tempers in check. Mid-century women clamored for it to use on their husbands. My great-grandmother's gift stopped heartache. Everyone desired that.

Our most guarded secret, the one known only to the top echelon of our most select clients, like Ms. Kang, is that the eldest daughter of every fifth generation has the power to summon one's true love. It's no small pressure to have the ability to create a perfume that will lure in the love of someone's life, ostensibly the reason for their greatest happiness.

I am the fifth daughter.

That's my gift.

Or it should have been.

I don't know if it was my older brother's silent but palpable gloating, my grandmother's unreserved disbelief, or Mom's grim-faced encouragement that hurt the most when Ms. Kang remained stubbornly single week after week. At least I didn't have to worry about Dad's reaction, because he insists the entire moli thing is superstitious bull. That stung in a different way, but it was one I was used to.

"I'm very sorry," Ms. Kang says now. "Your grandmother was an exceptional person."

She leans in with no more than a light hand on my shoulder to graze our cheeks together, but I stiffen despite the gentle touch. I know the scent that rises from her skin—a delicate, contradictory thing of cold incense smoke with a base of warm tonka bean. Twelve years ago, my mother had approved it with a single nod, causing the fireworks that went off in my chest to puff it out with pride.

Ms. Kang is wearing the failed moli perfume I gave her. I close my eyes, overcome by a brief dizziness.

"Luling." My mother's voice is sharp.

"That perfume," I say.

Ms. Kang beams at me over her sober navy dress. "I thought you might recognize it. I only wear it on my most special occasions. It smells just as good now as the first day I put it on."

"Like for a wedding?" I blurt out. I have to know. I *need* to know. Is it possible that my perfume worked, even after all these years? That she found true love? Surely Mom would have told me if she'd known. I force myself back to the floor because I've risen onto my toes.

Ms. Kang laughs. "Oh, no. No weddings for me. But I had it on when I met my daughter for the first time. I wore it the day I moved into my dream house and when I signed the incorporation papers for my business. Beautiful, lucky times."

My heart deflates. No...that would be a slow and steady action. My chest has been stomped on. My perfume is nothing but a celebratory scent, no different from Plage or thousands of others Ms. Kang could have selected off the shelf. There's no magic to it. There never has been. I remain a flop, although it's a good thing to have created a scent for Ms. Kang that she found meaningful. She's kind to linger on the positives and must have found ways to enjoy life despite my inability to deliver her true love.

Mom gives me a piercing look that communicates her desire for me to get it together instead of shaming her by breaking down in front of strangers. "Scent is the strongest emotional trigger," she says.

Ms. Kang nods. "Even in the midst of our grief, I'm connected to all of those other, more joyous moments. I should thank you, Luling. You made the olfactory accompaniment to every peak in my life."

Except love, which is what it was meant to do. That was my purpose and my duty, and sometimes I think it's the only reason my mother had me.

"Her grandmother expected more," Mom says. I can feel my lips tighten. Only Mom can fit in a dig about my failure at a funeral. I refuse to give her the satisfaction of a response, and the two women move on.

I turn toward the food, grateful for a break. Instead of a long sit-down meal, my mother opted for an open buffet to cater to the mix of guests. Crustless funeral sandwiches share space with steamed dumplings plump with shrimp and dotted with bright-green chives. Candies sit in bowls. The scent of the food covers the faint smell of incense and smoke from the joss papers burned during the ceremony.

"Hello, Luling."

My hand stills midreach for the steamed buns. The one minute, *one minute*, I stop scanning the room for Rafe Jin, he appears. The years have been unfairly good to him, and I take in the changes with a glance that I hope is more subtle than it probably is. As a teenager, he'd been tall and lanky, not quite sure what to do with his limbs. At thirty-two, he's grown into his eyes and nose. His dark hair is longer and falls in tidy waves around his face.

"Rafe. It's been a long time." I can't keep my eyes from drifting down to his left hand to note he's not wearing a ring.

"Luling, dear." Missy Jin moves her son aside to come hug me, the elegance of her gray outfit emphasized by the understated pearl jewelry decorating her ears and wrists. The Jins have always had far more money than my family, a situation that would occasionally lead my mother to comment that Missy Jin's new car or necklace was fine for her, but a little tacky for her own taste. Despite that, they were each other's closest friends.

"You have our deepest sympathy," says Ms. Jin, holding my hands in hers and looking into my face. "My, you haven't changed. You still look just like your mother."

I've always liked Ms. Jin, but I haven't spoken to her since Rafe and I... Well, there's not really a word for what happened. *Grew apart* is too organic, and *split* is untrue since we weren't together. *Stopped talking* is the most accurate, but fails to encompass the depth of how I feel.

Felt. How I felt.

"I remember when your grandmother used to bring us cut fruit in the summer." Rafe's voice has always been quiet, and although it's gained in resonance, his volume hasn't changed. "In the pink bowl."

This is an appropriate thing to say, although I hate him a bit for bringing up a shared memory when I want to forget that a *we* ever existed. "Thank you." My face refuses to fake a smile.

"Your mother tells me your shop is doing well," says Ms. Jin. "How wonderful for you—although I'm sure she'd love you to come back home."

The Jins have been moli clients of ours for generations, and Missy sought out my mother when she'd moved to Vancouver. After I'd left home, Mom concocted a story about how she'd generously allowed me to take time to follow my own craft before joining her to take my proper place as a Hua daughter. The lie hid the fact that I had no moli, and saved my pride, and hers.

I chat with Missy Jin as Rafe looks on without speaking. When I was younger, I had hugely gratifying fantasies about seeing Rafe again and what I'd say when I did. All of them resulted in a triumphant Lucy staring down a chastised Rafe, who would beg for forgiveness I wouldn't grant. This gave me a lot of solace, until one day it did nothing but leave me drained. I'd burned out on the witty, cutting things I'd pictured saying and on those scenarios that kept him alive in my mind. Slowly, the embers cooled, although the relief it brought was the release that came with being able to accept the pain, not from the disappearance of pain itself.

His crime had been relatively minor in the grand scheme of life. I know this. He was my first kiss. The Jins had come over to our house the day before they left for their annual trip to visit family in China. Rafe and I escaped as usual into the back garden, while our parents complained about the exchange rate and Dad joked about Mom working too hard in the store.

I was twenty, and so was Rafe, and I'd been telling him my news. "Mom says it's time to pick the date for my moli ceremony," I said, and I remember bouncing with excitement for my life to really begin.

Rafe nodded as I talked, and when I shivered from the damp, he wrapped his arm around me in a way that felt...different. I looked up and he looked down, and neither of us spoke.

As we stood in the misty garden in the shadow of the dark pines, my eyes went to his mouth. Perhaps if I'd been watching his eyes, I would have saved myself a world of heartbreak. I might have seen the warning to step back and away. Instead, I gathered my courage to do what I'd wanted to do for years.

I kissed him.

It was nothing more than my dry lips pressed on his, but those few seconds, brief but infinite, made me feel like I wasn't alone in the desire that had been with me for so long it was like a phantom limb, aching and impossible to soothe.

Or so I thought—until he put his hands on my shoulders and

leaned away. "I'm sorry, Lucy," he said, eyes moving from my face to somewhere past my shoulder. "I don't think this is a good idea."

"What? Why?"

He stepped back, hands running through his hair. "There's no room for me in your life right now."

"Sure there is."

"No, look how busy you are. That ceremony is all you've been talking about for days."

I was the one to move away then. "Because it's a big deal?"

"I know it is."

"Rafe—"

He wouldn't let me finish, his words like an avalanche, fast and relentless. "I'm sorry. I thought I could handle this. I'm happy for you, I swear, but all I can think about is that I like how we are right now. I don't want things to change."

The shaking that came from deep inside caused my teeth to chatter. "You mean you don't want *me* to change."

He kept shaking his head until I wanted to reach out and hold him still. "It's not you, it's me. What you have is so big it casts a shadow over everything. I look at your dad and your brother and I'm worried I'll end up the same—bitter and left out."

"Don't talk about my family like that." It was true, though, and my stomach clenched in humiliation that he'd noticed.

"I'm sorry. I don't want to hurt you, but you should be with someone who can support you in the way you deserve. I don't think I can be that guy."

He might have had more to say, but I'd heard enough. I don't think I ran back to the house, but I must have, because I remember panting as I reached the door. He was the person I thought I could count on no matter what, who would accept me for what I was—and he hadn't.

Dinner was spent in a cold bath of shame and confusion as I sat across from him. His bergamot-and-tobacco smell—one of my experiments he'd claimed for his own the second he smelled it on me six months before—lingered in my nose, and I felt smaller and sadder each time Rafe's gaze snapped down to his fork to avoid my own.

He left without a word, following his parents out the door to a chorus of best wishes for safe travel. The next day, the Jins left the country. Rafe didn't call to say goodbye, and pride prevented me from contacting him first. The chance of another devastating rejection was too intense for me to bear. After nights tossing and turning and wondering if my moli was only an excuse—Maybe I smelled? Or I was too desperate? Too ugly?—the mortification slowly transformed into resentment.

There was no room for him in my life? That was a lie. He didn't want me to change and grow. He wanted to keep me at his level instead of seeing how far I could go. Screw him. If that was the kind of person he was, I didn't need him. At all.

This was enough to drive me back to my work. It was time to choose my huo symbol and create my first moli perfume. I would take my rightful place in the great pantheon of talented Hua women, and I didn't need Rafe to do it.

I spent hours sitting with my mother and grandmother in the laboratory, doing my best to not relive that moment in the garden when everything had changed. They told me stories of scents they'd made and kept me busy with tests—create the smell of dry grass before a wildfire, blend these accords together to make something new—all in preparation of me becoming a worthy addition to our line. The gift of the fifth daughters has always been the most lucrative, by orders of magnitude. It was up to me to bring about a reinvigorated Hua family, backed by wealth and its analog, power. It was up to me to earn the money to properly invest in Yixiang. That was what I needed to focus on. Not a boy or my hurt feelings. I had a responsibility to fulfill.

Then I was the first Hua woman to fail in a thousand years. I couldn't measure up to the expectations of my own family, the same way I hadn't been enough, or possibly too much, for Rafe.

"I should let you go," says Ms. Jin now. She smiles. "Try to get some rest, and call if you or your mother need us."

She turns away, and Rafe looks like he wants to say something. Out of the corner of my eye, I see Kelsey waving, and as he opens his mouth, I say, "Excuse me, my sister-in-law needs me."

I don't look back.

3

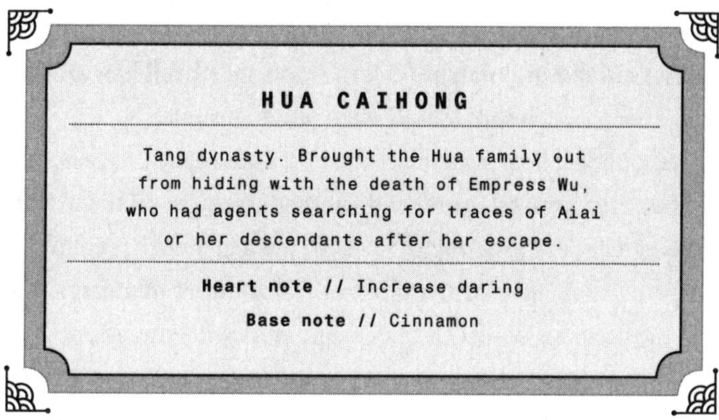

slowly circle back to the buffet, mechanically answering the people who stop me to share their condolences. A deep shakiness fills my bones that could be due to too much stress, too little food, or excessive caffeine. Kelsey waves at me again, this time more aggressively, so I give in to the inevitable and take my plate of sandwiches to the corner she's colonized with her children. My niece, Sophie, and her little brother, Owen, are curled up on the leather couch, playing on various devices.

"It's a long day for kids," says Kelsey when she tracks my gaze. "I usually limit their screen time."

I shrug, not caring in the least. If anything, I'm jealous they get to withdraw into their digital worlds. I don't know Kelsey very well, as she and Eric met after I left Vancouver, but my mother's politesse is indication enough that Kelsey isn't her favorite person. Their relationship isn't helped by the fact that my mother is suspicious of anyone coming close to the family. When they first started to get serious, she made Eric promise not to tell Kelsey about our moli. I'd been home on a rare visit and had never seen him so angry.

"What makes you think she'd care?" he snapped. "It's not like it's going to affect my kids if we have any. You made it clear enough growing up that I wasn't part of this."

"That's unfair and untrue." Mom stood to her full height, which brought her to Eric's shoulder. "I want you to promise."

"Jesus, do you hear yourself? Trust me when I say I have no plans to tell her. Her family doesn't need another reason to think I'm different. Being Chinese is enough." He shot me a glance that could have been either malicious or triumphant. "Not that it matters, since it seems the precious so-called Hua magic ends with you, Mom. Right, Lucy?"

I'm returned to the present by Sophie, who spies the plate in my hand and rises to her knees on the couch, digging her shoes into the cushions. "Mama, I'm hungry."

Kelsey smiles. "I'm sure your aunt won't mind sharing."

I do mind, as I haven't eaten since last night, but dutifully hand over the plate. Sophie pokes her finger into each of the sandwiches I stacked into a perfect pyramid, before making a face. "I want chocolate."

Kelsey glances over at me, her pale eyebrows raised as she hands back the plate, and I sigh.

When I return, it's with a plate overflowing with cakes and cookies, which I put down in front of the kids as Kelsey's lips thin. "That's a lot of sugar," she says.

"Is it?" I ask innocently.

She lowers her voice as the kids fight viciously over the single chocolate cupcake I included. "How much longer do you think this will last? Eric wasn't sure."

Although I'm also dying for today to end, coming from Kelsey, the question rubs me the wrong way. "I suppose as long as it takes for people to finish paying their respects." I try to keep my tone neutral.

"Right, of course," she says. "I'm glad to have caught you. I have a favor to ask."

"You do?" This gets my full attention, and I turn to face her. Kelsey is blond, and her natural freckles have been transformed into indistinct blotches under a thick mat of foundation. Her dark-burgundy dress—*red*, Mom muttered to me as she walked in, her tone saying everything—is tight under the arms and across the hips. Her hand keeps drifting down to yank it into a more comfortable fit.

"I'm sure Eric told you I've gone back to work," she says. "With the kids in school, I want to start exploring my personal growth through my career. Owen, don't hit your sister."

Eric hadn't told me, but it's not like we talk. "You were in banking before you had kids, weren't you?" I ask.

"Yes, but I wanted a change to something more creative. I'm doing luxury gift bags for special events. Very exclusive."

"Oh?" I look out at the crowd. On the other side of the room, my mother is speaking to a man who was one of Waipo's first clients, his back bent almost horizontal over his cane and his still-full white hair styled razor-sharp.

"It's not one of those pyramid schemes," Kelsey says.

"Of course," I say in surprise. "I wouldn't think it was."

"It's a young company with a lot of room for growth," she says. "Owen, what did I say? Sophie, stop annoying your brother." The kids ignore her.

"That's great about the job," I say.

"I knew you'd be supportive." Her dusty-rose lipstick has worn to a ring around the edges of her mouth. "I'd love for you to supply some samples of your perfume."

I stare at her, the dinging of some game coming from the couch, and she mistakes my look for interest instead of shock that she's trying to do business at Waipo's funeral.

"It's a good opportunity for you to build awareness for your little shop. We have an extremely discerning clientele for the luxury gift bags," she says. "I was thinking of asking your mother, but when I mentioned it to Eric, he said you needed it more."

"I bet he did," I mutter, wondering how many times she can say *luxury gift bags*. Well, Kelsey is family. "Email me the details, and we can work out a discount rate."

"Discount?" Her smile fades. "I thought you would do it for the visibility. Sophie, watch your brother. We supplied the Trantor Art Gallery opening, and the bridesmaid-proposal boxes and gift bags for Olivia Carlwood's wedding. This is a chance for you to get your product in front of people who matter."

I have no idea what or who those are, but I do know I don't have the capacity to negotiate this at my grandmother's funeral. "We can talk when you send me the details," I say firmly. "Oh, excuse me, there's someone I should speak to."

"Sure, sure. This is a great turnout," she says. "I'll be in touch."

I slip away and am in the corner eating a tasteless sandwich, the edges of the bread already drying out, when my brother comes up. "Lot of people," Eric says.

It's the third time he's said a variation of this since the event started, so I only nod.

"She left everything to Mom," he continues, eyes scanning the room. "Not a penny to you or me."

I don't want to talk about this here, but if I shush him in any way, Eric will go ballistic. It's easier to play along.

"Kind of to be expected, don't you think?" I ask.

"I need the money."

"We all need money."

"Yeah, but I'm the one with actual responsibilities."

I ignore that. "There wasn't much," I remind him. "It mostly went into Yixiang to support the business."

"Like everything in this fucking family."

"Not cool, Eric."

"Hey, I tell it like it is."

Maybe I can keep my temper by reminding myself that grief is causing him to act out like this. "Most of the value of her estate was in the heirlooms. The Qianlong vase is worth thousands."

"*Was* worth." He plucks the white chocolate macadamia-nut cookie off my plate and stuffs the whole thing in his mouth. He's always stolen my food.

"What do you mean, was?"

"It's gone."

My head whips up. "Your kids broke a 250-year-old family treasure?"

Eric glares at me. "My kids? Why do you assume my kids broke it?"

I glance over to where they're kicking at each other on the couch while Kelsey stares at her phone. "Huh, I don't know."

He takes a deep breath—deliberately, so I know it's entirely my fault if he loses his temper. "You know where that vase went? Mom sold it."

A cream puff falls off my plate when I jerk it up in surprise. "She what?"

"She sold it to pay rent on the store."

"The store. Yixiang? Why didn't Dad help?"

"Have you thought maybe Dad is tired of supporting Mom's hobby?"

I want to slap his self-righteous face. "You know it's not a hobby. That's her job. She owns a business."

"It's barely bringing in enough to support itself. That counts as a hobby in my book."

"Eric."

"Looks like you're the one left out of the loop this time." My brother grins at me, and despite the artificial brightness of his teeth, it's as cold as the ocean water that laps at the city. "Dad lost all his money, and Mom used what she'd saved to expand Yixiang to pay their mortgage and the store rent instead. When that wasn't enough—buh-bye, vase."

"You're lying." My reply is automatic, though. Eric would do a lot of things to irritate me, but making up a story like this is a stretch.

"Too bad someone couldn't cut it as the super-special super-daughter savior of the Huas," he says as a parting shot. "Then we'd have that one-of-a-kind vase for my son to inherit. Mom might even be able to keep her store six months from now. God knows she loves it more than us."

He leaves me there with a plate of crumbs, and instinctively I search the room, this time looking for my mother instead of Rafe. I've always been under the impression the shop made money, and if sales of regular perfumes were stalling, the astronomically expensive moli scents covered the difference. I didn't account for the fact that I'm not creating, and Waipo stopped making perfumes, both moli and regular, years ago. The store's revenue must have been drastically diminished.

The Huas have kept a store since Hua Zhengyi opened the first one in Nanjing over a hundred years ago. My mother and grand-mother dreamed about the money to expand Yixiang into the real-life version of Waipo's aspirational pencil sketch, framed and sitting in their lab. If Mom not only couldn't expand but also had to sell Yixiang, it would devastate her. Eric wasn't exaggerating how much she loves that place.

Dad crosses my field of vision and disappears through a door. I follow, needing confirmation but also hoping he'll assure me it's not that bad.

"Is it true?" I demand when I catch up to him, heart hammering.

We're in the corridor leading to the kitchen and the smell of old food sits in the stale air, ghostly celebrations for the dead.

"Lucy?" He glances down as he adjusts his blue tie. His brown eyes are bloodshot, as if he hasn't been sleeping. "What's going on?"

I don't bother to hint around, since my father prides himself on being a straight-talker. "Eric told me you're in debt and Mom will have to sell the store."

"Eric is blowing things out of proportion." Dad shoves his hands in his pockets, and the light glints off the new gray in his hair. "You know your mother would never sell the store."

"Then you have no money issues. None. At all."

He takes out his hands to adjust his tie again. "There's nothing for you to worry about. A few investments were made that didn't pan out, but it's nothing serious."

"Investments?"

"Eric came across an opportunity. It was the right decision, but sometimes unexpected things happen and no one can be blamed." He gives my shoulder a squeeze that feels more warning than loving. "We're fine. Worry about yourself."

With that, he turns away to head back to the reception. I watch him go. So Eric lost money as well. That must be why Kelsey is going back to work, however much she dresses it up as her own choice. I decide to send her the perfume samples for free.

I go back to the main room, which is emptying out as people put my grandmother out of their minds and return to their lives. My mother's calm voice comes from my right, sounding for all the world like her old self, not a woman struggling with debt and death and a failing dream. "Luling, let me introduce you to Henry Lai, one of..."

I smile at the man as I wonder how serious the money issue is. I can't help; I only bring in enough for my rent and supplies for Ile de Grasse. The one way I could contribute—by creating moli perfumes— is the one path closed to me. Moving back home? Not an option.

Jennifer: It's a unanimous decision from our judges: Lucy Hua is our champion.

Martin: She should be very proud of herself.

Jennifer: Oh, but she really shouldn't. Good night, viewers!

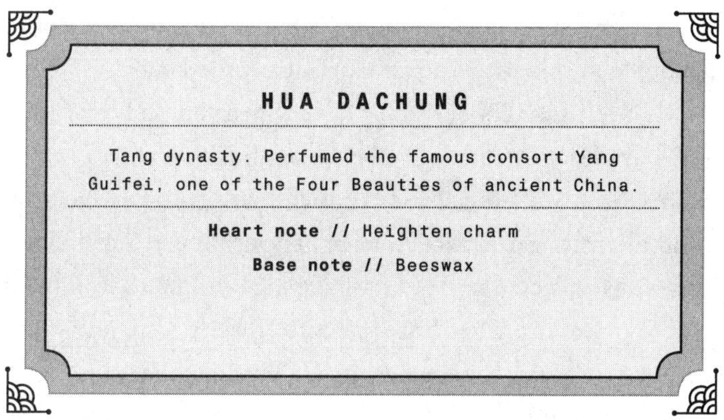

HUA DACHUNG

Tang dynasty. Perfumed the famous consort Yang Guifei, one of the Four Beauties of ancient China.

Heart note // Heighten charm
Base note // Beeswax

’ve only snuck out of the house once in my life, for a party when I was seventeen. I came home at three in the morning to find my mother sitting at the kitchen table in her quilted cotton housecoat. She didn’t say a word, but such was the power of her disillusioned expression and the accusatory bags under her tired eyes that I’d never done it again.

Until now.

It doesn’t take long to get to Yixiang Parfums in the light midnight traffic. Dad didn’t like the idea of Mom and Waipo working from the house because of the insurance cost, so the perfume lab is rigged up in the back of the store. It was a haven for me growing up, as I did my homework in the corner or sat at the table experimenting with my own scents while Mom’s soft conversation with Waipo filled the room. Eric rarely came by, but I liked it when he did. We’d compete to make up the strangest perfume names, with Mom acting as the judge. My brother almost always won.

Luckily, Mom hasn't changed the security code, so I let myself in through the back door and switch on the spot lighting over the table. Then I look around, searching for any variances between my memory and reality, like one of those find-the-differences pictures in the back of a children's magazine. There are some storage units and a new chair, but to my relief, the lab remains mostly the same.

At Ile de Grasse, I hooked up a table with a vent so I can create in a relatively safe and neutral-smelling space, but it's nothing compared to Mom's dedicated setup. Rows of brown vials sit in a huge horseshoe around a central workspace to form her perfumer's organ. Shelves with bottles collected from both the greats—Edmond Roudnitska, Dominique Ropion, Sophia Grojsman, Olivier Cresp, Jean-Claude Ellena—and up-and-coming perfume houses line the walls. I have a single shelf in our break room fridge to store more delicate ingredients, but Mom has two refrigerators.

This lab, a mainstay of my childhood, is where I would be working had life not drop-kicked me right off the field. Even moli-less, I could have been a perfumer like my mother and grandmother, building the very niche and respected Yixiang scents.

After all, it isn't bad being a Hua. Objectively, and on paper, I've been lucky. Our family's house is revered for its creativity and precise technical ability even among those who know nothing of the secret moli fragrances, and my years of perfumery training provided a marketable set of skills that started me off when I left home. There was some talk when I struck out on my own, since perfumery is a small world and an intergenerational fight makes for prime gossip. Those in the industry know my family connections and keep an eye on what I do.

But most of my clients are regular people who like good and interesting smells. Candy corn perfume is a thing thanks to me, courtesy of my Spookie Cookie Limited Edition Halloween Collection. Not a teeth-on-edge saccharine mess, though. The perfume had golden notes of caramelized sugar and champagne to evoke the smell of crushing dried maple leaves underfoot on Halloween night. I wanted the memory of kids calling *trick-or-treat*, fueled by the buzz of cheap candy and the exhilarating feeling of being out after bedtime.

If my mother would only mind her business and leave me alone, I would be entirely pleased with myself and my nongifted, apparently inadequate letdown of a life.

I put down the register I'd brought with me from Toronto—out of an atavistic need to return it to its proper home—and take a seat in Waipo's old chair. Only after I adjust the lumbar cushion does it occur to me that I've thoughtlessly changed something she'll never be able to change back. Her preferred position for that small cushion is gone forever, and gradually more and more of her will be erased from this world until nothing remains.

I reach out a shaky hand to straighten the battered notepad that sits on the corner of the desk. The list on the top sheet begins with limonene, which doesn't surprise me in the least. Waipo favors— favored—light citrus scents, and although she never would have worn perfume in the lab, it's like I can smell her preferred fragrance—a Greek lemon orchard, the sour-sweet fruit warmed by the sun and placed against the saltiness of the wild indigo sea.

Then I lower my head and let myself cry, really cry, for the first time since I unpacked that horrible book. I thought I'd been coping well, but I suppose the feeling of loss is as unpredictable as loss itself.

A few dozen deep breaths later, the hiccups fading further with each inhale, I gather my courage to open the thick register, which I've kept closed since it arrived in Toronto.

Except for the last four chapters, the writing is that of Hua Zhengyi. It's the responsibility of every fifth daughter to faithfully transcribe the work of the previous generations into a new register so the information is never lost. Fortunately, each daughter-scribe also made a point of updating archaic language and measurements, and inserting notes on changing vocabulary and dating systems, so it remains intelligible to twenty-first-century me. Since transcribing the register is a task that apparently takes years, I'll have a massive new entry for my to-do list once I start.

I flip through the pages, and it's only when I find it that I realize I was looking for a note from my grandmother. It's short, only two small characters in her signature purple ink. The first is the huo symbol that adorns all Waipo's moli bottles. It's the symbol that focused her power on the scent within, the conduit that helped transform the contents from a regular fragrance to a moli perfume. The second is my own huo symbol. I haven't used it since I left, although in dreams I trace every one of the fifteen strokes over and over until I wake up with my hands still moving.

I check the chapter where she placed it for me to find and instantly wish I hadn't. It's tucked in the section written by the last fifth daughter.

The duty of the fifth daughter is simple, Zhengyi wrote decades ago. *It is to maintain the family, like a pillar supports the vine. Others say power or fear or joy are most desirable, but I disagree. The need for love combines those and is paramount in all. The fifth daughter can offer this, and through her offering ensure the success, safety, and hope of her family. The fifth daughters are both foundation and keystone of a family which will wither without them. But they cannot exist without the family. Each nurtures the other.*

The door opens and I jump. My mother flips on the overhead fluorescents to eradicate my atmospheric puddle of light, turning the room back into a laboratory.

"What are you doing here?" I ask. It's late, and she should be in bed.

Her eyes fall on the register, but she says nothing and comes over to open the upper drawer of Waipo's desk. Sitting under a half-used pack of tissues is an almost identical book, but the leather is pristine, the golden peony sharply defined. She takes it out and opens it to show the blank pages.

"Waipo had it made for when you decide to start," she says. "You know the tradition."

The tradition is that the transcription begins when the register comes into your possession. "It's not my turn yet," I say. Mom is the eldest Hua, after all.

"Waipo sent it to you."

"You're next in line after Waipo, not me," I say, giving the book a little shove away from me. "It belongs here with you. So here you go. You can have it back."

"I hope you haven't let your Chinese lapse, the way you give up on everything else. That book is your heritage. She wanted you to have it."

"To remind me of how I failed?"

"To remind you of who you are." My mother's voice is usually gentle, a misleading veneer over her steely personality. Now it has the sharp edge of broken stone. "Harnessing your moli is not where you failed. You failed when you ran away instead of persevering."

"Okay, thanks for the clarification. Glad we can agree that I am, in fact, a failure, even though we differ on the details of exactly how that manifests." I want to check my watch to see how long we were in the room together before the fight started. I'd say about forty-three seconds.

"You can't be happy denying your gift," she says. "I can tell it burns in you."

I make a face. "Like an STI?"

"Language, Luling. Don't be vulgar."

"You know what, Mom? Nothing's burning. I don't feel incomplete. What I do feel is frustration about having this conversation with you again, and especially now."

"You are the fifth daughter," Mom says, as if I've somehow

forgotten. "The family has waited years for you to claim your gift. I have been very patient, but you need to stop wasting time and come home. You need to fix your moli. I was ashamed today to have so many people ask why you still lived in Toronto, with not even a store of your own."

That hurts, but I know the real reason why she was ashamed. It's because her bags aren't designer and the funeral catering wasn't done by a Hua family personal chef. Family lore says the massive wealth—like, "rooms filled with gold" levels of wealth—brought in by our genius Ming ancestor Xiaoting was increased by subsequent fifth daughters until the Huas were as rich as emperors. The whole shebang was lost after the Second World War when my grandmother's uncle poured it into supporting the nationalists over the winning communists, who took what was left of the money along with the house.

The family managed to sell the store and used the proceeds to set themselves up in Vancouver. The Huas—now reduced to me and my mother, since Dad insisted Eric have his last name—became denizens of the average middle class instead of the obscenely rich. This weighs on my mother. I may have accepted my life, but she dreams of a time dripping with jade and gold, where the Huas properly belonged.

"I know it's the money. You want the money, and you're tired of waiting." She's going to have to wait forever, though, since my moli simply isn't there.

"Having money keeps our family safe, but that's not the reason I want you to keep trying."

I make a disbelieving noise. "No? That's not what Eric said."

She doesn't blink. "Eric exaggerated."

"You don't know what he told me," I point out. "He said you'll need to shut down the store in six months."

"I will never shut down Yixiang." Her mouth tightens. "The Jins are helping me find a new location, that's all. The rent has gone up again. That's not your concern."

Not since you walked away remains unsaid, but the words linger in the air as if she'd shouted.

"Sure," I mutter.

"You have a power that's meant to be used." She pauses with meaning. "Then passed to your daughter."

This call for grandchildren isn't new, so I ignore it. "I don't. That was what we learned when I went away."

"Being too scared to try again doesn't mean you lack your moli. It needs to be cultivated. You are a Hua, and the gift is there but you're ignoring it. I don't know if it's pride or fear holding you back, but it's time you grew up."

I wonder at what point a jury would consider matricide justifiable. "I'm not scared."

"No? Perhaps it's plain laziness, then. You could have stayed and worked at Yixiang with me and your grandmother. We could have helped you. You have the best nose the family has seen in generations. Instead, you ran away at the first challenge."

A challenge—that's putting it lightly. It's also one no other Hua had to face. "I wanted to make my own way."

"You belong here, with us." She taps the register Waipo sent me. "With me. You have a responsibility and should come back."

"No." The word is out almost before she closes her mouth. Perhaps if I thought she wanted me for myself, my answer would be different, but she only wants what she can get from me in her pursuit of past Hua glory.

"Luling…"

"I said no."

Mom shakes her head. "You have too much of your father in you," she says. "A Hua would fight, but you abandoned your heritage and your gift at the first obstacle. Such a waste."

There's a long silence as I decide to take the slightly higher road by not answering. Mom breathes in and looks at the two registers on the desk. "Remember your history, Luling," she says softly. "All I ask is that you try to be the woman you're meant to be. Not this shadow."

"I did try."

She shakes her head. "Not hard enough. Double-check the door when you go." She heads back out into the night. That's it. She always has the last word.

If I were a different person, I might rip the registers into shreds of unapologetic and defensive defiance. Then an extra dose of daughterly guilt hits me, as it usually does after an interaction with my mother. Why am I doing this to her when Waipo is so newly gone? Why can't I control myself? Yet every comment from her is a sliver that I have to pluck out immediately before it can burrow deep.

I abandon the desk and go to the rear of the lab, where a heavy metal door, painted white, leads to the small walk-in vault my mother had installed at what must have been exorbitant expense. I haven't been back here since I left, and unaddressed and unnameable feelings pummel me like hail. My grandmother believed in my power, and so does my mother, both clinging to the idea that I have to possess my moli because—as with NASA Mission Control—failure is not an option. I might have accepted that I'll be the one to break a thousand-plus years of family tradition, but they can't.

Too bad they have to. Or at least my mother does, since Waipo is hopefully beyond caring. Moli perfumes only change emotions, not the future or the past. My mother can't make a perfume to fix me, although she clearly wishes she could.

Filled with words I wish I had the nerve to say, I stab in the key code and shove open the door to the small vault. The lights flicker on and the air, cool and quiet, settles around me like a blanket. The vault has the same environmental controls as a museum, necessary when protecting ancient perfumes. From the entrance, I can scan my entire family history. Every eldest Hua daughter kept samples of her moli fragrances along with information on the notes or ingredients, vitally important since most of them have long faded. The earlier ones, to the far left, are powders and incense, meant to perfume clothing with a subtle scent. Later ones in the middle include oils and waxes, and then on the far right are the essences and alcohol-diluted formulae I was mostly trained in.

These perfumes are a record of power, of the empresses and aristocrats and merchants who benefitted from my family's ability and could pay for our talent. It's also a collection of counterfactual histories, as each sample represents a changed emotion, something that could have meant life or death for a person—or a nation. When I was younger, my mother spoke about being able to move the collection to a better, more secure place, the implication being that my moli would pay for it. That's another dream I killed. No wonder she's had it with me.

I move to the other side of the room. My grandmother's perfumes sit in an orderly line, her name in neat English beside the characters below. Beside them are my mother's. The shelf next to those is where my fragrances should be. Only one sits there, a testament to hope but a record of failure.

I drop to the floor beside the battered steamer trunk that had brought these riches across the ocean and reach down to touch my right thigh. Each eldest Hua daughter has a birthmark that declares her as one of our line. Mine, like the others, is a small silvery blotch that looks like a peony, if you squint. Whenever I see it in the bath, I long for home like a drug I've only told myself I've kicked.

I rub my eyes. It's too late to try again. It had hurt when I'd failed; the pain mixed with an almost comic sense of disbelief, which caused it to bite bone-deep before the combination eviscerated me. I can't do that again. Moving back to Vancouver to make regular perfumes for regular customers would be almost as unbearable. Mom would be on my case every day about my moli, and it would hurt to turn down orders I couldn't satisfy. It would hurt more to watch the requests peter out as word of my inability spread.

I did my best twelve years ago, and that will have to be my legacy. "Sorry, Waipo," I whisper to her shelves.

When I stand to leave the room, my joints ache and creak. The door clicks behind me and the locks fall into place.

That part of my life ended a long time ago. If I remember anything from the register, it is the words from Hua Xiaoting when she abandoned her Nanjing home in exchange for safety: *There is no room in the future for regrets.*

The door shut softly behind Hua Aiai, closing like a trap. For a moment she stared, open-mouthed, at the private room draped in pink silk that glowed in the morning sun, the luxury unexpected given the plain decorations of the rest of the nunnery. Then she saw who was seated on the low platform and dropped her eyes as she bowed.

Lady Wu might have only been a fifth-rank concubine of the dead Emperor Taizong, but she still far outranked Aiai, a poor distant relation. She felt Lady Wu's eyes boring into the top of her head and fought an intense need to reach up and scratch her scalp, despite the ruthless way her mother had checked her for lice before she'd left home several days ago.

"Let me see your face, girl."

Aiai raised her head but kept her eyes low. Her hair, painstakingly wound into two drooping buns that she had thought so sophisticated when getting dressed, now made her feel dowdy and small, a brown mouse in front of a sleek tiger.

Finally, the buzzing in Aiai's ears cleared enough for her to discern words instead of noise. "I've heard of you," Lady Wu was saying, in a voice trained to be as sweet and soft as a ripe peach. "My aunt told me of your power."

"It is a poor thing, unworthy to speak of, my lady." Aiai tried not to mumble, tucking her tanned and callused hands together under her sleeves to hide their shaking. This was why she'd been summoned. Aiai gathered her nerve to peek up at Lady Wu's face to gauge how frightened she should be, but Lady Wu's expression was as smooth as the crimson blush that painted her cheeks and revealed nothing. Her maids, all wearing robes far nicer than Aiai's, stood beside their mistress, equally impassive.

"Yet speak of it, we will. Is it true? You can draw in one's true love with a mere scent?" She tilted her head to the side. The golden ornaments adorning the high bun of her gleaming black hair gave a pleasant tinkle as they brushed against each other. Not for her was the shaven austerity of the other nuns. Lady Wu was a phoenix among sparrows. Aiai brought her gaze back to the smooth wooden floor.

"Yes, my lady." There was no point in lying. "The Peony Goddess came to me in a dream and asked me for a scent to gift to the Queen Mother of the West. That was my reward."

"A girl who can please a goddess might be able to do the same for me," said Lady Wu. "Your perfumes are powdered?"

Aiai nodded, calming slightly at the idea that she could simply supply Lady Wu with an appealing scent and be dismissed back to the safety of home. "They can be burned or put in sachets my mother embroiders."

Lady Wu waved her hand as if the skill of Aiai's mother was of little importance, although the stylish ladies of the Xin family clamored for her designs. To one such as Lady Wu, perhaps even the haughty Xins were unimportant.

"Good. You will become my personal perfumer." She announced this in a regal tone, no doubt learned from the emperor himself. The thought of such familiarity made Aiai almost faint. When the rumors of Lady Wu's ascendance at court had reached Aiai's family, they had been eager to claim the connection to the emperor, however far removed. They said she had been a favorite who had worked as the emperor's personal secretary, invigorating him with her wit and spirit. After his death she had been banished to the nunnery to pray for his soul, as had the other imperial concubines who had not produced a precious son. The men in Aiai's family had noted this with disappointed satisfaction, gratified that a woman should be returned to her place in the background, where she belonged, but regretting the loss of perceived status.

"My lady?" This time fear mixed with disbelief gave Aiai the courage to risk another quick glance upward. Lady Wu had made the pronouncement without any thought for Aiai's wishes, but Aiai expected little consideration from one such as she. "Here in the nunnery?" That was the part that confused her. Nuns were not to indulge in worldly pleasures, although it was clear the woman before her cared nothing for temple rules.

Lady Wu's smile was mischievous enough to make Aiai's stomach churn. It was the same expression her younger brother wore when he was about to steal food and blame it on her. "We won't be here for long," Lady Wu said. "We need to be at the palace."

"The palace?" Although her father was a merchant, until she arrived at Ganye Temple, Aiai had never been farther from home than the nearby market town. That had been enough for her, with its noise and filth. She'd heard even more extreme beauties and follies could be found in the districts of Chang'an, where—they said—the streets were so busy from dawn to dusk that one could lift one's feet and be carried to one's destination by the crowd.

"That's where Emperor Gaozong is. He came to the temple to see me, but…" Lady Wu's voice trailed off. "He is a weak man. The Empress Wang has lost favor, but she remains a formidable woman."

"Yes, my lady," Aiai said, not understanding but knowing better than to say so. Court politics were beyond her. Her own life was simple, or had been until the Peony Goddess had blessed her. She had woken before the sun and spent her time helping her mother dry and grind the herbs they grew in their gardens and the spices that came from her father's caravans. Her great pleasure had been to create the fragrances that caused a wave of a lady's sleeve to perfume the air around her with indescribably lovely scents, like those of the fairies.

Lady Wu gazed at her so intently that it made Aiai shiver. "Tell me, to have the emperor fall in love with me, will I need him near enough to smell your magical fragrance?"

Aiai's arms pressed against her sides in involuntary protection as she scrambled for an answer. There was much she didn't know regarding her gift, including this. She had tried to eke out moments to test her scents at home to better understand the power wielded by her fragrance, fearing being unmasked and punished as a fraud. Her mother had locked her in a storage room when she'd tried to ask clients about their experiences, telling her no one would buy a true love scent if they thought Aiai herself was ignorant of what it could do.

Aiai suspected it was enough for Lady Wu to simply wear the scent to call her true love, but she wasn't certain. Nor did she know what would happen if one's true love had died or lived far away. It was convenient so many had found their love close by.

There were many unknowns, but there was one known, obvious even to a silly country maid like Aiai: If she failed, Lady Wu's disappointment would be vicious.

"Well, girl? How close do I need to be?"

The sharpness in Lady Wu's voice made Aiai recall another rumor she had heard. The previous emperor, Taizong, had once asked his concubine how she would make a horse obey. According to the rumor, Lady Wu had said she only needed three things: an iron whip, an iron hammer, and a dagger.

Aiai knew it was better to lie than be treated as Lady Wu had said she would treat the recalcitrant horse: body flogged with the iron whip, head smashed with the iron hammer, and throat slit if she still refused to submit. Not that she would ever rebel. Her mother often called her a mouse for the way she ducked her head and tried to scurry along the walls to remain unseen.

"Yes, my lady. Close enough to smell."

The lie would buy her some time, she thought with relief as the cramp in her belly subsided. After all, Lady Wu was here in the temple, not in the palace, and it might be days or months or even years before she managed to get into the emperor's presence. Perhaps Aiai would be able to discover whether her lie was true in that time.

"Good." Lady Wu looked out the window at the distant mountains shrouded in clouds. "You will make him fall in love with me. His desire is not love. It's not enough to turn him from the empress. He needs to love me to gather the strength to put her aside and make room for me."

"My lady!" Aiai openly stared in shock at Lady Wu's casual discussion of betrayal. Before Aiai had left home, her mother, forbidden by the summons to accompany her daughter, had warned her to be careful. Lady Wu was ambitious and cunning, she'd said jealously. Aiai cast her gaze back down to Lady Wu's silk robes, embroidered with pale ducks so detailed that each seemed to carry its own sly smile. Her mind spun at the danger she was in, now that she knew Lady Wu's plan and had been made part of it.

She needed to protect herself. She couldn't compel love or summon love from a specific target and had turned away those who demanded it. Perhaps they believed a purchased one-way love to be enough, and even preferable—for then they never needed to lose themselves.

"What if the emperor isn't your true love?" She risked asking the question in a voice so low it was a miracle it made it across the room to Lady Wu. She gripped her hands to control their renewed shaking.

There was a long silence, and when Lady Wu laughed, it was a deep sound from her belly that made Aiai drop her head in disgrace until her chin touched her chest. "How ridiculous," she said. "Of course he is."

Lady Wu's tone brooked no disobedience, and Aiai lost whatever courage she had. "Yes, my lady," she whispered.

"Good. You will tell no one else in Chang'an of your gift, and you will tell your family to put an end to any talk about it." She tapped her nail against her cheek. "In fact, we will tell them you are dead."

"My lady!"

"Yes." Lady Wu nodded decisively. "I will pay them well for you, little witch."

Her mother would like that, Aiai thought with a bitterness she usually kept caged, like the captive monkey in Lady Xin's courtyard.

Lady Wu's smile was playful, her lips gleaming vermilion in the center of her mouth. Her makeup was exquisite, the stylized gold lotus that decorated her forehead accentuating the long sweep of her eyes. "It is for your safety as well as my own."

"Yes, my lady." Aiai knew a command when she heard it. Her family had not been so good to her that she felt anything toward them besides duty, and even that had lain lightly on her shoulders. Had she been married, she would have been absorbed into her husband's family anyway. At least with Lady Wu, she might have a chance at some sort of freedom and to study her power. Those gifts were not to be disregarded.

"Then let's begin. We have much to do before I become empress." She smiled. "Along with the emperor, it is all I desire."

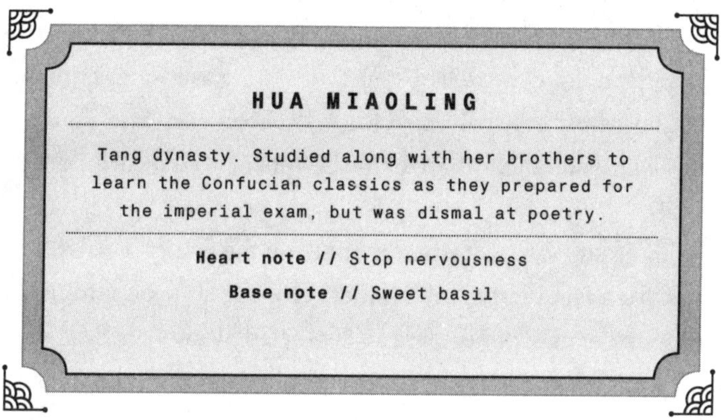

When I get back to Toronto after the funeral, the weight of the stale air in my apartment shoves against me the second I open the door. There's no life in my place. No pets, no plants. Not even the muted voice of my neighbor's television coming through the wall. It's so vacant that my usually latent loneliness swells to fill the expanse, pressing against the furniture and windows to seal me in.

I wish I didn't always have to live in furnished rooms. Despite steam cleaning every inch before I move in, I never feel like the space is mine. I'm only next in a long line of transients, making the best of a bad situation and hoping this is the move that will lead to something better.

Listening to podcasts helps, but it takes only three minutes of a lovingly detailed description of a serial killer murdering a woman in her bed for me to decide that perhaps music is a better choice. From the hall comes the ding of the elevator doors and the shuffle of boots on the thin carpet as someone walks past. A knock sounds somewhere, and voices lift in overlapping greetings before cutting off midword.

Leaving things unpacked makes me feel antsy, so I get to work after lighting a nutmeg-and-cardamom candle. Underwear and socks in laundry. Unworn shirt hung out to air, as it smells too much like my parents' house. I reach for my toiletry bag, and my fingers brush against something hard at the bottom of my suitcase, under my pajamas.

With no surprise whatsoever, I pull out the family register, which I know for a fact I left in my mother's lab. She snuck it into my bag, along with the blank one. I was so distracted by another fight we had before I left—about how she'd seen me talking to Rafe and if it meant we were friends again—that I didn't notice the difference in weight.

Mom is utterly incapable of taking no for an answer, especially if she thinks it's for my own good. Suddenly, I'm furious, and not only because of how easily I can apparently be conned into smuggling stuff in my luggage. Yet I can't help but run my hand along the worn binding, wondering if my memories match what's inside. Did one of my great-grandmothers really fight off bandits, or was that a story Waipo made up? I could find out, if I could stand to open the discolored cover.

Well, Mom can give me the register, but she can't make me read it. Sending it to Vancouver will only mean it comes back to me by return mail, so I empty the rest of the bag, place the books in my suitcase, and shove the whole thing in my closet under my summer clothes. *There.* I back out and slam the door to trap some of the emptiness in with the registers.

My phone rings. It's Ana, and she sounds out of breath. "Hey, are you home from Vancouver?"

"Is everything okay at the store?" I demand.

"Yes, yes," she reassures me. "I only wanted to know if you're home."

"I'll be in tomorrow, as usual."

"That's great—but, Lucy, are you home at this minute?" Frustration leaks through.

"Yes? Why?"

"Good." She sounds satisfied. "Then open up; I'm right out front." A tap comes at the door.

When I undo the lock, the dead bolt, and the chain, it's to see Ana standing there beaming at me. The light from the hall surrounds her with a pale halo. "Hi," she says.

"What are you doing here? How do you know where I live?" I'm so astounded at her audacity that I don't move out of the doorway.

She doesn't look abashed. "I told my mother about your grand-mother, and she put the fear of God in me for letting you come home to an empty house."

"Your mom told you to come over?"

"She said she would be ashamed of me if I didn't, so I guess." Ana shifts her weight from one foot to the other. "She's also right. Can I come in, or do you want me to drop the stuff in the hall and go?"

After my rudeness-and-rejection extravaganza in Vancouver, I'm too drained to do anything but acquiesce. I step aside and she comes in, shedding boxes, bags, and winter layers as she makes herself at home. Ana is dressed down—for her—with her brown curls held up in a bedazzled banana clip and a matching green velour tracksuit that makes her look like a very cozy Kermit the Frog. Her feet were bare in the boots, and her big toes sport bright-red varnish with white polka dots. The rest are painted bubblegum pink.

"How did you know which apartment was mine?"

"You put down your address when you signed the store subletting forms. Then I pushed the buttons until someone let me in. That's a security risk, by the way."

"I didn't include the apartment number."

"You didn't have to. I went to each floor until I smelled you." She heads into the kitchen with the bags she plucks off the couch. "Grab that box?"

I resist sniffing under my arms. "You smelled me?"

"Your candles," she calls over the banging of cupboards. "They make the whole hall smell homey, and I walked up and down until I zoomed in on the origin point."

Am I another stray Ana thinks needs rescuing? I can feel my expression hardening at the thought that she sees me as being on par with the foster kittens that parade through her home. I don't need her pity.

"Are you coming or what?" She pokes her head out from the kitchen and turns suddenly serious. "I made these cookies because I was procrastinating doing some inventory, and I could use help eating them."

"I bet Jayne would like them," I say, wavering. Company would be nice, I guess.

She glances down. "It's possible I wrapped some up to give her tomorrow."

This makes me laugh, and she adds, "You'd be doing me a favor. I've been lonely at the shop with you gone, but I understand if you're tired. I can leave if you want."

Ana is so good to phrase it in a way that lets me feel like I'm being the considerate one instead of the other way around. I join her in the kitchen, and she does me the courtesy of not making a fuss. She works with cats, I rationalize. She understands skittishness.

"Weird that we've known each other over a year and this is the first time I've been here," she says.

"It's a furnished rental—not the most comfortable place for guests," I deflect.

"Sure." When she cracks open the box to reveal the cookies, the cinnamon-sugar scent chases out any lingering hesitation. Ana grins at me. "I can't cook worth shit, but I do make a mean snickerdoodle."

"I don't bake at all," I admit. It's not one of my skills, although, like my mother, I excel at burning things. Mom might be a master of mixing perfume, but she dislikes anything to do with combining ingredients for dinner.

"Good thing you know me, then." Ana wiggles the lid off the ice cream container as I take out two bowls. "I can do three things well in the kitchen. These lovely snackies, sugar pie, and a chocolate chip cookie you bake in a saucepan. It's as big as your head."

"What's sugar pie?" The deliberately light conversation is enough to almost relax me.

"Like a fruit pie, but the filling is a mix of sugar, butter, and maple syrup. Sort of like a gigantic butter tart."

"What about those cheese breads you brought to work last week?" I ask.

"That was my mother. She and my sisters are kitchen goddesses." Her light dims for a moment before she shrugs. "I beat them all at cookies, though. They always tell me I only need to try and I'll make some man a good wife one day."

She rolls her eyes before she slathers ice cream between two cookies and hands the stack to me. The cookies are warm, despite Ana trekking them through the winter cold and then doing a floor-by-floor sniff-vestigation to find me.

God, these are good. That sugar pie Ana mentioned must be amazing. How have I never used the earthy sugariness of maple syrup in a perfume? Sugar and fire, with a line of icy water running through the fragrance to reference the spring sap. Or perhaps I would focus on the sugar shack, as the sap reduces in big copper pots standing over wood fires and the walls breathe out the scent of saunas.

"I know that face," says Ana. We haven't bothered to sit. I glance down to see crumbs littering my sweater, and move to the sink to dust myself off, careful not to get any on the counter. "That's your thinking face."

"I don't have a thinking face."

"Uh, yes, you do and that's it." She gives me a faint smile. "We work together, Lucy. I know you better than you think."

Before I can react to this remarkably inaccurate statement—Ana knows nothing about me—she pulls over a bowl and layers cookies along the bottom. "I'm not going to ask you how you are or what happened back home unless you want me to. Do you?"

I shake my head.

"Got it. Did I tell you about my new fosters?"

She talks about her latest kittens, bonded tabbies named Houdini and Dietrich, as she covers the cookies with ice cream, which is then topped with the dulce de leche sauce she pulls with a flourish out of one of her bags.

We pour out generous amounts of chocolate chips and I uncork a bottle of red before we move over to the couch. Dimming the lights makes the shadows from my candle flicker across the wall like a dancer's hands.

"I went on a dating thing last night." Ana's stack of Bakelite bracelets clack as she shoves up her sleeve.

I nod to indicate interest and take another bite. The chocolate chips have hardened from the ice cream and crunch between my teeth.

She frowns at her bowl. "I don't seem to be getting anywhere with Jayne, so I figured I'd try something new, you know?"

Living on the periphery of people's lives for years has made me an expert in drawing them out while keeping my own secrets close. In the end, most people like to talk about themselves more than they like to hear about others. Even sweethearts like Ana.

"How did it go?" I asked.

"It was kind of strange," she says, tucking her feet up on the couch.

"The event was like a maze. In each room, you picked a game to play that eventually led you through one of two doors."

"Like an Asian death-match game show?"

"Not gonna lie, I made that exact joke but no one laughed. That should have been my first clue I wasn't going to find my true love there."

"What happens when you finish all the games?"

"You find yourself in a room with the people who made the same choices." She trades in her ice cream for wine. "At least you could talk about the game, which made it less awkward to be in a room with people actively looking for ways to get someone to stick things in their orifices. Eventually, I mean—not there. It wasn't an orgy."

"That was not a visual I needed."

"It's the visual you get." She sighs. "In the end, none of them were Jayne."

"What's going on with her?" I should have considered a backup career as a therapist.

"I don't think she's interested," Ana says, stuffing her toes down the crack between the couch cushions. "We've been talking for a month already."

"A month isn't a huge amount of time," I point out.

"It is for love," she says stubbornly. "She would know if she liked me."

"That's different from taking action on it. She talks to you, so she clearly likes you."

"She talks to everyone," Ana says, jabbing her spoon into the bowl. "She owns a bar. It's her job."

"True. However, as a dispassionate observer, let me say that Jayne treats you much differently than me." She does, too, softer and more attentive. She looks at me, but she watches Ana.

"No, she doesn't."

Ana is committed to feeling sorry for herself, so I try a new tactic. "What do you like about her?"

Ana looks offended. "What's not to like? You've seen her."

Jayne is mixed, with a Haitian father and a Japanese mother—a tall, rangy, gorgeous woman who wears ripped jeans and tank tops that show off her tattoos. There's a lot to admire. "Besides that. Also, you've known her for longer than you've been into her, and she's always looked that good."

Ana's eyes shift away and she gets a little smile. "It's because she was nice to the cats in the alley."

"What?"

Ana puts her glass down, the better to talk with her hands. "You know that alley down the street? Where the garbage cans are?"

"Yeah."

"I always thought Jayne was a dog person because of Roscoe, but one day I noticed someone had been leaving food for the cats. Good food, too, the same as I buy."

"It was Jayne?"

She rolls her eyes. "Of course it was Jayne. This story wouldn't make much sense if it wasn't."

"Sorry."

"We showed up to feed the cats at the same time one day, and that's when we started talking." She smiles. "She's a kind person, you know? Not only nice. *Kind*."

"Then you know she'll be respectful and honest if you talk to her about how you feel."

Ana buries her face in the couch cushion, so I have to lean close to interpret her muffled words. "You haven't heard a thing I've said. I don't have the guts. What I need is a magical potion to make her fall in love with me so I wouldn't have any doubt. I'd give anything for that."

People say this so often that I've long since learned to avoid an obvious reaction, but this time I'm unable to help myself. "Would you?" I blurt out. "Really?"

She pulls her head out of the cushion and blinks, a little taken aback by my sudden apparent passion. "Why, you got one?"

"Of course not," I scoff. That's true enough.

"Perfumes are kind of like that, though, aren't they?" she asks. "Smells attract people."

"Attract, yes. Make them want to spend their lives with you and see how miserable you are in the morning before coffee, not really." I'm pleased with my insouciant tone.

"I wonder if any of your perfumes have done that," she says dreamily. "Caused people to fall in love."

I do my best to keep from wincing and train my eyes on the streetlight shining through a gap in the curtain. "I can assure you they have not."

"What if they did, though? What if you could spray on a love attractor?"

I pick up the bowls to take to the kitchen in an attempt to change the conversation. "Do you want more?"

"Wine's good." She chugs it down as if to make her point. "Don't you think that would be cool?"

"What?" I pretend ignorance.

"A spray! A love-attractor spray!"

I come back with some water. "Yes," I say. "It would be cool."

That satisfies her, and to my relief, she says, "What are you working on now? Not a love perfume, I bet." She laughs as if this is a hilarious joke, and it takes everything I have not to scream in frustration. She doesn't mean it. I drink the wine and force a smile.

"A client came in with her new baby the other day while you were out. She wants a perfume to celebrate being a mom."

"Will it smell like exhaustion and diapers?"

I laugh, a sound rusty from disuse over the last few days. "Absolutely not. Her daughter's name is Anala. She says it means fire, so I was going with something like roasted chestnuts, pepper, and coffee. A bit of guaiac wood for depth." I'm dying to get at it. I can already smell it—a lush, comforting smell that Anala will forever associate with her mother's love. And the opposite of my own mother's favorite scent, a cool, silvery iris.

I grasp around for anything to talk about that isn't love and notice Ana's necklace. "That's pretty."

"Thanks." She grins big enough for me to see her gold tooth outlined by red wine and chocolate, then leans forward with the chain stretched out to me. It's made of interlocking daisies and is like nothing I've seen before. A delicate pendant shaped like a hand holds out another flower with a tiny citrine in the center of the petals. It's stunning.

"I made it," she adds.

"You what?"

"Yeah, I trained as a silversmith. Made the chain and the pendant. Won a few design awards too."

I sit back. "Why did you stop?"

She bends her head down to look at it. "I had a partner and we were going to open a business. When he dumped me and then flaked on the business, I gave up."

"I'm sorry."

"Hey, you know what? I moved on to open Auntie's Closet. Life of an entrepreneur. ABH. Always Be Hustling. Don't look back, only forward, and all that jazz." She runs her finger along the chain while she speaks, then her mouth twists to the side as she bites her lip.

We spend the next hour chatting about the store, and Ana's cheerful voice floats over me as I turn on a few lamps. By the time she leaves, the smell of cookies and the echo of her raucous and infectious laugh have shrunk the emptiness of my apartment. It feels warmer.

At least for the moment.

7

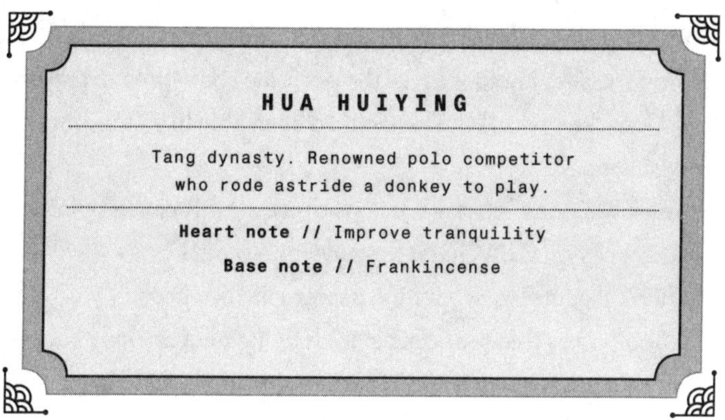

The rest of the month passes as Februarys do. I wake up in the dark, go to work in the dark, and return home in the dark. At least the store has been busy in the aftermath of Valentine's Day, as frantic lovers try to make up for forgotten plans or subpar gifts.

Ana comes out from the back, frowning.

"What's up?" I ask.

"Do you think we have room for another workspace here?"

"Sure." Not to mention it's her store, so I would feel like a cad for saying no. "What are you planning?"

"You asked about my necklace when I was at your place." She looks out the window at the snow swirling outside. "I've been thinking I want to make jewelry again. I want that back in my life."

"Then we can definitely make it work."

Ana grabs a measuring tape, and I drift around like an anchorless ghost before settling back at my counter. Two seconds later, I'm at the window. I have work to do, but the weather is making me itchy.

Ana joins me. "Should we close early?" she asks. "There won't be any more customers coming in off the street, and they've issued a severe weather alert."

"You go," I say. "I have to finish off this order." I have one last modification for a client before I give the perfume some time to macerate. It could have been done hours ago if I'd been able to sit for more than twenty seconds.

"You sure?" Ana lets the curtains down, and their dull pink gives the room a cozy feel. "What if the power goes out?"

"Then I'll go home, where the power will also probably be out."

We look up as the door opens. It's only Jayne. I say *only* because I want it to be someone for me—anyone—but Ana's face says our visitor isn't an *only* but an *everything*.

"Hey." Jayne smiles at me and takes off her black toque to brush off the snow. "I closed the bar early but saw your light still on. You two okay?"

The question is for both of us, but she's looking at Ana.

"Ana's heading home," I say. "Right now."

"Cool." Jayne hasn't moved her gaze, and Ana melts under its warmth. "You want company? We go the same way, and we can check on the alley cats."

"Oh, sure." Ana goes a mottled red. "Let me get my stuff."

After the two leave, I yawn and collapse in a chair. I haven't been sleeping well lately, and the warm store drags my eyelids down. It doesn't take long before I'm dozing, my mind wandering in a dream that ends with me holding a bottle of my moli perfume and standing on a cliff over a large lake. I've had this dream regularly for years, and it doesn't take Freud to analyze its deeper meaning.

I've tried to convince myself I chose my path because it's what I wanted, but it's hard to accept that I'm any happier here than I would be at home. Maybe it's weak, but I want to be the daughter and granddaughter my family expected. I want to stop being an exile. I want to not have the guilt of knowing the Hua family ends with me. I stare at my empty hands. If I could use my moli, I could go home and take my place where I belong. I could rest for a while and be a little less independent. A little less lonely.

Or maybe Dad's right about the Hua power being explicable through science, and I'm torturing myself for nothing. "Psychosomatic nonsense," Dad would say anytime Mom mentioned our moli. "An average family dying to make themselves feel important and preying on the hopes of others."

He never believed our perfumes were anything special. On bad days, I think he's right. There's enough science to prove scents can shift emotions; perhaps my ancestors' real gift was an early understanding of psychological manipulation. The mind is a powerful thing, after all.

On worse days, I know he's wrong.

I look at my perfumes. It's been so long since I tried. No one is here to watch me fail.

Before I can second-guess myself, I grab one of my premade scents, cradling the cool glass bottle in my hand. The process hasn't changed fundamentally since the Peony Goddess first showed Aiai the truth of her gift. It's passed on from mother to eldest daughter once she's old enough to understand how important it is to keep our secret. The first step is writing the huo.

In my bottom drawer is a stack of tags I haven't looked at since I moved into the store. The years haven't dimmed my memory of the order of strokes that create the character. They're easy enough, although the first lines are wobbly. My fingers peel off the sticker and smooth it on the bottle.

Time for the next step. The Hua gift is a mix of nature and nurture.

One has to be born with the power but taught how to access and use it. I'm to gather small elements of energy from myself and my surroundings and release it into the fragrance.

For the first time in forever, I want my mother with me. The woman has a multitude of flaws, but right now I need her bulldozer approach. She'd tell me to stop overthinking every step and do it, albeit in classier language. Her conviction that all I need is hard work and a good attitude would override my own doubt.

Of course, this is when the phone rings. I'm not surprised to see it's Mom. When I was a child, she always knew when I needed her. Sometimes she'd only have to call my name from another room to calm me down.

"Luling, I was thinking about you."

"I'm fine." I don't want her to know what I'm doing. It's better to keep her in the dark until I can report success—*if* I can report success—because the pressure that would come from the other side of the country would be strong enough to power electrical grids right through the prairies.

"I looked at the weather and there's a storm coming. Are you dressed warmly?"

"Are you checking the weather reports for Toronto?" I ask, astonished at this level of surveillance.

"Of course," she says. "Do you have your emergency kit ready the way I told you?"

I blow out a breath. "Yes, Mother, I do." I don't at all.

"Good. Make sure you fill some pots with water in case the power goes out."

"Okay."

"Make sure your phone is charged."

"Okay."

"Is it charging now?"

"Okay."

"Luling, are you listening to me?" she demands.

"Yes. I said I'm fine, Mom." I glance outside through the curtains, where I can barely see through the white. "The snow hasn't started yet," I lie.

"Mmph." There's a rustle like she's looking out her own window to check my words from four thousand kilometers away. "By the way, Missy Jin says hello."

"Okay?" Weird to think they're talking about me. I don't like it.

"Rafe might be coming out to Toronto."

"Good for him." This means nothing to me, so I ignore the nauseous feeling that could be either revulsion or anticipation.

"You should welcome him," she says. "You can talk about Vancouver. He can get you up to date. There are so many changes these days."

As if. I'm desperate to get off this call. "Snow's starting. I'd better get something to eat."

This has the desired effect, because along with *Are you warm enough, Have you eaten* was a constant question throughout my childhood.

"Be safe, Luling."

The call has broken my concentration, but also, in a strange way, removed some of my stress. I go back to my work feeling more confident.

Time to gather the energy. It sounds simple enough, but how? It's like telling someone that breathing is easy and all you need to do is suck in the air. That glosses over the muscles they need to contract, or how to make their lungs expand. I'd thought I managed to do it when I was twenty, but I clearly had it wrong.

I sit back, staring at a glass of water that was left on the table. The store is desert dry, thanks to an ancient radiator that knocks and hisses, and laminated rings have been etched along the sides of the glass as the liquid inside evaporated. Water.

After my failure with Ms. Kang, my mother reminded me that even

Aiai, the OG Hua, had trouble in the beginning. The Peony Goddess herself had to lay out instructions for the novice Aiai, and water had been key.

After filling a novelty glass from a Chinese buffet restaurant at the tap, I bring it back to my desk and sit down with a towel on my lap. Then I pour the water into my cupped hand and close my eyes. It's cold, but there's nothing to feel. Water's strange like that, like air—so present but ephemeral. I swirl my hand slightly and feel it creep up and then drip over my palm. Apparently, each molecule in the water is thrumming with energy. I need only a touch.

Try. My grandmother's voice whispers in my ear from the past, echoed by my mother. Mom had, surprisingly, been a patient teacher when training me on both the technical side of perfumery and how to handle my moli.

"I don't know what to do," I say to the bottle. "I need the right steps to know what I'm doing. The exact process."

That doesn't matter, my mother's voice comes again. *You're always so worried about being perfect; it prevents you from taking action. You get in your own way. That's why you don't succeed.*

How can I not, when my entire life is based on getting the correct number of drops into a bottle? Mom liked to say precision was the servant of creativity, but it was hard to take that seriously from a woman who made me re-create a rose forty times because it wasn't faultless.

I light a tuberose-scented candle with a mild astonishment that I'm considering praying to a flower goddess in this day and age, but it can't hurt. After all, the power exists, and it came from somewhere, so the Peony Goddess might be out there tending her celestial gardens and be willing to help out a poor human supplicant.

Please help. I send the thought out to the universe and the Peony Goddess. *Please. I'll do anything short of moving back with my parents. I'll give up french fries. I'll sacrifice a bottle of wine a day, and not the cheap stuff. I think you'll like rosé.*

I try to whip myself into a positive mindset. I can do it. I want this too much for it not to work. I pour more water, then close my eyes and channel the learnings from the single mindfulness class I took last year to let myself feel the swirling energy. I think I feel the tingling Mom said I would, that I felt once before, and raise my other hand to touch the huo sigil.

"Please work," I whisper as my birthmark gives off a sudden warmth.

Then I sag down, suddenly exhausted as the cold water spills into my lap and makes me twitch. That's the way it should be, as reported by generations of Hua woman, and the way I felt when I was twenty, but it hadn't worked then. Did it work now? What if everything I'm feeling is only mental? I shake the bottle in frustration, the bright work light gleaming on the glass. I should feel a tug from the bottle and a generalized feeling over my body originating from my birthmark, but I've learned I can't trust that. Do I feel it or not? I think so? I don't know. It's the same as the other times I've tried, with Mom hovering over my shoulder, asking if I'm sure.

I close my eyes tighter to focus more, until all I can feel is the bottle I'm squeezing in my hand. I don't feel different at all.

Nothing. Nothing.

With a scream of rage, I pitch the bottle across the room, where it bounces on the sagging couch instead of shattering on the linoleum floor. I'm exhausted at the dashing of my hopes. Then a horrible satisfaction tinged with *I told you so* rises. I was right that my moli was a bust. Mom was wrong to pester me. I was right that I was a failure, and I've proved it again. She's right to be disappointed.

I've had enough. I can't cry, but I move on autopilot to close the store. When I go to my computer to shut it down, a message appears from Kelsey.

> Lucy, where are the samples? We were expecting them
> today and it's holding up the luxury gift bags.

Oh, for the love of... I check the email thread. It's long, thanks to the back-and-forth required to convince Kelsey that if I did the samples for free, it would be for twenty and not the hundred she wanted. I check the last message. The event is called 'Searching for L♥VE' and it's for singles who want to find their soulmates. Something romantic would be perfect. Do you think you'll be able to manage that?

Then Kelsey buried the deadline under some updates about Sophie's baking adventures. I didn't ask for this, but I feel guilty about letting her down. Damn it. I snatch the failed bottle from the couch in a fury and spend the next ten minutes noisily rage-preparing her samples and swearing at each step.

Quickly decant the bottle into small vials. I should have known better than to try with my moli. I should have learned my lesson all those years ago.

Tuck the vials into paper packets that describe Ile de Grasse and the fragrance, a fresh and appealing—although non-adventurous—unisex scent with pink peppercorn, musk, and rose that melts into the skin. What was the matter with me?

Dump all twenty packets into a box and shove in some inflatable wrap. Why the hell was Mom talking about me to Missy Jin, anyway? What happened with me and Rafe was none of their business.

Print out a label for the box. Rafe. I can't believe this still bothers me after so many years. I'm such a loser. Why can't I move on?

Leave the package in the back on our makeshift mail desk. Kelsey. Why couldn't she take no for an answer?

At least her perfumes are done, and I promise myself to hold firm next time she asks. I send her a quick reply to tell her they're on the way.

By the time I yank the store door shut behind me, my feelings are in a bigger swirl than the snow that's falling from the intensifying storm. High drifts pile along the sidewalks and against the buildings; I drag my legs through in a sad imitation of wading through shallow water at the beach. At least it's quiet. Most people are smart enough to be indoors, and the snow itself insulates me from the surrounding sound, leaving only the swish of my own footsteps.

Although I hoped to clear my head by walking home, the huge glittering flakes heighten the sense of isolation. It's like I'm in a novelty snow globe, separated from the rest of the world by thin curved glass. This feeling, which used to be as familiar as a necklace I wore so often I no longer felt it against my skin, now tugs and chokes.

Enough of this wretchedness. I'm tired of it. I'm tired of me.

So your mom pokes her nose in your business. Suck it up; she does it out of love.

So your shop is tiny and you think your perfumes are nowhere near as good as your mother's or your grandmother's. Practice makes perfect.

So a guy kissed you and then rejected you. So it was a sharp enough stab at a fragile moment that you've thought about it every time a man has kissed you since. It was years ago. Go to therapy and get over it.

So you failed at the one thing you were born to do. Maybe the magic skipped a generation. It's never happened before, but what if someone miscounted, or there was a hidden eldest daughter? It could happen. It's not your fault.

By the time I get to my apartment, I'm cold, wet, and—like a loser—have made myself totally miserable with my own thoughts.

"Stop being an Eeyore. Thoughts are not facts," I say to the flakes falling in front of my face.

The pep talk might work better if those thoughts weren't true. Too bad they're the factiest facts that ever facted. Mom thinks I'm a disappointment, my perfumes are an eternal work in progress, Rafe pushed me away, and I never brought my clients true love, thus ruining Mom's dream for the family business and apparently sending my parents into debt. Fact, fact, fact. And sad, true fact: I'm tired of this life and too stuck to know how to fix it.

I press my bare hand into a snowbank, letting it sink down until there's a perfect handprint in the drift. When my skin turns so cold it burns, I shove my fist into my pocket for warmth. Then, without warning, the streetlights blink off, along with the glow of the building windows. Only the red emergency lights peek out from the stairwells.

Blackout.

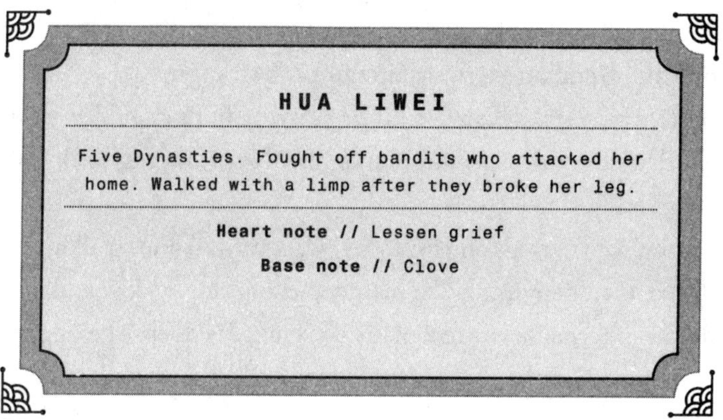

Naturally, there's a blackout. At this point, I'm past being upset. To be honest, I should have anticipated a power outage. It's one more shitty thing in a day of shitty things. I send a mental apology to the rest of the city. This is clearly my fault, as the universe angles to snap me like a twig, forcing everyone else to suffer as collateral damage.

At least I'm at my building, and although the front door is partially buried, someone has recently arrived and done the work of yanking it back and forth until enough snow has been cleared to let me squeeze in. A hot shower is what I need. No, there's no power. Food will do. I always make sure to have convenient comforting things on hand, like Kraft Dinner, or cheese ramen, or rice and ginger for congee, and I have a gas stove and the matches to light it.

With my phone flashlight in one hand and my keys gripped in the other, I hug the wall of the stairwell and make my way up, jumping at every noise until I arrive at my floor. Then I stop dead. A man is silhouetted in the dim light of the hallway, muttering at a door three down from mine. Is it safer to wait until he's inside?

I look again. I instinctively recognize that profile. My heart speeds up.

"Rafe?" It comes out as a whisper. I'm sure I must be wrong and don't want to embarrass myself in front of a stranger.

Rafe whips around so fast his bag drops off his shoulder, jerking his body to the side. Around him on the floor is luggage. A lot of it. "Luling."

"Lucy," I correct automatically as I walk toward him. Walking is an exaggeration. If anything, I'm merely inching closer, slow and deliberate, as I internalize the fact of his presence. He doesn't belong here. Not on my side of the country; not in my building, my hall, or my life. "Why are you here?"

"I'm staying here." His voice sounds normal, and that's enough to turn my surprise into anger. The unexpected usually does, as it jolts my calm and orderly existence into something unpredictable and possibly, to my primal brain, dangerous. Rafe isn't a physical threat, but he's a psychological one that I've dealt with by trying to forget him.

"Why aren't you in a hotel?" My voice sounds accusatory, although I know, rationally, that he can stay wherever he wants. Him being here is simply too much of a coincidence, one that indicates a purposeful, if malicious, hand at work. I'm close enough to see him give me a similar suspicious look, which is rich since I'm the one who lives here. It's like we feed off each other's bad energy.

"I can stay where I want," he says.

How petulant. I stare at him, and eventually he shrugs.

"I don't like hotels, and I need to be in Toronto for a few months on business. My mother recommended this place. She said a friend suggested it, and…" He stops talking as we follow the chain of events as easily as if we drew the map ourselves. The woman who lives in that apartment is an assistant producer who rents out her place when she's away on film shoots, something I'd mentioned to my mother while trying to make conversation. I never guessed she would hoard the information like a treasure dragon, waiting to deploy it at the right moment. There's my hand of God. My mother. I feel a wave of admiration for her cunning, one that passes as soon as it appears. That's why she hinted about Rafe. She had it planned.

There is nothing to say, so I say nothing as I go into my apartment and very loudly throw the locks behind me.

Then I lean against the door. Prickles run over my skin as multiple years of compressed emotion percolate through my blood like a scuba diver getting the bends. I'm self-aware enough to know holding a grudge for so long means it's more about the grudge itself than the original offense, but can I be blamed? The man down that hall is the avatar of all my deficiencies, the physical embodiment of the time when everything changed for me, and not for the better. Rafe offered me the first rejection in a series of failures and might as well be wearing a sandwich board that reads "Lucy, remember you're an undesirable washout." I wish things could be different, but I can't chisel through the feelings that have accumulated like cooled lava.

Even if the feelings faded, after so many years, I wouldn't know how to back down.

When the knock comes at my door, I sag. Somehow, I'd been waiting and hoping for it, but in order to achieve what kind of resolution, I don't know. All I know is, if the knock hadn't come, I would have been up all night thinking about why. That makes me more upset because I shouldn't care at all. Not after all these years.

"Luling?" Rafe calls.

"Lucy." I'd used Lucy for school and when I left home, but I'd always been Luling to him. I don't want that intimacy—not now.

"The key doesn't work, and the host isn't answering my calls."

I walk to my closed door. "I don't have an extra."

"Luling—"

"Lucy."

"Lucy. I didn't know this apartment was in your building. There's a blizzard outside and no way I can safely get another ride to a hotel."

"What do you want me to do about it?" I know what's coming, but I'm not going to offer. He has to ask.

Rafe doesn't hesitate. "I swear I'll get it sorted out in the morning if you let me in."

I weigh the satisfaction of making him sleep in the hall against dealing with my mother's pointed comments about hospitality and her friendship with the Jins. I sigh loud enough for him to hear but know what my answer will be.

"One night," I warn as I unlock the door.

Rafe drags in his luggage and stands there dripping melted snow on the floor, looking as utterly done with his day as I am with mine.

"You can hang your coat to dry on the hook," I say.

He nods and shrugs it off. Underneath, he wears a thick, soft-looking gray sweater with a turtleneck. It's not a look every guy can pull off with confidence, but he makes it look good with the black business-casual slacks still caked with snow at the cuffs.

"Bathroom is down the hall." I wave my hand in the correct direction and try to sound, if not cool, at least unaffected. It's hard since my resentment is still seething, although below it lingers another feeling that I don't want to fish up. "There's no spare bedroom, so you can sleep on the couch."

"Thank you." He directs his reply to the floor, and his awkwardness is enough to make me somewhat more civil. After all, I let him in. It's churlish to be rude for the sake of it, and I have a feeling it would only broadcast my own mixed feelings about the situation. The best-case scenario is we treat each other with the distant polite attention one would give a stranger sharing their train compartment.

Rafe watches as I circle the apartment to light candles, providing the ambience of a séance. They're fat white pillars left over from my shop from last summer and combine a variety of scents that don't necessarily complement each other. He sniffs the air. "Do you have any that don't smell like vanilla or geranium flowers?"

He's right. The room will soon be a headache-inducing symphony of combating smells, but I don't admit it.

"Geranium's scent comes from the leaves," I mutter as I bend to light the last one, a spicy orange clove. He doesn't move, but when I go to the kitchen, I hear the sound of luggage being unlocked.

The distraction of lighting the burner and putting water on to boil for pasta gives me enough time to calm down. He's in my space, but he's only here briefly. I want him to leave me alone the way he has for years, not once trying to contact me, but I'll be rid of him soon enough.

Shivering, I go to my room to change my wet clothes. The temperature is dropping, and I reach for my thickest sweats. I could make an effort to not look like a slob, but what's the point?

The point is that I want him to see I don't care enough to make the effort, which is kind of...caring enough to make an effort.

Rafe calls my name from the kitchen, and it gives me a jolt. He called me Lucy this time, but he drew out the *u* the tiniest bit, the same way he did when we were teenagers. A sickening wave of nostalgia overtakes me, and I lay my hands on the dresser for some deep breaths before I go back out. Rafe is dressed in a black hoodie, with jeans that fit him too nicely. I run my eyes down his body. He filled out in ways I hadn't expected, and I wrench my gaze away. He doesn't seem to notice my attention, because he's looking around my kitchen. Thank God.

"Your water is boiling over," he says.

Right, dinner. I pour farfalle into the pot. It's the only kind of pasta I buy, because the fun little bow ties cheer me up every time I look at them. I'm glad they work their usual magic today. Rafe moves away to stand in the living room.

"It smells like an aromatherapy shop," he says.

Since I'm on alert for anything that could be construed as criticism, I react badly. "I invite you to leave."

"I like it," he says quietly. "It reminds me of you experimenting with your perfumes."

"Oh. Thanks." I can't help but glance over. He's frowning at a candle, one finger tracing a line down the side, but then he shakes his head and moves to the window, where he twitches back the curtain to check the storm.

I use my phone light to find the Parmesan Reggiano in the dark fridge, then grate a bowl to go with the pasta as I worry about how to get through the evening. What could we talk about when forbidden topics include home, work, relationships, and childhood memories?

The thing is...it's hard to avoid these issue-laden areas since so much of a friendship is based on reliving shared histories. That's why I have so few friends. None, in fact, or maybe a half or three-quarters of one with Ana. I was never around enough to build those joint experiences. It doesn't matter, though. Rafe and I might have been friends once, but after so long, we're worse than strangers.

Distant politeness, Lucy. You can do this. We sit across from each other at the counter to eat.

"This is great Parmesan," he eventually says.

"I got it from my favorite cheese store. Half my profits go to their cheddar." We used to compete to come up with the weirdest names we could give a place, and I wonder if he remembers. I have an urge to connect with him that's at odds with the story I've told myself all these years—that I don't want him at all. It's confusing and I don't like it, but I know I'm going to give in.

"Cheesateria?" I say it tentatively.

"Cheesonette?" he says.

"Fromagaterama," I counter.

This makes him laugh, a real laugh that I haven't heard since I left Vancouver. It's like a punch, the way it affects me. The sound is filled with the afternoons we spent giggling at old screwball movies, or the weekend we decided to bake cookies and dropped the flour on the floor. Rafe laughed so hard he fell down, causing another massive explosion of white powder to settle around the room and send us into coughing fits.

I want those days back so bad I ache.

In the candlelight, Rafe's face is soft with fatigue. "I missed this," he says.

"Snow? You get that in Vancouver." I deliberately misunderstand him so he has to take the lead in the conversation I suspect is coming.

"Not the snow." His eyes close as if he doesn't dare to look at me. "Lucy. Can we talk?"

Here it is, and my heart beats in my throat when I bend my head to look at the counter. "What do you want to talk about?"

"Us." The little word is like a bullet. "I want to talk about us and what happened."

"Why?" I shift my gaze to what's left of my pasta. "It's in the past. Why dredge it up?" I both want and do not want this talk.

"Because it bothers me." Rafe's voice is hard. "It's been years, but it's a shadow I can't get out from under. I'm sick of it."

I want to get up and run out of the apartment. Surely a Hague tribunal would categorize this as torture. Then I glance at my generic furnished apartment and, like Rafe, know that I'm sick of the shadow as well. He's giving me a path out and my internal debate ends. I'll do it like a Band-Aid. Rip it off.

"You know what happened. I kissed you, and you pushed me away because you were scared of my moli." I can't look at him, so I focus on an old gouge in the counter left by a previous tenant. "I was too much for you."

Rafe stares at the ceiling, his throat working as he struggles for the words. "I never should have done that. I said it all wrong, and I ruined our friendship and what we had. I regret that, Lucy. I regret it. I'm so sorry."

"You said it wrong? There was a right way to tell me you wished I wasn't who I was?"

"No, never! I never thought that." He almost lurches out of his seat. "I think what you and your mother do is incredible."

"Sure didn't seem that way."

"I know, because I fucked it all up. I made it sound like you were too much for me, but that's not what I meant. It was the opposite. I was worried I wasn't enough for you. I didn't think I could be."

I examine him, the familiar boy in the unfamiliar man. "Because of Dad and Eric."

He looks me in the eye. "And because I was young and immature and self-centered."

This makes me laugh, although it's not funny. "Yeah."

"When I was in China, I thought about what I'd said and how you looked at me. I felt sick, all the time. My aunt made me drink this shitty broth she got from some Chinese medicine shop for a week straight."

"Gross." I don't feel bad for him. He made me suffer as well.

"I meant what I said, that it had nothing to do with you, Lucy. It was all me, and what happened in the garden confirmed I didn't deserve to be in your life. I thought that for years."

"And now?"

"Now I do." He says it simply. "I want to be, if you're willing."

I eye him. "Just like that, huh?"

"Well, no, you're seeing the end result of a decade of experience that younger me didn't have the benefit of—and therapy."

"You have a therapist?" I'm impressed by this. Dad and Eric would rather gouge out their eyes than admit they could be improved in any way, and of course, I don't go. There's no point, if I have to keep my moli secret, which I would. I also move around too much. There are always reasons.

"I live in Vancouver," he says. "Everyone has a therapist or a dog. Most have both."

I sigh. "I'm glad for you—but what do you want from me, Rafe? To forget it happened and start fresh because you can now name your feelings?" It might be rude, but I have a lot of hurt swirling.

"No. I want you to let me back in, at whatever speed you want." He waves toward the door. "Me being here gave us another chance. I understand if you need time or if the answer is no, but I miss you. Let me prove to you that I've changed. Let me be your friend again. That's all I want."

We sit in silence as a siren wails on the street, rising in volume before fading away in the distance. Lassitude overtakes me, and I sway in my seat, almost as if I'd been saving my breath and finally released it. A strange grinding noise comes from the radiators as the kitchen light flickers on. We look at each other as the microwave blinks a yellowish 12:00.

"Power's on," I say.

Rafe has already moved to check the radiators. "Heat," he declares before sitting back down.

"This is like..." I pause. "I think I need a second to recalibrate." Talking to Rafe is strange and disjointed. He knew so much about me, and then he knew nothing. I can tell building a bridge to connect those pasts and presents will take time and effort. I think I want to, but what's unclear is whether I want it to soothe my feelings about the past or create something for the future.

"Me too." He picks up his water glass and puts it down. "Do you have any wine?"

Finding a bottle and uncorking it brings a semblance of normalcy that lasts until we huddle up next to the radiator. The heat is taking its time to seep through the lingering cold of the room, and we're wrapped in blankets from my bedroom. I've turned the lights off to leave only a couple of the less-fragrant candles burning, and it feels peaceful as we look out at the snow. The space between us is less charged.

"I sent you a birthday card," he says. "That next spring. I did send one. When you didn't answer, I figured you didn't want to talk to me."

"I didn't get it." When I gather my nerve to look up, Rafe is watching me with the same expression I glimpsed when he showed me that first sea star. That's when I know this conversation is not to rectify the past. I believe what he's telling me, and it's enough for me to dredge up the confidence to offer him a truth. I'm not extending the full olive branch, but I'm walking back from the tree with my hands full. "I wish I'd called you."

"Me too." He puts his glass to the side. "I thought the feeling of you not being there would go away. It never did."

"I know," I say. "Same."

He snorts. "Do you think we imprinted on each other?"

"Like ducklings?" I think about it. "Maybe."

"It's been a long time, but we could get to know each other again," he says, not moving his eyes from the radiator. A sliver of lamplight shines on his hair, which has always been a true blue-black compared to my own chestnut brown. "If you want."

I don't hesitate. "I'd like that."

When he meets my gaze, I can't help but smile. It's been a long time since I felt anything like home, but a bit of it comes back to me now.

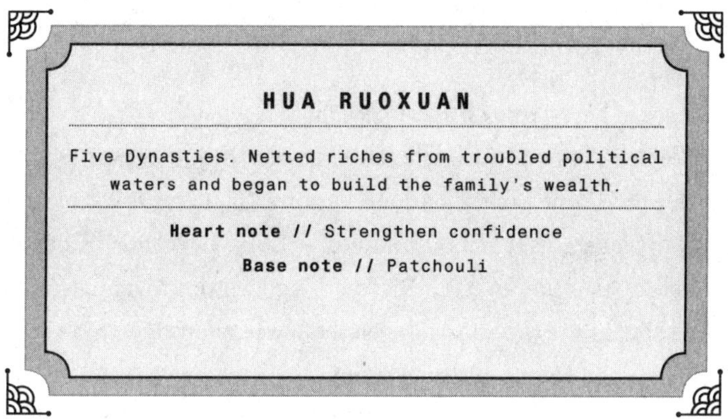

At least March came in like a lion, so it'll be out like a lamb," Ana assures me as she flips the page on her Humane Society calendar. "Oh, look, this month is hamsters."

She grabs the pen she uses to mark in special events and glances at me. "When's your birthday, by the way?"

"March," I say.

"So it's coming?" She's all fluffy hair and black overalls, cinched tight with a wide elastic belt and rolled up to the knees to show glitter socks.

"It's today."

She freezes, horror writing over her features. "I missed-slash-am currently missing your birthday?"

"Did you say the slash out loud in that sentence?"

"How else would you verbally indicate it?" She frowns. "Also, don't change the topic."

"It's not a big deal to me." A good coping mechanism for years of uncelebrated birthdays is to convince yourself you don't care.

"That's cool." She writes my name in the correct calendar square with a fun bubble script and a few hearts. "To each their own, and all that. How old are you? How do I not know this stuff?"

"There's no questionnaire," I say. "I'm thirty-three."

"Me too! Fun fact, that's the same age Jesus was when he was crucified."

I stare at her. "How do you know that?"

"Thirteen years of Catholic school, and my mother pointed it out in order to ask me what I've done with my life compared to Christ. She didn't take it well when I told her he didn't have kids, either, and the Bible doesn't mention our Blessed Virgin getting on his case about it." She checks the time and flips on the white neon OPEN sign before smiling at me. "Happy birthday, Lucy."

When was the last time someone said the words to my face? To my astonishment, tears prick my eyes. Luckily, Ana turns to glance out the window, so I can get myself under control. "Oh, gross."

"What?" I should have known it would be the teenagers, whom Ana has named Elvis and Priscilla. This time they're leaning with their foreheads together like one of them is about to go off to war. "Shouldn't they be in school?"

"I love those crazy kids," Ana says.

"You do?"

"No, but I read a thing about loving-kindness meditation, so I'm trying to reframe my loathing at having seen both their tongues as having hope in young love."

I have no such desire, so I go to hang up my jacket in the back but stop on the threshold. It looks much different than it did yesterday. "What's this?"

Ana jumps past me into the room with jazz hands. "Surprise! It's my new jewelry workspace. I set it up this morning."

Across from the couch, there's now a battered worktable and a collection of drills, solder guns, goggles, pliers, and what looks like a crucible under a bright light with a swinging magnifying glass. Mistaking my silence, she says, "We can do up a schedule if you want me out of your hair when you're working."

I can feel my face going purple that she thinks me so selfish. "Oh my God, no. I'm sorry. I was taking it in. It's amazing."

"Thanks. I can't wait to get started." She carefully scratches her arm. On her bicep is her latest tattoo: an American traditional design of a mermaid with a heart. The bold colors and strong lines match her vibe, and I didn't say anything when I noticed the mermaid's features look a little bit like Jayne's.

The morning is slow, and Ana leaves to run some errands in the late afternoon. The door opens and I look up with my customer-service face. To my surprise, Rafe walks in.

"Hi?" It's been a day since the blackout, and I think we're both struggling with what's next, because a decade of not talking and some soul-baring isn't something one simply forgets or gets over. I thought maybe we'd have at least a few days of uncomfortable texts as we tried to feel each other out, but it's a relief to have Rafe simply arrive, potential awkwardness be damned.

"Happy birthday, Lucy." He hands over a lovely glossy-leafed jade plant and a small box that reveals a cupcake through its cellophane window. "I know you're working, but I wanted to bring you these."

I'm floored he remembered, let alone bought me a gift. "Oh my God," I say. "I mean, thank you."

He smiles, the left side of his mouth lifting higher than the right and making my face warm. "Your mom told my mom to remind me that today was your birthday."

"Oh." The jade plant is still lovely, and it was good of him to come by, but the leaves look duller when I run my finger along them.

He shrugs. "I didn't need the reminder, although I appreciated her sharing your address."

"She did what?" *So she knows we've seen each other, although I decided not to mention it to her. I didn't want to know what she thought.*

"Your mother has always been very detail-oriented."

That's a polite way to say *controlling*. I take the Funfetti cupcake and divide it to share. Rafe makes a slow turn to examine the shop. "You were more emo when you were younger," he notes.

"That part of the store isn't mine." I point at the counter. "That is."

"That feels more like you," he says before biting into his cupcake half. "You had a sketch of your perfect store when you were eighteen, and it looked a lot like this."

"I did?"

"In that black notebook you used to carry around. The one with the sticker of a fox on the front."

"Oh, my scent notebook. I wonder what happened to it." It's easy to talk to him when we're reminiscing, and I relax. Only a bit, though, because I can't help but wonder what it means that he remembers such a small detail of our shared past. Even at such a distance, it feels good to have been seen. Rafe always did that for me.

I show him my workspace in the back and he laughs. "God, this is like going down memory lane."

I know what he means. "You used to come by the lab on Wednesdays after soccer."

He winces. "Your mom installed an industrial fan after that time I brought McDonald's for you. I felt bad."

I grin at him. Mom was furious and made me wash down the entire lab to get out the smell. "The Big Mac was worth it."

He picks up a vial with a questioning look, and I hand him a blotter. It's a gourmand of praline with marzipan and lychee, given depth by patchouli. He used to test all my creations, and it's a pleasure to share my perfumes with Rafe again. I used to wait, barely breathing, for the hum he always gave when he found something he liked, and the same happens now as he sniffs a few more of my works in progress.

"This is incredible," he says. "Your mother said you wanted time to be on your own, and I can tell how you've changed over the years. These seem more complex? Maybe layered? I'm not sure of the right word."

"Thanks," I say, unable to control my smile. Unlike my mother, Rafe has always been complimentary of my perfumes.

He glances at his watch. "I'd better go. I have an event with some clients."

"Oh, of course." I try not to sound disappointed that he fit me in between commitments. After all, he came by the store. That means something.

He looks at my perfumer's organ. "Do you think you'd like to grab dinner soon? You can show me a place you like in the city, or we can try one new to both of us."

Is this a date or a catch-up between two old friends? It occurs to me that I'd prefer it to be the former. I could ask where he wants to go with this, but I lack the courage. It's too soon, and I'm unsure of him, and myself. Despite our history, this is new. Also, he did make a point of stressing he only wants to be friends.

"Sure," I say. No matter which it is, I need to get to know him again before we can move forward.

We decide on a few days from now, and then Rafe leaves, pausing to wave through the window from the street. I swipe my finger along the last bit of icing on my plate, smiling at my new plant and feeling good for the first time in ages despite my earlier moli failure. It's like rediscovering Rafe has taken some of the sting out of it. He was always the sugar to get down the medicine, and it seems he still is.

I should have known this buoyant feeling wouldn't last, because when I get home, a package waits for me in the mail room. The second I'm in my apartment, I throw it on the sagging couch like a hot potato at a child's birthday party. I know what it contains, because every March for the last twenty-eight years, my mother has created a birthday perfume for me. When I was younger, I used to make requests. *Make it smell like the sky, Mommy. Cats, cats, cats! I want a unicorn.* The last was an effervescent cotton candy that somehow was exactly how seven-year-old me had imagined a unicorn would smell.

In what is rapidly becoming the closet of monsters from my childhood nightmares—the werewolves and ghosts transformed into more adult fears about duty and obligation—sits a plastic tub holding twelve identical bottles to the one I know is wrapped up and lying on that couch. They're labeled Luling21 to Luling32 and I've lugged them through multiple cities and living arrangements. I could have shipped them with my other perfume stuff, but despite never uncapping the bottles, the idea they could be lost in transit devastates me.

I grab a glass of wine before I reassess and take a shot of tequila. It's medicinal, like field surgery in some old war.

When the phone rings, it disturbs the hush of my dark apartment and startles me so much I drop the shot glass into the sink. The phone rings twice more before I manage to pick it up.

"Happy birthday, Luling." Despite our distance and the push and pull of our relationship, my mother's voice settles deep into my bones, then travels up to form a lump in my throat.

"Thank you for the perfume. I was about to call you." It's a lie I've offered so often it feels like truth.

"Did you like it?"

"Of course." Another lie.

She pauses. "Ah. Good. I'm glad."

Our conversations usually follow a format as strict as a nun's schedule. From Mom's comments about what I'm eating or have eaten or am going to eat, it moves to my day and then straight into something that will irritate me. The last topic changes, but in the past has included: my love life (lack thereof), how I run my shop and why it should be more like hers, the weather, and any mention of Vancouver or coming home. The breadth of potentially dangerous topics is wide-ranging and capricious enough that a tone is enough to set us off. Or, more accurately, set me off.

Today, though, Mom deviates from the routine. "I started cleaning out Waipo's rooms."

"Oh." Waipo lived in an annex off my parents' house for the last few years. Remorse jabs another bruise on top of the others it's left around my heart. I should have known my mother would be trimming the threads of Waipo's life. I should have asked.

"There's more to do, but I'm putting some boxes aside for you to go through when you next come home," she says. "Keepsakes. She didn't have much. She gave you the thing she valued most."

"The register?" I ask tightly. "I said it belongs with you." We still haven't addressed the fact that she ignored me to send it back to Toronto. There's no point.

"Waipo thought not, and I can't debate with a dead woman."

I recoil at her harsh tone. My gaze lands on the anodyne pastel landscape that came with the apartment and the small table under it that should be covered with framed family photos. It's where I put my junk mail.

Instead of fighting back, which is my first inclination, I take a deep breath. Neither my father nor my brother would have offered to help sort through the room. One of the terrible consequences of a death is filling garbage bags with the remains of a life, and Mom had to do it alone.

I don't want to fight, not when Mom is dealing with Waipo's things and it's my birthday. I muster every ounce of kindness I can excavate from my soul to say, "Thank you for keeping some of her things for me."

"Of course, Luling." She sighs. "I should go. I'm closing the store. Take care of yourself."

This is brisker than usual, and when she hangs up, I stare at the phone, almost hurt. I'm the one who hangs up first, and this reversal unsettles me.

I pluck the shot glass out of the sink and check it for cracks before washing it and putting it away where it belongs. She said she was closing the store. Why those words? Not "I'm closing up the store," or "I'm getting ready to go home." I weigh the pros and cons of texting Eric. Pro: Finding out what's going on. Con: Listening to him crow over knowing more about Mom's business than I do. It's an easy enough choice.

I shut the cupboard to go slump at the table and decide how to spend the rest of my special birthday night. I can watch *My Neighbor Totoro*, my comfort movie. I can take out *Anne of Green Gables*, my comfort read and the only book I've allowed to get dog-eared from use. I can have a bath laced with sandalwood, my comfort smell. I can work on my new autumn line or some of my commissions, my comfort coping mechanisms. I can go to bed, since it's already after ten, although that will bring no comfort.

None of the options are appealing because of those bottles lined up in the cheap dollar-store container in my closet.

Ah, goddamn it. I haul myself up from the chair and pour a second shot of tequila before shuffling back to the bedroom to stand in front of the closet again. The earthy smell wafts up from my glass, laced with honey and citrus. I finish it before snatching out the container, putting it on the bed, and sinking down to the floor so the bottles are at eye level.

Why have I never smelled Mom's birthday creations? Does she know? I'm punctilious about my thanks—truly the least I can do—but I never give her details of what I think about them. What secrets am I about to find that she assumes I know?

I drag the box down to the floor and pull out Luling21. It arrived at my studio apartment in Halifax, which was about as far away as I could get from home without landing in the Atlantic. The bottles are the classic Yixiang design, created by Hua Zhengyi in the early 1900s, a low, wide bottle reminiscent of old incense censers. The designs etched on the side all feature peonies, but subtle changes in the way the flower is depicted indicate which fragrance family the scent falls into: floral, ambery, woody, leather, chypre, or fougère. When I was younger I wanted to simplify it to amber, floral, woody, and fresh, the more modern standard scent families, but Mom refused.

"This is our tradition," she told me firmly. Waipo agreed, and as head of the family, her decision was what mattered most. I took my defeat gracefully because I was nineteen, with no reason to think I couldn't make the changes when Yixiang inevitably passed down to my stewardship.

I lean over to grab some blotters from my dresser drawer, settle back down, and give the black cap a slight twist.

Then I spritz.

It's jasmine, an intoxicating single-note floral. I wave the blotter and sniff again, the memory coming to me not in bits and pieces but fully formed. When I was sixteen, my mother told me to re-create the jasmine she grew in the small garden behind the house in all its different moods. Jasmine in the rain. In the sun. Playing up the indoles for the pungent smell of mothballs, and then its green notes. I'd done dozens of jasmines, refining and learning each time. The one my mother had chosen for my birthday was a light and sweet interpretation, something suitable for a girl.

Luling22 makes me gasp out loud. It's a rich, spicy bomb, not typical of my mother, who prefers soft fragrances designed to stay close to the skin and respect the olfactory space of those around the wearer. This is the opposite, an amber overdose with notes of opopanax, civet, and vanilla. It's said when Giorgio Beverly Hills was released, it was so overpowering restaurants posted signs asking people to tone it down. Luling22 could give that, Angel, and Poison a run for their money. It's the 1980s in all its lavish excess, and it pulls a surprised laugh out of me. If it were a relationship, it would be the love-bombing of a narcissist.

The more of them I smell, the more I'm convinced my mother is trying to tell me something—but I don't know what. There's a tea scent with a breath of buttery pastry that reminds me of Sunday mornings, a leather that smells like a supple old handbag, and a powdery rose I recall from one of Waipo's old cosmetic compacts.

I sit with Luling28 for a while, as it's a feat of technical brilliance that brings me an unusual feeling of envy. I knew Mom was good, but this good? She's combined the ozone of an approaching storm in the top notes with the petrichor of the rain-soaked earth, giving the entire story of a summer shower, with an epilogue of fresh leaves trembling with rain. I don't know how she made the green linger, when its volatility means it should be one of the first notes to disappear.

Then I open the package that came today. All the accompanying note says is *Happy Birthday, Luling,* and I put it carefully in the pile of identical notes from years past, tucked under the bottles in the bottom of the tub.

The mist from Luling33 settles on the blotter, turning the white paper translucent. Then I sniff.

There's nothing.

I try again, but again, nothing.

Bringing my arm up, I bury my face in my sleeve and inhale to reset my nose. Coffee is a myth for fighting olfactory fatigue, since it only replaces one smell with another. I take another breath and turn back to my blotter.

Still nothing.

It's ridiculous to think she mailed a scentless bottle, and Mom doesn't make mistakes. I spritz it on my arm in case it's some novel formulation that has to interact with heat or something.

There's definitely nothing there.

I put the blotters in the kitchen garbage and the bottles neatly away, all except for Luling33, which I keep on my night table. If I previously suspected the perfumes were a message, now I'm sure. I leave it and head to the shower to clear my nose and my mind, but once I'm back in my room, damp and warm, I pick the bottle up to spray it again.

Nothing.

"Why can't you just tell me what you want to say instead of playing these games?" I mutter.

Because you never listen, her ghostly voice says.

Wounded by this internal debate that I made up myself, I get into bed, still staring at the bottle. Is she saying I have a blank canvas to play on now? Is she saying my life is empty? I want to ask her, but then I groan, remembering that I already thanked her. I can't go back and tell her I hadn't smelled it.

I put the box of perfumes away and take two melatonin gummies. Then I curl around Luling33 like a lover and wait for sleep, hoping to puzzle out the mystery of my mother's empty perfume in my dreams.

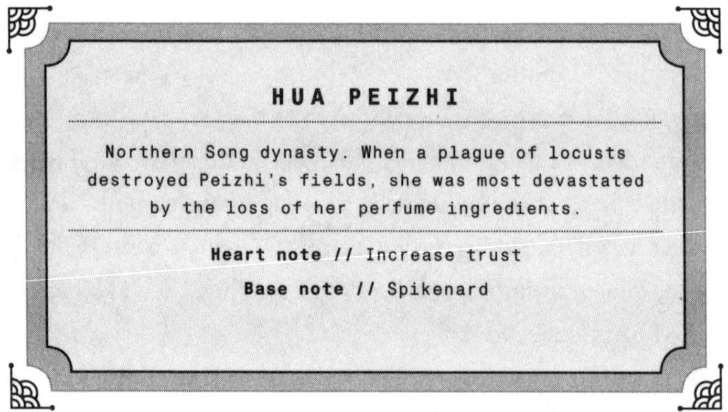

The morning finds me standing in the dim apartment—gray clouds staining the sky the color of a faded shirt—and staring at my closet.

Smelling my mother's perfumes last night was like opening the floodgates. I woke craving a connection to what I lost when I left home. Mom is too direct and intimate a link, but those long-dead women from generations past can't pressure me. I can't disappoint them the way I have the women in my immediate family.

Yet simply taking out the register and starting to read makes me feel somehow like I'm letting Mom win. I pull the closet door back and forth, the suitcase blinking in and out of sight, until I eventually come to the conclusion that I'm being almost childishly immature. I want to read the register. There are no winners or losers involved. I open the closet fully and grab the suitcase, feeling as though I've grown, very slightly, as a person.

The stained ivory pages are almost limp with age and use, and lay out my family history starting from the days of Hua Aiai in the Tang dynasty, a distant millennium ago. It runs to the final, empty pages at the back, where my own story should be and isn't.

Despite Mom's skepticism, my Chinese is adequate enough to read the orderly columns of characters outlining the lives of fifty generations of Hua women. Other kids had fairy tales as bedtime stories. I had the highlight reel from our family register. Some stories are so familiar I can repeat them by rote, such as my thirteenth great-grandmother watching her brothers being forced to grow queues when the Manchu overthrew the Ming. Others need three or four lines to jog my memory. Many I don't remember at all.

Literacy was prized among Hua women simply because of this register, as each woman is responsible for writing her own chapter. I pause to read one entry from Liqiu in the Southern Song dynasty, describing the steps taken by her mother to ensure her education, which had to remain secret from a disapproving father. At least Ming-era Dongmei had fewer problems, and her own father, a scholar, had insisted she be educated in order to appreciate the beauty of his poetry.

I return to the page at the back of the book and let my finger slowly trace down the characters as I read, mouthing the words as I go to make sure I translate them correctly.

I am Hua Aiai and the first of this line, which will be counted only among daughters. This is a record of my troubles so you may learn from this humble and ignorant woman. I leave here the words of the Peony Goddess, who came to me in a dream and told me the fragrances we create will be unique. She said my gift was to make hearts become whole. For my daughters, other gifts would stir.

I was born in the reign of Emperor Taizong…

I squint at a character I don't recognize, then grab a notepad and jot it down to check later. I can get the gist from its context and I don't want to be distracted by hunting through the onionskin pages of my old Chinese-English dictionary, which I prefer to anything online.

Some chapters run long, while others are only a page or two. Occasionally, there's a note that the chapter was finished by a daughter or granddaughter after an untimely death. Zhengyi had kept the traditional format, and the book reads backward to my Western eyes. Should I do the same thing? How about an English version? These are decisions for later.

I turn to the first page, which has a few additional comments from Hua Zhengyi dating from 1953, with a straightforward explanation of changes in measurements from taels and catties to the new metric system, along with a laughably short side note that covers the end of the Qing dynasty, World War II, the rise of Mao, and moving the family to Canada in 1950.

I pen this note far after my six years of work on our family register, she writes at the end. *May I be forgiven any errors.*

Six years of work. Good to know.

Then I turn the page, my initial reticence subsumed under an intense need to know everything about the women in my family. It's like I'm trying to absorb the information like a sponge, skipping all around the register to the sections that catch my eye.

What I soon realize is that there's not a new problem under the sun. After an hour, I take a sip of cold coffee and stretch out my legs. I'm in the distant Yuan dynasty and poor Jing is worrying about not being found desirable enough to marry; how would she carry on the family line? If she does marry, what if her future husband is unkind or doesn't wish to keep her girl?

There's a note from Mom here. *Better to leave the man than damage the daughter,* she'd written. Of course she'd say that. Huas need to protect their investments, after all.

Other burdens echo through the generations. Fears of sickness, of strange lumps and unexplained bleeding. Worries that they're getting too old to work, gnarled hands unable to handle the delicate materials. Concerns about no longer being able to contribute. Frustration about never being able to rest. Fury at having to hide who they are. Rage sits on the pages among the everyday updates of life, as if the anger itself was banal.

What none of them have—or at least, none that I've seen so far—is a lack of conviction. My ancestors, for all their differing personalities over a period spanning a thousand years, had one thing in common: an overwhelming confidence in their power as a Hua. I rub my eyes, remembering when I felt the same way. I knew exactly who I was and what I was born to do. Unlike them, it was taken from me. I don't know whether to envy them their stability or pity their lack of choice.

That's a lie. I know.

I put the register away and drain my cup. It's time for me to go to work.

The next few days fly by, and I spend my nights reading the register. Rafe and I have been texting, but he's busy as he tries to get used to working in Toronto, and I don't mind as much as I thought I would. It's nice to be able to have some casual conversation without pressure. Kelsey calls to talk about the luxury gift bags as I'm about to leave work for the evening.

"People loved them." She's marveling slightly, like she can't believe it. "Your perfumes were a real hit."

"Thank you," I say. It's nice to have my work appreciated.

"We're getting all these client requests for wedding and engagement parties, which is amazing."

"That's good to hear," I say.

"It's why I'm calling! I said you could supply us with more samples. I'll need something people will like."

"I'm fairly busy." I'm going to stick to my guns this time.

"You're never too busy for family." She laughs. "Jo Malone is popular, so something like that would be perfect. A Jo Malone dupe."

"It might be an idea to get Jo Malone samples, then."

"I would, but it's important I use you," she says. "Clients love it when I can tell them we support diverse women-owned businesses. Oh, let me get back to you. I've got another call."

Ana comes by as I'm making a face at the phone and gives me a searching look as she pulls on her shearling mittens, one of the few solely practical items she owns. "That seemed fun," she says. "I'm here if you want to chat, you know?"

She reaches out and gives me a quick squeeze on the arm, which, given the size of the mittens, feels more like the tap of a bear's paw. I do want to chat, I realize. I want the comfort of Ana's conversation and laughter. I want to talk to someone about Rafe to help me figure out how I feel about him. Our date—although I still don't know if *date* is the right word—is tomorrow, and I've already mentally gone through my closet twice trying to decide what to wear. I open my mouth to ask if she wants to go for dinner when Jayne comes through the door and Ana's eyes go huge. My jaw shuts so fast my teeth clack together, and I do my best to feel only good things for people whose lives are working out.

I tell Ana I'll finish closing, and she goes to check on the cats with Jayne, which is the furthest their relationship has progressed, much to Ana's chagrin. After I set the alarm and double-check the doors, I stand shivering on the sidewalk before forcing my feet homeward. I'm in no mood to cook, so I toast an English muffin and crunch it dry over the sink, where I eat many of my meals, then make two more to block the emptiness inside me.

I don't think twice before cracking open the wine I bought over the weekend and filling a glass almost to the top before I pull out the register again. I wonder why it gives me comfort even though it's a summary of everything wrong with me. In the collective wisdom of a thousand years, some other woman must have faced the same feelings I have. Yet if I found that validation, what would I do? After my recent attempt, I've given up ever finding my moli.

Instinctively avoiding Mom's chapter, I open it to my grandmother's writing and grab a box of tissues just in case. I was welcome to look at the register whenever I wanted, but when she was alive, it seemed like an invasion of her privacy, even though she'd written it for posterity. It's strange to read because Waipo didn't like to talk about the past. Mom told me not to ask about Waipo's uncle, the one who lost the family fortune, because Waipo had never gotten over the shame. I can see traces of it in my great-grandmother's chapter as well, in the heavy scratch marks through her brother's name and then its disappearance altogether.

Waipo was a bridge between two fifth daughters and was over twenty years old when Zhengyi died. She lived through some of the most momentous changes in history but documented almost none of them. Her chapter carries no mention of the first time she used a cell phone, but she describes my mother's scent as a newborn in tender detail. I don't know when she first saw a computer, but she wrote about her faded memories of the old Nanjing store.

I slow my pace to read every word Waipo wrote after she activated her moli for the first time. Her handwriting is shaky with excitement.

It was as I'd been told, she wrote. *A tingle and then a profound knowledge and confidence in myself and what I could do. I could feel the meaning of my power through to my bones, and it made my mark feel alive. To know I was doing what I was born to do is extraordinary. I can see why we never need to test our fragrances. The knowledge is innate.*

Excellent, good for her. There's no mention of my lack of moli, only a single line that I'd left Vancouver. I put the register down to stare at the ceiling and wonder why I torture myself like this. Then, for the first time in a long time, I call my mother.

"Hi, Mom."

"Luling." She keeps her surprise hidden, as if this is a normal occurrence. "How was your day?"

The conversation is pleasant enough. Mom tells me Eric was over with the children for an early dinner. "On their screens the whole time," she complains. "Your brother didn't care, and they would only eat chicken nuggets. I had to make two meals."

"How are they?"

"Fine. Kelsey mentioned the perfumes you sent for her gift bags."

"Yeah? She called me and said people liked them." I straighten my jade plant pot and take a small cloth to wipe away the specks of dirt that have collected on the edge from overenthusiastic watering.

"That's good, because she told me the scent you provided seemed unusual."

"Unusual?" I describe what I sent to her. "That's as basic as you can get."

"Kelsey would go to the store and ask for the most popular scent so she can smell like everyone else," my mother says. "She is not a good judge."

Unfortunately, Mom's assessment of Kelsey's taste is probably accurate. She continues, "By the way, did you see the latest review of your perfumes?"

"You know I don't look at reviews."

"Watch Maryska's."

She leaves it at that and starts talking about a new house she's heard of from Thailand that uses traditional cooking spices in their perfumes, like basil and green peppercorn, as well as the fragrance of a candle called a tian op, most often used to scent desserts. I listen with a sick feeling in my stomach, knowing Maryska's review is probably not going to make me happy.

When Mom hangs up, I immediately pull up the video. Maryska Popova is a critic I respect, with a large following. Unlike some other reviewers, self-proclaimed experts who make a show of waving blotters around before sniffing them dramatically while looking at the sky, Maryska is astute, insightful, and has incredible taste.

Too bad she doesn't like the perfume she bought from me. Or at least that's what I gather, from the little sad-face emoji in her video summary.

"I've heard people rave about Ile de Grasse, so I was interested in trying these fragrances. The pedigree of the nose, Lucy Hua, is impeccable, as her family owns Yixiang, one of the world's underrated perfumeries. My most treasured scent is Blue Lotus from Meilin Hua, whose watery notes are utterly sublime. All of this is to say that I had high hopes for Ile de Grasse, and it gives me little pleasure to say I was…disappointed?"

Here, I pause the video and take a break to breathe before directing my middle fingers at the screen in a private juvenile tantrum that doesn't make me feel better. Maryska stays frozen, her long sandy hair tied in a neat bun and her face as ascetic as a ballerina's. Then I pour some more wine, drink it, pour more, and start the video again.

She sprays Thera on a blotter and waves it gently. "Technical perfection," she says between sniffs. "This is clearly the work of an experienced and creative perfumer who is willing to take risks. The notes are unusual and harmonious, without any of the harshness or imbalance I sometimes get from indie houses." She puts the blotter down and sprays the other, Petra, on her wrist. "Same here. It melts into the skin. Lucy Hua shows true and undeniable talent."

Then what's the problem? I'm on the edge of my seat, leaning forward as if that will make her speak faster. She enlightens her audience soon, her mobile face thoughtful.

"The problem is that it lacks heart. It misses the emotion that transforms a perfume. These fragrances are like listening to a robot play Bach. Every note is perfect, but the sum total exudes a cold impersonality that's detrimental to the work. Don't get me wrong, these are excellent fragrances. If you wear Ile de Grasse, people will be impressed by how good you smell, but you might find yourself unsatisfied. It's a true shame."

I slam down my phone and jump to my feet, spilling wine down the front of my shirt, which, of course, is white. Swearing, I rip it off and don a black T-shirt and sweats. She has the nerve to call my work heartless. Soulless. A shame. How dare she?

I tumble onto my couch and stare at the ceiling, troubled by a single question. What if she's right? Moreover, what if she's so right that it's the reason I can't make the moli perfumes? I'm not worried I'm some ghoul, but what if I'm missing the ability to connect with people emotionally? That there's not something wrong with the perfumes but with me?

Also, what the hell is my mother's problem that she takes such pleasure in a public takedown of her own daughter's creations? It's sick.

I call my mother back immediately. "Why did you feel the need to share that with me?" I demand, voice quivering.

"To tell you she's wrong. It's not soulless."

"What?" I was expecting her to point out that I should look at the video as constructive criticism.

"It's not lack of heart Maryska observes," she barrels on. "It's too much heart. An abundance."

"What do you mean?" I sit up.

"Longing," my mother says simply. "That's what's in your perfumes. A longing so intense that it's unbearable and has to be hidden."

My early anger deflates and is replaced by a powerful distress, as if my mother has walked in on me doing something secret. "I have to go."

"Think about what I said, Luling. You need to come home. You need your moli. It's part of you."

I hang up on her, not bothering to be polite, although part of me already regrets not saying goodbye. Mom has always been more on the tough-love side of the parenting equation, but this is too much.

I jump to my feet, needing to get rid of my excess energy, and the register tumbles to the floor. It's not damaged, but my feelings about Maryska's critique and Kelsey's off-the-cuff lack of enthusiasm about my samples have collapsed to create a pinhead wormhole in my heart, bleeding my energy and self-control into another universe.

I burst into tears. The gross, snotty, wailing kind you can only indulge in when you're absolutely alone.

So of course, midsob, a knock comes at the door.

"Let me in, Lucy."

It's Rafe.

Hua Xiaoting left her room with steps as quick as she could manage on her bound feet. It seemed the rumors were true—Zheng He's fleet had finally returned home, laden with strange animals and mysterious artifacts from distant and mythical lands.

The courtyard was chaos as servants unloaded wooden crates and carved chests from the carts that continued to roll through the gates. Her gaze sought out the tall man speaking to her head maid, his voice booming over the din. "Fetch me your mistress, for I would speak with her."

"Such a racket, Admiral," Xiaoting called from the shade of the pavilion where she stood.

Zheng He strode across the courtyard when he saw her, servants scurrying out of his way. "We must talk, you and I."

"Welcome home." Xiaoting hid the fear his tone created in her heart and kept her voice light and playful. "You honor me with a visit. I thought you would be regaling the emperor with tales of potential conquests."

She nodded at her maid to prepare the suitable presents for Zheng He to take back with him. There would be nothing special—some bolts of a rare silk she'd been gifted from a grateful client, said to have been woven by the legendary Empress Xi Lingshi herself, and a gold statue of a tiger so expertly crafted the animal looked as though it would slink off into the night if left unwatched. They were inadequate compared to the bounty he'd brought, but it would be enough to serve politeness. Xiaoting itched to see her new treasures: the herbs and flowers and resins and woods and spices she could craft into beauty. Lucrative, magical beauty. She schooled her expression. It would never do to appear too eager. That gave away the advantage, something Xiaoting hated to do.

"You've upheld your part of the deal," she observed to her longtime friend as they walked through the corridor, he matching her much slower pace. Perhaps *ally* was a better term, for one rarely had friends in Nanjing. The Yongle emperor's capital was a fetid cesspool.

"Not as well as you. My holdings have increased threefold since they've been in your care."

Xiaoting smiled, pleased. Zheng He trusted few at court, and she had monitored his people and estates in return for items of interest he came across in his voyages. She had ached to see the foreign lands herself, but her place was here. At least Zheng He had more than returned her investment, judging from the riches now filling the courtyard.

He followed as she tottered into the workshop, where small bottles and jars were meticulously lined up on the shelves. As usual, her apprentices—orphan girls rescued from certain death or sold to Xiaoting instead of brothels—worked with nimble fingers as they created the bases for the moli fragrances for which the Hua family was known. The magical scents. Xiaoting's mother, An, was busy in another part of the compound with Xiaoting's own daughters, though usually An would be here to teach the girls as well. An was not a fifth daughter like Xiaoting, but her moli was in high demand from those who wished to increase their bravery. The admiral was a repeat customer.

Unlike her mother's moli scent, which was made in abundance for those who could afford it, Xiaoting's was strictly rationed. The ability to find one's true love would only be sold to those who could pay well, and scarcity created need. Xiaoting priced her wares high, and the profits filled the Hua storerooms.

Zheng He stood by the door, restless eyes roaming over the space, the girls, and the jars. His gaze rose to the dried herbs and flowers that hung from bars on the ceiling, covered with silk to prevent dust from settling, then down to the bowls of spices stacked tidily along a wall, some of their contents whole and some already ground to a fine powder. He was always like this, a man-size ball of barely contained energy, sharp gaze constantly assessing his surroundings for both threats and opportunities. Wherever he went, the admiral brought the power of the waves on which his armada sailed. It was his greatest charm or most repellant trait, depending on who was judging. Xiaoting liked it. She found it stimulating, like standing in a hard rain.

"Empty the room," ordered Zheng He.

Xiaoting's eyebrows rose, but she pushed back her wide sleeves to clap her hands. "Girls, go and walk in the garden. I want each of you to come back with a single flower or leaf to describe to me." There was no need for them to waste time when they could be improving their craft.

There was a small hum at this unexpected treat before the girls filed out, their voices fading as they clattered down the corridor. "Xiaoting, you have made a mess of things," Zheng He said. He sounded regretful.

Her back stiffened at the informal use of her name. Allies or friends they might be, but this was an unwelcome intimacy. Nor did she like his insinuation that she was naught but a silly woman. It was as bad as her husband's resentment of her for being too much like a man. "I don't know what you mean."

"You sold to the wrong people, ones with flapping tongues. The power of a witch who could call love was the first story I heard when I came into the city. By the time I reached my own compound, it had grown to a sorceress who could create both love and hate."

Xiaoting laughed and pushed aside the unease that tingled along her arms. The Hua family gift had been shrouded in the shadows for generations, their scents selling only to a tiny insular group of concubines and rich matrons. No longer. She'd looked at her little daughters, with their soft cheeks and wide eyes, and had known that it had to change. The Huas were wealthy, but not wealthy enough. They needed to be able to protect themselves, and that meant wealth.

After mulling over the problem, she'd come to the only solution and had expanded their client list to anyone willing to pay. Her mother had protested at the beginning, but Xiaoting was a fifth daughter. Her moli fragrances were the ones that brought in the caskets of gold and taels of silver, the ivory and the jade. It gave her the right to make the decisions.

"Better for business," Xiaoting said, leaning down to tidy Liaobing's workspace. The girl was talented but messy. "I'm curious as to why you think I need to explain my actions to you."

Zheng He frowned at her. He might be a eunuch, but he was still a man and did not appreciate impertinence from a mere woman. "You sold to the Li family."

"Only to one." The second wife was a confident woman, small, sure, and discreet—or so Xiaoting had thought. She didn't usually misstep.

"The first wife has died."

She fixed her sleeve. "The first wife has been unwell for over a year. My perfume has nothing to do with that. The second wife only wanted to confirm her place in her husband's heart as she aged." The woman had been certain her husband was her true love and wanted a moli fragrance to bind them tighter.

Xiaoting hadn't bothered to correct her as to the truth of the moli power—that sometimes one's true love was not who one thought or wanted. After all, money was money, and if the woman was so deluded about her role in the household, so be it. Let her mistake safety for love. Perhaps her real true love would change her heart, if she was open to it. Or perhaps not. She might be grasping, as well as gullible, and reject true love if it came in the form of a servant or maid.

"They think she poisoned the first wife," said Zheng He.

She laughed lightly. "They say that every time a first wife dies. If men could keep themselves to only one woman as we are constrained to one man, there would be fewer problems."

"They say your perfume was the poison she used," continued Zheng He. It was as if he hadn't heard her.

Now Xiaoting became angry. "How could that be? It's a fragrance."

"They say it was cursed. That you cursed it because a witch who can bring love can easily call death." He raised his eyebrows. "Especially if that death creates an opportunity for an adversary."

"That's ridiculous," she said, giving Liaobing's workspace another swipe with her sleeve. She would have to punish the girl by making her clean the whole workroom again. "It was a sachet of camphor and cinnamon, nothing more." Not very original, but neither was the second wife.

"They also say that the perfume has been lost and now anyone can use it, even against the emperor himself."

Xiaoting wanted to slap her hands on the wall to release some of her anger, but the impulse died quickly. "That's not true. The first person to use the scent is the one to get its benefit. It's not a cloud, indiscriminate in what its shadow covers, but a stream poured from a pot into a single cup."

"The truth never matters. You know that."

She looked at him closely. "What do you know, Admiral?"

"I know such rumors are already being planted by the Lis. They are your rivals at court, and they've taken the opportunity to blacken your name to the emperor."

"We are already powerful enough to withstand those little arrows." She tried to keep the prideful note from her voice.

"The Lis are also powerful. More than that, they are snakes and they will poison the emperor further against you. The eldest son is one of his advisers. Are you greater than innuendo and rumor? Than the pleasure people take in bringing down a woman with power?"

She shook her head. "I bought a place at court for my uncles." Not her husband, who was good only to curse at her from his studio, where he drank wine and composed bad poetry while pretending his failure as a scholar didn't sting. "They will fight for us."

"Your uncles have not been there long enough to fortify their power base," countered Zheng He. "They have no weapons to fight against the subtle attack the Lis have brought. Plus, your mansion is elegant and your gardens the talk of the city. The emperor already looks upon such things with envy, and the Lis have used that to their advantage."

She had assumed they had another few years to transform the Huas into the emperor's most trusted advisers—time to buy enough favors and prove themselves. Her uncles had been making progress, but only with those in the lower ranks, who wielded mostly household and unofficial power. It was a start, but not enough to combat the Lis.

"There is no direct threat," she said as calmly as she could. "I have time."

Zheng He raised his hand. "No. I came as soon as I heard the whispers. The Lis plan to have your husband summoned and possibly arrested. I don't know when."

"My husband!" Xiaoting laughed out of astonishment. "This has nothing to do with him."

"No, but either they don't believe it, or they wish to scare you. It doesn't matter. Your uncles will be able to do nothing, and it says much that no one has warned them. This will happen unless you act quickly."

A cloud covered the sun, and Xiaoting shivered. He was right. Xiaoting had misjudged, and now it looked like her family would have to pay for her errors. She could see her husband's triumphant face once he found out. A cruel, small part of her, the part that had absorbed his insults and gibes for so many years, the part that had been forced to beg him to keep her workshop and to apologize through swollen lips for having only daughters, wished she could allow this to happen to see him trembling and prostrate before the officials.

However, she had to think of her children.

She eyed Zheng He distrustfully. "Why are you telling me this? Why are you helping me?"

"Friendship." He smiled at her cynical look. "We are intertwined, for better or for worse. I helped your uncles at court. Should the Huas fall, it will be a shadow on me."

"You're the emperor's favorite," she said.

"The Yongle emperor will not last forever, and who can anticipate the whims of the Son of Heaven?"

"No," she said slowly, thinking it through. "You would survive even if tainted with more than a shadow. Tell me the truth. *Friend.*"

Zheng He traced his fingers along a bamboo strut used to hang pots. "You will make me a perfume in thanks. One of yours."

"You wish to find your true love?" Xiaoting kept her voice neutral.

"I've had all I can desire, save this. Even eunuchs have hearts."

She pretended to consider her options to save some face. Finally, she said, "Protect my uncles at court. Make sure we have safe passage out of the city, and find a place for us near enough to Nanjing that we can get the supplies we need but distant enough to be safe."

"I have a compound far to the east of the city on the river." He gave her an impish grin that looked incongruous on his big body. "I've been looking to sell for some years."

Xiaoting sighed. "Admiral."

"It's suitable," he assured her. "I'll tell my servants to prepare it for your household."

She nodded. Zheng He was not the kind of man to take advantage of a simple house sale. "I'll check with our astrologer for an auspicious day to travel."

"Speed is your friend now, and you need to move faster than jealousy and fear."

She bit her cheek. "That's very fast indeed. I'm sure the astrologer would agree tomorrow is a good day." After all, an inauspicious day to travel was better than a summons.

"I will have some servants accompany you," he said. "Can you be ready at dawn?"

She thought of the hundreds who made up the household, and packing their belongings, and the family's. The fight she would have with her husband, who acted as if he were the one who brought in the money for the gardens and the silks. Then she gave a decisive nod. "Yes."

The admiral turned to leave, then looked back. "My payment?"

This time Xiaoting laughed. "Delivered after I see how suitable this compound you're selling me is."

"Then I expect the best, because you'll be pleased."

The moment he left, roaring out for his servants to ready his horse, Xiaoting sent a maid to summon the girls. They came, chattering and red-cheeked from their time outdoors, and she watched them with fond eyes, glad they'd had one last happy memory there. She had hired the best landscapers and artists in Nanjing to create the garden. It was like a poem, complete with vistas and a pavilion, where they put on theatricals in warm weather for the household and guests. She had based it on Aiai's description of the Peony Goddess's realm and named it the Garden of Everlasting Aroma.

"Everlasting," she muttered. "Except for my judgment." She had no time for self-recrimination, not when there was so much work to be done. Anyway, her husband would be happy to point out her missteps, on the journey and thereafter. She looked at the flowers clutched in the girls' hands. She would gift the garden to the emperor, Xiaoting decided. If it assuaged some of his covetousness and made him better disposed to the Huas, it would be worth the sacrifice. Better to give him the mansion as well.

"Ma'am?" asked Liaobing. Petals rested in her hair, but now was not the time to berate the girl for untidiness.

"Pack it up," she said, indicating the shelves and the workshop. "All of it. Quickly, before nightfall." Xiaoting would inform her mother once the girls were at work. It was more important to act than to endure endless debate with the others in her household over the best action to take.

"Everything?" repeated Liaobing. She might be messy, but the girl was the workshop's best perfumer and the apprentices' unofficial leader. "What's going on, ma'am?"

Xiaoting sighed. "It's time for us to move on."

This time, she would be more careful. Power and safety dwelled together with secrecy. In her hurry to make the Huas invincible, she had made them vulnerable. In her eagerness to demonstrate their power, she had made them powerless. Regret coursed through her as she looked at her workshop, where generations of her ancestors had toiled and experimented, refining their craft and learning their power. All gone, thanks to her misjudgment. She had moved too fast and too openly, and trusted too easily.

She would never make that mistake again.

Nor would the daughters of her blood.

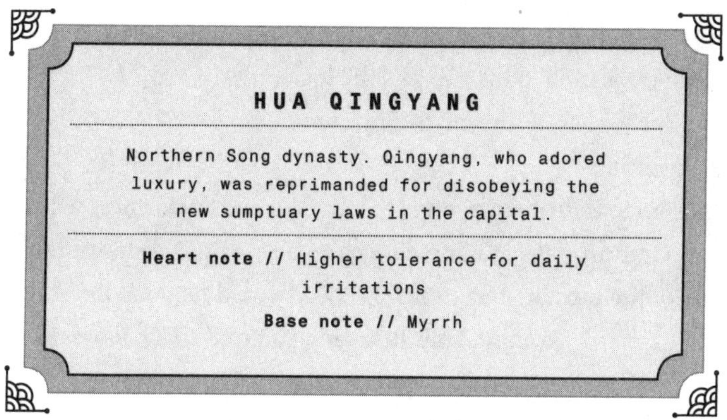

Rafe knocks again, but I cannot deal with him or anyone at this moment.

"Go away," I yell.

"Please, Lucy." His voice is soft. "Just...let me in."

I'm not ready to be weak in front of Rafe, but I need the company. I'm tired of the empty room. Tired of trying and failing. I'm too tired to keep saying no, and although we may be estranged, we're not strangers.

The wine means I struggle with the locks and, because I haven't put down the glass, spill more on my clean shirt. Finally, I crack the door open and step back.

Rafe stands in the doorway and we stare at each other for what seems like an eternity. He's in a gray zipped hoodie—worn, frayed, and faded, like the one he wore almost every day when he was seventeen. I could be convinced it's the same one, except there's no way the hoodie that had draped over his angular teenage frame would fit the man in front of me. He's also in jeans and bare feet with ratty slides. He must have been putting the garbage out or something equally domestic. No, a square white bag hangs from his hand. He met a delivery person in the lobby.

I step aside, then turn around and walk into my apartment. Behind me, Rafe closes the door and sets the locks.

"Wine?" I ask, sitting on the couch.

"I'll get it."

I listen to Rafe move around the kitchen and try to guess what he's doing. Getting plates down; that's easy. There's the click of a lighter; is one of the burners not working? Why would he need the stove? I could turn around to see, but that seems like so much work when I can barely lift the glass to my lips.

It takes only a minute or two before he comes into the living room and puts a cup down in front of me. "Water," he says.

As I sip, he opens the bag to reveal Korean fried chicken and tteok-bokki, and what look like corn dogs but with an oddly textured exterior. "You should eat," he says. "Luckily, I bought too much because I didn't know what I wanted. Is there anything you don't eat? Meat?"

"No, but I'm not hungry."

"Lucy, don't let the food go to waste." He pulls on the translucent gloves that came with the food and picks up a chicken wing.

He's halfway through the chicken when I give in and grab one of the corn dogs, its surface cratered with what looks like hash browns. "Does this have potato on it?" I ask, hefting it in my hand by the wooden skewer stuck through the center like a handle and turning it around curiously.

"It's cheese with potato." He pushes over the white Styrofoam tub of tteokbokki. "Dip it in this."

I do, the weight of the food making my hand slip on the skewer, and take a bite. The coating is soggy from the delivery, the cheese congealed from cooling, but this is a comfort food par excellence. I take another bite, then another, and before I notice, I've finished it without offering any to Rafe. Mom would be deeply unimpressed with my greed, but all Rafe does is hand me the second, this one covered in what looks like toasted ramen noodles with a half–hot dog, half–cheese interior.

I drink down the rest of the water—the food is salty—and Rafe pours me another glass from the carafe he brought out. I can already feel the headache coming and rub my temples with my fingers to try to alleviate some of the tension. Then I drink some more wine. Might as well put off the hangover for as long as I can. I've settled into a miserable and introspective drunk, not a happy, hyper one.

"What's going on, Lucy?"

I screw my eyes tight. "You know when people say they want something so bad it hurts?"

"Yes."

"Have you ever wanted something so bad that it went beyond pain? So deep that it almost numbed you?"

There's a short silence, and then Rafe says, "I have."

"I want something like that, but it's something I never had. I thought I did and I was wrong. What's wrong with me that I can't let go? Why can't I accept the loss of something that was never mine in the first place?"

My eyes squeeze shut to keep in the tears the wine has loosened, but I hear Rafe rise and then feel the dip of the couch when he sits next to me. He's close enough that I can sense his presence. "What did you want?" He sounds severe, but when he reaches out to lay a hand on mine, it's gentle.

I can't stop, because deep down, I desperately want to tell someone. "I want my power. My moli power."

"What do you mean?" Rafe sounds a little staggered, as if he hadn't expected this. Which—fair.

When I don't answer, he examines me, his bottom lip caught between his teeth before he speaks again. "Lucy. Are you telling me that you don't...that something happened to your moli? I thought you were taking time for yourself before you joined your mother. That's what we were told."

I still don't say anything.

"I promise I won't say a word to anyone, including Mom." Then he adds, "Swear on Stevie."

I had forgotten about Stevie. It was the name we gave a little harbor seal who liked to swim around the beach rocks when we were exploring, recognizable by a perfectly round dark patch between the eyes. Swearing on Stevie had become our inviolable code for promise-keeping and truth-telling.

"That was a lie, about me taking time." I force it out. "I don't have my moli. I never did. Mom came up with that story to cover it up."

"What happened?"

I spread my hands in my lap. "No one knows. The power might have skipped me. I might not be doing it correctly. There might be some other reason we haven't thought of."

Rafe's face is intent. "How can you tell?"

"Well, nothing changed for my first client. So that was a big indicator. But there's a feeling. My mother asked if I was sure I felt it, and I thought I did. It's a little tug. Every woman in the family felt the same thing."

"You didn't?"

"No, but I thought I did." I curl deeper into the couch. "When I was younger, I expected the power to work for me like it did for everyone else."

"Like the sun coming up in the morning?"

"Exactly. It never crossed my mind that it wouldn't. Then it didn't, and I couldn't bring myself to try again."

"Why not?" The words are gentle.

I lie on the couch and talk to the ceiling. "Because this way I still had hope. Deep down, I could tell myself maybe that initial failure had been a fluke. That if I tried again, it might work. The possibility kept the hope alive."

"I assume you tried again."

I sigh. "Yeah, a while ago. I don't have it. I never did." My eyes drift down to the discarded remains of our meal. "You know what's at stake. Mom was depending on me to rebuild the family fortune. The moli fragrances are the moneymakers."

"People pay a lot for love." He leans back. "I realize I don't know how this even works. I never asked. How did you find out your family could do this in the first place?"

It feels a little strange to share my family's history. "The original Hua woman—her name was Aiai—gave some incense to a maid, who fell in love after she burned it. Aiai's mother realized her gift was to call someone's true love, to make their hearts whole."

"Can you test it on yourself?"

"It doesn't work on us. Mom can make people happier, but have you met a more miserable woman?"

"That's not fair," he reprimands me gently.

I press my lips together, embarrassed and resentful that he's called me out, and Rafe looks over at one of my candles. "It's perfume, though. Wouldn't everyone who smelled it be falling in love or feeling happier?"

Somehow, it relaxes me to chat about the logistic side of what we do. "Some moli are more inward and only affect the wearer. For instance, Mom's does that. It wouldn't make all the people who smell it happier as well. Some are more outward, and they cause changes in others."

Rafe looks fascinated. "Like what?"

"Like my great-grandmother seven or eight back, who could make the wearer look more attractive to others. The moli's impact was on those who came in contact with the one who wore the perfume but didn't change the wearer's mood or perception at all." I consider this. "Although I guess they'd be happy everyone thought they were hot. So it had a secondary impact."

"What about the true love?" he asks.

"I suppose that's the only one that does both," I say, surprised I haven't thought of this before. I'll need to add that into my transcription as a note. "True love goes both ways and needs to be reciprocated. If it's one way, it's only an obsession."

I let my voice trail off at the end, realizing I'll never be able to see that impact firsthand. I'll never witness two people achieving their love thanks to me.

Then Rafe touches me softly on my arm like the hundreds of times he'd wanted my attention when I was reading or zoning out. It's been so long since someone touched me like that, and never someone who knew the truth. Humiliatingly, I start to cry again. I can't help it. All of this has been stuck inside, and that touch has drilled a hole in my flesh where it can leak out.

Rafe doesn't hesitate. He wraps his arms around me and tucks my face into his chest to simply hold me until my tears fade and dry.

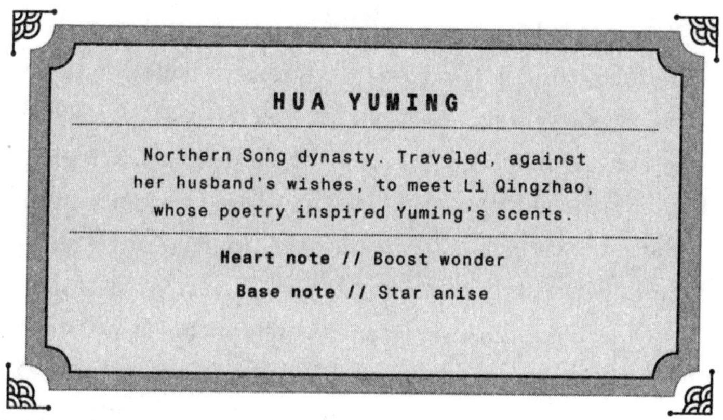

don't know how many hours later it is when I wake, suddenly alert, my heart pounding. Was there a noise in my apartment? I reach for the illegal can of pepper spray I keep by my bed and sit up, hand pressed to my chest, to listen in the darkness. There's nothing, and once I get the nerve, a quick check of the apartment shows all is in order.

I lie back in bed, staring at the ceiling and trying to analyze the cause of this inexplicable dread, when it becomes extremely explicable for two reasons. The first is the edge of the hangover tugging at my brain. The second is that I told Rafe my secret.

I stuff my face into my pillow, yelping when the sudden movement causes my head to throb. I sift through my memories of the night. He'd stayed with me, holding my hand and occasionally patting my back. It was the same as when I was a teenager and angsting over a fight with my mother, and the soothing familiarity had calmed me down.

Was he more distant than usual when he left? It's hard to say, since I delivered a bit of a whammy. All those years wasted because he'd been scared he couldn't live up to something that never materialized.

I lie in bed and worry about it for a good hour, looking at every potential bad outcome, and each time reminding myself there is little I can do about it at three in the morning. My mind flutters from thought to thought, from the inane to the truly worrisome, without fully landing on anything. The store display needs to be changed again. Will this change how Rafe feels about me? Ana's new idea of live streaming the cats in the alley. Kelsey's samples. It's strange how she suddenly needs wedding-based fragrances. I could have some fun with them. No florals at all. She'd go nuts if I left out the orange blossom, but she wouldn't know why. What Mom said about my perfumes. Am I stagnant? Will Mom be mad I told Rafe the truth when she's spent so much effort covering for me? Do I have to tell her? Whatever happened to that failed bottle from my last moli test?

Then a cascade of thoughts clatter down like I pulled the wrong block in a game of Jenga.

I know why this feeling of impending doom hasn't dissipated. Something very bad has happened.

Kelsey is excited so many women need engagement-themed luxury gift bags.

Women get engaged when they're getting married.

People get married when they find their true loves.

My incipient headache vanishes with a rush of adrenaline. While it's possible those women could all be a part of some mass-marriage cult, I think not. What I do know is they all received perfume samples from a boutique called Ile de Grasse.

Whose nose, Lucy Hua, had decanted those samples from a single bottle she'd seized off an ugly break room couch after failing in an experiment to access her ancient ancestral magic.

Or *had* I failed?

Kelsey sent me a follow-up email, and I scramble for my phone, never in my life so eager to read a message from my sister-in-law. A quick scan confirms I didn't fantasize the entire conversation. All signs point to the idea that not only was my bottle a moli fragrance, but it was distributed unknowingly to a random group of women.

Oh my God. I drop my phone. The most important rule in our family is to never talk about our moli.

I blew that a few hours ago.

The second most important rule of our family, but one I never had to consider much, is that we only give moli fragrances to those who ask and who know what they're getting. And, more significantly, *pay.*

It looks like I've screwed up the second rule too. Seriously, can not one thing go well for me? I was born cursed. That's the only answer.

Then, bursting up through this inner torment, it dawns on me what this means.

I have my moli.

The realization is so big I can't comprehend it. The Kelsey problem fades as I poke around the edge of this huge thought. I have my moli. I have it?

I need to call my mother.

No. I need to be sure.

After getting out of bed so fast I almost tumble into the wall, I right myself and run to the bathroom to grab a perfume. I usually keep a few of my own around. Standing on the chilly tile, holding my bottle of Jade Bracelet—a warm but green chypre—it hits me that I don't know what to do. I emptied out the bottle I'd decanted Kelsey's samples from, but even if I didn't, I have no idea how to test it for my moli. I don't think I felt anything from them, but I'm not certain. I can't know if I have it for sure.

Goddammit, I'm back to square one.

I go to the living room and hunker down on the couch. First things first: I need to talk to Kelsey. It's only two thirty in the morning in Vancouver. Still too early. I'll have to wait at least four hours.

Never has time gone so slowly. I do my best to keep busy by having a shower (ten minutes), brewing coffee (ten minutes, but most of it standing there waiting—so, not helpful), and making my bed (less than a minute, because I only need to yank up the duvet). This still leaves many hours, since I reconsidered and decided to wait until a civil eight in the morning Pacific time to call Kelsey.

There's no point trying to sleep, and I can't do anything that requires an iota of focus. The bottle I took from the bathroom with the vague idea of trying my moli again sits on my kitchen counter. I take it with me to lie on the couch and watch a reality show about psychics battling it out over a deck of Zener cards. Lady Bliss is in the lead with an impressive run of knowing the tester had held circle, square, square, circle, and star.

Finally, halfway through the finale, where the psychics are helping solve a cold case, my phone turns from 10:59 to 11:00. I immediately call my sister-in-law on the West Coast.

Thankfully, she picks up right away. "Hello?"

"Hey, Kelsey, it's Lucy." Then I pause, wondering if I need to clarify. "Lucy Hua. Your sister-in-law."

"Lucy, hi." She sounds confused. "What's up?"

"I was thinking about your call—"

"You'll have the samples to me soon? So awesome. I should thank you, but honestly, it's the other way around because you're getting amazing visibility! Did I tell you that I've had so many requests for luxury gift bags suitable for chic tastemakers I'm now my company's number one in sales?"

"That's great." My heart skips a beat. "I wanted to check a few things with you."

"Sophie, get your brother's bag from upstairs. Start getting him ready for school, and don't forget he has soccer." She comes back to our conversation. "What do you need to know?"

In the many hours I've been waiting, I've come up with a perfect way to get the answer I need without making her suspicious. "The clients asking for the wedding and engagement bags—were they all ones who got my original samples?"

"Mmm, I think so."

"Could you confirm it for me?" I press. "I want to make sure I don't repeat the fragrance notes."

"Is it that big a deal? I'm a little busy, and I'm sure it'll all smell the same."

"I suppose not," I lie. "It's just that you made a point of mentioning how sophisticated your customers were. Of course, women like that would notice. If you don't think it's a problem, I won't worry about it either."

That does it. "Give me a second, my laptop's right here." She pauses. "Let's see, Hailey, Madison, Amanda, Courtney... Yes, all ten were on my original list."

"All of them are getting married?" I feel sick with adrenaline.

"Unbelievable, huh?" She sighs. "They were in the perfect mindset to find love, and it came to them right away. Manifestation works. You'll get me the perfume soon, right?"

"Sure thing." I hang up while I still have my voice.

Then I lie on the couch and feel my heart beating so fast I worry about passing out. It's true. I have my moli. I hug this knowledge to myself, waiting for a sense of completion to come to me. I've finally achieved what I've wanted my whole life.

I should tell my mother. Should I call her now? I can prove I'm a worthy daughter. A good daughter. I work through the conversation in my head, knowing I'll be thinking of every possible way to tell her until I say the actual words. None of them seem right, though, and I shift to what her reaction could be. She'll probably take it calmly, with a small tinge of *I knew you could do it if you tried* or *It's about time*. Some of my excitement dies. It's not like I want a party, but it would be nice to be left with something more than finally living up to an expectation.

Hold on. If I tell Mom, not only will I have to experience that lackluster response, but I'll also have to run her gauntlet of questions delivered rat-a-tat under the guise of caring. It might be best to keep this to myself as I think it through, because I need some answers ready. For instance, why? Why now and not when I was twenty, like every other woman in my family?

Also, I'm in a very slight panic about this wedding stuff resulting from Kelsey's bags and having provided a powerful moli scent to twenty strangers who have no idea of its impact. I can take one day to myself to figure this all out. One day will be fine. It can wait for that long.

I try calling Rafe with no answer, which increases my overall nervousness although I know he's probably in meetings. I shoot him a text asking him to call, then sit, turning the bottle in my hand. The knowledge is too new and uncertain for me to be happy yet, leaving me tense and jumpy.

"I have my moli." I say the words to the empty room, and with that, it finally sinks in enough to let me feel it. The fears and worries disappear under a deep relief and then a burgeoning joy I thought was permanently excised from my life. Finally, I'm the person I was meant to be, one who's worthy of the women in my family. I'm not a failure. I'm a fifth Hua daughter in more than name. Tears leak from my eyes as if I'm literally overflowing.

The only damper on this is that I don't know why it happened, and that nags at me. No, I won't let it take over. I have my moli, and for once in my life, I won't look at what-ifs or wait for the other shoe to drop. I will allow myself to be happy without strings. I fall over on the couch, hugging the bottle and grinning at the ceiling.

The phone rings, disturbing my inner celebration. It's Ana. "Are you coming in today?" she asks.

Shit, I'm late. Huge epiphanies have a way of shoving aside daily worries, but daily worries are insidious enough to distract me from the huge epiphany. It's the modern circle of life. "Sorry. I got delayed."

"Are you okay?" she asks. "You sound a little wild."

I stop the hysterical laugh from bubbling over. "I'm good. Be there soon."

I'm not usually a morning shower person, but I take one to get the lingering smell of metabolized alcohol off my skin. I throw down one of the shower bombs I've been experimenting with, and overdose myself on an energizing blast of tangerine that makes me sneeze. I'll need to tweak the formula, but even this product fail makes me feel like singing. After wiping the steam off the mirror, I examine my face and see my lips have tilted up in a smile. It grows wider as I watch, and my mother's face smiles back at me. I haven't realized I've started to resemble her so strongly, and I give our reflection a small salute, then shake my head. I'm crossing over into silly. Time to rein it in so Ana doesn't ask more questions about my mood.

I finally arrive to find Ana staring out the window so avidly I want to ask if she needs popcorn. "They're fighting," she says as I come in.

"Really?" At least everything at the shop is normal. I join her at the window to see Elvis and Priscilla. They're not making out this time, but staring at each other with crossed arms. Priscilla is the one to throw up her hands and walk away.

"Ohh, she's not looking back," says Ana.

"Boss move."

She glances over. "You look happy."

I shrug. "Having a good day."

"We all need those." She holds out her hand and I high-five her. "It looks good on you," she adds.

My mood slowly erodes as the hours pass. It's busy, and I begrudge every customer because all I want is to read the register I brought with me to try to figure out what's happened. I've been taking peeks at it all day, each time getting a rush of adrenaline that gradually turns into trepidation as more what-ifs cross my mind. What if I'm wrong? What if there's something bad about my moli? What if Mom doesn't believe me?

Plus, Rafe hasn't called, although he does send a brief reply to my text, asking me how I'm feeling and telling me he'll be in meetings all day but wants to talk. I say okay. We should talk, although my guilt at telling him my secret last night has been minimized by the thought that I have my moli. There's no doubt in my mind Mom will forgive the Rafe indiscretion if I can show her I've finally proven myself.

Finally, Ana heads out with a cheery goodbye, locking the door behind her, and I'm left alone.

I heave out the register, thankful to finally be able to concentrate. First, a quick scan. I start with the Tang dynasty's Aiai and page through at a steady pace, focusing on the women's accounts of the days when each were able to access their power.

After an hour, I start to get depressed. After two hours, my arm cramps from flipping pages and I'm only at the Song dynasty.

Eras of Chinese history are unfolding in front of me like a fan, and not one of them has a single bit of useful information. I slam the book shut and stick my legs out until I'm stiff as a board in the chair. With my mind mush and frustration looming like a nova on the edge of my patience, I pick up one of my perfumes. This time I work with a confidence I haven't felt since I was twenty and Mom and Waipo were standing at my side with their silent support. It comes to me as easily as it did that day, each movement part of a ritual dance that feels exactly like it needs to. Once the last huo stroke is complete and the sticker placed on the bottle, I force myself to calm down. I've done it before. It worked. It's going to work again.

This time my power rushes into me like I'm opening a gate. I take a moment to feel that oneness with the surrounding energy before I direct it at the bottle.

I slump down as the energy rushes out, leaving a sense of rightness, a ghostly sensation of absolute certainty I assume is similar to what one feels when faced with one's true love. I twist the bottle in my hands and stare into it as if I can see the change. How much easier this whole thing would be if the perfume glowed, or glittered, or a circle of flower goddesses appeared out of the sky to holler, "It worked, Lucy, don't worry!"

None of these things happen. I uncap the bottle cautiously to give a test sniff, knowing it's useless since the smell doesn't change.

I put the bottle carefully on the table and check myself over. I'm a little tired, the way I should be. Then the misgiving assails me again, evaporating all my excitement. These are all the feelings I felt while Ms. Kang waited impatiently for me to change her life, and look what happened. Nothing but endless quizzing from Mom, so intense that by the end, I doubted my own name. It's the same way I begin to doubt myself now, although I've followed the instructions to a T and completed every step perfectly. That's enough, isn't it?

Or am I simply so desperate for it to work that I'm overhyping the very reasonable outcome of a bunch of women of marriageable age getting married? If my moli really had worked, wouldn't all twenty of those women from the list be ordering their Jo Malone dupes in luxury gift bags emblazoned with BRIDE in fancy gold script, instead of only half of them?

I don't know.

But Mom will.

I look at my phone and shake my head. For this, I need to go back home.

I stand in Toronto's Terminal 3, poking through some unappetizing sandwiches with limp Boston lettuce leaves hanging over the edges of the bread. By the window, a pair of bald toddlers in matching overalls stare at the planes that sit on the tarmac like gigantic birds. They break into gasps when their father points out one lifting off in the distance.

I told Ana I had a family emergency, which was true enough, although I felt a little bad for the way she fussed over me. Rafe wanted to know if everything was okay when I canceled our planned dinner, but accepted without question that I needed to go home. He's texted twice to check on me, and I fought the urge to tell him what's happened. That would be wrong; Mom has the right to know first.

My flight is full, but luckily I have an aisle seat next to a teenager who doesn't bother to look up from their phone and keeps their elbows and knees tucked into their space. It's the second-best-case scenario for flying. I stuff in my earbuds and listen to the soothing sound of British men talking about fast cars going around glamorous locations until a bump wakes me up. I've slept through the whole flight. Excellent for my nerves, since I didn't have to spend five hours worrying, but now I have a limited amount of time to come up with the correct wording that will tell Mom what she needs to know without me getting messily and unacceptably emotional in front of her. If I break down, it will confirm how badly I wanted this. The years of me pretending to her that I didn't care, necessary to save my own heart, will be proven useless and I'll have no choice but to fully acknowledge what I suspect she already knows.

Thanks to a delay at the gate in Vancouver, which sends a repeated chorus of grumbles up and down the plane as people hover in a half crouch over their seats and glare at the lucky few standing in the aisle flexing and stretching, I'm running later than I planned when I get a cab and head downtown. Although the first Yixiang Parfums was established in Chinatown—for safety and convenience, because at the time most of their customers were Chinese—Waipo moved the store to what she considered a fancier location on Burrard Street, betting on my fifth-daughter income to eventually make it worthwhile. Looking at the buildings as we pass, I wonder if Mom regrets the move. Chinatown rents are some of the cheapest in the city, and the big Tiffany and Hermès showrooms are indicators that Burrard is definitely not.

The boutique is a gem, though. The shiny brass Yixiang Parfums sign sits in a clean sans serif font over the door. It gives the impression of a stylized art deco Chinese gate, with a dragon and a crane edged in bronze, surrounded by peonies. The storefront is perfectly symmetrical, and each of the display windows features thick jade-green velvet swathed around perfectly lit perfume bottles. There's not a mote of dust in sight, and the entire vibe is one of deep luxury. I stand across the street in the fading Vancouver sun and watch the store. I can't see inside, and no customers go in as I wait. It's close to six, my mother's usual closing time on weekdays, when I finally roll my bag across the street.

I haven't been in the store since I left home, limiting my visits to the lab in the back, and entering Yixiang now is like walking into my childhood merged with an alternate future I never had a chance to experience. I look around with greedy eyes. Here are my family's perfumes, arranged in elegant collections through the store. Small signs sit near each bottle to list the notes and the scent story, and a brass plaque tells an abridged history of Yixiang. The entire store is designed to delight Asian customers with the details while ensuring others are confident enough to come in and buy. As my mother cynically points out, it's exotic enough to be exciting but comfortable enough to not scare people off.

I note every change with a faint sense of disapproval. That chair in the corner is new, as is the floor. Before, it was gold-and-red carpet, with swirls that looked like clouds, and now it's a dark-brown wood. Not a single footprint mars the shine.

While I'm looking at the floor, my mother comes out of the back with a smile on her face. "Welcome to... Luling?"

As well as never seeing my mother cry, I've rarely seen her shocked. Her hand flies up to her chest. "What are you doing here?" she asks, her eyes wide. "What's wrong?"

"I need to tell you something," I say.

It says much about my mother's self-control that her only reaction is to nod. "Let me close the store first."

She hands me the mop, and I do a quick wipe of the already spotless floor as she locks the door and closes out the cash register.

Then she takes the mop, not having said a word the entire time, and leads me to the back. Unlike the hodgepodge room at Auntie's Closet / Ile de Grasse, my mother's break room is orderly and clean. Boxes sit on proper storage shelves, and there's a spotless mini-kitchen with a small table and chairs. No food smells permeate the air, nor does a dish sit in the sink. Mom is as exacting about the appearance of her personal spaces as she is about the store.

"Tea, Cloud?" she asks. I look closely at her. She's more tired than at Waipo's funeral, and I think she's thinner. Although she might have celebrated this in the past, I worry about the way her clothes hang off her. Mothers aren't supposed to waste away. They should get more solid with time.

"Where did that come from?" She hasn't called me that since I left, and curiosity distracts me. "The nickname. Cloud."

Mom smiles. "It's from when you were a little girl."

"How old?"

"Five? Six?" Her voice gets the faint exasperation that always appears when there's something she thinks she's supposed to know and doesn't. "Do you want to hear the story or not?"

"Yes."

"You wanted the smell of clouds, for some reason. You had something in your head, and nothing I created matched. I tried pine. I tried my favorite aquatic accord. Your grandmother tried." She pauses. "One of the mods ended up being the foundation for Mist, by the way. One of our most popular scents. Very profitable."

"Yeah, glad you could monetize a gift for your daughter so it wasn't wasted."

Mom sighs. "You should be proud you were the reason it exists, not angry we sold it. Do you want to hear the rest of the story?"

I nod, clinging to it as a way to procrastinate telling her my news a bit longer, while I can still pretend she'll hug me and be proud, instead of the response I know I'm going to get.

"You insisted on doing it yourself, so I took you to the lab and had you smell things until you had three you wanted." She gives a small laugh. "The strangest things. Lilac. You always loved those, and in the spring I'd find you hiding under the tree, behind the lowest branches. Then mint, but you called it gum. Peppermint, not spearmint. You were firm about that."

"What else?"

"Cucumber." She smiles. "You took the pipettes and kept adding drops until you had the smell you wanted."

"Did it smell like a cloud?"

"Of course not. It smelled like the water in an upscale spa. Very refreshing. You didn't tell me if you want tea."

"No, thanks."

She puts down two full cups. "Tell me your news."

I take a breath. "Mom." Then I stop, unable to put it in words. The thing I've wanted the most for years is here—to be able to tell her I'm not a failure. Yet I can't find the proper *words*.

"Sit down, Luling." She waits until I obey. "You always worry too much about the right way to do things. Everything has to be flawless. Just tell me."

"I have good news and bad news."

"Bad first."

"There's an issue with Kelsey. One I caused with my perfume samples."

Her face doesn't change. "All right. We can talk about that after you tell me the good news."

In response, I reach into my bag and pull out a perfume bottle. She looks at it curiously. "You have a fragrance for me?" she asks eventually, the bags under her eyes puffing as she frowns. "Why did you bother to fly across the country for this? What a waste of money and time."

This spurs me on. "No. I came to tell you this is a moli fragrance. Mine."

It takes a moment for my mother to understand, but when she does, her eyes widen. I wait for the little dig, the *Are you sure?* That doubt she's always had in me, that inability to believe in me, and her endless and debilitating need to test and question.

Mom says nothing.

To my shock, she comes over and hugs me, clutching me close and then closer as her arms tighten. I stiffen. This wasn't what I expected, and I want to pull away but I can't. All she does is repeat my name into my hair, and I give up on trying not to cry. Crying in front of my mom is usually a no-go zone because I can't handle showing that much vulnerability in front of her. Here, in this moment, it's like all our history has been filtered out, leaving only the two of us and what we used to have.

It lasts seconds before she moves back, hands on my shoulders, her elbows stiff. "Tell me everything, Luling. Everything. Now."

It takes a while, but to Mom's credit, she doesn't say a word as I stumble my way through the story. Then she asks if I brought the register with me.

This is more normal, and it calms me down. I pull the book out of my bag and hand it to her. "I've been reading but haven't found anything."

She flips through as she mumbles under her breath. Finally, she stops, fingers spreading over and down the page as if to smooth out the words.

"Your grandmother wondered if this could be the same for you," she says.

I read the entry. "I don't get it," I say. It's a straightforward account of a woman's moli ceremony. A successful one at that.

Mom jabs a finger at the dates, and I resign myself to doing some mental math. Okay, Jiali was born in 1670 and then found her moli in 1696. So?

I frown. So. That's not twenty years—that's twenty-six. "She was older, but I'm not sure how that matches me."

"There was another note, a small one." My mother takes the register and finds the page she wants. It's a woman from the Ming dynasty, which I'd barely glanced over because most of it was long-winded descriptions of the landscape that would only interest a geoarchaeologist.

My daughter is ten now, the entry reads. It's after a lovingly in-depth overview of their new pigs. *She is young, but ready to learn about her moli. Some girls are ready to be trained earlier. All girls are different, I told her, the way all our power is different.*

"You think I'm a late bloomer?" I ask.

Mom shuts the book. "I don't know. We thought if some girls could be trained earlier, it was possible for others to only access their moli later. Twenty might have simply been the age set out by Aiai because that was the age her own daughter's gift appeared."

"It could have been a calendar error," I say. "Also, why are you only telling me this now? Didn't it seem like important information for me to have?"

"I did tell you," she says. "You didn't listen, and every time I brought it up, you changed the conversation. I decided you were capable of reading the register yourself when you were ready."

"I don't remember this." Did she tell me? It's possible I did shut her down, but shouldn't she have kept trying?

Mom doesn't say anything but shifts her gaze to the door that leads to the lab. I know what she's thinking, the way I've always known what she's thinking. If I'm a late bloomer, then I should be able to access my moli now. I should be able to go to her perfumer's organ, mix a fragrance, slap on a huo symbol, and do my thing, the same as I did in my own lab.

Thank God she doesn't ask me to prove myself. I would have lost it. Unfortunately, it's because she's homed in on the negative. "You gave samples to your brother's wife."

I know that's a big problem because they didn't pay, but I thought we'd have at least another minute of celebration, sixty measly seconds more for me to feel appreciated. But Mom is in action mode, and there's no choice but to join her.

"I sent her twenty samples."

"Then what happened?"

My hackles rise. "How do you know something happened?"

"Because you told me it was bad news," Mom says, narrowing her eyes.

"I don't know if it's an issue or not," I say. "Kelsey said ten of those clients want engagement or wedding luxury gift bags." Here I am, repeating Kelsey's favorite phrase.

"Ten of the twenty," Mom says.

"I guess the other ten didn't smell it yet?"

"What are you planning to do?"

I stare at her in confusion because I thought my surprise arrival made it clear I had no clue what to do next. "Tell Kelsey?" I hazard. That seems like a reasonable step.

She shakes her head. "No, no. She can't know."

The frustration that is part of every conversation with my mother spikes. "Then why did you ask me for my opinion?"

Her phone rings and Mom glances down.

"It's your brother." She picks it up. "Hi, Eric. Don't be silly. Tell your father I have a special surprise."

Mom hangs up, then looks between me and the bottle, brow lowered as if thinking. "We'll have to discuss this later," she says. "We're late for your father's birthday."

Right, Dad's birthday, which I'd completely forgotten. I pack up as Mom finishes closing the store. Speed walking to the restaurant—Dad considers tardiness the eighth deadly sin—means there isn't a chance to talk, as I'm panting from dragging my suitcase and am weighed down by the register in my knapsack. Although she offered, I would rather die than have my aging mother carry my baggage. I steal glances at her as we walk across Robson Street; her lips are slightly downturned. Whether that's from my news or knowing we're late, I don't know. All I know is that, as usual, I've failed. Even my good news is laced with bad.

Hua Zhengyi kept her head low, a gesture of obedience at odds with her words. "I won't marry him."

"You need to have daughters, Zhengyi. Daughters to keep the Hua line alive. Do you plan to have fairies deliver one to you?" Her mother wasn't usually sarcastic, but exasperation had leached away her patience. "You are twenty-two years old."

Zhengyi glared at the ornate inlaid table before her, crowded with the moli fragrances she'd spent years learning how to make. It was unfair of her mother to bring up her age. Although other girls were considered marriageable when they put their hair up at fifteen, the eldest Hua women didn't marry until after they had their moli ceremonies at twenty.

"I am not ready to marry."

Her mother waved her hands, her jade bangle clinking against the gold. "No woman is ready to marry, yet it must be done."

"I don't love him."

Her mother didn't bother to answer this, and Zhengyi knew it had been a silly thing to say. Although her mother admired the strength of the fifth daughter's power in her, Zhengyi resented that she could so easily bring love to anyone who could pay but not to herself. The Hua moli gift was layered with a curse—they could never use their perfumes on themselves or other Hua women. Only luck could bring Zhengyi her own true love. If one existed for her. One thing she had learned from reading the register was that the women in her family were not lucky in love. Their stories had shown her indifference was one of the best things she could hope to receive from her husband, because that meant freedom to work on her perfumes.

As she was being scolded, she shifted her weight back and forth on the thick-padded cotton soles of her embroidered shoes. She was grateful to her mother for not binding her feet, much against the wishes of her grandmother, who saw it as a badge of their heritage and class in the rare moments she was lucid enough to argue a point. Zhengyi's mother, although conservative in matters of love, had been determined her own daughter would be able to stand for hours working on her perfumes if she wished, without suffering the pain that so racked her own body.

Her mother's words drifted over her like woodsmoke as ice crackled on the river outside their isolated country home. The compound had grown over the centuries, incorporating new annexes that housed additions to the family and bigger, airier workshops for the women to experiment in. There was a storage wing where Zhengyi and her mother kept their oils, herbs, and spices, separate from that of the kitchens, although they shared many ingredients. Each was meticulously labeled with the date it had been created or acquired, and sorted by purity or grade. Apprentices tended the large flower, herb, and fruit gardens to the west, where the soil was better and large fences protected the delicate plants from any animals that broke free from their enclosures.

The Huas had avoided cities for generations, obeying an ancestral edict to keep attention away from them. "Secrecy is paramount," Hua Xiaoting had told her daughter, who passed the rule to her own daughter. "Secrecy is safety." Over the years, they'd sold their moli fragrances only to a select and trusted group of clients, and stockpiled their riches to make themselves unassailable.

It had worked for five hundred years. But times were changing. Zhengyi could almost taste it in the air, a buzz that came from people traveling and bringing back what they'd learned. There was a curiosity that pulled as much as it pushed, and would eventually be turned on the secretive family living in the guarded compound the way photographic cameras focused on the grave faces of those who posed for them in the city studios. Her mother, who rarely left the compound, refused to believe change was inevitable. She'd only seen her first foreigner last year, and the sight had knocked her almost speechless. "Her nose," she had whispered to Zhengyi as the woman passed. "Her hair. So white for such a young woman, and with no shine! The poor thing. She must see ghosts with those pale eyes."

Despite her mother's disapproval, Zhengyi wanted to know more. She needed to know more, if they were going to survive and prosper in this ever-changing modern world. She insisted on going with her brothers when they went to Nanjing, to feast her eyes—and nose—on the hectic streets where the reek of sewage competed with the aromas of cooking and hair pomades and skin creams. It was a cacophony of scents that would sometimes give Zhengyi a headache. She didn't care. She would go home and write notes for hours, trying to make sense of all she'd smelled.

"I'll make you a deal," she said, interrupting her mother. Rude, but she was being scolded anyway.

"No."

Zhengyi shrugged. "Then I will never make another perfume. How unfortunate the fifth daughters create the most profitable scents and your sons enjoy luxury."

There was a long silence, and Zhengyi wondered if this would be the thing to finally earn her the next beating her mother constantly threatened.

Zhengyi's grandmother Miaoyu chose that moment to hobble into the room, dressed in her usual dowdy rough robe. She was already unsteady on her tiny shoes and broken feet; age had wasted her knees and bent her back.

"We have enough," the old woman croaked. She rarely spoke, and when she did, it was usually to rebuke Zhengyi for anything from eating too much to smiling.

"Mother," said Zhengyi's mother carefully. "How do you feel?" Yitong was always formal with her mother.

Miaoyu ignored her. "We have enough. Our greed and selfishness cause pain. We meddle in the lives of innocents and will be punished by the Almighty God for our arrogance and pride."

Yitong had only beaten Zhengyi once when, as a child, she'd said she wished her grandmother were dead. Zhengyi had learned to keep those unfilial thoughts to herself, but she couldn't prevent them from arising occasionally. Miaoyu dimmed the light of any room she entered, and although Yitong extorted Zhengyi to be kind and respectful, Zhengyi's flesh crawled whenever she faced her grandmother and saw the emptiness behind her eyes.

Although most Hua daughters had moli that could be used for good, occasionally the gift misfired, leading to plaintive prayers and exquisite offerings to the flower-covered shrine for the Peony Goddess built in the corner of their workshop. Miaoyu was one of these. Her gift, to create devastating sadness, was one that was in demand only by evil people who wanted to spread unhappiness. It was a rule in the Hua family that those with malevolent gifts would never create or sell them.

Miaoyu had disobeyed.

Zhengyi watched her grandmother leave the room and saw her

mother take a deep breath. "It's like her moli has infected her," Zhengyi said. "She's the walking embodiment of misery."

"Don't say such things," admonished Yitong. "She's paid for her error."

"Not as much as those people did."

"Daughter! Enough."

Yitong's terrible expression cowed Zhengyi into submission. "Yes, Mother."

Her mother sighed. "It's difficult for her to accept she caused so much death and pain. She only wanted to save our home. Her crime was to put our family first."

Zhengyi wasn't as certain, having heard her grandmother's incoherent ranting about the Heavenly Kingdom promised by the Taiping Rebellion's leaders and her hate of the country's Manchu rulers. "She didn't have to give Hong so much of her moli," she said.

Yitong roused herself to defend her mother. "She rarely made it and had no idea of its potency. Plus, how could she know what he had planned?"

It had been a diabolical plan by the Taiping leader. Since the Hua scent only worked on the first person to smell it from the bottle or sachet, Hong had apparently held his breath as he decanted the moli into dozens of smaller containers, which he then had spies dressed as Buddhist monks smuggle into the besieged city. As the Nanjing commanders fell into intractable sadness so intense they dropped where they stood, the city's defenders found themselves unable to withstand the Taiping rebels, who poured in like a spring flood, slaughtering tens of thousands.

"The screams haunt me," Miaoyu had once told Zhengyi. "They never give me rest." It was true. Her grandmother rarely slept.

In the register, where every eldest Hua daughter and her gift were logged for posterity, was another story of one like Zhengyi's grandmother. Hua Haifen of the Tang dynasty had been able to create intense fear. They'd had to hide that skill, lest people try to take advantage of her gift during battle and cause the deaths of innocents. It was unfortunate Miaoyu had ignored that precedent.

Now Zhengyi glanced behind her mother. In the other corner of the workshop, buried in a locked chest, was their answer to those more evil impacts, although it had been too late to use against Miaoyu's moli. Zhengyi had been trusted with this information when she turned twenty and began to contribute to the family in the way she was destined.

With an unreadable expression, her mother looked at the door through which Miaoyu had disappeared, then turned back to Zhengyi. "You spoke of a deal."

"I did. I marry who I like."

Before Zhengyi finished, her mother was shaking her head so hard one of her silver hairpins flew out to land on the floor. "Impossible. You can't bring simply anyone into this family. We need to trust them."

This was a valid concern, and Zhengyi had an answer. "I marry who I like, as long as they won't betray us."

"How will you know?" scoffed her mother. "A girl in love is no judge of character."

Zhengyi thought of Jun's broad shoulders under his trim black jacket, the perfect shine in his black hair, and she was honest enough to admit this was true. "I will take your guidance."

This silenced her mother. They might disagree, but her mother had an eye for people and she loved Zhengyi. She would be a good judge of an appropriate husband. "You will?" she asked slowly.

"Yes, but I have the final say."

Her mother considered this, tilting her head back and forth so her gold filigree earrings tinkled. "What do I get in return if I allow this?"

Zhengyi adjusted her padded jacket. Nanjing was oppressively humid in the summer but cold in the winter. Cold for her, that was. She'd heard Beijing was worse.

"In return," her mother prodded.

"In return, I will make this family safer."

Her eyes narrowed. "How?"

Zhengyi had her plan prepared. She'd been thinking about it for months, ever since her elder brother had come home from Paris, where he had met a Monsieur Jacques Guerlain and visited his shop in the Rue de Rivoli. He'd come home filled with barbed comments about the Huas being old-fashioned, so she knew he at least would be open to the idea. "There are houses in the West creating fragrances," she said.

Her mother made a face. "Heavy, cloying things. They smell like animal behinds."

It was true, but Zhengyi ignored that. "We will do the same."

Her mother stilled, her earrings silenced. "We do not create for farmers."

"We will now. We will be a perfume house, and we will sell to anyone who can afford our wares."

"We can't simply provide everyone with our moli. Safety, Zhengyi. Safety. We must have trust with whom we deal. Remember your grandmother's mistake."

"We will continue to do so, in secret and with select clients. We will also make perfumes for others, with no magic. Regular perfumes people can wear simply to enjoy. Hair oils. Powders. Whatever will sell. We will become known around the world as perfumers, not as holders of moli. That will remain the knowledge of a chosen few while we hide in plain sight."

There was no doubt in Zhengyi's mind that her mother considered this a demotion in prestige. Their family had never been able to strut their wealth the way others had, and her mother chafed under the restrictions that hid their power instead of displaying it to garner the appropriate respect.

"We've never done such a thing." She frowned. "All our perfumes are moli scents." Zhengyi heard the unspoken words. How would they save face if they became mere craftswomen, no better than weavers or builders?

"We're skilled technicians, Mother, and there is no shame in that." Zhengyi walked to the window to look at the river, already rising up the banks with the coming spring, and waved north to Beijing. "There may be no empresses soon."

"Perhaps not, but there will always be the rich." Her mother joined her and lowered her voice. "Lady Yu contacted me the other day. This is what this family is. We are only for the select."

"That world is changing," Zhengyi said. "We aren't limited to China, and we aren't limited to only one kind of perfume."

"Your father will not approve."

There was a long silence as Zhengyi thought of her poor father, a scholar who loved nothing more than his books. And, unfortunately, opium. His wing of the house reeked of the acrid smoke, which fuddled his brain and made him by turns maudlin or wistful.

"We need to do this for Father," she finally said. It hurt to have to be a parent to her parent, but the moli power had always resided in the women. They were used to wielding authority within the house and on behalf of the family, to varied levels of bitterness from men who assumed that authority should be theirs alone.

"It's proper for your eldest brother to make this choice for us," her mother said stubbornly. "You're only a girl."

"I am the fifth daughter," Zhengyi reminded her.

Her mother bit her lip, knowing Zhengyi was right but that her brothers would resent having it thrown in their faces.

"We'll find jobs for them," Zhengyi assured her. "This will be a business, and we will find more customers in China and beyond. We'll send my brothers to school in America and France so they can become fluent in the languages foreigners speak and make important connections."

Her mother nodded slowly. "They'll like that."

"They'll like the money too," Zhengyi said dryly. "Elder Brother especially. I saw his bills from Paris."

Her mother frowned again, returning to her main objection. "I don't like selling our wares to simply anyone who can afford them."

"That will change," Zhengyi said. She already had a name in mind: the House of Yixiang. The House of Rare Perfumes.

"Do I have an alternative?"

Zhengyi smiled. "No, Mother. None of you do." Because she could see their future, even if her mother could only see ahead to her marriage.

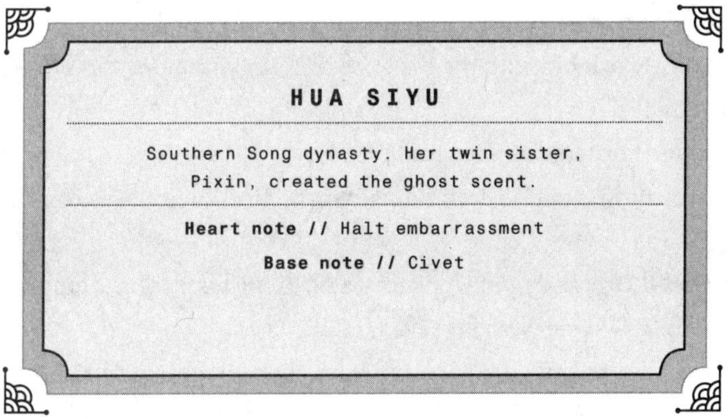

Dad always has his birthday dinner at the same steak house, one of those old-fashioned places with blinding-white tablecloths, dark-red velvet seats, and service bordering on obsequious. We arrive to a thoughtful smile from the hostess—always a woman and always serious, for steaks are a grim business—before heading to the back corner to Dad's favorite table. One year, when Mom had reserved a different one, he insisted on waiting for an hour until it was free. In accusatory silence, so we all knew Mom had messed up.

The server takes our coats and my carry-on, but when he reaches for my knapsack, I clutch it so protectively he eyes it with concern.

"Happy birthday, Dad," I say, waving across the table. We're not much of a hugging family. "Eric, Kelsey, nice to see you. No kids tonight?"

"They're at home with the babysitter," says Eric. "I guess you're the surprise?"

"You're late," Dad says. "Lucy, glad you could make it, but you should have told me you were coming. This table is set for four."

"It's no problem at all, sir." The server is already there with an extra table setting, followed by a woman holding a chair. In seconds, he's made one of the long sides of the table into two spots for Mom and me. Eric looks into the distance as Kelsey motions for a top-off on her wine.

"We've ordered appetizers," Dad says.

"You didn't wait?" Mom stares at him. "Eric knew we were on our way."

Dad shrugs and pours himself water, filling his glass and emptying the carafe. "Dinner was for seven, Meilin."

I try not to chug the wine but have soon caught up to Kelsey. I'd forgotten the pressure of the constant low-level hostility that filled the house and followed us like a fog. Occasionally, it would lift for a meal, or a day, or sometimes a week, and they would get along well enough that it wasn't a stretch to see how they'd fallen in love. Then one of them would make an oblique reference to an old hurt, or take offense to a phrase or gesture, and they'd be back to their cold war. When we were younger, and before they started using us as proxies, Eric and I would try to buffer each other. Those days are gone.

"Even though it's Dad's birthday, I brought something so you don't feel left out, Meilin," Kelsey chirps, handing over a small package. She always says Mom's name as *My-leen*, instead of *May-lin*. I startle at Kelsey calling my father *Dad*, but no one else blinks. Mom opens the package to reveal a small bottle of oil, which she uncaps and sniffs. I twitch my nose as the harsh, cheap smell wafts over.

"Thank you," Mom says politely.

"I knew you would like it." Kelsey crinkles her eyes graciously over her wineglass.

"How's Toronto, Lucy?" Dad asks as the cheese bread comes. He pulls it toward his plate from the center of the table. Shrimp cocktails arrive for Eric and Kelsey, who begin eating without a word.

"Good. Kensington picks up with the warmer weather."

"What's the difference in the number of customers?" he asks.

"Oh, I don't know exactly, but it's significant."

He shakes his head. "You should know, Lucy. You need to track this kind of thing if you want to be successful."

I don't bother telling him my sales are steady throughout the year and depend on much more than foot traffic. Dad and Eric consider themselves experts on whatever topic is at hand, speaking confidently and expecting to be unchallenged. During the pandemic, they were epidemiologists. Then economists. Now it looks like he's a retail consultant.

The server rolls up the cart with the Caesar salad ingredients and begins to prepare it tableside. Kelsey turns to me. "Do you have those samples on you?" she asks. "The girls loved your scents. So modern. Meilin, you should think of doing more like that. It might increase your sales, you know?"

Even Eric stiffens at this, but before I can jump in—no one rags on my mother but me—Mom gives her a generous smile. "Thank you, Kelsey. I'm sure your customers are women of discerning taste."

"Oh, they are," Kelsey assures her. "One of them has an amazing brand deal for her social media. She could probably do something for you if I put a word in. It would help you attract a younger crowd."

The server finishes plating the salads, saving Kelsey from a devastatingly polite but knife-sharp reply from my mother, which would probably have gone over her head. Eric doesn't bother to look interested, and Dad stabs at his lettuce.

I'm drinking too fast, and the server tops me off again as we finish the salad, which is garlicky and delicious. Kelsey isn't helping. She keeps making little digs at my mother, like mentioning how nice it is for the kids to spend time with GramGram, who is retired and has plenty of energy to give to her little treasures. She mentions nothing to Dad about Gramps, who I believe spends a lot of time playing golf. My mother only nods and turns her attention to the scallops the server puts down in front of her. Dad scoops one off her plate and makes a face. "Overcooked," he says, taking another. "You should have gotten the salmon."

Then Kelsey starts talking about those damn gift bags again.

"My event was so successful," she says for the third time. "I can't believe all those women found love through my luxury gift bags. It just goes to show that the right curated items can give a woman the confidence she needs to go out there and find her man." The silence at the table is emphasized by the hum of conversation surrounding us. "You know, Lucy, I should have kept back one of the bags for you. Everyone deserves love, and it looks like I'm the fairy godmother who made it happen for those girls."

The stress of the day, travel, and wine all combine, and I've finally hit my limit. "You don't know what you're talking about."

Kelsey gives a little laugh. "You'll understand if you eventually get a boyfriend."

It's clear Kelsey thinks this is a wicked burn, but Mom's the one to react. "Luling is perfectly happy. Not everyone needs a partner. Sometimes they're more trouble than good."

Dad puts his fork down. "What's that supposed to mean?"

She looks at him. "Nothing. Why do you assume it's about you?"

"I didn't until now."

Eric and I share a look across the table in a rare moment of sibling understanding. Then we both look down, knowing that to interfere will only prolong the fight.

Too bad Kelsey fancies herself a peacemaker. "Oh, let's not ruin dinner. Everyone's feelings are valid here—right, Dad?"

Eric's eyes flicker and we share another look. She might as well have waved a red flag in front of a bull, because if there's one thing Dad hates—one of many things, actually—it's being told what to do. He also prides himself on acting calmly and rationally at all times, especially when he's being both overdramatic and emotional. Like now.

The server comes by, and Kelsey glances at Dad before she says, "My father-in-law would like another scotch, thanks."

I roll my eyes and Kelsey, unfortunately, catches me. "What's that about?" she asks.

My defensive side kicks in. "Nothing."

"Obviously it's something," she says through an afterthought of a smile.

"I'm not sure why you're ordering for Dad."

"Someone has to take care of this family," she says.

That's it. "First, we're all adults who are perfectly capable of speaking to a server ourselves. Second, you don't know anything about this family." She's not part of it—not really—and it bothers me that she's acting like she belongs more than I do.

"What's that supposed to mean?"

Eric gives me a look, and I back down so I don't ruin Dad's birthday. "Nothing."

"Do you not consider me part of this family?" Her voice climbs higher with each word. "When I've been married to Eric for ten years and we have two children? Is that not enough to belong?"

Dad looks up from his meal. "People are looking."

"I want to know," insists Kelsey, lowering her voice slightly. The alcohol-induced slur is more noticeable. "Am I part of this family or am I not?"

"Of course you are," I say, not wanting to cause a scene in a restaurant.

"Then what don't I know?" She's not letting up, and I look to Eric for support, but he's staring at his plate.

"Nothing. Anyone want the last bit of salad?"

"You're lying."

"Let it go, Kelsey," mutters Eric.

That's the wrong thing to say, because she pounces on it. "Then there is something to let go. I knew you've been keeping secrets from me."

"What makes you say that?" I ask.

She curls her lip. "You're not as subtle as you think. Tell me."

I'm trying to think of some lie when Dad leans forward. "Enough of this. It's ruining dinner. What Lucy is referring to is that your mother-in-law imagines her perfumes are magical and it's a family curse or something. Absolute nonsense, but she feels strongly about it. Are you happy now? It's nothing important."

Mom's face goes completely blank, and Dad looks pleased with himself, as if he's finally won a battle in their ongoing war. My eyes dry out from how far they've widened. How could he? *How could he?*

It takes Kelsey a moment to react.

"Oh, funny." She rolls her eyes. "Sure. Nice try."

No one answers, and Kelsey's expression fades to confusion while she looks at my dad as if trying to figure out whether he really was joking, in that unfunny way some men use to replace talking about how they feel. Unable to find an answer on his face, Kelsey turns to Eric. "Baby?" she asks.

He goes for his steak with such force it skitters off the plate. "It doesn't matter."

"Eric!" Mom's voice isn't scolding, but it's definitely a reprimand.

Kelsey leans over her plate to stare at us, one by one. "You can't think I'm going to fall for this. Curses? Come on."

"That's right," I say. "Dad was just putting you on."

This is a mistake, because Kelsey has been around Dad long enough to know that's not something he does. "Wait," she says slowly. "You can't be serious?"

"I said drop it," warns Eric.

Kelsey puts on her playground-mom voice. "I insist you tell me the truth."

The silence around the table tells her what she wants to know. She bursts out laughing. "Figures. This figures. I knew this family was weird from the first time Eric introduced me, but this is too much. Magic perfumes?"

Eric stabs his fork into his mashed potatoes. "It's not real. The Huas have probably exaggerated it over the years for social status."

"Hey," I say.

"Corporations study the impact of scent on mood and use the data to influence consumers," he says, looking at me. "They create big mood maps from a database. There's no magic. No power. No mystical shit. Nothing but science."

"You researched that?" I ask, my hands clenched into fists under the table. "Were you that keen to find a way to put us down?"

He shrugs. "Dad told me."

Mom hurriedly covers her look of betrayal, and Dad glares at Eric. "Enough."

"This isn't the point." Kelsey speaks loudly enough that the people at a nearby table put down their knives to listen harder. Mom's face is pink. "The point is I had a right to know."

My mother stiffens. "A right? It has nothing to do with you."

But Kelsey's mind has ticked over to a new track. "Oh my God," she says. "My samples. My luxury-gift-bag samples. Did you do something to them?"

"Don't be ridiculous," Mom says.

Kelsey ignores her and stares at me, no doubt correctly pegging me as the weaker link. I don't look at Mom this time because I know I can't lie. "They may have been..." I search for a word that will resonate with her but is less judgmental than *cursed*. "Enchanted."

With an almost flawless sense of comedic timing, the server comes up to ask if we're enjoying ourselves. "I was until two minutes ago," mutters Dad, like he didn't start this, while my mother, in a slightly louder voice, says everything is fine, thank you.

Kelsey's attention has moved from me to Eric, who looks bored and irritated. "Is this true?" she demands. "You're *cursed*?"

Mom stiffens beside me at the fear in Kelsey's voice. "It's a gift," she says.

"Meilin, stay out of it," says Dad.

"How can you say that when you brought me into it?"

"You didn't think this is something I had a right to know before I married you?" Kelsey says to Eric, ignoring the rest of us. "What about our children?"

Eric snorts. "I didn't tell you because it's got nothing to do with you or the kids. It only impacts Hua women." He glances over. "Besides, I thought it didn't matter anymore."

"Fuck you, Eric," I mutter in a low tone, not daring to say it louder.

Dad throws down his napkin and gets up without saying a word, his old trick of simply walking away from anything he doesn't want to deal with and leaving Mom to take care of the situation. He brushes against the server, who takes one look at the table and then discreetly waves away his colleague, who was about to clear the plates.

Eric watches Dad leave, his jaw twitching. Kelsey dabs at her eyes with a napkin, which only succeeds in smearing her makeup. She gets up, swaying slightly. "I can't believe any of you."

"Kelsey—"

"I don't want to hear it, Eric!" Kelsey doesn't look at us as she grips her purse to her chest like a shield before swinging on her heel and running out of the restaurant.

Mom blows her breath out softly. "I apologize, Eric."

Eric looks furious. "You ruined Dad's birthday. No wonder he's miserable—married to someone who never puts his needs above her own."

"Shut up, Eric," I say. "Dad caused this in the first place. How supportive has he ever been about Mom and her store?"

"What the hell are you talking about? He let her do it. What more can she ask for?" Eric glowers at me. "What do you think would happen if the attention was off you for a minute?" he says with fake solicitude. "Do you think you would literally explode?"

"Eric, that's not fair." Mom has put her napkin down. Her color is high but her body is straight and still, unlike me, who's shaking.

"My wife left crying, but whatever. The second Lucy gets upset, it's not fair. Of course. You know what? Even if that perfume shit were real, I don't know how you think any man could put up with it."

"What are you talking about?" I demand.

"What do you think it's like, not knowing if your own wife is using it to control you? Your own daughter?" He glares at me. "Your sister?"

I snort. "Since Mom's gift is a mood booster, I think it's clear she's never used it on any of the men in this family."

"Like I believe that."

I want to slap him. "Just because it's something you'd do doesn't mean that we would. Stop projecting."

"Eric, how could you think such a thing?" Mom sounds fierce. "That I would be such a person?"

"I never got to know the person you are. After all, I'm not special like Lucy." He shoves his chair back hard enough that it almost hits the man behind him. "Thanks for the support, Mom. Good to know whose side you're on. I need to find Kelsey."

He leaves, and a swell of silence comes down over what feels like the entire restaurant. Mom looks straight ahead before motioning the server. "We're ready for the bill."

He nods, casts his glance over the uneaten food, then leaves the bottle of wine on the table by my hand. I grab it and fill up my glass. Why not.

Mom does not agree. "Don't you think you've had enough?"

"No. Do you see why you should have let Eric tell her before?"

She stares straight ahead. "Kelsey didn't need to know about us."

I take a sip large enough to make me cough. "Kelsey was going to find out when I told her about the problem with her samples."

"We could have found a solution without her knowing. Even Eric knew better than to tell her, but you, announcing it to everyone under the sun..." She gives a little wave around the restaurant. "A thousand years of secrecy, gone. Telling the wrong person can be fatal for us."

"It's not like your judgment is perfect. You married Dad and told him."

She pulls back like I've struck her. "We are not discussing that."

Good, because the second the words came out of my mouth, I regretted them. What a night.

"Mom, seriously. There aren't witch hunts anymore. No one's going to burn our house or take away our land."

"People don't change, Luling." Mom sounds disgusted at my naivete. "We are disadvantaged in a world that wasn't made for our safety. Look around and show me a powerful woman who doesn't have a sea of people trying to drag her down. Show me *any* woman who doesn't have that."

I open my mouth and shut it. She goes on, "You see so little of the world. The people on our client list are not used to being told no. They get what they want because they have money, power, and influence, and those things are all they value. When we lost them, we turned from people of regard to nothing but providers, to be ordered around without respect or deference."

"That can't be true."

"Powerful people don't see others as people in their own right. We're only there to serve their needs. No one calls them to account. How do you think we protected ourselves from their tyranny over the years? How do you think your past grandmothers avoided being taken hostage and forced to work for a noble or an empress, as Aiai was? Because they had power themselves."

"The world has changed." My voice sounds weak.

"No, Luling. You've been trained to think things have changed. You can't see it because you're not of that level. You're on the land, and your vision is limited because they are above the clouds."

"That's a nasty way to look at the world."

"It's a realistic one. That's why our perfumes cost so much. Respect. Supply and demand. When we lost our wealth, we lost more than money. We lost our status. If we can't replenish it, we are dead in the water. That's why I covered for you when you left, although you've kept yourself sheltered and ignorant so you don't need to think about it."

I look down, ashamed because she's right but irritated that, as usual, she's put it so bluntly. "Do you think Eric was right? About the men in the family?"

She shrugs. "Weak people will always find excuses to shift blame for their circumstances."

The server comes with the bill. Mom pays it silently as I grab one of the after-dinner mints, then quickly spit it out when it turns out to be spearmint and not peppermint. My luggage and our coats appear, and we weave our way between the tables. I'm not sure what's going through Mom's mind, but I'm thinking about what she's said. She thinks we can't replenish what we lost, but I have my moli now. At least, I think I do. I can make those changes. I'm uncomfortably aware Mom is right in her assessment of the world, but I can't bring myself to accept it the way she does. Mom wants to reclaim our place in that domain, but I wonder if we can change it.

The last glass of wine hits me hard, and I stumble out the door after Mom, the street wavering around me.

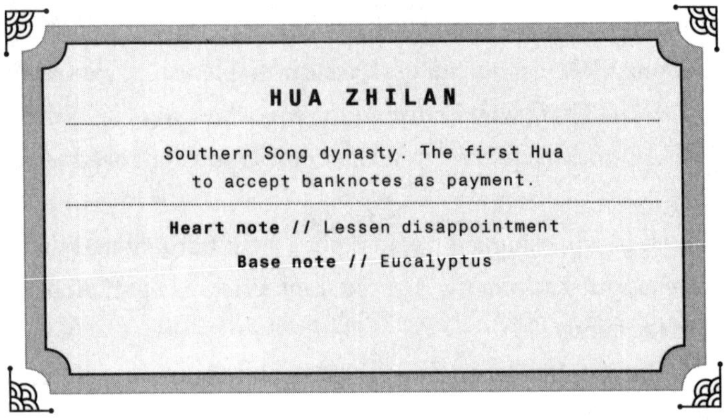

wake in my childhood bedroom, in my childhood bed. At least I hit the perfect spot with the booze last night, drinking enough to keep me asleep instead of waking me in the dark hours to worry. Now, however, nothing stops me. Why did Dad do that? There's almost no point speculating; I'm sure he thinks he has a perfectly inarguable reason for why he's right. For the very first time I wonder if Dad even respects Mom, let alone loves her. He seems to hold what she does in deep contempt, and if he thinks that about his own wife, what about his daughter?

Dads are supposed to love their kids, but no one says anything about liking them.

I want to talk to Rafe, but I'm not sure if it's an overstep. *Friends*—if that's what we are—is a vague term. One person's friend is another's acquaintance and yet another's bestie. A lot has happened since the night of the blackout, and we haven't had a chance to get to know each other as the people we are now. We've texted since I've been back to Vancouver, mostly him asking how I am and me sending photos of things that have changed, but does that mean anything? I like a single path, with no deviations that make me question myself more than I do already, and Rafe has set me down in the middle of a labyrinth.

Calling Rafe, however, would mean talking about last night and also telling him I might have my moli. That decides me. I put the phone down, worried a simple hello could lead to a conversation I'm unable to deal with right now.

The house is quiet. It's a reprieve to have my parents at work, although Dad's absence is a familiar feeling. When he's home, he's usually in his office with the door shut.

My clothes are in a mess on the floor, the pants in a figure eight and the shirt tossed over a chair. I don't like to wear clothes I've had bad experiences in until they're washed, so I pull out a fresh, if wrinkled, outfit to wear before moving robotically through my morning routine. What am I going to do about Kelsey? Why does Dad have to leave like that all the time instead of staying to say what he thinks? Does Eric truly believe Mom is lucky because she was *allowed* to continue our family business? That the men who live with Hua women don't trust them? What's Eric's problem, anyway?

When I'm fresh enough, I check my phone to see a message from my mother, ordering me to come to the store when I get up.

Instead, I climb back into bed and pull the crumpled sheets over my head. I don't want to go to the store. I don't want to talk to, or about, Kelsey. I don't want to look at Dad, knowing finally and for certain how much he despises part of me. I absolutely don't want to talk to Mom about my moli, which is causing as much trouble with its appearance as it did with its absence. I pull out my phone. Since the avoidance tactic I've used in the past—running away—has been thwarted this time by having a plane ticket that's not good until tomorrow, I might as well mentally escape by scrolling social media for hours. I make it through six videos of earnest but frazzled women cooking breakfast for their gigantic families—where are the men in any of these?—before I realize I'm not paying the slightest bit of attention to the surreal fact that these people own family chafing dishes.

I know what I have to do. I haul myself out of bed and head to the shop, where I find Mom sitting with a cup of ginger tea.

She looks up when I arrive. "We need to understand what happened with your moli."

"Good morning to you as well."

"Luling."

"Don't you think we need to talk about last night?" My question is pro forma, because I don't want to either.

"No. We need to prioritize."

"Shouldn't you be working? Since you're here at work?" *Stop stalling, Lucy. Mom is right.* Yet I don't want to be tested.

"Don't worry about what I should be doing. Right now, I am doing this."

She gets up and comes around the counter, where she fixes the sign to say CLOSED and gestures me toward the door. "We need to go to the lab."

I follow without arguing and stand blinking in the bright-white light. It looks the same as it did when I was back for Waipo's funeral.

"The most important thing is to fix this mess you've made." She walks to the back of the lab and taps in the code to access the archive vault.

It's true, I have made a mess, but her tone gets my back up. Naturally, having my moli isn't enough for her. She always has to focus on the negative. That it's a huge and worrisome negative isn't the point. "You said the priority is to figure out what happened with me."

"No, I didn't."

I'm so flabbergasted I almost leap forward. "Yes, you did! It was three minutes ago. You said we didn't need to talk about last night and we needed to understand what happened." As usual, my mother is able to light me incandescent with injustice. I know what she said. She said it. She does this all the time, insisting she's right to the point that I suspect reality has been warped in her head.

"No, Luling."

"Is this even a big deal? Finding your true love is a good thing."

Mom takes the register back into her hands to page through, the lines bracketing her mouth deepening as she pauses to read one of the more recent chapters. Then she looks up. "Finding your true love is a good thing," she says. "This is not."

"Why not?" I knew she would ruin this for me.

"Because that perfume is out in the wild and being used by people who don't know what they're dealing with. Our clients have always treated our work with the respect it's due and, moreover, knew what to expect."

"So?"

She thrusts the register in front of me. "Remember Miaoyu."

"Miaoyu?" I echo, looking down. It takes only a few seconds of reading to recall the story of my ancestor from a hundred years ago. Miaoyu's moli had been to create deep sadness, and her chapter was so filled with frantic religious exhortations it was uncomfortable to read. "What about her? She never made any. She wasn't allowed to." My family might like money, but they were also united in this one thing: that their moli never be used for evil.

She points to a line. "Here."

"'The gift is a curse and I was cursed by God, though I wielded it for His glory,'" I read aloud. Then I read it again. "Wait, she made some?"

"She was a follower of the Taipings and made one bottle for the commander, who told her it would end the siege of Nanjing and stop suffering. They decanted it without smelling and spread it around, causing the Manchu troops to fall and the slaughter of innocents to commence."

It's hard for me to not feel defensive that she's likening my actions to this horror. "True love is not the same as a war or sadness."

"People who sought their true love were prepared for it. What if you were in a relationship with someone you thought was your true love, but then a new love came along? How many lives could be ruined? Families destroyed? Hearts broken?"

"We don't know that," I say immediately. "Plus, that was always a risk for the person being summoned. They might have been in a relationship."

She made a face as if that was a negligible point, and I move on. "These people wanted true love. It was a gift bag for singles."

"They might have given the samples away as gifts. They might simply have wanted the bag and seen the love aspect as a marketing gambit. We don't know. We don't even know if the reason your moli was delayed was because there was something wrong. What if this time the scent doesn't call true love? Or it works on everyone who comes in contact with it?"

She doesn't wait for me to reply. "Even if the moli was perfect, we don't bestow our gifts willy-nilly," she says. "We are cautious about who we sell to, so they respect the power in those bottles. These women don't. We don't know the strength of your moli or the damage it can do."

While I don't love the language that makes it sound like my moli is a mass nerve agent, I can't disagree with the premise. I should have kept this to myself. I knew it. I double down, simply to be contrary. "I think it's fine."

"It's not. Luling, you can fight about this, or you can solve a problem that could wreck innocent people's lives."

She goes in and I stay back to do some deep breathing to try to find enough calm to deal with her. When I finish the last of about thirty breaths, and then put my hand against the wall because I made myself dizzy, I go into the vault to see Mom on her knees in front of one of the shelving units, pulling some dusty boxes out of the way. "What are you doing?"

"Moving boxes."

I asked for that one. "I see. Why?"

She reveals a small safe I haven't noticed in all the times I've been here. I'm fascinated. Mom mutters to herself, I assume reciting the code to the lock, and backs out holding a small tray filled with sealed beakers, like a chemistry experiment.

"What are those?" She takes the tray to the main lab, me trotting behind like a puppy. "Mom? What are they?" All my annoyance has disappeared.

It's not until she squares the tray on the table that she answers. "Hua Pixin's fragrance."

"Pixin?" I frown, thinking through the register. "I don't remember reading her chapter."

Mom doesn't look at me, instead riffling through the bottles. "She's not in it."

"Then how do you know?"

"It's information shared directly from mother to daughter."

"You didn't think it important to tell me this until now?"

"There was no need for you to know," Mom says, looking at me. Her eyes are darker than mine, almost black. "You never showed an interest in your history once you left."

That hurts, but it cuts deeper because she's right. I didn't deserve access to these secrets because, although I'm a Hua, I didn't put the work in.

She pulls out a stoppered vial, and I pause my introspection to read the label. "Ghost scent? Dramatic."

"It's a dampener."

"A what?" I reach out to one of the vials, but my mother's warning expression causes me to drop my hand.

"Pixin was one of a set of twins. Her sister made moli scents to reduce embarrassment, which was perfectly suitable and popular enough to bring in money to the family. Pixin was the younger and thought to be empty of moli, but she wasn't. Her gift was unlike any in the family, and it took years for them to learn what it did."

"Which is what? Stop our moli?"

"It negates the power."

"How?"

"The scent reduces its immediacy, the same way perfume fades if you wash your skin with water. The scent lingers, but its edge is gone." She lifts the tray. "They made the decision to not write this into the register for fear that one day an enemy would read it and use Pixin's power against us. She was a smart woman and made batches for future use in case there was another Haifen."

"The one who could create debilitating fear." I'd read her chapter a while ago.

"Pixin knew there might be more negative gifts in the family. She thought ahead. They would have used it against Miaoyu's moli had events not moved so quickly."

I look at the tray. There are about six jars labeled with Pixin's name in tiny characters, and another character etched into the side that I assume is her huo. "The moli fades with the scent. How old is this?"

"Extremely, but since she created them as incense, they've lasted longer." She points to the safe. "The cold maintained their longevity as well. It should still be adequate if we let it sit in oil, then add it to a perfume Kelsey's clients will find appealing."

That's great news, but I'm battling a sense of hurt that this has been kept from me. "You should have told me."

Mom tucks a stray hair behind her ear where it belongs. "Why, Luling? Do you think you should have access to privileges that are to be earned through trust and commitment? You wanted to be left alone. You wanted nothing to do with your moli. I respected that."

"Like hell you did," I snap. "All those phone calls?"

"I call because I worry about you," she says with a hand palm up, like this is obvious. "I am your mother."

"What about giving me the register?" I have her here.

"That was different." I can see her mouth harden in a way that, in my childhood, would send Eric and I scattering.

"Right," I mutter.

"Don't be angry at me for your choices," Mom says. It's her tone, so matter-of-fact, that stops whatever I was going to say next.

Instead, I accept I'm not going to win this fight and look at the vial. "How does it work?"

"Through scent, as usual."

I push aside my hurt at being excluded from a fairly juicy family secret because I'm not worthy, and it occurs to me Kelsey might have felt the same way. "What does it smell like?"

Mom takes her tweezers and pulls out the incense, a dark ball about the size of a blueberry, and hands it to me. It's subtle, almost a floral, but then not. I sniff it again before something occurs to me. "Won't this have an effect on us?"

She shakes her head. "It's the same as any other moli. No impact on Hua women."

I sniff again, then hand it to Mom. "Maybe magnolia?" She tries it and a line forms between her eyebrows as she thinks. It's usually not so hard for me to identify a note, but the scent is strangely mutable.

"Lighter, though, like plum blossom?" She sniffs. "With a breath of Japanese cypress?"

"That's it." As usual, there's a momentary sense of satisfaction as we identify the scent. "It's nice."

"It would make a good body lotion." She puts the incense in a vial of oil and caps it. "Interesting. I'm not sure how they would have made that scent back then. I thought plum blossom was too fragile for the techniques they used to render scent."

"Kelsey said ten of the women were requesting new bags," I say.

"We should assume all the women smelled it."

"There were twenty altogether. Do you think Kelsey smelled it?"

Mom is rummaging through her perfumer's organ and putting aside a few bottles of notes to mix with the ghost scent.

"I don't know. She must have, as quality control for her luxury gift bags."

God, we're all saying that phrase now. "That's twenty-one."

"Mix the oil with this," says Mom, holding out a bottle. I take a sniff. It's light and charming, with notes of freesia and apple, and would suit almost anyone on a spring day. "Tell Kelsey this is a special batch to congratulate her clients," Mom adds. "Don't tell her what it's for."

"I can't do that. That's wrong."

"We need to protect the family," she says.

I laugh. "There's no way she's going to believe these are only perfume samples. Not after last night."

"We have an unopened sample of scent that makes people more trusting," she points out.

"From the Song dynasty, and they were cautious about who they sold it to," I say, remembering the register. "She refused the prospective client who wanted to trick her daughter into marrying a different man than the original betrothed, who she loved. We're going to do this the right way."

"Kelsey can't be trusted."

"She has no choice," I say. "At least in this. What's she going to tell her company? That she gave their clients the equivalent of a love potion? That's not going to look great for her."

Mom glares at me. "It is not a love potion. We are Huas, not street hucksters."

"I'm ninety percent sure her boss will be more versed in the Western tradition of fairy tales. In any case, she's as stuck as we are."

"Luling, for once, listen to me. She might not want to change what she's done. She's making money off it; that's all she wants."

I keep the *like you* out of my mouth. "It's the right thing to do. It's also my problem and my choice how to solve it."

She blows out a breath. "No. This is what you constantly refuse to believe. It is not your problem. It is *our* problem because you are a Hua, and we are a family."

"Oh, now we're a family."

"We have always been a family."

Silence falls in the room. "I'm going to do it my way," I say finally.

She throws up her hands and walks away. "I can't stop you," she says over her shoulder. "I never could."

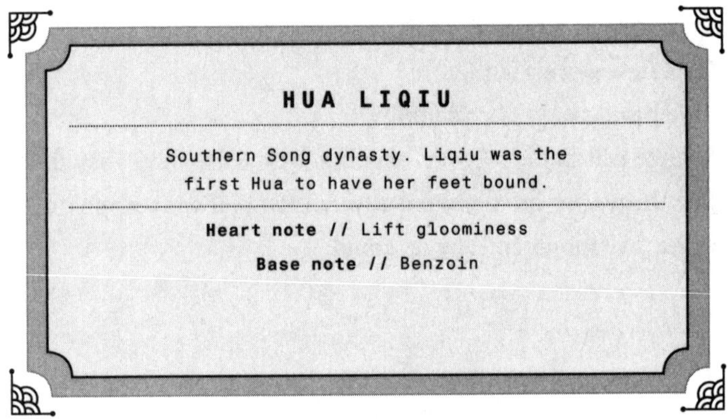

As always, although I know I'm doing the right thing, my mother's disapproval has me second-guessing myself. The best way I've found to deal with it is to simply do whatever the thing is as quickly as possible to reduce the chances of Mom getting too deep in my head. With that in mind, I prepare the ghost-scent samples and get ready to leave.

The store door slams open.

It's Kelsey. She's dressed, but her lips are pale without lipstick and her eyes are small and faded. I never realized how much of her face was painted on; like this, she looks brittle and exposed. Real. I feel a pang of guilt that she's been dragged into this, all because she wanted a pretty scent for her luxury gift bags.

"I came to talk to you." She doesn't take her eyes off my mother.

I can tell Mom is on the verge of telling her it's not a good time, so

I intervene. We might as well get this over with. "If we stay here, we'll have to watch for customers coming in. We can go to the break room."

I flip the OPEN sign around for the second time that day, and my mother sighs before she leads the way to the back. Kelsey looks around. "This isn't where you make the perfumes," she says.

"The lab is through there," says my mother, pointing to the door. I don't think either of us are surprised when Kelsey opens it to take a look without asking permission.

"Were you lying last night? About the witch thing?" She speaks to the empty room.

"We're not witches as you think of them, but it's close enough," I say.

She turns around and runs her tongue over her front teeth. "My clients weren't falling in love because it's spring, or whatever. You manipulated them."

I don't appreciate her word choice, but I suppose it's technically accurate, so I nod.

"I want to know more about this."

"What in particular?" asks Mom. She sits down on an armless chair and crosses her ankles.

Kelsey shuts the lab door with such determination it's almost a slam. "All of it. What it means for my kids. What it means for Eric. Me. My clients."

"It doesn't mean anything for you, and apart from this mess, it doesn't impact you at all." Mom speaks with the authority of a professor giving a lecture. "Your children inherit none of the Hua ability, as the gift only comes through the eldest daughter. That's Luling."

"So, Eric—" Kelsey starts.

"Has nothing," finishes Mom. "He is completely normal."

Kelsey rouses herself. "He's a good man."

Mom's brows rise almost imperceptibly at Kelsey's defensiveness, and she catches my eye. "We're only talking about our moli power," I say, trying to smooth it over. "It's not about Eric personally."

Mom takes my bag of fragrance samples, which I've done up to look elegant and expensive, and puts them in front of Kelsey. "Give this to all the people you gave those original gift bags to. Tell them this is a special blend, limited edition, from a world-class perfumer who wants their opinion since they're clearly people with taste. That should fix the problem."

Kelsey's expression turns mulish. "What if I don't?"

"This is in our best interests. All of our best interests."

"Do they have to wear it?" She wrinkles her nose as if the fragrance couldn't possibly come up to her exacting standards.

"That's best, but as long as they smell it, it's fine." My tone is low and pleasant. Nonthreatening. "Imagine it like an antidote. There's one in there for you as well."

"I didn't smell them," she says. "I lied to be polite."

I suppose that's a relief. We don't have to worry about her leaving Eric if her true love comes along.

She pulls out one of the samples and weighs it in her palm. "If I do this, I'll lose those commissions."

Mom warned me about her greed, so it's not as shocking to hear as it might have been. "You might."

Kelsey pushes the samples away. "I need this job."

"This isn't something to mess around with," I say. I might have fought with Mom earlier, but on the off chance she's right, it's better to close ranks.

"I don't believe you," she says. "Witches? Please. Those people would have fallen in love without your perfume."

"You don't believe me?" I repeat the words because I can't absorb what I'm hearing. After the fuss she made last night?

"My God, listen to yourself. Your father is right. You and your mother perpetuate this self-aggrandizing story to make yourselves feel important. A magical perfume?" She laughs. "You've got to be kidding."

"It's not a joke," I say, my voice rising.

Mom intervenes. "Kelsey, this is a problem that must be addressed. Immediately."

"So you say, but I disagree. My clients are happy, so I'm happy. You don't want me in your special family perfume club? Well, that's on you."

Oh. She's bleeding hurt and rejection. I feel bad for her, but I don't have the time to work through her emotions. It's time to lean on fear.

I speak up before Mom makes it worse, and deploy the plan B I'd thought of earlier. "We would prefer not to deal with any lawsuits, to be honest. That wouldn't be great for your company either."

"Lawsuits?"

I look at her as if in surprise. "People place a lot of importance on their love stories. How do you think they'd feel if they found out their relationships were based on you trying to influence them? They might not sue, but I don't think they'd be supporting you after that. Then there's the damage that will come from word of mouth." I shake my head.

She sags against the counter. "I can't believe this."

"So, you can see why you need to do it."

Kelsey glares at us. "Trust me when I say I'll take you down with me."

"We'll deny it. Then who will look more foolish?" I say. "If anyone asks, I'll tell them what you seem to believe. That we are simply perfumers who understand the psychology of scent, and you were the one who took the opportunity to try to influence your clients in the hopes they'd buy more from you." I pause. "Didn't you say you became top in sales?"

I suppose Mom is right. When it comes down to it, I'll protect the Huas over anything else.

Kelsey stops and puts her hands on her hips. "You're manipulating me to make me do what you want."

"People do it all the time," Mom says. "They wear red when they want to feel powerful, sit in higher chairs when they want to intimidate."

"That's not the same thing. What you do is immoral. It's wrong."

There's the gotcha she's been looking for, and her smug expression infuriates me because I'm trying to help her. I don't hold back.

"You don't think you do the same? You've got one kid in ballet and the other in sports. You tell your daughter she's responsible for her brother. You don't think you're influencing the way *they* think? Their expectations? You don't think calling Owen your 'big smart scientist' and Sophie your 'pretty little dancer' makes an impact?"

"How dare you?" She's clutching the table as if to stop her hands from reaching for me.

"It's not daring to tell the truth," I say. "I accept that we manipulate people. I even admit I'm not completely comfortable with it. At least I'm open to understanding what it is I do."

She paces again and then stops. "Eric said you told him not to tell me," she says. "Is that right?"

"Yes," says my mother. She stands and walks to the sink, hand resting lightly on the counter. "We are very cautious about who we trust with this information."

Kelsey glares at her. "I didn't make the cut?"

"As we said, this has nothing to do with you," Mom says.

I groan internally. That won't go over well.

My sister-in-law's lips thin. "As you delight in telling me," she says dryly. "Tell me, Meilin, what is it that you hate most about me? That I married your son? That I'm white? That I don't kiss your ass and let you control me the way you need to control everyone else in your family? Do you have a magic potion for that, too? A perfume you wish you could hook up to the vents of my house so we'd finally fall in line the way you want us to?"

"Whoa," I snap before Mom can answer. "That's uncalled for."

She bursts out laughing and then gives an exaggerated wipe under each of her eyes for the nonexistent tears, as if to demonstrate how downright amusing she finds this. "You, of all people, know better," she says. "You left town to get away from her."

"Kelsey," says my mother, stepping in front of me. "You're wrong. None of that is true."

"Oh, yeah?" Kelsey tilts her head to the side.

Mom nods and looks her in the eye. "I would need to care about you much, much more to bother doing any of that."

The flinty words land like a slap, and I take a little step back. Kelsey is going to lose it. Instead, her face crumples and her nose twitches as if holding back real tears.

"The hell with you." That's all she says, and this time I don't intervene, because Mom deserved that. "You know, I thought Eric was exaggerating about how bad a mother you are. I made excuses for you. Said you were allowed to have your own interests. He was right all along."

She snatches up the bag with the samples and leaves without another word. Neither Mom nor I bother to stop her, something she seems to be expecting, because she pauses at the door as if waiting for us to call out. When we don't, she gives her hair a shake and snaps the lock back with such force I wonder if it's going to break.

Once she's safely gone, Mom turns the sign back to OPEN. "I told you—"

I hold up my hand. "I don't want to hear it."

She creases her mouth. "Fine, but it doesn't change the fact that you should have listened to me about her. She's a bitter, jealous woman. The kind you can't trust."

The headache that has been lingering in the back of my head all day surges up to make itself known in a very nasty way. "Have you considered that all of this could have been avoided had you welcomed her into the family in the first place?"

"Like your father did?"

I frown. "What did Dad do?" I can't imagine him throwing a party.

"He did absolutely nothing, and I don't see you or Kelsey getting upset with him the way you are with me." Mom rolls her shoulders. "I made the right decision to not tell her. This proves it."

"Okay, Mom." Years of experience tell me arguing is useless. In the end, we got what we needed, which is Kelsey taking those perfumes. I have a feeling she's going to do as we asked, but it might be prudent to point out the consequences to Eric if she doesn't. I'll do it later, because right now I want to be away from any family members, be they by legal decree or by blood.

Before I can escape, Mom pulls out two dusters and returns to the main room, where she hands me one and starts on the shelves. "I made her a wedding fragrance," she says to the wall. "Kelsey. As a gift."

I wipe the counter free of specks as I search my memory. "Didn't she wear Marc Jacobs?"

"Yes. Waipo and I worked on her wedding perfume for weeks. She thanked me and put it aside without smelling it."

There are no words for how deep a cut Kelsey gave my mother, and worse, she probably didn't realize the care, time, and consideration that had gone into the gift. My family makes scents for some of the most important people in Asia, and Kelsey rejected them for an off-the-shelf Daisy flanker. Any hope of a relationship would have died between them that day, and Kelsey probably has no clue. Mom would never tell her, and Eric wouldn't care that it had been Mom's way of welcoming her to the family.

I change my mind. Kelsey deserved that hit from my mom.

"It doesn't matter," Mom goes on. "We need to talk, Luling."

"About—"

"Not about Kelsey. We are going to talk about your moli," she says firmly.

I know this. I absolutely know we need to talk. This situation is worthy of many talks. There are countless unknowns, lots of ground to cover. However. I don't want to. I just don't. I don't want to talk about the future. I don't want to go over how any of this could have happened.

"I need to get back to the house," I say, turning my attention to removing nonexistent dust from a chair's arm. "I have some work to do before my flight leaves tomorrow."

"You can work here," Mom says. "In the lab. Where you're meant to be."

I can't help the shiver that rises between my shoulder blades at the thought of working in that space. I'm no longer an impostor, the way I felt when I had no moli. I'm a true Hua. I belong, although I don't feel like I do.

"Actually—"

"Sit."

I am an adult, but lower myself in a chair, unable to withstand her tone. I wonder if that's something ingrained in babies from the time they're in utero. When Mom speaks in that voice, my instincts take over and I obey like a lemming. A lemming child, double cursed to do as she's told.

"I know you don't want to talk about this," she says.

Somehow, having Mom point out my reluctance makes it worse. "What if I don't want to use my moli?" I say, knowing I sound like a sulky teenager. Mom brings out my worst self.

She looks at me. "Don't lie."

It makes sense that she's pushing me. Mom can see the dollar signs dancing around my head, ready for harvesting. One fifth-daughter fragrance sold, and she has the store's rent for months, if not longer. A few more, and she can expand the way she's wanted to for years. There it is, her heart's desire right in front of her, if only I cooperate.

For a single, evil moment, I wonder what she would do if I said no. Not having my moli is one thing, but to have it and refuse to use it for her benefit or for the continuance of the Hua family fortunes? Unfathomable and unacceptable.

I can't do that. I know I can't, the same way I couldn't leave Rafe in the cold hallway or lie to Kelsey. I give in.

"I don't know how to test it to see if it worked this time," I say. "I'm almost certain it works."

"Almost is not enough." She takes my duster. "We can find a client. I'll tell them it's a test and it might not work."

This is the most reasonable course of action, but I have an immediate and visceral response. "No."

"Luling, what would it take for you—"

"I said no." The fierceness in my voice surprises both of us, and I find I'm halfway out of my chair. In the subsequent silence, I drop back down and stare fixedly at the floor. Please let her not ask me why, because I definitely don't want to talk about feelings I don't understand myself.

At least I can scratch that last concern right off the board. Mom does not do feelings talks, and in this, I recognize that she's been a role model equal to Dad. She claps her hands together, the sound loud in the sharp, hard surfaces of the showroom. "Fine."

I look at her apprehensively. "Fine?"

"We have many other questions to answer, such as why. We can look at those until you reconsider."

Until I reconsider. She says it like a certainty. "I've made my choice."

"I heard you."

"I need to do a few errands before dinner. I'll see you in a couple of hours."

It would be an exaggeration to say I run out before I can hear my mother's response, but not by much.

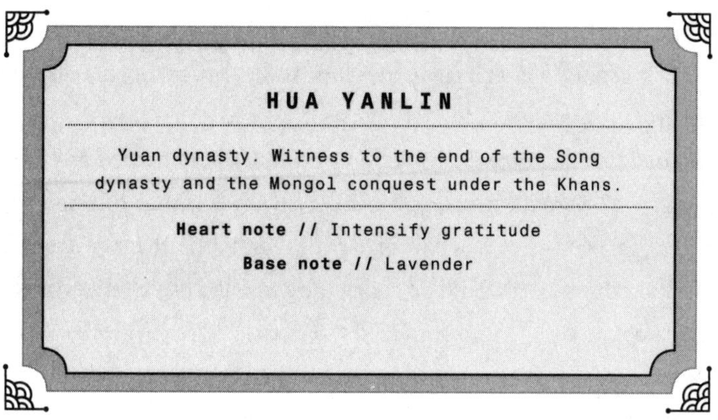

return to the house in time to share a strained dinner with Mom and Dad. She's made stir-fry, and I'm reminded again how time-intensive cooking is when you have to cook for others, since there's no way I'd bother cutting all those vegetables just for me. The second the meal is over, I plead more packing and escape to my room. Dad comes to say goodbye while Mom does the dishes.

"It was good having you home," he says. "Your mother wishes it would be more often."

"Dad, about last night."

He holds up his hand. "All in the past, Lucy. You know I'm not the kind of man to hold grudges."

That's a lie. "Which means that there's something worth holding a grudge about?"

"We can all agree it wasn't an ideal situation, but as I said, it's in the past."

"Dad, did you mean what you said about our moli?" I ask, almost desperately. I don't know why I can't let this go, even when I know the answer will hurt.

"Have a good flight. Call your mother when you arrive so she doesn't worry."

A few seconds later I hear the door to his office close. I suppose that's answer enough.

Since I don't actually have packing to do, I sit on my bed and check my phone. There's a message from Ana with a photo of one of the designs she's working on, a pair of earrings with little cherries dropping from silver threads. It would be cool if they smelled like cherries as well.

"Are you busy?" Mom stands at my door.

I want to say yes to avoid whatever conversation she wants to have, but it's obvious I am not busy at all. "What's up?"

"I thought you could go through the boxes from Waipo's room."

Mom's tired expression drains my initial unwillingness. She did all the heavy lifting: the removal of the intimate leavings such as used toothpaste tubes and wrinkled bedsheets that retain the imprint, if not the heat, of the body. I should have been there to help or at least offer support, but I wasn't. I can look at a few boxes.

"Sure," I say, standing up. We go out the back of the house to the little annex where Waipo lived. It's about the size of a reasonable one-bedroom apartment, and when Mom turns on the lights, I stand in the door for a moment, the same way I did at the Yixiang shop. In front of me is an empty space, apart from appliances and a pile of boxes in the corner. It smells of nothing except bleach.

"I sold off the furniture," says Mom. "Luckily, we'd done a big purge before she left the old house to move here, so there wasn't much."

She points to two boxes that have been set apart from the rest. "Those are yours."

"What's in this one?" I tap an unlabeled box sitting slightly to the left. The others have Mom's tidy writing listing what's inside. Clothing for donation. Dishes. Books. I never saw Waipo reading. She was always busy. Busy cooking, and creating, and running Yixiang, and then, as she got older, playing games on her tablet.

Mom glances over from the kitchen, where she's unplugging the refrigerator. "Nothing."

I've always been able to read Mom well, no doubt because humans are evolutionarily wired to pay attention to threats, and I know she's hiding something. "Really?"

"It's late, Luling. You should go through your boxes. You can do what you wish with them."

There's no point in putting it off, so I turn away from the box of books and open up the ones meant for me. The first is accessories—lovely silk scarves and supple leather gloves that still have the tags on them, which makes me ache almost as much as seeing the ones that have been well used. The best method is to do this as dispassionately as possible, like Ana sorting through a bin at the thrift store, so I get to work. Three scarves and all the gloves are instant keepers, and I put aside a few to give to Ana, or that she might like for the store. The last scarf I pick up is printed with peonies in various shades of pink and has the faint smell of lemon. I keep that one as well, folding it as small as I can to try to preserve the scent forever.

Mom watches me. "Did she tell you why she loved the smell of lemon so much?" she asks.

I shake my head and pack away my treasures. "I assumed she liked how refreshing it was."

"The old family compound outside Nanjing had a lemon tree that had been gifted to them by a prince," Mom says. "The tree had been tended religiously through the generations but had to be left in China when the family came here. Her mother harvested the last lemons for the oil."

"She liked it for the memory of home?" Waipo never talked about leaving China.

"I suppose. The oil is somewhere in the vault. She never let me smell it."

"Did you open it after she passed?" I ask.

"No."

Mom doesn't say anything as I pick up the second box. It's much smaller and rattles when I open it. No surprise, because inside is a handful of vials, each labeled with my own laborious child's writing, complete with the little circles I used to dot my I's.

I examine them closely as the memories resurface. "I did these when you were teaching me how to mix accords," I say. It took me a while to understand how several notes could combine to create a new smell. I didn't play any instruments, so Waipo's attempts to explain it through musical notes didn't help and led to an argument between the two women on why I hadn't learned piano. It was Mom who finally figured out how to explain it to her food-oriented child. She brought me to the kitchen and pulled out ingredients. "Look, Cloud," she said as she mixed. "Eggs, flour, and sugar are their own things. When we combine them what do we get?"

"Batter?"

She poured a circle into the greased pan, then handed me a blueberry before tossing some on top. "Pancakes. A new flavor from many different ones."

I thought about that as I ate, and after, Mom set me up with two notes in the lab, jasmine and tuberose. She told me to begin with a 1:1 ratio, then to keep adjusting until I had something that smelled new. The results are in this box. I unscrew one of the caps and take a sniff at the faded scent. "Too much jasmine," I say.

Mom watches me. Then she says, "I'm coming with you to Toronto."

I nearly drop the vial. "What?" In a thousand years, I never would have anticipated this. "You can't come to Toronto. What about the store?"

"I'll put a manager in charge."

The words pour out. "Where will you stay?"

"With you."

"I only have one bedroom."

"You have a couch, I'm sure. Or we can pick up an inflatable bed."

That I will use, because although I'm a rotten daughter, I'm not low enough to force my mother to sleep on the floor.

"What about Dad?" I don't know if I'm trying to throw up obstacles or get information.

Mom turns to reorganize the boxes so I can only see her back. "What about him?"

"What does he think about you going to Toronto?"

"I'll put meals in the freezer for him to heat up." She puts a bottle down with more force than necessary. "I already booked the flight. We can go together."

"How? You don't know which one I'm taking."

She gives me a withering look. "Of course I do. You hate getting up, so you wouldn't book early, and you want to get home at a reasonable time, so you wouldn't take one in the evening. I'm on the ten-thirty flight with you."

That is, in fact, my departure time, so I move on. "Why do you need to come back with me?"

She folds up the box, tucking the top flaps into each other to close it. "We know nothing about what's going on with your moli. You refuse to talk to me. You refuse to engage with me to discover a solution. You won't move home and come back to Yixiang. You've left me no choice."

"You have a choice! The choice is to not follow your grown daughter like a stalker! You could leave it alone." As always when I get upset with Mom, my voice reverts into a high-pitched almost-whine.

"No. I will not."

"We can talk now," I say.

"There's no time. We will talk and work when we are in Toronto."

That's all she says about it. After that declaration, she looks around the room. "Finish packing," she adds. "You know I like to get to the airport early."

Rafe texts me later that night, after I've taken a shower so long my fingers have turned pruny.

> **Rafe:** Sorry I was AWOL all day. I was learning about the commercial zoning bylaws in the greater Ottawa region. Do you have any questions about arterial main street zones?
>
> **Me:** Mom is coming back to Toronto with me.

Whatever is going on with our relationship, Rafe has known me for years. He'll understand.

The phone rings. "What?" he asks.

I keep my voice low so she can't hear. "Do you remember what I told you before I left?"

"Yes. I haven't told anyone. I swear."

"Thank you. Do you remember I told you that I couldn't do it?"

"Yes?" Rafe pauses. "Lucy, are you telling me..."

I'm almost giddy from being able to say it out loud to someone without fear of judgment.

"I have my moli. I think I have it." I wait for Rafe's answer with bated breath.

"Lucy, this is incredible. Is that why you're in Vancouver?"

"I had to tell Mom and figure out what's going on." There's no need to go into the mess about Kelsey's samples.

"Figure out what? Isn't it enough that you have it?"

"We don't know why I couldn't do it before. Mom has decided I can't be trusted to get to the bottom of things by myself, or trust that I can control it."

"That's why she's coming to Toronto with you?"

"So she says."

There's a silence, then Rafe says, "It'll be nice to have her around, won't it?"

I nearly throw the phone. "What are you talking about?"

"Lucy, she loves you. She probably misses you."

"That doesn't mean we can cohabit for an indefinite time," I say. "You've seen the size of my apartment. We're like matter and antimatter. We always have been."

This time the silence is so pointed that I sigh.

"Whatever you're thinking, just say it."

"You haven't always been," he says.

"Of course we have."

"When you were younger, you spent every moment with her. When I came over, you were always in the kitchen together, or gardening. Or hidden away doing perfume stuff."

"Well, naturally we spent more time together when I was younger. I was a kid." I adjust my towel and scowl at my wrinkled fingers.

"No, Lucy. You loved being with her. I read the full Akira series while you two planted an herb garden. You sprayed me with water and got the pages wet, and I went home because I was mad."

"I made lavender cookies as an apology." I grin into the phone. "You thought you were going to smell like lavender after you ate them, and I caught you sniffing your arms."

"I was disappointed to keep smelling like a sweaty teenage boy. That's not the point. You liked spending time with your mother, Lucy."

"Things change."

"I know relationships change, but I don't think it's good for you to shoehorn your memories into some new narrative."

I twist my neck around, trying to stretch it to alleviate some of the tension. "My place is still too small."

His sigh comes through the phone. "When are you coming back?"

"Tomorrow evening."

"I'll see you at home, Lucy."

Rafe may have been right about my mother's and my relationship, but that was in the past. We haven't found our way to interacting as adults instead of mother and child. The register is in my bag, and I reach in to touch it with tentative fingers. Maybe it's time for me to read Mom's chapter, if we're going to be stuck with each other for the foreseeable future.

Then her voice comes from the other room. "Luling!" she calls. She appears in my door before I can answer.

I pull my hand away as another thought occurs to me. "What happened to the bottle I brought?"

She knows I'm talking about the moli. "Safe."

I'm too tired to go back to the lab and fetch it. The bottle will be fine locked up in the lab behind that huge door.

Mom casts a critical glance at my suitcase. "You should roll your clothes. Fewer wrinkles."

Already managing my life. She leaves and I stuff the register in among my flat-folded clothes, deciding to leave Mom's chapter for another day. I'm not ready for her inner thoughts when I have her outer ones to contend with.

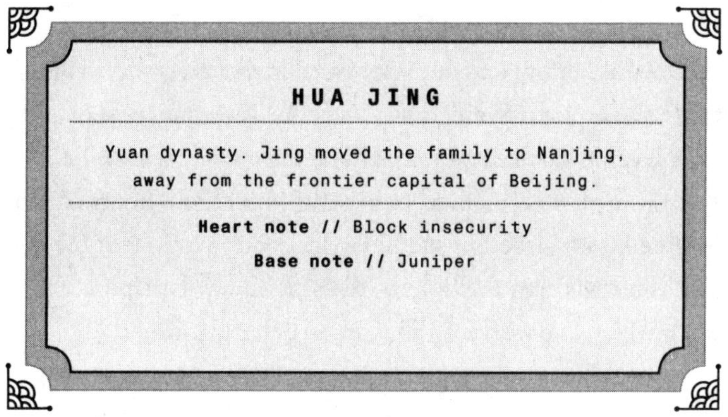

Mom and I take the SkyTrain to the airport, since Mom, despite saying we can save money by sharing a cab, decides to save more by skipping the convenience altogether.

Ana sends me more photos of her jewelry, interrupting Mom's disapproving commentary about the shoddy nature of goods in the airport stores and women wearing leggings as pants. Despite lifting my shoulder to block her line of sight, she looks at my message.

"What's that?"

"My shopmate, Ana, is a silversmith and decided to start designing again." I scroll to the next photo, which is similar to the daisy chain she showed me, but with pineapples.

"Very nice," my mother says. This is high praise. "The central pendant could hold a scent to make it stand out."

"I thought so too." I'm a little surprised we had the same idea;

I thought it would be too cutesy for her. "She had cherry earrings that would be nice with a touch of rum and vanilla. Sweet, like maraschino."

"Or go further with chocolate and ginger."

I like to talk perfumes with Mom, and we swap a few more ideas before she says, "Enough of this. You need to focus on your moli. No time for little side projects."

She opens her bag and unpacks the sandwiches, granola bars, and cut fruit she brought from home, citing the exorbitant cost of airport food. We eat in silence before boarding the plane. To my relief, we're not sitting next to each other, and I settle in for a few hours of peace. This time I don't sleep but spend the time worrying about the logistics of Mom's visit. By the time we're flying somewhere possibly near Medicine Hat, I've worried about, in no particular order:

> Whether we'll have to share all our meals. Corollary: Who will cook? Probably Mom. It honestly feels weird to cook for her, like an inversion of our roles.

> Work. Will she want to go with me?

> If she *doesn't* come to work with me, what will she do all day?

> If she *does* come to work with me, what will she do all day?

> What will Ana think?

> What about Rafe and our postponed date? Can I do that with Mom there?

> How long is this visit going to last?

On the plus side, all these concerns have sidelined the reason why she's coming, which is to test my moli. That's a whole other list of problems that would take a flight to Auckland to resolve and that I currently do not have the capacity to deal with. It's easier to agonize over how many towels I have and why I didn't wash them before I left.

The plane lands, and everyone too cheap to buy in-flight Wi-Fi immediately turns to their phones to see what they've missed over the last four and a half hours. I'm no exception, and see a few texts from Ana wanting to know if things were okay. I tell her my mom is staying over and they'll probably meet at the store.

Ana: I'll be on my best behavior.
Me: She'll love you.

This is true, because despite my mother's many failings and what I view as her painful traditionalism, she'll respect Ana in the same way she's able to enjoy all people who aren't me. Ana can be admired for what she currently has, not her potential. Her is-now rather than her could-be.

There's also a text from Mom, directing me to wait for her when I get off the plane and designating an exact location (to the left at the first corner out of the sky bridge). I push aside my juvenile desire to wait about ten meters away, and watch as she comes up the ramp. Have her shoulders narrowed? Are they more slumped? She might be tired from the flight. She already has on huge sunglasses that cover half her face, and I wonder how long it will be until she succumbs to the inevitable visor I also see in my future. Suncare is self-care, after all.

"Did you pop your ears?" she says as she comes up. "You'll get a headache otherwise. Did you bring gum?"

"I'm fine, Mom." Her voice is muffled, but I don't want to tell her that.

"It's so easy to do, Luling. I taught you when we went to Shanghai. Do you remember all those flights? I think it took us a full day." She laughs. "You and Eric fell asleep in the customs line and nearly fell over. You were both holding those big Toblerones your father bought you."

That had been one of our only family trips, taken when I was ten and Eric twelve, so Dad could see his family. I remember asking Mom if we were going to see the old Hua compound or the Nanjing store, but she said we couldn't manage it.

"I remember," I say, tugging my ear.

"Here." She hands me some gum and I take it. "Now, yawn."

"Mom, I am fine. Let's go." When she turns away, I stretch open my jaw and feel the pressure lift.

We wait for her luggage—although I went carry-on, Mom has a large rollie—and head home. This time we take a cab, because I'm paying and it's already past six in the evening.

"It's been a long time since I was here," Mom says as we drive along the highway, the city shadowed in the distance as we come around the swooping curve of the overpass. "At least twenty years."

"I wonder if it's changed much."

"All places change and are the same."

When I was younger, these kinds of gnomic pronouncements would leave me puzzling for days. Now they've started to make more sense as long as I don't think about them too deeply. Perhaps this is one of the benefits of age.

She's quiet as we edge our way to my neighborhood, the cab swerving around the parked cars and oblivious pedestrians on their phones. I look out my window, preparing myself for the upcoming barrage of criticism about my living arrangements. When we arrive, I'm happy the setting sun gives the street a honeyed glow that's usually reserved for a late-summer afternoon. The yellow brick of my building looks like a design choice instead of merely being dingy, and when I open the door, the light glints off brown tile floors that would be right at home in a 1970s shopping mall to reflect pretty patterns on the wall.

I hope Mom doesn't comment on the elevators. On a good day, they make a worrying creaking noise that gives the impression they're being hand-cranked by a pod of gnomes in the basement who could get tuckered out and let go at any moment. I consider it atmosphere but accept she might see it as a health hazard.

We make it upstairs without incident, and I drag Mom's suitcase to my apartment. Mom walks in, her nose twitching, but even unburned, my candles have negated the stale smells that could have accumulated in the dead space while I was away.

She takes off her shoes and explores, mumbling the room names to herself as if marking them off a mental tally sheet. "Bedroom, good size. Luling, you have socks on the floor. Bathroom, fine. How often do you wash your towels? Use bleach. Kitchen. Gas or electric? Gas."

Meanwhile, I stand in the middle of the living room, wondering if there's food for dinner. Thank God I changed my sheets in a fit of nervous energy while waiting for my flight to leave. I pull in Mom's suitcase while she's checking the refrigerator and take the opportunity to discreetly spray some lavender scent on the pillows.

A knock on the door brings us out like curious mice. I check the peephole before unlocking the door. "Rafe?"

Rafe stands in the hall, but before he can greet me, Mom comes up. "Rafe Jin." She says it with a satisfaction I don't think I've ever heard her use with my name.

"I came over to see if you wanted to join me for dinner," he says. "I thought you'd be tired after the flight."

"You cooked?" I ask. This is unexpected. What's he up to?

"Over at my place, so you don't need to clean up or anything," he says. "If you already ate, no problem. I love leftovers."

"A good boy," Mom approves. "Let me wash my hands. Luling, you too."

Rafe's navy T-shirt carries the faint smell of cooking, those homey scents of garlic and onion and oil, and I lock up behind Mom. The two of them chat casually about the flight and how Missy and Eddie Jin are doing. I relax. Rafe and Mom have known each other since he was a teenager, and between them is a mellow ease.

He lets us in. I'm not sure if it's my neighbor's natural style or what she thought would work best for a place that's rented out half the time to strangers, but the decor is very old Hollywood. Framed posters from movie classics line the far wall in a tidy grid of mirrored frames, and there's what I hope is a fake zebra-skin rug on the floor. The furniture is gilt and red velvet, but with knitted throws made of an ivory yarn so thick the needles must have been the size of a wrist. They also look like they would snag at a touch.

Rafe follows my glance. "I'm too scared to use them in case I wreck them," he says.

Dinner is already on the black-lacquered table, family-style with covered dishes. "Wine?" he asks, already pulling out the water because he knows Mom never drinks.

"Thank you, yes," she says.

This isn't the Hua Meilin I know. Rafe and I share glances, but he fills both their glasses. Not mine, because I know myself. It's better to not drink at all than risk having the first glass that leads to another three or four because of tension and stress.

Rafe serves a simple meal of rice, braised chicken thighs and tofu, and green beans. "The shops are finally getting fresh spring vegetables in," he says, handing Mom a plate.

That starts a conversation about produce seasonality that lasts a good ten minutes. Which is convenient, because although Vancouver only has a three-hour time difference, the strain of the last few days, plus the jet lag, is catching up to me. I listen in a half doze as they chat, only occasionally adding something. Mostly I observe.

Although Rafe and Mom are familiar with each other, it's clear they're both skilled at drawing out the other person's opinions to keep a conversation going. From vegetables, they turn to Rafe's work and then Toronto and Vancouver real estate prices. She quizzes him about costs per square foot for the different neighborhoods here. I bite into a green bean, which Rafe has cooked so it keeps the snap, and try not to think about the reason for all the questions. Mom is here to help with my moli, not expand her empire, which Eric seems to think is almost bankrupt.

How well the store is doing is something I'll have to bring up with her during her visit as well, and it's another conversation I'm not looking forward to having. Luckily, I might not have to. If I have my moli, any problems she's having will be solved. I nod to myself. Another reason to get to the bottom of this.

Rafe brings out dessert, with fruit for Mom after she refuses the burnt-toffee ice cream, and then we wish him good night.

"Rafe turned out to be a very good cook," Mom says as she goes into my room.

"He is."

"Very handsome too. He looks like his mother."

"I suppose." He did look good tonight, with his dark hair a bit messy and the casual outfit that he filled out to perfection. I had to look away when I found myself staring too often.

"I'm glad you two are talking again. Missy and I often wondered what happened."

She's in my room, so her voice comes to me like a disembodied judgment. "I guess we grew apart," I say. I don't want her in my personal life at all, let alone in my business about Rafe, and talking to my mother about relationships is embarrassing at best.

"You're prickly to deal with," says Mom. "I'm sure it was over something that you blew out of proportion."

"Thanks."

Mom comes out holding a small toiletry bag. "Are you together?" she asks.

It takes a moment for me to recover from her asking me this. I can't believe she has the nerve, and right after blaming me for the estrangement.

"We've started talking since you managed to get him living down the hall, if that's what you want to know."

"It would be easier to have a relationship if you moved back to Vancouver," she says.

"No need to worry about that." I grope around for a way to change the topic, because Mom will be in my space for a while and I don't want to deal with more negativity than I need to.

"We'll start looking at your moli tomorrow," she says in answer before she goes into the bathroom and shuts the door.

I sit on the couch, wondering why all conversations with my mother are like this. Why can't she accept that I have a life away from her and Yixiang? I wouldn't be surprised if she maneuvered Rafe here in another line of her multipronged attack to get me back home. If guilt failed, she'd rationalize, maybe love would succeed.

I text Rafe to thank him for having us over.

Rafe: I owe you another dinner from the one we missed
when you went home. I know your mom's visit changes
things, so tell me when you want to rebook. I can make
any day work.

Part of me had wondered if he would let it slide and we'd continue on as we were now, with the occasional text, until he went back to Vancouver, and I hug myself knowing he still wants to go. I pick a stray thread on the couch. I don't want to put our dinner off, at least not for long. I want to see him so I know where his head's at and perhaps figure out my own.

Mom finishes in the bathroom as I'm tucking the sheets into the couch, not wanting to sleep with my face pressed against fabric that's been sat on by so many others. I've already put a glass of water on her bedside table and taken out my pajamas, book, and a change of clothes so I don't have to wake her if I get up early.

"Tomorrow," she reminds me. It sounds like a threat.

She leaves the door open, and I lie on the couch, listening to the sound of another person and wondering how long it will be until I get my peace back.

Although I guess it's good to have the company. At least for a while.

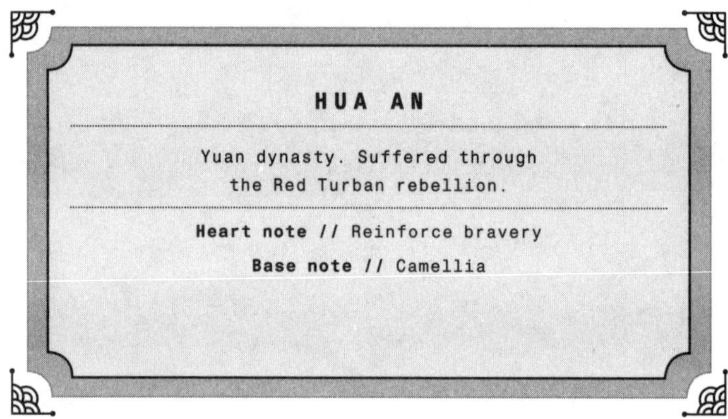

Fragments of dreams drift around me as I edge toward waking, and I cling to them as a way to keep in the sweet zone of unconsciousness.

That's until a firm hand shakes my shoulder. "Luling."

It's my mother. I roll over and curl back under the blankets like I'm fifteen again. "More sleep."

"Luling. It's morning."

I crack my eyes open to see she's correct in the sense that dawn has risen. "The store opens at eleven."

She makes a tsking noise. "What do you do until then? Waste your day by sleeping?"

Sitting up on the couch with the duvet wrapped around me, I yawn. "Sometimes."

"No. The day is for working. Waste your time later."

"Tell me what you really think," I mumble to the pillow.

"What?"

"Nothing."

By the time I get out of the bathroom, Mom has made her bed, started boiling water for breakfast noodles and tea, stripped the couch, folded all the bedding, and brought it to my room. I don't have to check to know her suitcase is empty and the two drawers I gave her are filled with neatly organized piles of clothes. My suitcase remains open on the floor near the couch, and she eyes it with disapproval. I'm not thrilled with having it out of place, either, but it seemed easier than going into what is now my mother's room to get things I need.

I take down two cups and put them on the counter with tea bags, which she brushes aside. Out comes a tin of her own blend, plus the teapot Ana gave me from her collection when I moved in.

I've dressed up a bit today, with my nicest jeans and a black sweater I spent ten minutes fixing a pulled thread on to make it perfect, but my mother has outdone me in a pair of tailored slacks, a striped blouse, and a blazer she's pushed up at her elbows like an old-school J.Crew model. Her hair is smoothed back and small gold studs adorn her ears. Like me, she wears nothing on her fingers or her wrists, and all our necklaces sit close to our throats, a habit to keep ourselves and our jewelry safe at work.

She says nothing about my appearance, which I take as a blessing. "Your lab is at your store," Mom says as she pours the water over the leaves. It's a scent so intertwined with my childhood, that for a moment, I can't answer as I stop and breathe it in. Her favorite milk oolong is lighter and more floral than a regular oolong, with a buttery, creamy taste.

"Drink first," she says, pouring me a cup. "We'll eat after."

Mom never likes to mix her morning tea with food, saying it wrecks the taste of the tea. Although it's a habit I've let go over the years, as I sip the tea with her, I can see the meditative benefits.

Or I could, if she didn't fix me with a gimlet gaze across the counter. "Your lab is at your store," she repeats.

"Yes."

"We'll go after breakfast."

"Ana may be there," I say, as a warning that we might not be able to have the moli talk Mom wants.

"She may not. We have time to work around her. I'll be here until we solve this."

On that ominous note, Mom grabs the old bamboo chopsticks to dish out a bowl of spaghetti noodles she's mixed with soy sauce, sesame oil, garlic, and ginger. It's one of those mishmash meals most immigrant families have, using the ingredients available at the grocery store to make equivalents to beloved dishes when they can't get to a specialty grocer. Although lo mein and ramen noodles are available most places these days, I prefer it this way, with store-brand pasta, but feel a little queasy at the sight of the food.

"I don't usually eat breakfast."

"I can tell. Your skin is dull. You need more vegetables." She puts the bowl in front of me, and although I want to push it away out of spite, I eat a few bites to get her off my case.

It's only nine by the time we leave for the store. A morning walk is sacrosanct to her, and as we head out, I realize it is to me as well.

"Why did you choose this neighborhood to live?" Mom asks as we step out into the spring sunshine. It's going to be warm today, and this cheers me.

"The rent was low." This is true enough, although I gradually opened to the charms of the location. I point out a few places I like—a coffee shop, a tiny gift store, and a corner store with the best selection of fresh herbs I've seen, all year around.

"Do you walk to work every day?"

"It's only about thirty minutes, so yeah."

"Good. Exercise works the brain." She glances over. "It might help with your skin too."

I clamp my mouth shut. We get to Kensington Market and Mom

looks around with a little smile. "I came here years ago when I was last in Toronto. There was a place on the corner that made vegan muffins bigger than my hand. It must have shut down. Too bad."

I like Kensington in the morning, when its shops are closed and streets quiet. In the day, especially on a summer weekend, it can feel chaotic, but at times like this, it seems like a secret only a few know.

Mom stares in open interest when we get to Auntie's Closet. "Where's your sign?"

"I told you, I rent. The store belongs to Ana."

"Did I hear my name?" Ana comes up from behind me, then holds her hand out to Mom. "Ana Garcia. You must be Ms. Hua. I'm so pleased to meet you."

Mom's face is a study as she checks out Ana's outfit, a black sheath with a sequined snake sewn around the shoulders like a boa and a leather jacket draped over it. In the time I've been away, Ana has bleached her hair Marilyn blond and styled it like a 1950s pinup. She looks fantastic, and I pray Mom doesn't say something rude or judgmental.

Then Mom smiles. "Thank you. I'm looking forward to seeing your space."

"I'd be happy… Oh, Jayne, hi." She goes bright red as Jayne comes up, and I introduce her to my mother.

Mom holds out her hand and they shake. "Do you work in the store as well?" Her eyes dart between Ana's makeup, which has little star stamps by the eyes, and Jayne's classic white shirt and jeans.

Jayne laughs. "Clothes aren't my thing, although Ana is inspiring." Ana goes limp as Jayne continues. "I own a bar down the street. You should come for lunch, if you're staying awhile."

"She probably won't be here that long," I break in, rattling my keys as I open the door.

"I know about your company, of course, Ms. Hua." Ana gives Jayne a wave goodbye as we enter the store. "I'd love to talk to you about how you manage to both keep it current and incorporate the history of your perfume house. It's fascinating content for marketing."

"Of course." Mom goes in to stand in the middle of the room. "Engaging displays," she says. "Luling, are you responsible for the room scent?"

"Yes."

Ana waits for me to say more, and when I don't, she shoots me a look and jumps in. "Lucy changes the scent based on the season, but it always sort of smells a bit the same to make sure repeat customers recognize it."

Mom turns to me. "A base?" She closes her eyes and breathes in. "Black currant and fig. With some bay?"

I nod and Ana looks impressed. "I can't believe how well you two can do that," she says.

Mom smiles. "There's a lot of memorization. My mother made me keep a scent diary."

"A scent diary?" asks Ana.

"A notebook where you write down what you're smelling and how it makes you feel," says Mom. "I have Luling's."

"I didn't know that," I say. So that's what happened to it.

"I keep it with my own." Mom walks over to my counter, her block heels knocking on the floor. "This is your space."

Ana goes to the back workroom and I join Mom. "It is."

Mom's already spraying blotters, sniffing her way through my collection, much in the way a master chef would judge her apprentice. I can't handle the stress, so I take her coat and go to hang it up in the back.

Ana peers around me to make sure Mom isn't there. "I don't know what to say," she says urgently. "How bad was this emergency? Should I be giving condolences?"

"No, no, it's nothing like that. Sorry to worry you. I had to talk to Mom about some family stuff. It wasn't big. No one died. Your hair looks great, by the way."

"Thanks. I wanted to surprise you." She takes a breath. "Whew. Your mom has, like, an aura, doesn't she? I want to be on my best behavior and also get her approval."

"Trust me, I know."

She laughs. "I bet."

"She's going to be hanging around for the next few days," I say. "Is that okay?"

"As if I'm going to kick out your mom. Sure. If she wants to work back here, we can figure it out. Or is she on vacation?"

I shrug as Mom comes to the back. Unlike other people, who would poke in their heads, Mom simply fills the doorway.

"You're a silversmith." She circles Ana's table. "My daughter showed me your work."

Hearing her refer to me possessively like that instead of by name makes my heart give a strange lurch.

Ana looks up from the container of overnight oats she's opening for breakfast. "I started back up a little while ago after putting it aside for years."

"Very nice designs," Mom approves, looking at the board where Ana has printed out some of her tablet drawings and a few sketches torn from her notebook.

"Thank you." She frowns. "The result is decent, but the process doesn't feel right—or at least, not like it did. I was used to working with a collaborator."

"I know that feeling," Mom says. "Although Luling's grandmother stopped working years ago, she enjoyed being in the lab. I hadn't realized what a comfort it was to have her there to discuss ideas."

I'm listening so hard my face tingles. I didn't know that either.

Ana nods eagerly. "That's how I feel. These are good—I know they are—but it's a struggle because they can be better." She droops. "I thought it would be fine to be on my own. I don't know."

I stand over Ana's workspace as they go to look at the store. I've always worked alone, too, but I remember the days I would join Mom and sometimes Waipo in the lab, each of us tossing out thoughts or simply holding out a blotter or wrist in a silent request for opinions. To me, Ana's jewelry looks spectacular, but I can see what she means about how hard it is to work in isolation. It bothers me, too, sometimes.

Reaching out, I take a blotter and roll it between my fingers, frowning at the narrow cylinder when I'm done. Mom comes back to sit at my perfumer's organ without asking permission, her eyes flickering over it. At least she won't be able to find any issues here; the workspace is spotless. A squirt bottle of alcohol sits near the neat collections of wipes, pipettes, and blotters. Although she and Waipo preferred to organize their materials by note family, I work with a more curated collection, and alphabetical suits me. Each small brown bottle is labeled with the date I created or bought it, the dilution, and the name. The fire extinguisher is within easy reach. There is nothing she can find fault with, but I brace myself for her criticism anyway.

None comes. She merely sniffs a few of the materials and nods. "Excellent," she says.

"Thanks?" Is she fattening me up for the kill?

"The first thing we'll do is create a scent for you to work with," she says. "The same as if you had a real moli customer."

"Speaking of, I've been away and I do actually have customers," I say, grateful to have an out that can delay this, at least for a few hours. "Real ones. I have some commissions I need to finish."

The one thing I'll say about Mom is that she takes business seriously. Despite her intense need to get to the bottom of my moli puzzle, she stands up immediately. "I'll explore the city while you work," she says. "When I come back, we'll talk."

She's a grown woman, and far more capable than I am, but I can't help a twinge of unease as I watch from the store window as she walks down the street. There are so many things that could happen to her.

Why I never worried about this before, I don't know. All I know is that I'm worrying now.

Ana comes up beside me. "She's not hanging around?"

"I told her I need to work."

Ana looks amazed. "That was it? She didn't tell you family comes first and work could wait?"

"Nope."

"Wow, she should sit down and have coffee with my mom to share that perspective."

"Don't you think it would be weird if someone else's mother was yours?" I say idly.

"Yes, but that doesn't stop me from wishing she could be a little more like other ones, the same way she wishes I were a better daughter. Or any other daughter." Before I can respond, she points at the window. "I didn't tell you. Priscilla and Elvis are back together."

"What happened?"

Her face lights up. "It was awesome. To set the scene, I was doing the window. Do you like it?"

"Very springlike." It has a stuffed bunny offering a purse that looks like a carrot to another bunny. Perfume bottles line the back like a fence. I've already adjusted the bunnies so they're more centered in the window, and although it's a little twee for my liking, I don't want to hurt Ana's feelings by changing anything else.

"Elvis walks by. Then I see Priscilla go by a few minutes later. This happens a couple more times until they're on the same side of the street. I couldn't hear them, but there was lots of staring at feet and I assume groveling, but from which of them, I don't know. Then they started making out again."

"Gross but emotionally satisfying."

We putter around the store for a bit, me casting glances at Ana and trying to decide whether I want to suggest my jewelry-fragrance idea. Ana says, "Why don't you just say it?"

"Say what?" I drop the broom with a clatter.

"Whatever it is you want to ask me."

"How do you know I had something to ask?" I demand.

"I am an empath."

"Shut up, you are not."

"God, Lucy, you're as easy to read as a Dr. Seuss book. You keep giving me these looks out of the corner of your eye like a Victorian housemaid wanting to ask for an extra hour off so you can meet up with the milkman."

Only Ana would use such a weird analogy. I give in. "I had an idea."

"Is it that we should install a huge wooden bear out in front of the store?" she asks eagerly.

"What? No. Why would you think that?"

"Oh. No reason! Spill."

I do my best to not worry about whether I'm going to come into work one day and find a new decoration to deal with. "It's for you, but you don't need to take it."

"Understood." She waits another few seconds and then does a tick-tock motion with her hand to hurry me up.

Well, if she doesn't like it, she doesn't like it. My mom said it was cool. "I was looking at your drawings and your work." I walk to the back and she trails behind me. "Those cherry earrings, for instance. If they were hollow, you could put in scent. Perfumed jewelry used to be very fashionable."

Ana picks up a rose locket she's crafted out of filigree. "How would it work, exactly?"

I point to the back. "You could add a small box or cage with a removable ceramic pellet that would absorb the scent. You can also sell the pellets along with the jewelry for top-ups when the scent fades."

"I like it." She nods. "I'm in."

"In?"

"Yeah, obviously we're going to collaborate on this."

"We are?" That was fast.

"Don't you want to?" I don't need to see her hopeful expression to know that yes, I do want this.

"I might have a few ideas for scents," I say.

She laughs. "I thought you might."

"You really like it?" A relaxed feeling licks up from the depths of my chest.

"Love it, and more importantly, it's unique. Stands out." She puts down the duster. "I thought you were going to say you were moving back to Vancouver."

"Why would you think that?" I'd never mentioned that as an option.

"I don't know, you were being all mysterious and mopey! I thought it was bad news. This is great." She looks over. "What gave you this idea?"

"I told you, looking at your drawings."

She shakes her head. "A few months ago, there's no way you'd be interested in a partnership. You're the epitome of a lone wolf. The ultimate sigma female."

"That theory on power dynamics has been totally debunked."

"I don't care and you know what I'm saying." She runs her hand through her hair and swears when it gets caught thanks to the hair spray.

"I had an idea," I say dismissively, not wanting a therapy session. "Nothing deeper."

"Sure, Jan."

I make a face at her and she makes one back. I tap a sketch of an earring. "Behind the ears is a traditional place for women to put fragrance. What if we did a collection that's all around the pulse points? Earrings, a choker for the throat, and bracelets for the wrists. Everywhere a lover could smell it."

"Don't forget anklets."

"Anklets?" I frown. "That's not really one of the usual spots."

She raises her eyebrows. "Trust me on this one."

We go through the designs, and within half an hour, we have the basics. We'll go simple and offer a choice of three fragrances: a light floral, a sexy amber, or a delicious gourmand, all of them gender neutral.

"They can also customize a fragrance," I say. "For a price."

Ana notes that down. "I love this."

"Me too." I beam at her, happy to be doing a project that gets me away from Mom's moli focus and distracts me from Rafe. Something just for me, but with a partner. It's nice.

HUA AIAI

655 CE, EARLY TANG DYNASTY

IMPERIAL PALACE, CHANG'AN

There is no trusting a man," Empress Wu said to Aiai. They were, unusually, alone in her rooms without any attendants, and Aiai was hard at work creating one of the scents her mistress demanded be changed daily. "Especially one with no power of his own."

"Yes, my lady." Aiai took some tangerine peel she had dried and sniffed it carefully. She had access to so many materials of exquisite quality in the palace it sometimes boggled her mind. She was often in the kitchens to take spices and fragrant fruits and herbs for her experiments, such as the time she had steeped star anise and chrysanthemum in tea, then dried the liquid and ground it. She had added it to a wax, which the empress tried on her skin and disliked, ordering Aiai to keep to incense and sachets. She took her mortar to crush the peel with jujube and a dry magnolia bud, hoping to alleviate some of the bitterness.

The empress seemed satisfied with her answer and did not bother to explain herself. Aiai expected nothing else. She had been with her mistress for five years and feared her as much as she had the first day they met at Ganye Temple. The nun had quickly become Consort Wu and, only months ago, had maneuvered herself to be elevated from consort to empress. Aiai had heard low-voiced talk about the people who suffered if her mistress felt they were more obstacle than person. Although she knew some of it was due to envy, Aiai had long decided safety lay in being the smallest, quietest thing in the empress's rooms, much the same way she had survived in her father's house.

The empress glanced down at Aiai's hands, moving quickly among her ingredients. "I've heard some of the others have been asking you for your scents."

"I told them I only create for you, my lady." Aiai had enough self-preservation to refuse the riches offered by people who sought to attract the emperor. They knew nothing of her moli, but her everyday perfumes were famed at court, and people searched for any advantage to raise their status.

However, not all of Aiai belonged to the empress. Anxious to understand more about her moli, Aiai had been taking action on her own. Daily prayers for guidance to the Peony Goddess had gone unanswered, so after setting up a shrine, Aiai decided she was on her own to understand what she was capable of. She began creating moli scents for others without them knowing. Maids, mostly. That was who she had most access to, thanks to the watchful eye of the empress, and no concubine in her right mind would allow a woman known to be close to Empress Wu near them with a mysterious powder.

She had learned a few things in the rare opportunities she had to slip a moli scent to an unsuspecting maid. It took over a year for her to understand that a person's true love didn't have to smell the scent themselves—as she had told the empress—but was summoned by the seeker wearing or lighting the scent. She had watched avidly as a eunuch from another part of the palace had come, lovestruck, to find one of her chosen maids. Luckily, the empress hadn't known their love was due to Aiai's interference and had decided it was amusing enough to buy them a small house in the city and release them from service.

Another had left her secret lover and had become inseparable from another maid, and the two cried if forced apart. Three of the maids had disappeared, and Aiai hoped it was because they'd found their true loves and had run away with them. Why else would they leave if not for love? She felt no guilt about her shadowy actions. She was giving people true love as a gift, after all.

"Good." The empress settled back. "You belong to me, and that secret power you wield is for my use only."

Aiai said nothing, but this rankled. Every time she succeeded in a test behind the empress's back, Aiai felt like she was regaining part of herself.

There were days her life gnawed at her. Her time at the palace had been spent in sumptuous luxury. What Empress Wu spent on cosmetics would feed half a district, and Aiai couldn't help but think that money could be better used to help the lives of the others in the city. She was wicked for thinking that way. Everyone had their place under the Son of Heaven, even lowly perfumers who wished they could work for everyone instead of a single ambitious woman who desired to hoard everything for herself—be it love, power, or Aiai's perfumes.

Still, Aiai would give anything to be able to create in peace and without fearing her patroness's cold smile. One day, she would be free.

Their solitude was interrupted by one of the river of advisers who flowed past the empress. The adviser spoke in a low voice, and Aiai tried to prevent her hand from shaking as she rubbed the powder from the ground peel into her wrist to test the scent, then jumped at a loud sound from the corridor. The maids' gossip about strange happenings in the palace had become more lurid since the death of the Empress Wang, strangled by order of the emperor after the death of then-Consort Wu's baby daughter.

Wu had cried over her daughter's death. Aiai had seen the redness in her eyes and the trembling of her pale lips before the maids had painted them vermilion. However, her grief hadn't stopped her from taking advantage of the situation.

At the thought of the lost baby, Aiai's hand instinctively went to curl around her belly before she brought it to her knee in the most casual gesture she could manage. Fuqian had been the first to notice the changes in her body, wondering at the expanding curves during one of their clandestine meetings. Her monthly periods had ceased for five months now, and it was becoming difficult to hide her shape. Luckily her mistress had been busy, and Aiai had made a point of eating more at meals as an excuse for the new moonlike roundness of her face and figure.

The adviser left, and Empress Wu looked at Aiai with the intensity of a hunting tiger. Aiai made sure to keep her face down and her robe fluffed out over her body. Only bad things happened when her mistress looked like that. "Aiai."

"Yes, my lady?" She might sound like the emperor's prized parrot for the frequency with which she repeated those three words, but they kept her safe. Had she been caught? Which secret had been unearthed? Fuqian? The maids? Both? Either could get her killed if the empress felt ungenerous.

"I never thanked you properly for bringing the emperor to me," said her mistress in a honeyed tone that had Aiai on breathless alert. "How things have changed in the last several years, and you by my side the whole time. So loyal. So honest."

"My lady." She kept her head lowered to her work. Would it be better to brazen it out or to admit everything and beg forgiveness?

"Do you truly think he came because of your scent?" Wu asked in a deliberately casual tone. "That he is my true love, as you led me to believe?"

Aiai distinctly remembered doing the opposite, but knew better than to say so. "Few men can resist you, my lady." She was grateful to get words out past her tight throat.

"Enough," Wu snapped. "No sweet deceiving words, Aiai. Tell me the truth, for I have learned some fascinating information."

"I told you what I know," said Aiai urgently. "The Peony Goddess came to me. She said hearts will become whole, and my scents have brought love to others before."

"Yet I have just been told something I've suspected for a while," said Empress Wu. "That it was not at the emperor's own request that I came back, but that of the old bitch Wang."

Aiai did her best to act naturally. "The entire palace can see the emperor's love for you, my lady."

To her relief, Empress Wu nodded thoughtfully. "Yes. Yet this is confusing to me, that he would not have moved heaven and earth to get to me if your fragrance had worked. Wang should not have had to interfere if he was my true love, don't you think?"

"He made you his empress," said Aiai.

"So he did."

The ensuing silence meant Aiai was free of questioning for the time being, so she forced her icy hands to work again, pouring her blended powders into a sachet for the empress to tuck in her clothes. She thought the bitterness was faint enough to not be noticed. The work helped focus her mind and calm her heart, although it was difficult to work with the empress's eyes on her. What was she thinking? How much danger was Aiai in? She knocked against the tray, spilling the powders.

"Ah, Aiai. What a mess. That's not like you. Are you worried about anything?" asked the empress, her jade ornaments tinkling.

Aiai found the courage to take away some of the empress's pleasure in playing with her. "Only the ratio of orange peel, my lady."

The empress took the sachet that Aiai had placed on a tray and waved it in front of her nose. Then she tossed it back. "Too bitter. Try again."

It took two more blends before Aiai found the right combination, and when the empress swept out, she nearly fainted in relief.

Yet she could not get the dead Empress Wang's face out of her mind. The Empress Wu had already killed Aiai as far as her family was concerned when she took her to the palace five years ago, sending gold and rare goods for trade along with the note about how Aiai had succumbed to a filthy disease racking Chang'an. She might not hesitate to do it for real if she thought Aiai had misled her.

"You must leave." Fuqian's voice was urgent once Aiai had told him an edited version of her discussion with the empress. "There is no time to waste."

"How?" Aiai sat up and wrapped her robe around her shoulders. "Where would I go?"

"Come with me to Youzhou. It's far to the northeast, and she won't look for you there." Fuqian sat up as well, his black hair loose from his futou. She fished around in the bed and handed him the headscarf.

"To Youzhou?" She'd heard Fuqian speak of his home with affection.

"I need to return soon, and you can come with me." He stroked his thin nose. "I was to leave in ten days. I can have my servants take you in advance to wait for me. You will be bored while you wait, but then we can travel together. We can live in Youzhou, and you'll be safe."

Aiai gaped at him. "You want to take me home?" She had been wondering what would happen to her after Fuqian left, but had been too frightened to ask.

"I have been thinking of it for some time." He smiled and stroked her stomach. "I was going to ask you, but I was worried you couldn't leave the empress."

"I bring nothing. No dowry. No family."

"You bring my child." He looked conflicted. "You would not be my wife, Aiai. My family has a woman for me to wed when I return. The bride is not my choice, but my father's."

A concubine and alive with her child, or her pride and possible death. Aiai nodded, knowing she had no choice. "I understand."

Fuqian leaned over to hold her tight enough to feel the beat of his heart. "I will make sure my wife is kind to you. Perhaps you will become friends."

"I must be able to make my perfumes." After years with the empress, Aiai cared little about kindness or companionship. All she wanted was to keep creating.

He nodded. "You may. I'm sure my wife would be pleased to have her robes smell like those of an empress."

"I will also create for others." Finally, she could share her gift freely with the world.

Fuqian shrugged. "I would not stand in the way of your harmless hobby, and will see that she does the same."

Aiai frowned. Perhaps it would be safer to keep her gift limited to those she chose instead of open to everyone. What if there was another version of the empress or her mother, someone who would try to control her for her gift? Perhaps Fuqian would change. Money and power did strange things to people. Aiai had not told him of her moli. Even had the empress not forbidden her to tell anyone, she would have kept the information secret out of self-preservation. The empress had been right when she said men could not be trusted, even if the man was fiercely handsome with gentle hands. Aiai would extend that mistrust to the women in her life as well.

She considered him. The flickering beeswax candle cast a dim glow over his pale skin, turning it golden and scenting the air with a light sweetness. "You will teach me to read and write."

Fuqian looked at her, his dark eyes widening in curiosity. "Why?"

"I would write down my perfume ingredients for my child," said Aiai. "I have nothing else to give."

"You and your little perfumes!" Fuqian's laughter was fond. "My love, you will find it frustrating. Learning is easier as a child, and you are but a woman."

"Will you?" Aiai pressed. Although she spoke the truth about her reason, she had seen how Empress Wu's ability to read could be used as a weapon to protect herself from the trickery of others.

"Well, we have far to journey and it may help pass the time. I will teach you."

Fuqian told her it was safest for her to leave immediately. "You shouldn't go back to the empress," he said seriously. "She acts as quickly as a snake strikes, and you don't know what she will do with you."

"It may be nothing." Here, with Fuqian in their secret room, it was hard to believe anything could happen to her.

"Perhaps, but it's not a risk that you should take—not with my son." He ran his hand over her belly. "You will do as I say, Aiai."

She lowered her head, knowing he was right yet feeling a pang at leaving the lovely tools the empress had gifted her over the years. She almost asked if she could go back and retrieve them before coming to her senses. Fuqian's way was best.

"Will she come after me?" she asked as they dressed. She adjusted her silk sleeves. Her years in the palace had improved her appearance, and she looked more the lady than the Xins of her old home.

He shrugged. "Chang'an is a large city and she is a busy woman. There are dozens like you. She'll easily find another to scent her clothes."

There are none like me. As usual, she kept her thoughts to herself. With luck, the empress would think she had fled in fear of being discovered a cheat. With more luck, she would let Aiai go instead of bringing her back to face the empress's version of justice. If she was very lucky, Empress Wu would soon be too busy running the empire she desired above all things to think of Aiai at all.

If she was unlucky, Aiai would join Empress Wang.

Fuqian left after reassuring himself that she understood where to go to meet the servant he would send. She lingered for a moment in the small room in the corner of the palace Fuqian paid a eunuch to use. Their liaison was over a year old, after Fuqian, a government official, had come to pay his respects to the then-Consort Wu as a member of an entourage of officials from Youzhou. Aiai sometimes wondered if her own moli worked on herself and Fuqian was her true love.

The thought, however, never lasted long, and eventually she confirmed what she had suspected since the beginning—the true love power had no effect on her. She assumed she would wish to share everything with the man she loved, but she had no keen desire to tell Fuqian about her gift, the same way she knew she would hide her hope that her firstborn would be a girl instead of the boy he craved. Fuqian was a good man, though, and he would take her and her daughter to safety.

She touched the sachet, sewn into layers of thick fabric to block the scent, in her pocket. She had made it months ago to give to Fuqian when she was in the first throes of a love she now recognized as base lust before it deepened to affection. She had avoided giving it to him at each meeting, and the scent had eventually faded.

Aiai sat up straight as a long, low noise sounded from the corridor, and she cursed the muttering maids. She shivered, wrapping her arms across her chest, and wished for Fuqian's solid body.

Then she pinched herself. There was no time for such silliness. Not when she had real fears to confront. That was enough to help center her. Her life, and her daughter's, depended on her ability to keep her wits for the night, at least.

Aiai took a breath to prepare herself for this new adventure. How odd that she was already missing Empress Wu, for her mistress was the only woman who understood Aiai's power. She would be going to live among strangers, and it would be wise to keep her secrets to herself, at least for now. Aiai looked ahead to the solitary years, already seeing Fuqian's attention wane and waiting for the time her daughter was old enough to learn at Aiai's knee.

Her daughter's name would be Mingyue, she decided as she lowered her head to walk down the corridor, trying not to startle at every noise from behind the wooden lattice walls. It meant bright moon, for her girl would be the one to light the lonely night of her isolation. Mingyue would make it all worthwhile.

Mom texts to ask what I want for dinner as she's on her way back to the store. Although I want sushi, Mom is skeptical about uncooked fish, so I direct her to a dumpling place nearby. She arrives as Ana is leaving and presses a box of dumplings into her hand. "For a snack," she says.

"Thank you, Ms. Hua!" Ana is overjoyed. "I love your mom," she calls back as she leaves.

By the time I get to the break room after closing, Mom has pulled out plates and arranged the dumplings on them in perfect semicircles. No eating out of containers. She used to do the same with pizza, but instead of annoying me as it used to, I appreciate it. Why not make things nice, even if it's just for yourself? Isn't that partly what perfume is? A personal luxury, something that has to please you before it pleases anyone else?

"How was your day?" I ask, feeling almost like I'm talking to an acquaintance. Having Mom in my space is stranger than I thought it would be. I mean, we lived together for two-thirds of my life. You'd think I'd be used to it.

Mom pours me water. It's embarrassing how easily I've reverted to a child, letting her do things for me. "I went to the lake."

"What did you do?"

"Walked."

I take a dumpling, this one pork and chive. All of them are delicious. "Are you tired?"

"Not too tired to work on your moli," she says.

I should have known better than to think we could have an easy conversation about what her day was like, since her conversation revolves around work and the store, which is basically work. She puts another dumpling on my plate. "Mushroom," she says. "You love mushroom."

I used to love mushrooms, but a bout of food poisoning in Ottawa left me with a distaste for them. I take it without comment. "Did you go anywhere besides the lake?"

"A perfumery store I heard about online." She looks affronted. "They never heard of Yixiang, but they claim to be luxury."

I'm offended on her behalf. "Was it Olafactopia?"

"Yes."

"I know them. I don't think they're going to last long."

"No, they had poor service and I was the only customer." She takes her plate to the sink. "Bring me your dishes when you're done."

I want to stretch out the last few bites because I know what comes next, but the sooner we do this, the better. And, to be honest, I've been thinking about it all day. I'd be a liar if I said I wasn't excited. *Not excited*, I correct as I gather the rest of the dishes and bring them over to the sink. Mom is clucking about the lack of rubber gloves, so I hand her a pair of latex ones from my worktable.

The feeling in my gut is the same as going down a roller coaster, and I rename it. I'm apprehensive. That's a good word. Over the course of the day, I kept sneaking into the bathroom with the register to try to find another ancestor—any one—who had the same fear as me. None of them did, or if they had, they didn't admit to it. They only felt anticipation.

"Let's begin," says Mom, peeling off the gloves. Despite wandering around the city for the day, she looks as put-together as when she left the house this morning, and not a drop of water from the dishes has dampened her shirt. "Sit."

I sit. "Do you know what you're doing?"

She ignores me, but the question was rhetorical anyway. Mom isn't one to admit ignorance or wrongdoing. The mental gymnastics she can do to prove herself right, even when confronted with proof otherwise, are boggling. Dad flipped out the time she said she'd locked the door when she clearly had not. She kept insisting she had despite him taking photos of the door, intent himself on being declared correct.

She looks down at the table. "What's this?"

"One of Ana's designs. We're going to work together to make them into a new line of fragrant jewelry."

Mom is shaking her head before I finish. "You need to focus on understanding your moli, not this kind of silliness."

"You said it was nice," I say, trying to keep down my hurt. "You thought it was a good idea."

"For someone else. Not you. You should have bigger goals. Bigger ambitions for your work."

I feel my shoulders go high. "I want to do this."

She takes a deep breath and lets it go. "Think about what I said."

My entire body feels unruly, but Mom, having dispatched something I was excited about with a few quick words—efficient as always—points to the worktable.

"Show me," she demands. "We're going to go through the process from the beginning. I want you to start by making a perfume."

There's no point in arguing, so I move the register out of the way with a violence that is all the rebellion I can handle. Well, Mom can have her opinion on what I do, but I'm an adult. I don't need to listen to her about the jobs I take on. Mom grabs my notebook as it's about to fall off the table, and of course, she opens it.

"What is this?" she asks.

It's the list I've been working on as I read through the register. "Chinese characters."

"I can see that. Why are they in a list? Are you practicing them?"

"No, they're characters from the register I don't understand. I'll look them up later."

"Always putting things off. Do it as you work so you gain full understanding of what you read." She points to one. "This is a plant with purple flowers."

I'm not thrilled to have disappointed her again, but she's saving me precious time looking up the words, so I let her continue as I jot down a few notes for the perfume. This helps calm my nerves, at least for a moment. I can make a perfume. That's something I can do well, without failure. She writes down the name next to the character in English and pinyin, then goes through a few more. She laughs at one entry.

"I remember this. It's from Jingjing's chapter, when she was trying to capture the smell of lily of the valley. You could feel how frustrated she was trying to get it."

"Too bad she lived two hundred years before hydroxycitronellal was created," I say, putting my notes aside to bring out the register and find Jingjing's chapter. Mom's right, you can almost taste her rage at her inability to capture the scent.

"Synthetics changed so much," Mom agrees. She pages through the book, and I notice with interest that, like me, she avoids the two most recent chapters, her own and Waipo's. "I always liked Jingjing. She had personality."

"Like when she gave the perfume to the tax collector's wife to put him in a generous mood."

We flip through the pages, commenting on our ancestors like they're characters in a book. "Do you think they were really like this?" I ask. "Or that they wrote themselves the way they wish they were?"

Mom shuts the register. "Who can say? They knew they were writing for the future, and they could read what happened in the past. Can we blame them if they wanted to be seen for themselves among all these unique women?"

Did she? Mom pushed the register across the counter. "Get ready," she says. "Time for work."

I can do this. I need to do this. I want to do this. I look at the rows of fragrances and pluck out a few vials without hesitating. I know exactly what I want to make. Ambroxan with some cardamom. Frankincense. Like my very first fragrance for Ms. Kang, this is a play on incense, but instead of cold smoke drifting to the ceiling, it's warm with embers before it turns to ash. I add in some iris for the faint metal of an old, treasured censer and give it a sniff. It's not perfect—too much iris is giving more bite than I want, and it requires additional velvetiness— but it's fine.

Mom takes it from my hand. "Good enough," she says. This is possibly the only time she's accepted less than perfection. "You know what to do."

If I thought it was awkward and nerve-destroying when I did this the first time, doing it with my mother there to critique my every move is eons worse. She doesn't comment on my shaky strokes when I trace my huo or the crooked way I place the tag.

Mom looks at the bottle. "Now, Luling," she says in a hard voice. "Do it now."

I think through what I did last time—the sensation of the water, the connection as I drew energy from the world around me, the feeling of loss as I let it go—and dip my head forward.

Mom is there with a cup of cold rejuvenating tea she must have made this morning when I wasn't looking, and I remember the medicinal taste. It's the same as what she gave me after my first attempt.

I drink it and we stare at the bottle. Mom takes it from me and holds it to the light. "Can you see something?" I ask, wondering if I've missed a vital testing step.

"No." She puts it down. I take the bottle back and, like Mom, hold it up to the light. I made it in clear glass, but all I see is the pale hay of the juice. I give it a shake.

"Do you feel it?" she asks. "That tug?"

I close my eyes and let myself be filled with the power from the perfume, the bottle pulling at me. "I do."

"Really?"

"Yes." I try to keep my hand from shaking.

"You're sure? Absolutely you can feel it? You aren't imagining it?"

I keep focusing, but now I don't know if it's a tug or simply gravity pulling down my hand. I'd been sure before and it didn't work. I rub my birthmark. "Maybe?"

"You need to be sure," Mom says intently. "Are you? A lot depends on this, Luling. You must be absolutely and one hundred percent certain."

I begin to doubt myself. "I don't know."

"How can you not know?" She sounds more disappointed than angry, which is of course so much worse.

"I thought I did, but then you came in asking if I was sure!"

"Because you need to know."

I put the bottle down carefully, because what I really want is to slam it through the window.

She doesn't say anything for a moment, but then pushes my bottle aside with a decisive gesture.

"Watch," she says firmly.

The first thing she does is riffle through my vials with blue-gloved fingers, nodding and pursing her lips. In a moment, she has five lined up in front of her in a wavering line, along with a beaker and pipettes. "I was thinking about this today," she says in a soft voice, as if speaking to herself. "By the water. The difference in the smell between a lake and an ocean when the sun hits it."

I nod, but I'm not sure what she means.

"It reminded me of Xiaoting and what she wrote in the register," Mom says. "Our moli is like a sea in our souls. You need to dip into that sea with your hands and pour a little of that energy into the perfume. You will channel the current as it moves through and around you."

I brush off my renewed frustration because I thought I had done that. I need a GPS map, and all I'm getting is a pastel sketch.

She adds galbanum and petitgrain with other ingredients and automatically notes her measurements on one of the paper formula sheets I keep in a small wheeled cabinet that fits under the desk. It has rows for the materials and columns for the amount that goes in each modification. I simply sit and wait. In any other situation, I'd be looking for my phone or anything else to distract myself, but there's a deep pleasure that comes from watching my mother at work. This is her as a professional, and I have the strange dissonance that comes from understanding our own parents are deeper and more complex than we give them credit for in our minds—almost as complex as we are ourselves.

Mom's hair is tucked behind her ears, as it always is. Although we look alike, I inherited Dad's more jug-like ears. When I was younger, Waipo used to laugh and call us to join her in front of the mirror so she could see the three generations together. Our similarities were exaggerated whenever she did, and I could see the connections between us through our hands or our noses. It was easier to mark those physical traits than it was to see how my mother and grandmother shared other characteristics, like high-handed stubbornness, and wondering if that was passed to me along with our eye shape.

Mom sits back with the blotter in her hand, eyes distant as she smells it before handing it over. I sniff and, much like smelling the Luling scents, awareness of Mom's ability crashes over me. She's not only my mother but also an artist and a craftsperson, with an expertise that extends far past my own. I would feel envious if this were anyone else, but instead I'm in awe.

"We're doing an experiment," she says. "I want you to watch. Give me your huo stickers."

She's going to transform it right in front of me? She frowns when I don't move. "We don't have all night."

I still don't budge. "What are you doing, exactly?"

"I am going to go through every step to make sure when you do it later, you know exactly what to do."

"I know what to do," I remind her. "I did it already. That's why I came to Vancouver. It worked for Kelsey's samples. I just don't know why, or if these do."

"We also don't know if it works all the time. Let's start at the beginning and make sure it's not an issue with your process."

I wait for her to mention giving them to a client to test again, but all she does is say, "Watch, Luling."

I do. The first thing I notice is Mom's calm. She writes her huo with bold strokes, the characters so familiar that she would probably hesitate more if forced to think of each movement individually rather than letting them flow. Unlike me, who held the bottle with hands shaking with dread, Mom exudes casual confidence.

She doesn't look at me before she closes her eyes.

Then nothing.

Mom droops and nearly drops the bottle. "There," she says with satisfaction before she sips from the tea she gave me.

"It looks the same as when I do it." I frown. "What did it feel like? Walk me through it."

She looks exasperated. "I told you to watch."

I keep my temper. "I can't see your thoughts."

Mom puts the bottle down, and I go to the sink to get her some water. "I thought of the world around me and put the energy in. It's best not to think too much, Luling. You need to feel it."

I bring her the water and sit down again. "That's fine for you to say now, but when you were starting out, I bet you thought about it. Every step."

"No," she said, looking at the bottle. "I believed. That's the difference."

My brain feels like it's going to explode. "That's not the difference! I believed. You don't think I believed?"

"You were distracted." She points at her huo. "I remember when you chose your huo," she says. "I chose mine by instinct. So did your grandmother. You kept saying yours had to be perfect, it had to be right. You never understood the huo is only a conduit. It could be a sketch of a squid and work, as long as you believed it would. You lacked confidence in your ability to get it right."

"I wasn't distracted."

"No? That summer was hard for you, when you were so sad about Rafe. You looked through every book in the house searching for the right huo. I have the notebook where you tried different ones."

I stay silent. She noticed I was miserable. She knew it was about Rafe. Yet in my memories of that summer, she didn't say a word about it or once mention his name. Odd—at the time, I took her not talking about Rafe as another rejection, that she was so caught up in my first moli she saw me only as the continuation of the Hua line instead of as a person. Was I wrong? Perhaps she was giving me space, waiting for me to come to her. Not mentioning Rafe was a kindness she tried to extend me.

She rubs her hands together to stop the shaking. Making a moli fragrance takes a lot out of someone.

"I'll call a cab," I say. "Let's get you home."

"I want you to—"

"It can wait," I say.

Then she nods, giving in to me for the first time in her life. It doesn't feel like a victory, because I'm not thinking of winners and losers. Perhaps one day we can simply be us, and it can start here.

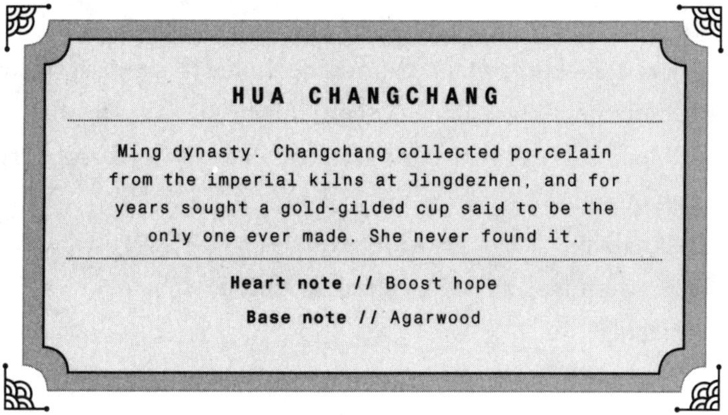

HUA CHANGCHANG

Ming dynasty. Changchang collected porcelain
from the imperial kilns at Jingdezhen, and for
years sought a gold-gilded cup said to be the
only one ever made. She never found it.

Heart note // Boost hope
Base note // Agarwood

The next day is rainy, and Mom decides to stay with me instead of going for a walk. "I have some ideas I want to work on," she says as we share coffee with Ana. "I'll stay out of the way."

I thought Mom's presence would get on my nerves, but it's peaceful. She takes one of my empty notebooks and spends the morning with the concentrated expression I know I also wear when I'm focused on following an idea. Occasionally, she gets up to take one of my vials, slipping in a blotter and holding it to her nose with distant eyes before going back and jotting more notes down. If I look at them, they'll be full of small squiggles and letters, her personal shorthand that I learned to decipher years ago.

Rafe is in another round of meetings but texts me around noon.

Rafe: What do you think about going out for dinner tonight?
I understand if you need to put it off because of your mom.

I tell him I want to go. This date has been built up so much in my head it's almost a relief to simply have it happen. Although our ongoing text conversation makes me happy because I like talking to him, it's unsatisfying. I can admit how hard it was to have him out of my life now that he's here again. I want to see him. I want to see his face as he talks and to make up for our lost time. He suggests a place and time, and is off to another meeting.

The weather keeps all but the most dedicated shoppers away, and by early afternoon we're alone, with the rain beating hard on the windows. Mom calls us to the back for a tea break. It's a pleasant, lazy Sunday-afternoon feel.

As Ana sips, she looks around my worktable. "How do you become a perfumer, anyway?" she asks curiously. "Is there a school or something?"

"There are, and there are also apprentice programs with the big fragrance companies," I say. "Our training for Yixiang is done in-house."

"In-house?" Ana looks at my mother, who nods.

"The women in our family have always taught the next generations," my mother says. "My mother and grandmother taught me, and we taught Luling."

"At first, I didn't know what Mom was doing," I say. "When I was a kid, she talked to me about how things smelled to make sure I was aware of scent in my life."

Ana points at the gardenia I have in the back waiting for more soil. "Like flowers when you went on a walk?"

"That, but everyday things too." Mom takes an orange from the bowl and holds it out to Ana. "Take the difference between the oils in an orange peel"—she sinks her nails in and the room sings with zest—"and the orange itself." She peels into it to reveal the bright pulp, and Ana leans in to breathe deep.

She sits back. "How do you go from that to making perfume?"

"Awareness is the beginning," I say. "Most people take smell for granted, but by the time I was twenty, I could recognize almost two thousand scents."

"Are you kidding?" Ana looks stunned. "There are that many smells in the world?"

Mom smiles at her. "Far more. You can't write without words, and you can't create perfumes without knowing scents and materials, so you need a vocabulary for what you're doing. An olfactory library."

"A library of flowers," says Ana.

"And spices and herbs and chemicals," Mom says.

"How do you do that?"

"Practice," I say. "Lots of patience."

"I taught Luling to connect smells to memories," says my mother. "That helps. We process smell in our olfactory bulb, which is connected to the parts of our brain involved in building memory."

I pull out a vial and dip in a blotter, then hand it to Ana. "For instance, dihydromyrcenol is synthetic, so it's not something you can instantly connect to, like a rose. The first time I sniffed it, I happened to be looking at my grandmother's purple scarf," I say. "Now, in my head, it's a cool purple scent, and that's how I remember it. The scarf matched the lavender notes."

"It totally smells like purple." Ana looks fascinated as she waves it in front of her nose, then sighs. "I've always wanted a signature scent but never found one that matched me."

"I can make you something, if you want. One just for you." I can see the kinds of fragrances that will suit her. Chocolate and red chili, with amber for a scent as expansive as Ana herself. Creamy balsamic. Or gardenia and frangipani—big, gorgeous blooms that will fill a room if she wants to take up space.

"Really?" She looks thrilled.

"Absolutely. Do you have something in mind or want a surprise?"

She gives me a look. "What do you think?"

"Surprise it is." I'm a little astonished I know her well enough to say it with such certainty. Friendship was sneaking up on me solely through proximity.

The door bells ring, and Ana runs to the front of the store so fast the socks she's sorting tumble to the ground. She's back before we've finished picking them up.

"It was only the mail." She's obviously upset.

Mom watches her. "Did you want it to be someone else? You look like there's something on your mind." I didn't know Mom's voice could go that gentle. She certainly doesn't bother to use that tone on me.

"It's not a perfume thing," says Ana.

Mom laughs. "Most things aren't."

"You met Jayne, right?"

"In front of the store."

"I thought it might be her. I like her," Ana says. "Then I saw her laughing with another woman the last time I went to her bar." She looks at me. "You know, the one with the crystal store?"

"Krystal, yeah," I say.

"No, it's called Karma. Or Karma Gems, I can't remember."

"Her name is Krystal."

"Seriously?" Ana rubs her face as Mom tries not to laugh.

I nod. "She ordered a perfume from me and wanted it to smell like radiance." I gave her a twist on a classic Chanel No. 5 neroli with sparkling aldehydes to go with the patchouli that permeates her clothes.

"I'm jealous of a woman named Krystal who owns a crystal store." She groans. "How is this my life?"

"You shouldn't be," I say. "Talking doesn't mean anything."

"I know." She frowns as the soundtrack for *Amélie* plays in the background. Mom has busied herself taking the teacups to the sink, but I can tell she's listening.

"Ana. Go over there and say hi. You talk to her all the time anyway."

"Yeah, but now she's more real, you know? She's not going to be this perfect being I've built up in my head. She's going to have issues because she's a person, and it's scary and making me act weird around her." Ana starts removing vinyl belts from their crinkly plastic bags. "What if I end up disappointed? Then I don't have Jayne and I don't have the dream of Jayne. I'll have nothing. It's easier not to try."

This hits me hard; I know what it's like to lose both the dream and the reality. As I'm trying to think through a response, Mom answers.

"Disappointment is a part of life," she says. Ana looks taken aback, as if she expected some sort of a *You got this* pep talk. She doesn't know Mom. "People will disappoint you in many ways. They'll make promises and break them. They'll raise expectations and dash them. They'll leave you wondering what you've done wrong when you've done nothing at all."

Is this directed at me? It must be. Ana's eyes are wide. "Okay?"

"However, they will also surprise you. We often misread people or project assumptions on them." Her voice turns thoughtful. "What we see on the surface is nothing like the person below. Much like a perfume, you need to give time and warmth for a person to reveal themselves fully."

"Even if they end up disappointing you?" Ana's voice is small.

"Even then, because the risk is worth the reward," says Mom. "Sometimes that person blossoms for you, and only you."

Ana wriggles her shoulders as if fighting against the weight of her insecurities. "What if I disappoint her?"

Even I, with my limited emotional intelligence, can jump in here because there's only one honest and conveniently acceptable answer. "Impossible. She'd be lucky to have a chance to be in your life."

This is true. Ana is sincere and giving, open in a way that's totally foreign to me.

"Yeah," says Ana, neck lengthening like a swan. "I'm a catch."

"You are," says Mom.

"I have a lot to offer."

"Tons," I assure her.

"You know what? I'm not made for pining. I was forged for action." She fluffs her curls until they rise in a platinum halo. "I'm going to get my woman."

Before I can reply, she grabs her coat and umbrella, then leaves. It's so sudden I expect to see a little puff of smoke where she sat.

"Goodness," says Mom after a pause. "What an interesting girl."

The door slams open and Ana comes rushing back in.

"What do I say?" she moans.

This time I almost shove her out the door. "Just make conversation. Like usual, the way you did before you started having this crisis."

"Right." She draws herself up tall. "Be cool. I am cool."

"As ice."

"Ice." She gives a decisive nod. "I can get a drink."

"You can," says Mom. "You said it was a bar."

After a little more cajoling, she's off again.

Mom looks at me, eyebrows high, and I shrug. "That's Ana," I say.

"I think a scent with a long sillage would match her," says Mom, walking to the window. "Very long."

I trail after her and watch as she adjusts the curtains. "Did you mean what you said about people disappointing you?"

"I was speaking in generalities," she said. "Do you disagree?"

"I don't know." Feeling a little uncomfortable, I turn to my phone and see a new commission has come in. I show the brief to Mom to break the silence.

She reads it over. "All the instructions say is that it should smell like 'home.'"

They didn't tick any of the boxes I include to help narrow down their preferences, but wrote a cheery "Dealer's choice!" in the Additional Notes box, which is less than helpful.

"I'm thinking flowers and apple pie," I say to tease her.

"Apple pie." She makes a face at these uninspired choices. "Really, Luling. I trained you better."

"I was kidding," I protest. "What would you make?"

She looks at me, and her smile is mischievous in a way I haven't seen in years. "Waipo and I used to compete over client requests sometimes," she says. "We'd each take the brief and see who interpreted it better."

"You want to compete?" This is so not like Mom. Or maybe it is and I'm only just now learning.

"Who can create the best 'home' perfume," she says. "Two hours."

"You're on."

After a brief delay to help a customer who braved the rain because he wanted to surprise his fiancée with matching his-and-hers scents for their upcoming wedding, I pull out my notebook to think about the home scent.

The shop feels calm, but my mind is somehow simultaneously empty and frantic, making it impossible to settle on an idea. It doesn't help that when I glance at Mom, she looks serene as she pulls the ingredients she needs. *Home. Home. Home.* The word repeats in my head until it loses meaning.

The strangest thing that happened when I left home was how badly I wanted my mother, who was one of the very specific reasons I was leaving in the first place. I knew it would be asking too much for her to reassure me I was doing the right thing by leaving—Mom made it crystal clear she thought I was acting like a child and making a huge mistake—but I would have settled for a mom who at least cared enough to check in and shame me out of living from my suitcase for two months because unpacking was too overwhelming. She never did. I'd thought she would always be there, but once I left, she faded away. No, took herself away. That upset me, because how could she be the one to separate herself from me?

Only I was allowed to do that.

I sigh and hunker down to my work. I decide on the smell of night in the garden at my parents' house. I put in black water and wet sand and rocks, then cover it with the butterscotch of a ponderosa pine. I consider adding an echo of Rafe's cologne, that smoky light tobacco that's nothing like a cigarette and instead is everything sexy. I find myself reaching for a pristine and chilly iris. Mom's scent.

She's writing away on one of the formula sheets. A discarded pair of gloves and a capped vial sit in front of her.

"How are you doing?" I ask.

In reply, she holds out the vial. I exchange it for my own and we dip in our blotters. It takes me a moment to absorb what my mother has done. It's almost identical to my own, minus the iris. Instead—I close my eyes. Yes. She's incorporated the Turkish rose note from the scent I wore in high school, a deconstructed version of a high-end perfume that I didn't want to spend hundreds of dollars on, and over it, a breath of citrus. Waipo's lemon.

"You did the garden," she says with satisfaction.

"What night is this?" Because somehow I know her creation is referencing a specific memory.

"It was a Saturday night. You were sixteen. Your brother was out with friends, and your father was on a business trip. We'd spent the day in the lab with Waipo and then went home and ordered a pizza to eat outside."

"You picked fresh basil from the garden and put it on the top." I remember that night.

"Always better than what the restaurant uses." She waves the blotter. "Cheaper too."

I want her to comment on the iris, or that we had the same fundamental theme, but she says nothing except, "The winner?"

I take her vial. "I'll send samples of both and let the client decide."

She puts away the gloves and I watch her. She hasn't mentioned my moli once today, and I wonder if that was the thing standing in the way of us getting along all these years. If perhaps Kelsey was right and the moli is a curse, at least for me.

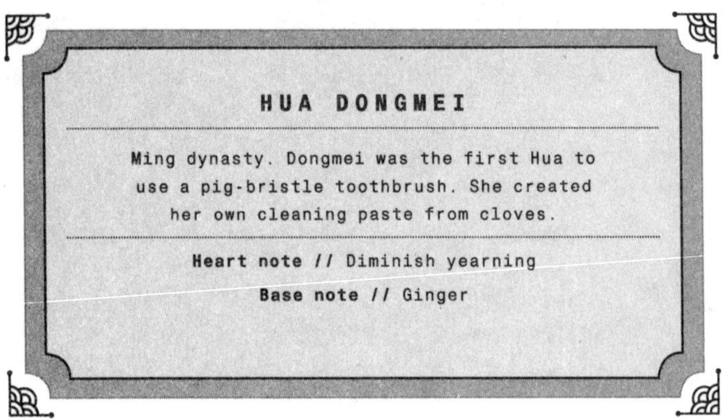

After work, the rain stops, leaving the air cool and fresh. Mom is happy for me to go out for dinner with Rafe, although she tries to convince me to go for something other than sushi, muttering darkly about parasites and worse. I lie and promise her I'll stick to donburi. She heads home and I go to meet Rafe, who is waiting outside the restaurant on Spadina.

When I catch sight of him lounging against a wall as he waits, I stumble. How did I not realize I compared every man I met with him over the years? They were all lacking and I never understood why until now. They simply weren't him. He waves when he sees me and I speed up.

We've hit the tail end of the dinner rush and are seated at a small table for two that's far more intimate than I anticipated. After the initial conversation about our day and how Mom is settling in, we stop.

We've been texting, but there are huge gaps in what we know about the last thirteen years. This makes it hard to be completely easy with each other, although the echo of that comfort remains and resurfaces often enough to give a false sense of familiarity. Rafe holds his mug of green tea in both hands and looks at the table. A frown has drawn long lines across his forehead, and we listen to the couple beside us gossiping cozily about their work colleagues.

Finally, he smiles at me and I take my courage in hand. "We haven't had a chance to talk about what's happened to us over the years," I say. "I don't even know if you have pets."

He nods. "It's weird to try to catch up on so much time. I don't remember half of it. Maybe most of it."

"What if we do a highlights reel?" I suggest. "We'll trade the top five things we should know."

Rafe puts aside his cup. I watch him greedily, hungry for his face after all the years of telling myself I didn't care. Lies to yourself are almost impossible to get over. "My top five life highlights." He sounds baffled.

Although it was my idea, I'm also struggling. It's not so much a list as a judgment call about what I find valuable. What do I want him to know about me? By the time the server comes by for our order, I've only got three items and second-guessed a dozen others.

"Who goes first?" Rafe asks.

"You asked."

He groans. Our tradition is, the one to ask is the one to go first.

"Fine. No comments until we're both done." Rafe clears his throat. "These are in no particular order," he warns.

"Mine neither."

Rafe thanks the server for the Asahi Super Dry and takes a sip. "Work. You know I work for the family real estate business. We branched out from residential and I want to move us into the luxury space, more high-end real estate."

He glances at me and I nod.

"Pets. I have two cats named Trixie and Lola. While I'm here, they're with my neighbor." He pays the cat tax and shows me a photo of a sleek brown tabby and round black cat sitting side by side like judgmental sphinxes.

"Home. I live in a condo near the water in Kitsilano. Hobbies." Here he flounders. "I don't think I have any. Most of my time is working. Relationships. None. My last girlfriend was two years ago, and we dated for three years." He looks up. "Your turn."

I stop myself from asking what broke them up, because I don't like thinking of Rafe with another woman. "I make perfume under Ile de Grasse. Also, I know Grasse isn't an island. Mom points it out all the time. The name is conceptual."

"I had no doubt." His grin makes me laugh.

"I move around a lot. I've lived in seven cities since I left and I don't go home very often. I don't have any pets. I..." I peter out. "No relationships."

"That's four," he says.

"It's five," I argue. "Perfume, moving, seven cities, not going home, no pets, no significant other. Six, now that I count them out. I overdelivered."

"I consider moving, the cities, and not going home all variations on a theme." He crosses his arms. "Give me one more."

"I–I don't have..." I falter, trying to think of something, anything.

"Not a negative," he says. "Not anything missing. Something you have."

That shuts me up completely because I've defined the last decade more by what I lack. "I have a friend," I say finally. "Ana. She owns the store. At least, I think we're friends."

We sit across the table, looking at each other. "If this were my eulogy, everyone in the funeral home would cry from pity," Rafe says finally, frowning at his cup.

"At least you didn't turn into a kayak guy," I say to lighten the mood.

"I was one for a while." Rafe goes red. "I sold it last year and got back into hiking. Hey, I guess I do have a hobby."

"We used to hike all the time," I say. "Remember when we climbed the Grouse Grind?"

"It was in October," he says.

"You slipped."

He snorts. "Because you missed a step and fell on me."

"Then those Japanese tourists took photos of us because we were covered in mud."

"Right before that eighty-year-old couple in the head-to-toe Patagonia beat us to the top."

"They made fun of us for being slow."

Rafe frowns. "Yeah, if we'd known it was a race, we could have totally beat them."

"We probably should have known. Doesn't it automatically become a race the second someone passes you on the trail?"

We laugh, and for that brief moment, it feels like no time at all has passed.

"We could go hiking again here," he adds. "I found a nice trail out by the zoo I want to try."

Another date, pulling us from the past into a shared future. I nod enthusiastically.

Rafe eats neatly, which is something I forgot. Missy Jin drilled manners into him, telling him a Realtor needed to exude a sense of class. The conversation is easier than I expected, and with the basics of our lives out of the way, I feel better about simply talking. We move from his trip to Ottawa to my time living there, and then to a jasmine-mint scent I'd been working on.

"I put it on before I left." I hold out my wrist, where I'd sprayed it.

This is a mistake, because Rafe cradles my hand over the table. I keep my arm still but can feel the trembling start in my knees as he pushes my sleeve up to nose along my skin, his eyes closing to concentrate on the scent.

I do my best to cover my reaction to his touch. Having Rafe back in my life again leaves me feeling strangely untethered. It's as if part of me never moved past the twenty-year-old who'd been stunted with hurt. That Lucy was stuck in time, but I have options I can take if I grow through the past like a sapling reaching for sun.

The problem is that I've been in this space so long I don't know if I can get out of it. Loneliness is treacherous; it trains you to its needs and makes you think that you crave it. Ana was the first one to start kicking at my walls, knocking out a block here and there, but with Rafe, they could all come tumbling, leaving me vulnerable. Deep down, I'm still the girl who thrilled at that chaste garden kiss before the crushing disappointment came, but there's a lot to learn about a man who's going back to Vancouver in weeks.

He leans back and blinks. "It smells pretty," he says slowly. "Like a spring day where you wake up energized after a long winter. Fresh."

I manage to find my voice and pull my arm back. The imprint of his hand sits heavy on my skin. "Thanks."

We keep going with the conversation, but the vibe has shifted to one that could be leading us to where we broke off so many years ago. When we leave, the weather is warmer than it has been in the last few weeks and still carries its post-rain crispness. "I'd like to walk for a bit," I say, hoping to keep the spell over us.

He falls into step beside me, and we go up Spadina, me pointing out places I like. Then Rafe stops in front of a sign. "Oh my God," he says. "They're playing *Big Trouble in Little China*. We saw that in the rep theater, and we were the only people there."

I laugh. "We tried sitting in every row to figure out which was the best, because we could."

"One row up from dead center. Sitting in the front row nearly broke my neck."

I read the rest of the poster. "Hey, it starts in twenty minutes."

We immediately head over to the theater, a small screening room at the university, and get tickets from the apathetic seller.

"Popcorn?" asks Rafe.

I nod and we buy a huge and surprisingly fresh bag that I sniff with delight. Hot popcorn has a lovely toasted smell from the sugars heating, and the coconut oil lends it a delicious lushness. I dip my hand in at the same time as Rafe, and we both pull back.

"Sorry," we say.

The next time it happens, he only smiles at me and doesn't move his hand. Nor do I.

The room itself is a little strange since there are no chairs. Everyone sits on big blocks placed like an experimental amphitheater around the screen. A few have brought half chairs with built-in backrests. The lights dim soon after we take our seats on the last block, one with enough space for two people to sit beside each other. There are no trailers and the movie starts right away.

"What if it doesn't hold up?" whispers Rafe as Egg Shen appears on the screen. "I haven't seen it in fifteen years."

I fold my legs to sit cross-legged. "Then we've blown a couple hours and twenty bucks, but on the plus side, we got popcorn."

"True." He settles back.

Rafe holds the popcorn between us, the way he always did after the time I got scared by the vampires during *30 Days of Night* and tossed the bag so far in the air that it rained popcorn over the surrounding seats. Sitting next to him in the dark transports me back, and I close my eyes for a second to let myself wonder what if. What if I had stayed. What if I had called him. What if, what if.

What if we can pick up where we left off? What if I can have him back like nothing happened?

It's almost one in the morning when we leave the theater, but we're buzzed. "That was incredible," he says.

"I'd forgotten how good it was." I feel giddy. "You know there's a bar named after the movie on Dundas?"

"No way."

"Ana told me about it. Apparently, it's got red lanterns and everything."

We swap some favorite scenes, and it's like being with Rafe again, my old friend. I gaze at his mouth, wondering if that's all we'll be but knowing for certain I want more.

The walk home is relaxed, as if Wang Chi has kicked the ass end of our estrangement along with the bad guys, and Rafe lingers at my door. "That was fun," he says.

I nod, but I need to ask something before we get too deep. Eric's words from the other day have been gnawing at me. *I don't know how you think any man could put up with it, not knowing if your own wife is using it to control you.* I have to know. "Can I ask you something?"

"Sure."

"Are you scared I'll use my moli on you?"

He shook his head. "Never."

"That's certain."

"I know you, Lucy. I trust you would never do that."

I look at him, and I believe him.

"Okay," I say.

He grins at me. "Doubt I could afford it anyway."

"I'd give you the friends-and-family discount."

"Thanks, but I'd prefer to use it on one from your mom. I need the occasional mood boost. Yours, though? Not necessary. I've got it covered."

He waves at me and heads down the hall, as I stand in front of the door, puzzling over what he means. My moli isn't necessary? Why not?

It's not until I'm in bed that I realize what he might have meant, and I fall asleep with a big smile on my face.

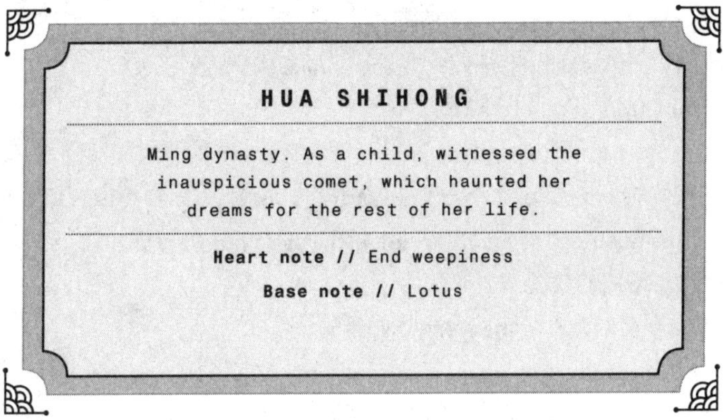

Mom doesn't come with me to work the next day but waves me off at the door the way she used to when I left for school, saying she would keep herself busy. Time passes slowly at the store, where Ana works on her jewelry in between not-so-casual spontaneous mentions of Jayne, and I try to focus on my commissions instead of wallowing in what happened last night. When I come home, Rafe is outside my door.

"Hi, Lucy," he says, taking a couple of steps in my direction.

"Were you waiting for me?" I ask, a little confused.

"Your mom asked me to drop by." He takes another step. "Hey, I was thinking—"

The door opens behind me. "Luling?"

We turn to see my mother. What a party. "Rafe, you're still here," she says. "Will you join us for dinner?"

"Thanks, Ms. Hua, but I'm meeting someone."

"Are you sure? Luling is here now."

He glances at me. "I'd love a rain check."

"Next time, then." She goes back in, and I follow after giving Rafe a quick nod.

"What was that about?" I ask.

"Rafe looks skinny. He should get a good meal."

"No, why was he here in the first place?" I ask.

"I wanted to talk to him."

"About what?"

She gives me a look over her reading glasses. "Over things that are not your business at the moment. Go wash your hands."

"Like what? The shop?"

She points me to the soap. "Hands."

"Mom, is Yixiang okay?" I ask tentatively. This is finally my chance to ask.

"It is, Luling." Her voice is assured. Can I believe her? Or do I believe Eric? Why would she lie to me? I decide to wait and see because that's the coward's way out of a conversation I don't want to have.

Dinner is delicious. Mom made spaghetti and cheesy garlic bread. The flavors are perfect in their simplicity, the tomatoes simmered down with basil. Yet it also makes me sad. Maybe *pensive* is a better word. *Forlorn.* Like everything she's cooked, it's one of my favorites from childhood. Everything she thinks she knows about me is from the past.

"I can do dinner tomorrow," I say. "I make a good tuna couscous salad, and the asparagus is good this time of year."

"You don't like canned fish," she says.

"I didn't," I correct her. "I do now."

She's quiet for a second. "That would be nice. Perhaps you can make it for Rafe as well. He can join us."

"Maybe."

We tidy up after dinner—or I try to tidy while Mom sits down, but she insists on helping. While we work, she asks if I've heard back from the client about the home-perfume options I sent (no) or have any new commissions. I fight against taking the question as a commentary on my ability to generate business and do my best to answer her words, not any perceived tone, like an emotionally actualized adult. "I got one today."

"Oh?" she asks, looking interested. Before the moli issue got in our way, talking to Mom about perfume had been one of my favorite things in the world. It still is.

"It's a young woman. New job. New boyfriend, new apartment, and everything is exciting instead of causing her stress. She wants to bottle that feeling so she can remember this moment when she needs it."

"Intriguing." Mom takes the kettle off the stove. "I wonder why she doesn't think her regular scent will do that, the one she wears every day."

"I asked the same thing. She's never worn perfume."

Mom's hand halts with the kettle midair. "Never?"

I share her disbelief. "Her father hates all fragrance. He didn't allow anything—not a scented candle or detergent or shampoo—in the house. He wasn't allergic, the woman said, just didn't like it. She moved away from home recently and wants to explore."

My mother vibrates with ideas, and I give her the opening instead of hoarding this challenge for myself. "What do you think?"

To my surprise, she only smiles at me. "What do *you* think?"

I settle down at the table. "Something light so I don't overwhelm her?"

"Did you do a consultation?"

I grab my bag and pull out the sheets I'd brought home with me. Mom pages through, tapping her fingers on the table. "She doesn't know what she wants," she says. "Did you have her smell anything?"

"She liked all of it," I say. "It's truly wide open, but I don't know where to start."

Mom thinks. "Sometimes it's better to watch instead of listen when a client is trying the blotters. Do you have the register?"

I fetch it, and Mom flips through the pages until she finds Zhengyi's chapter. "Here," she says. "Zhengyi's rules when she opened the store cover this."

"What didn't they cover?"

Mom laughs. "She was a thorough woman. Your grandmother said Zhengyi went to the store each day until she was bedridden to run her fingers along the baseboards. After that, she made your grandmother do it and demanded she come home without washing her hands, to show her the place was dust-free. Waipo refused and they compromised on using a tissue as proof."

I didn't know that, but I can imagine the look on a young Waipo's face as she tried to negotiate with a crotchety old woman born in the previous century.

I skim the chapter and then point. "Is this what you were talking about?"

Mom nods. "Zhengyi was before her time. 'Scent is instinctive, and although the client may feel shy about stating her preferences, there will be some she reacts to more strongly than others without knowing herself. It is your job to draw these out.' Do you remember if your client reacted?"

I close my eyes to put myself back in the moment. The client was a delicate, colorless woman, with mouse-brown hair, pale-gray eyes, and slightly freckled skin that looked like it might have had a tan several years ago. Her clothes were taupe and camel, her shoes unexpectedly stylish brown Victorian lace boots.

"Yes, I was surprised." I describe what she looked like and then say, "I thought she would like spring flowers, like muguet or lilac."

"She liked heavy woods? Oud?"

"No, oakmoss."

Mom looks pensive. "Curious."

"Aromatics too."

"A gorgeous combination. You could do a lot with that. Rosemary and oakmoss. Perhaps pine."

"Yeah." I'm listening as I write down ideas. "Maybe with a touch of fruity sweetness, like raspberry."

By the time we're done, I've jotted out a few sketches as a starting point. Mom is still reading Zhengyi's chapter, and I look over her shoulder. Besides rules for keeping the store clean and organizing stock—probably useful information, as Zhengyi was the first shopkeeper in the family—were tips on selling that were still applicable.

"'Be present but not hovering,'" says Mom, tapping the page. "Good advice."

"I like that she's willing to recommend other shops, to make it look like you only want what's best for the customer."

"Zhengyi was a marvel." Mom takes our empty cups and puts them into the dishwasher, then comes back to look at my notes.

"That second scent might be good for Yixiang," she says. "You could do it when you come back home."

Instantly, I'm on alert. "When I what?"

"Nothing," she says quickly. "I misspoke."

"I live in Toronto," I say. "I don't have plans to leave."

"I didn't mean anything by it," Mom says. "I just thought since Rafe is back in your life and you have your moli, you might be thinking about the future."

I get a prickly feeling when she mentions Rafe's name, but I brush it off. "We're only friends, and I'm not going back to Vancouver."

"Of course." She gives in with more grace than I expected.

As I'm thinking how nice this is, to be able to just talk to her, Mom goes to her room and comes back with a box. She places it in front of me and I recognize it from Waipo's room.

"What's this?" I ask.

In front of my increasingly alarmed gaze, she pulls out the red fabric tucked inside to display the low collar like she's a host on a home shopping channel. A line of knotted-rope buttons run down the front of the garment, and the red cord of each fastening is woven around an imperial jade bead the size of a hazelnut. According to Hua Xiaoting, the jade dates back to the Song dynasty.

The robe is a magnet drawing my iron-cold hands close. A faint whiff of smoky wood rises from the fabric, which she must have scented the old-fashioned way by airing it over burning incense.

I accept the robe when my mother hands it over, her expression blank as if she understands the slightest hint of triumph will result in the robe tossed at her feet and me out of the room. The silk has the same feel as when she first draped it over my shoulders when I was twenty, a slippery lightness with disconcerting warmth. Despite the substantial ornamentation, it was like wearing a cloud. I did a twirl for the sheer pleasure of feeling it billow behind me and whisper around my legs as Waipo looked on with a proud smile.

I shove it back at her.

"Why did you bring this?"

"I thought it would inspire you," she says.

I'm hit with a red-hot rage, made worse by how comfortable I felt fifteen minutes ago. I should have known not to let my guard down. "Can we have one night without you getting on my case about my moli?"

"You need to try."

"I need you to leave me alone!" This is rude and I know it.

She rolls her eyes. "So dramatic, goodness. I gave you space, but now it's time to work. You must get to the bottom of this, Luling! Don't you want to be fixed? We need to know."

It's like she's punched me. I was wrong to imagine we could simply be us one day. Or in a way, I was too right. I was thinking of it in the wrong way, because we already are us, today and right now.

The problem is that Mom and I, as an us, are not compatible.

"I'm not broken," I say.

She waves her hand. "Don't you understand what this could mean for you?"

I shut off completely. By *you*, she means *us*—or more accurately, *her*. It always goes back to the store. Back to what I owe her for the priceless gift of allowing myself to be born the fifth daughter. "Fine."

"You need to practice until you're sure," she says with finality. "The way you used to be. Dedicated. Not like a butterfly, going here and there to scent jewelry or make pointless things that smell like a fall fair."

"Sure, Mom," is all I say, but it hurts to know that's what she thinks of my work. The anger has drowned under the soreness that simmers inside me whenever she's near.

I smooth my hand over the embroidered band on the wide sleeve, the material catching on my rough fingertips. The silk might be light, but the garment is heavy with the weight of hope. That's why I'd left the robe and all it represented behind when I started a new life as a nomad.

"I don't understand you," Mom says, sounding exhausted. "I don't."

"What don't you understand? That I don't want you bugging me about my moli all the time? That I want you to leave me alone? That my life is better when you're away from me?" I draw in a ragged breath as she flinches.

Then she does the worst thing possible. She runs her hand gently along my hair and touches my shoulder. Her face is filled with pity.

"Go to bed soon," she says softly. "You need rest."

Before I can reply, she gathers the robe tightly in her arms, then leaves. Her bedroom door closes.

She didn't deserve what I said to her. Luckily, we'll pretend it didn't happen and I won't have to think of it again, except to add it to the list of shameful acts that parade through my brain at three in the morning.

I don't deserve to be a Hua at all.

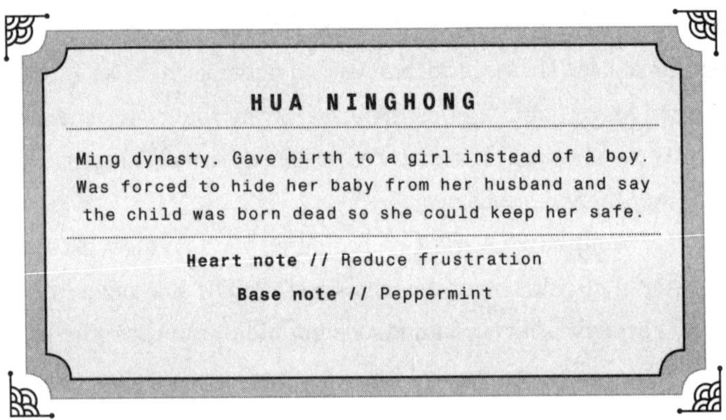

The next day, Saturday, I wake up with a fever. Mom takes one look at me and says, "You're not going to work."

"It's my busiest day." I wipe the sweat off my face. I hate being sick. I'll have to get dressed and drag myself down to the corner store to get some ginger ale.

"I'll go."

I curl up on the couch, grateful to be prone. "You can't work my perfume shop. Don't be ridiculous. Ana can handle it."

The fire from her gaze is hot enough to spike my fever. "Do you know who you're talking to? I was selling perfumes before you were born."

I pull the covers over my head. "Sorry." At least my sickness has given us something to wrangle over that isn't my behavior from last night.

"Get into the bed," she says, pointing to the bedroom. "I'll be back."

I stumble in, relaxing into sheets permeated with my mother's light almond-scented hand lotion. I text Ana to tell her about Mom standing in for me.

Ana: Can I bring you anything?

The instinctive *no* rises, but this time it's justified.

Me: Mom's getting some stuff from the store.
Ana: Did your dad ever take care of you when you were sick
as a kid? I don't think mine did.
Me: Once. I had a sore throat and he brought me a bag of chips.
Ana: Yikes. Well, don't worry, I can give your mom a hand if
she needs. I'm going in a couple hours early, so tell her
to knock. I'll let her in and lock up after her tonight.

Mom comes back and a few minutes later brings me a glass of Canada Dry ginger ale, a tangerine nestled in the peel like a flower, and honey-lemon ginger tea. She hands me two Tylenol and a glass of water. Having so many hydration options makes me feel rich. "Ana will be at the store to let you in."

She nods. "There's more fruit in the kitchen and I bought some white bread."

I close my eyes. "You hate white bread. You think it's tasteless pap."

"That's true, but you're sick."

Mom puts her hand on my forehead and it's nice and cool. "Go to sleep, Luling."

I guess I listen to her, because when I wake up it's a few hours later and the apartment is empty. There are texts from Ana.

Ana: Your mom is here. All good! She brought me tea with a
big-ass flower in it. It was super pretty but tasted like hay.
Don't tell her that because I told her it was yummy.

Ana: Holy shit your mom is a selling machine.

Ana: Jayne came over and took her to the bar for lunch.

Ana: Your mom is working in your lab space. Also she put a
sign for Ile de Grasse in the window. Looks good.

Ana: She went for a walk and Jayne told me she came in,
said the bar smelled, and I quote, "like poor people," and
gave her a bottle of diffuser oil, which Jayne says and I
quote again "Is the best fucking thing I've smelled in my
life."

Ana: Oh my God, that blogger from BlogToronto came in
and your mom sold her so much of your stock, then told
her to go to Jayne's to check out the diffuser. I told Jayne
so she's ready. Your mom is something else.

I let the phone drop.

A sharp knock on the door wakes me up again, but I ignore it. Then
my phone buzzes. It's Rafe, asking me to let him in.

I stumble to the door, the sticky taste of ginger ale filling my mouth,
and open it.

"How do you feel?" he asks.

"How did you know I was sick?" I run my fingers through my greasy
hair to tidy it. I look like a mess, but Rafe has seen me look worse.

He comes in. "Your mom told me and suggested I come by."

That spiky feeling rises with this further evidence of Mom's med-
dling. "She didn't need to do that."

"I wanted to, once I knew." He raises a white bag. "I thought you'd
like some congee. You always liked that when you were sick."

I brush my teeth and do some basic grooming as Rafe sets out a
bowl. Only one, so when I come back, I ask, "Aren't you eating?"

He makes a face. "I ate so much of this and ramen in university, I can't stand it anymore."

I sniffle and drink the glass of water he's put out. "I did the same with hot dogs."

He laughs and I eat about half the bowl before I risk a look up. Rafe is sitting on the other side of the counter with his sleeves rolled to the elbow, gazing at the wall, chewing on his cheek. Then he smiles at me and my heart gives a running jump. I wondered if being alone so long had made me susceptible to any attention that came my way, but no. It's Rafe. I want him in my life, smiling at me just like this. I want to care for him the same way he's caring for me.

I spoon up more congee and Rafe chats about his day, making me laugh. He pours me ginger ale and tidies the kitchen while I have a shower. Returning in clean sweats, with my hair damp, I accept the tea Rafe hands over, taking pleasure in him being there. Rafe is the only one I can be silent with as well as chatty.

The door opens and my mother calls a greeting. Rafe stops talking and stands as Mom comes in the room. "I'll leave you to get some rest," he says.

He and my mother exchange pleasantries before he leaves and my mother pulls out a pan. "You ate?"

"Rafe brought congee. He said you asked him to."

"I only said you were sick and he might want to drop by on the way home."

"Mom, don't do that." I don't need her shoving us together.

"Why? He's an old friend. He lives down the hall. It's not like he traveled to the moon."

I need distraction so I don't make this a fight. I go to lie on the couch as she moves around the kitchen. I pull out the register and drape my blanket over my head like a cowl and keep reading. There aren't many mentions of the men in my ancestors' lives, I notice. Some didn't tell their husbands at all, and others told and regretted it because the men tried to take over the business, telling their wives they knew how to do it better. Some were flat-out exploitative or resentful. I hesitate over Mom's chapter and then avoid it like I usually do. I don't need to read about Dad's attitude; I heard it enough growing up.

Surely there has to be one truly supportive man in our history, but even the ones who loved their wives begrudged the time the women spent on their moli or were unhappy moving into the Hua compound instead of bringing their wife home to their own family. I give up after another half hour.

I don't understand why. Wouldn't the men in the lives of my ancestors have appreciated the money and power? The register seemed to indicate some husbands resented this too. But if they could take their wealth from their fathers and think it was their right to have it flow between generations, how was it that different from receiving it from their wives? They still didn't have to work for it.

Mom drops something, and I suddenly remember the question I can't believe I never asked.

I throw back my blanket wimple. "Mom."

"Are you hungry?" she asks.

"No." It doesn't matter what I say, because a bowl of light-yellow Asian pear slices appears on the coffee table. "How did you tell Dad about your moli?"

She doesn't look up. "I didn't until we were married."

"What? I thought it would have been before that. Like a condition of marriage."

Mom shakes her head. "He planned to go back to China after school, so there didn't seem to be a point in telling him while we were dating. Then he got a job here, a good one, and after a while, his family told him to stay. It was more than he could make back in Shanghai."

"You told him then?"

She sits down and crosses her legs at the ankle, a ladylike posture she tried in vain to have me adopt. "I was going to, but our engagement was short. He could be in the country because of his work, but it would be better if he was married."

"Wait, were you in love?"

Mom avoids my eyes. "Of course. We had similar goals."

That does not sound like a ringing endorsement, and Mom gives me a look.

"Love comes in many ways," she says.

"He doesn't believe in our moli," I say.

Mom's work-worn hands are flat on the armrests. "He didn't need to. All I asked was that he let me do my work."

I'm actually shocked at this. I would have thought Mom would have insisted on more than simple noninterference. "Then when did you tell him?"

"After our honeymoon. We went to Shanghai so I could meet his family, and I told him when we got back."

"Wow." That would be a shocking bit of information to lay on a new husband. Poor Dad.

"I didn't get a chance to do it earlier."

"Really?"

She stands up. "God, Luling, how can I remember from so long ago? I told him when I told him, he understood, end of story. Ancient history. Now, do you want more pear? An orange? You need vitamin C if you're sick."

Part of me wants to push further, but the bright-red spots high on her cheeks tell me her patience is running thin. "No, thanks," I say.

It's not until later, when she's gone to bed after changing the sheets and I'm lying on the couch staring at the ceiling, that I realize being sick has some benefits. She hasn't mentioned working on my moli all day. Nor has she referred to our fight, and I've been too ashamed to bring it up because I know I owe her an apology I can't give. I shouldn't have to apologize for telling the truth.

I shouldn't.

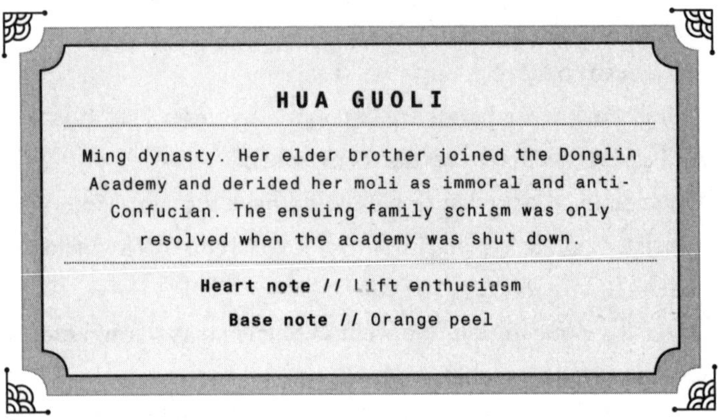

When I wake up on Sunday, I feel like myself again. Mom makes me toast and butter, and I feel cared for in a way browning my own bread never achieved.

"You'll be late for work," she says.

"The store opens at noon on Sundays." I pick up the buttery crumbs with my finger.

She slaps my hand away and takes the plate. "Disgusting, licking your fingers like that. Fine, Luling. Perhaps I'll go for another walk."

It's well within my abilities as an adult to thank Mom for the help yesterday and tell her she should go enjoy herself. I can run my counter alone.

I say, "Do you want to come with me?"

She initially demurs. "No, no. I'll be in the way."

This always irritated me when I was younger, how this confident, headstrong woman would always become diffident and need to be convinced when it was something she really wanted to do. I used to take it at face value, so I didn't get sucked into her mind games, but the toast and tea have made me generous.

"It looks like rain, so it might not be good for walking," I say. "You should come with me. Ana loved having you there yesterday."

Mom looks at the fluffy clouds in the blue sky, and I think she's going to call my bluff. Instead, she nods. "All right."

We're there an hour early, and I see Ana's correct and the Ile de Grasse sign does look good. I'll leave it, but I won't tell Mom I like it. I don't want to encourage her interference. Mom doesn't seem to notice and checks over my counter while I prepare myself for a litany of suggestions based on her experience yesterday. It sets me off-balance when she says nothing about my marketing or branding or mentions the sign. She only touches the soil in the jasmine and points out a new bud.

I follow her, almost bemused and waiting for the real Mom to come out, as she goes to the back and looks at my table, where I'm working on a few things for Ana's jewelry. I pull out the vials and a few blotters. She puts aside her dislike for me wasting my time on non-moli work to sniff them.

"I'm not sure about this one," she says, pointing at the third scent. It's the floral, and I'd bristle except I'm not happy with it either.

"It's too bland and typical," I agree. "I wanted something fresh. It's for a flower pendant."

"Why not a green scent?"

This stumps me. "I don't know. I got florals in my head because it's a flower?"

She smiles. "When I was first learning, your waipo told me to think of my ideas like a triangle. She'd learned the technique from her mother. The three vertices are the top, heart, and base notes of your fragrance. Take one corner and find two more notes that fit.

That's your second triangle. Then you keep repeating the exercise to see what you get. That's how I made World. It was a chypre before it became a marine floral, after pages of little triangles."

I like this, and Mom goes to make some tea as I let my mind drift. It's an amusing way to brainstorm ideas, and by the time she comes back, I have a few different directions to work in. "I'm much happier with these," I say. "Thanks."

"How about some Iso E Super?" she asks, tapping a finger on my last triangle. "To amplify it?"

"I like it." I make the addition.

"I did a scent like this," she says. "Maybe four or five years ago."

I frown. "I don't remember that." Although I flinched at my Luling series of birthday perfumes, I always smelled the new Yixiang scents Mom sent to me.

"It was for a moli scent," she says.

"Oh."

"It was one of the only ones I did that year."

This makes my head shoot up. "So few? Are you serious?"

"Demand dropped," she says. "People seem to care less about the magic of our perfumes. Or they don't believe. Like your father, they think it's all science and they can find a solution for themselves online. Or they don't need my mood boost because they have so many other options they're told will make them feel better. My moli was always one of the weakest, especially compared to your great-grandmother's. She had people begging for her to cure their heartbreak until she died."

Mom doesn't sound defeated, only like she's sharing facts.

"Tingwen said her moli was a curse," I say.

"I understand why," my mother says, causing me to stop working in surprise.

"You never thought it was a curse," I say. If ever there was a moli cheerleader, it's my mother.

"When I had to watch each word I said? When I was already too different thanks to being Chinese? We didn't live in Chinatown—you know that—so I had no community at school. It was hard enough to make friends without telling them I couldn't go out because Waipo was punishing me for forgetting to macerate a scent, or she wanted me to re-create the smell of a hyacinth in salt water, or something ridiculous. I had to spend every spare minute in the store. Of course I hated it. And loved it. That's why I thought of it as a curse. The hate in the love and the love in the hate is what makes it so difficult."

I don't know what to say, and Mom shrugs at my expression. "I got over it. You need mastery before you can enjoy a skill, and that takes time and effort. Like your moli."

Ana comes in then to say that someone wants to talk about perfumes. Both Mom and I stand up before Mom waves me on. When I come back after giving the woman a sample to try at home before she buys, Mom is hovering over my mods for Ana's jewelry.

"5D is the best," she declares.

It's as if our argument didn't happen at all. I watch her apprehensively for the rest of the day, waiting for her to come back at me with some underhanded comment about my moli, or work ethic, or our fight, but she doesn't. It's as if she listened to me for the first time in my life and got off my case.

It's what I wanted—what I demanded—so why do I feel abandoned? Am I like my mother, needing to be coaxed into doing what I truly want? Because part of me, perversely, does want her nagging at me.

Like it's proof she cares.

It's early afternoon when Mom decides to go for a walk. The second she's out, Ana turns to me with huge eyes. "Your mom is great. She's so knowledgeable."

I lean against a table, surprised at Ana's enthusiasm. "About perfume, yeah."

"Oh, that, absolutely. The room fragrance she made for Jayne?

Like, who would have thought a bar should smell good? The way it matches Jayne's ambience is incredible. She's going to ask your mom if she can sell it."

"That's cool." Although I'm not sure if Mom would think of it as a comedown for the Yixiang brand.

"She talked with me more about Jayne."

"How are things there?"

"Good." Ana's face is dreamy. "We went to her place last night, and Jayne rigged up a blanket tent fort thing, and we huddled in there with the dog, and it was perfect—except the dog had really bad breath."

"Yeah?"

"I think I have a girlfriend now, and we're in love and going to have beautiful fur and non-fur babies."

This seems like a moment where people would hug, so I smile at her. "I can't believe you were going to give up."

"I was wrong," she chirps. "Thanks to your mom."

I raise my eyebrows. "Sounds like you two had a great time."

Ana sighs. "I know you weren't home for a long time and family dynamics are messy, but I think she wants to spend time with you."

I stare at her. "She what?"

"It is my belief that she misses you and wants to get to know you again. Your grandmother died a little while ago. Were they close?"

I open my mouth to answer yes, but then reconsider. Waipo lived in the house and they worked together, but were they close? I only assumed they were. "I don't know."

"Whether they were or not, it's a sure thing she misses her mother and she's reassessing a lot of her life, don't you think?"

I poke at the glittery tiaras on the table. Mom was right: Repositioning them under the light gives them an eye-catching spar-kle. I want to buy one so I can be a princess. "Probably."

"You were gone from the time you were twenty," Ana says. "They say your teen years are the formative ones, but I think that's wrong. After twenty is when you turn into a person."

"'Miss Stacy told me long ago that by the time I was twenty my character would be formed, for good or evil,'" I quote idly.

"*Anne of Green Gables*, nice one."

"Thanks, but it was *Anne of the Island*. Mom could have reached out during those years."

Ana picks up one of my blotters and sprays it absently to wave under her nose. "Again, I don't know anything about your relationship, but you seem almost closed off with her now. Would you have been open if she'd asked you to come back home?"

"She never did," I mumble.

"Oh." Ana bites her lip. "Because she was giving you space?"

I shrug. The lack of invitations stung until I reframed them in my mind as what I'd wanted in the first place. If Mom was more welcoming, would I have actually ended up going back home? She seemed content to have me gone, as if with no power, I had nothing to offer. It wasn't my plan to have this turn into a therapy session, but the words come out before I can stop them.

"It's fine to say she wants to catch up on lost time now, but the only thing that matters to her is the store. It always has been."

"Then why is she here and not there?" Ana asks.

"Because she wants me to come back and run it with her," I say firmly. Ana doesn't need to know the real reason Mom's in Toronto.

Ana's eyebrows rise. "Really? She didn't give me that impression at all. She was asking me a lot about how I structure my online store and why I decided to share the space."

"Trust me, it's what she's always wanted."

Ana shifts her weight from foot to foot. "Did she say that, or did you assume it?"

The door opens and we spin around, expecting to see Mom. It's two women, one of whom calls out, "Excuse me, can we get some help here?" before we can greet them. She's pointing at Ana's stock, so I go to my counter to make some notes about my new collections.

"What do you mean, you don't have it in red?" The nasal voice breaks my concentration.

Ana's low voice drifts over. "We're sold out. The last one went yesterday."

"Go to the back and check. Don't you know who I am? I have almost ten thousand followers on social media. I can, like, break your store."

I watch Ana walk to the back, where I know she'll count to twenty and come back out full of apologies, then peek over my laptop to better see who she's dealing with. They're in their twenties, one dressed in high black boots and a black miniskirt that looks like it's made of recycled sweatpants. The other has blue shadow covering her eyes like a bandit mask, and a baby doll head on a white plastic chain around her neck. I can't tell which one is bitching at Ana. They both have their phones out.

"Hiiiii, pretty babies!" squeals Lady Color into the screen. "Oh my God, you know I am obsessed with sequins. I'm crying right now."

"Sorry," Ana says to the pair, who are giggling over some long gloves. "We're sold out, but I did find this."

I peek across to see her hand over a pair of suspenders with rainbow sequins. Lady Color wrinkles her nose. "Eww, do you think I'm a clown or something?"

Ana, to her credit, does not look at the baby doll–head necklace. She laughs. "Oh, sorry. No worries. You're right, they're hard to pull off."

There's no way the influencer's going to fall for that, but to my surprise, it's the woman in the sweat skirt who snatches them. "I love them."

"Olivia, those are mine," whines her friend. "I'm already obsessed with them."

What *isn't* this woman obsessed with? I turn back to my screen as Ana magically finds another cool item—a pair of black iridescent legwarmers—to make both women happy.

"Good Lord," I say when they leave.

Ana has her hand pressed against her forehead. "At least they bought them instead of taking a photo in the store and leaving."

"What if they return them after taking photos at home?"

Ana sighs. "I made it clear returns were only for store credit. That might stop them. My returns are increasing each month."

She looks defeated, which is such an unusual look on her I don't know what to do. Mom came in at the end of the conversation, and although I think she's going to jump in with advice, she doesn't.

Ana glances at her watch, a vintage Rolex she found for a song that is one of her prized possessions. "I have to go out for an hour," she says. "Can I leave the store with you?"

After waving goodbye to Ana, Mom walks through the displays, twitching a glove here and a hat there.

"I went through and added some more definitions to your list of characters you don't know," she says as she takes out a duster. "Also, you need something that traps dust. This only spreads it around." She gives a demonstration swipe, then points to the air where little motes drift through the sunbeams. "Zhengyi would be horrified."

That makes me laugh. "Ana likes the retro look of the feathers."

"Then keep one for show and get something that works to hide in the back. No one wants to buy dusty stock. Makes them think they have poor taste because no one else wanted it."

A man comes in to find a gift for his daughter's birthday. With a few simple questions, Mom directs him to the tiaras and then suggests a few accessories. After I cash him out, I think back to the register and the characters Mom is helping with.

"It's so ridiculous, anyway, how this works," I say.

"What is?" Mom adjusts the tiara display.

"That the fifth daughter isn't supposed to start transcribing the register until everyone else is dead," I say. "It makes no sense. How can she ask questions? Get clarification or bounce ideas off the other women if no one is left?"

Mom straightens up. "What on earth do you mean?"

"I mean, she has to transcribe all alone. All the people who could have helped her are gone." It's easier to think of the transcriber as some distant fifth daughter and not myself.

"You're thinking of it the wrong way."

"How? Is there a necromancy component I didn't know about?"

"Don't be glib." She moves the tiaras again. "Zhengyi didn't work in a vacuum, Luling. She lived with her grandmother and mother and even her great-grandmother."

"So?"

"They talked," she says, irritated she needs to spell it out. "Zhengyi would have been talking and listening to them all the time, hearing their stories as they worked. Asking questions. Telling jokes. By the time she started transcribing, she had those memories to rely on. She would have been reading and rereading the register for years while her elders were still alive, checking in with them if there was something she didn't understand."

I think about this as she goes to the back. For generations, the Hua women lived in the same compound, sharing their whole lives. I learned a lot on my own, but what wisdom could I have learned if I had stayed? What stories will die because of me? Mom didn't blame me, but I feel the family responsibility. I didn't appreciate what I was missing.

The door jangles again and I look up. "Hiii," says one of the influencers from earlier. "I need to, like, return this?"

Before I can answer, Mom steps into the room. "Ah," she says. "What's the issue?"

"It's not, like, for me?"

Mom clucks. "It certainly is. Let me show you how to style it."

I never thought I'd see my mother demonstrating how to wear rainbow suspenders, but here we are. By the time Mom has shown her how to wear them with a tube top—thankfully, not on herself—the influencer is almost dancing up and down. "I'm obsessed, my pretty baby," she says as she leaves. "Obsessed."

Mom waits until she's out the door before she turns to me, mouth twitching. "Pretty baby?" she asks.

I roll my eyes. "Don't ask. And please never call me that."

This makes her laugh and I smile. I forgot how much I loved it when she laughed.

HUA XIAOTING

1425, MING DYNASTY

OUTSIDE NANJING, ON THE YANGTZE RIVER

Xiaoting looked at her younger daughter's pretty face as it contorted with fury, and wondered why her mother had never warned her of this. Was it out of revenge for the time Xiaoting had hidden in a chest to avoid the evening meal as a child? To this day, she refused to eat goose, disliking the too-rich taste of its meat, especially after her mother had fished her out from the chest and forced her to eat a full bowl as punishment.

Xiaoting had never done that to her daughters. Did she get praise for it? She did not.

Her elder daughter was so *good*. Guilan listened. She understood. Yingtai had been born resentful, and that bitterness had expanded over the years, until it was as if the girl had a small cloud attached to her bracelets that followed wherever she went.

"All of this secrecy is silly," Yingtai said. "No one wants to hurt us. Anyway, how could they find us in this backwater?"

"You don't understand."

"Of course I don't. How could I when you never include me? You never wanted me as part of this family." Yingtai's lovely complexion had turned a spotty red. "You wouldn't allow me to learn with Guilan when you were teaching her."

"You were refused once, and it was because you were five years old," said Xiaoting through gritted teeth. "You weren't ready."

"Guilan is only three years older."

In age but not in attitude, but Xiaoting knew better than to say such a thing to her younger daughter, who even on good days was like a crackling fire, mindlessly burning all around her. Xiaoting sighed in unconcealed exasperation. "You bring that up all the time, but you were a child. You don't remember!"

"I don't need to." Her daughter's hair ornaments tinkled, and Xiaoting resisted the urge to fix them to make the display more graceful. Yingtai hated anything to match or show the beauty of symmetry. "You show me every day."

Xiaoting would have straightened her back, but it was already stiff despite the soft cushions of the platform where she sat. "I do no such thing."

"No? Then why does Guilan get all the attention?"

"She gets different attention because she is the first daughter. Different, not all." Xiaoting waved to her daughter's elegant peach robes. "What does she have that you don't? You have the same tutors and number of maids. You eat from the same dishes, and your clothing is made from fabric that comes from the same storehouse. The curtains on your bed are embroidered by the same women."

"Guilan has peonies on her curtains," Yingtai said.

What was the connection Yingtai was making in her own mind? Xiaoting had no idea. "You have wisteria. They are flowers, like your sister has flowers."

Yingtai glared at her. "They are not peonies! I am a Hua, and yet I'm treated like a servant."

"A servant?" Xiaoting couldn't believe her ears. She grabbed her daughter's hand. "With soft skin like this? What work do you do, you foolish girl?"

Yingtai snatched her hand back and yanked down her sleeves. "Oh, it's my fault you won't let me into the workshop. My fault I don't have the power of my sister."

"What are you saying? Not let you? You never wanted them. You know you're always welcome. The lessons I gave Guilan were meant for you as well, but you avoided them like they were cursed." If her daughter wanted to learn how to make fragrances, she knew all she had to do was come to the workshop. She simply never had, and Xiaoting was too busy to chase after Yingtai and beg her to attend.

"What was the point of me going?" Yingtai's voice nearly shook the painted paper panels decorating the walls. "Even if I did, my fragrances would always be second-best, the way I am in this family. You made it obvious you saw me as useless. When I marry, I'll have to leave for my husband's family, but Guilan will get to stay because you won't marry her to a man who will make her leave. I don't understand why I was born if you didn't want me."

She flew out of the room, slamming the sliding door so hard the wood splintered.

Xiaoting thought of fetching her back to apologize, but a soft cough from the corner made her turn.

"Let the girl go," said her mother.

"Such disrespect," groused Xiaoting. "You would never have put up with such behavior."

Her mother rose from the pearwood chair where she'd sat through the entire confrontation without saying a word. "Someone needs a dose of her own sister's moli," she said. "Envy is eating the girl alive."

"Yingtai has always wanted what her sister has and never wants to admit that her own life is easier than anything Guilan will confront." Xiaoting arranged her silken cushions, but nothing was comfortable. She'd noticed the same thing happening more and more over the last several years. Cold sank through her robes no matter how many layers she wore, while heat made her feel as if she needed to roll in mud like the pigs to cool herself. Occasionally, it seemed as if fire was erupting from her very blood, making her slick with sweat. Her bones ached, and when sleep came, it was brief and fitful.

Her mother waved away the maid who had come to investigate the broken door, and poured the tea herself.

"Have you thought, Daughter, that to her it isn't easier?" Her mother's smile was small as she handed Xiaoting the blue porcelain cup. Xiaoting didn't like the note of pity she detected.

"How hard can it be? She has no responsibility to improve her craft. She doesn't have a craft, for that matter. All she does is sit in her room and paint. You see the hours Guilan devotes to the workshop. She searches for new ingredients. She spends time in the gardens harvesting flowers and herbs, and in the markets shopping for new spices. You hear her worry about having a daughter, while Yingtai waits for her future to be brought to her."

Xiaoting drank the tea in a vulgar gulp, indignant on her eldest daughter's behalf. Guilan was responsible for continuing the Hua family line by having a daughter, leaving her little choice but to marry. Yingtai, the lucky girl, didn't have to marry if she decided not to, for Xiaoting would never force her—despite what her daughter said.

If Yingtai's husband joined the Huas, as was their family tradition, so much the better. That had been another fight, one of many, between Xiaoting and her husband, who had still not forgiven her for moving the family out of Nanjing so many years ago. Yingtai was like him. The two preferred to dwell on what could have been rather than deal with what was. They were fantasists who were allowed their dreams because Xiaoting was there to do the work, to make the hard decisions to keep the family together and safe.

"The admiral was right," said her mother.

The admiral? They had seen Zheng He only occasionally over the years, although he regularly sent messengers to check on the house as if he still owned it. Although safe from the intrigue of the new capital of Beiping, Xiaoting's moli sales meant she was still in secret contact with many of her old clients, who were happy to pass on gossip about what was happening in the capital. Zheng He must have consulted a fortune teller, for his prediction of the new emperor had been correct. In the last year or so, the Hongxi emperor had put a stop to the diplomatic treasure fleets and grounded Zheng He, who had been named the defender of Nanjing. It was pleasant to have the admiral—for she continued to call him that—close to her, but she knew it pained him to be separated from the open sea.

Had he known he would be back in Nanjing, perhaps he would not have sold Xiaoting the house. She wondered if he ever regretted it, for the property was exquisite. No doubt the gangling woman who shared the admiral's life would have loved it. At least that was one thing that had turned out well. Zheng He had wished for love, and Xiaoting had provided the answer to his most pressing desire. After all, she thought wryly, the man had experienced adventure, wealth, power, and influence. What was left to possess but love?

She had heard from her clients that his wife was as in love with him as he was with her. Jokes were made about them in the city, where Xiaoting rarely went, but she knew many of them came from envy that Zheng He had found such tenderness and loyalty in a woman. Although there were those who insisted love was nothing but a distraction from the greater goals of life, those who yearned for it would do anything to have it in their hearts.

Most people, she was convinced, fell into the second category. Luckily, for her money chests.

She took a brief moment to listen to the river and admire the grounds that were hers before turning back to the conversation with her mother. "The admiral was right about what?"

"Do you remember what he said on the visit when he picked up his moli?"

Xiaoting thought back. "He said many things. He's a man who likes to hear himself speak. Loudly and often."

"He said you were like a farmer."

"He did." Xiaoting remembered now. There had been an odd glint in his eyes that she had put down to the anticipation of meeting his true love.

"You took it as a compliment," her mother continued. Xiaoting knew that tone. She wasn't going to like what came next.

"I didn't take it as anything," Xiaoting said.

"It was because you drive this family like a farmer drives his oxen," said her mother. "Yoked to your will."

Xiaoting tucked her feet under her, then put them back down. "Say what you wish to say. I have much to do."

Her mother reached over and slapped her lightly on the arm. "You order this household around without a care for anyone else's concerns."

Xiaoting nearly dropped her cup in shock. "How dare you?" she said, forgetting to whom she spoke. "I do nothing but think of this family."

"You think of the family, not the people."

"They are one and the same." Xiaoting did her best to hide the quaver in her voice. Of all people to attack her, she would never have expected it to come from her own mother. "Who else will do it apart from me? It's my responsibility. I am the fifth daughter." What she left unsaid, because of the guilt that plagued her sleep like a stinging insect, was that it was her error of judgment that had required them to move in the first place and forced the Hua women to hide for the first time since the death of Empress Wu.

Still, the old woman continued, "There may have been other solutions than to leave our home for this village exile. You never asked, but made the decision on your own."

"The decision that saved us," insisted Xiaoting.

"Perhaps."

"Perhaps? You know the warning Zheng He gave us. What was I to do?"

Her mother's wrinkled face creased. "I don't know, Daughter. I never had the chance to take part in a discussion, although it was my right. Nor did your husband, although it was his right."

"As he has pointed out many times," muttered Xiaoting.

"Do you blame him? He came home and his wife had half the household ready to start out the city gate. You're lucky he allowed it."

"You know time was of the essence. He didn't have to come." She wished he hadn't.

Her mother doesn't bother to answer. "You need to stop treating Yingtai like an ox," she said with finality.

When she left the room, Xiaoting lay flat on the couch, furiously debating with the faint scent of her mother's robes since she couldn't do it with the woman herself. She didn't treat the family like oxen. Yingtai was merely jealous of her sister. She frowned. Xiaoting's own sister had never been jealous. In fact, her sister had been almost sad for her. "Imagine having to have a daughter," she'd said the night she'd left for her husband's house. "I was saved that, at least, along with this stifling life."

She had died in childbirth not a year later, the unwanted daughter dying as well.

Xiaoting sat up, the grief that accompanied thoughts of her sister coming to haunt her again. Xiaoting looked out the door in the direction her mother had gone, wishing she hadn't left. Then again, what would she say? She had made a mistake? It was too late now. They were here, and there was nothing to do but go forward. She was certain it was better to make a decision and live with the consequences than do nothing. The idea of wu wei and its release of control had never been understandable to her.

"Mother." Her elder daughter came in. "What did you say to Yingtai?"

Xiaoting waved her to a seat and Guilan sat down, as obedient as always. Xiaoting looked at her daughter, her long black hair neatly tied up and smelling like something new. "Too much camphor," she said absentmindedly. "You always put in too much."

Guilan nodded. "I know. Yingtai said the same thing."

Xiaoting poured tea to have something to do, wondering at herself. It wasn't like her to be uncertain, particularly with her daughters, but Guilan was twenty and had recently taken possession of her moli. She suspected that was when things had begun to degrade further with Yingtai. It would continue if Yingtai married and was lost to them forever, like so many other daughters.

"Your sister is angry with me," Xiaoting said.

"She is." Guilan's smile was brief. "She's never been able to hide how she feels."

"She says I neglected her for you. Because you are a moli daughter and she is not."

Guilan kept her expression as bland as unflavored barley porridge, but Xiaoting saw through it. "Guilan."

"Yes?"

"Have I treated Yingtai poorly?"

Guilan's eyes slid to the side. "What I think doesn't matter. If she thinks you did, that's the most important."

Useless. Both her girls were useless. Xiaoting waved her away, and her elder daughter swept gracefully out of the room. How dare her mother say she treated people as oxen! How ridiculous. She was the ox, if any of them were. All she did was work for Yingtai and the rest, to keep them safe and fed and clothed, and this was the gratitude she received.

She stood to pace the room and halted by a panel painted by Yingtai several years ago, the lines of the branches drawn with a passion that had surprised Xiaoting. Yingtai's father had been impressed a mere girl could manage to portray such power and insisted on providing her with tutors and the finest tools. Xiaoting stood before it now, looking at it with fresh eyes.

It was a scene from nature, three birds on a branch. Two were larger and looked to the left. The smaller one on the right looked wistfully at them. Light snow came in to cover the branches and the smaller, lonely bird, while the winter sun played on the other two.

Was this how Yingtai saw them? With herself on the outside, looking in? Xiaoting took another step back. Yingtai rarely shared her art with her mother, although she did with her father, and Xiaoting had known that to be presented with this piece had meant something at the time. But she'd been busy with a new commission, and Guilan had been ill with a fever that had spread from the maids. The fields to the west had been dying from too much rain. Although she'd taken the painting and hung it in a place of respect, Xiaoting hadn't contemplated it in the way she did now. She had not spoken to Yingtai about it.

She had treated it like decor and not art.

Raw, bleeding shame overtook Xiaoting. Her mother was right. She had looked at the family as more important than the individuals. In truth, there was no family without the people. Yingtai could not be treated like Guilan because she was not Guilan, and by treating her individuality as a problem, Xiaoting had forced her daughter away.

She looked at the painting, wondering if it was too late to shelter the small bird under her wing. Her daughter would be suspicious at first and wonder at Xiaoting's motives. Xiaoting knew from experience she would occasionally fail and slip back into her old pushy ways.

She refused to dwell on the mistakes of her past. The sale to the second wife. Leaving the capital. There was nothing she could do about them, after all, so what was the point? With Yingtai, though, she could make a difference. She could perhaps make up for her mistakes going forward. She could have Yingtai know she belonged here as much as her sister and her value was as great.

She was about to leave to look for Yingtai when a maid came in to announce a visitor.

It was Lady Pan, and in her hand, she held a flask Xiaoting recognized. "You lied," Lady Pan said, her usually sweet voice high and cracking. "I found no love."

"Lady Pan." Xiaoting faced her, wondering about the best way to deal with the enraged woman. Although Lady Pan was robed to perfection and her hair dressed beautifully, tears of anger trembled on her lower eyelashes. "You tried the moli."

"I wanted love," Lady Pan said. "Love, my true love. Yet I remain alone with only my husband. You know how cruel he is and what a true love would do for me. It would give me some joy. A little happiness is all I desire. You lied."

Xiaoting sighed. "I'm sorry," she said. "This happens sometimes. When the moli fails, it means your true love has died."

Lady Pan took a deep breath and Xiaoting watched the fury dissipate into bleak acceptance, the quick resignation of a woman who was used to living without hope. How much of the payment would Lady Pan demand back? She would be within her rights to want all of it, and Xiaoting prepared herself for a hard bargaining session. She had to appear reasonable—she didn't want Lady Pan to spread rumors— but at the same time, it wasn't her fault the woman's love was dead.

As she was about to offer Lady Pan tea, a commotion was heard in the corridor. "Lady Pan! My lady!"

It was a small maid, who stumbled into the room, followed by Xiaoting's own maids, all exclaiming at this breach of manners. Lady Pan twisted. "Sheyue? What is the meaning of this?"

The maid stood tall, her eyes wild and hands working the front of the robe in anxiety. "Lord Pan, my lady. He was coming after you on his horse."

Lady Pan went white. "How far is he?"

"No, my lady, no. He had been drinking and his horse threw him. His head hit a rock. He died."

"He's dead?" Lady Pan whispered. "Are you sure?"

"Yes." The maid looked at her. "Very sure, my lady. His manservant was there and saw everything. He managed to get Lord Pan's body back home."

Xiaoting murmured some words of sympathy but trailed off when she saw Lady Pan's face. Her dark eyes were shining not with the unshed tears of grief, but with ecstasy. "He is dead," Lady Pan whispered. "Dead." Her voice grew more confident as she repeated the word. "I must return home."

"Of course."

Lady Pan looked at the maid. "Prepare my carriage, Sheyue." She seemed to have forgotten the reason she was here at Xiaoting's residence, as she left with her step light and head held high. *Strange,* thought Xiaoting, *but a lucky occurrence.* The gossip she'd heard said Lord Pan was a monstrous man. Lady Pan was lucky to be rid of him, and Xiaoting had no pity to spare for a man who enjoyed causing fear and pain to his wife and others who could not defend themselves.

Thinking of love and Lady Pan, she went over to the register that sat in the corner of the room and was where she listed all her sales. Lifting her brush, she drew a line through Lady Pan's name. With a dead true love, it was unnecessary to add her to the list of people Xiaoting had helped when it came time to write the final version of her chapter for generations to come.

The sound of a breaking vase came from the direction of Yingtai's room, and Xiaoting put her brush down to look at the painting again, tracing the line of sight of the little bird and wondering what she should do about her wayward daughter. Then she leaned in and frowned.

The bird wasn't looking at the other two birds. It was looking higher, to a small break in the branches, as if yearning for freedom. The bird didn't care at all about the other two. It wished only to escape.

Ridiculous. She was being ridiculous. It was only a painting, and if she looked closely, she could see the errors made with the brush. She had more important things to consider. Yingtai was a child and she had a child's perspective, limited to what affected her.

With a final look at the painting, Xiaoting gathered her robes and went to look for her daughter. Guilan was due in the workshop. As for Yingtai? She could do as she pleased.

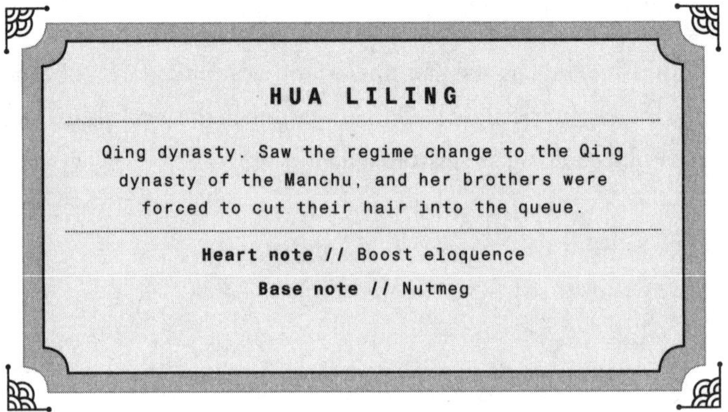

When are you leaving for work?" Mom asks as I stretch on the couch. It's snug enough for sleep, but there's a break between the two cushions that I end up partially wedged into each night.

"It's Monday," I remind her. "Store's closed." We should do something so I don't spend the day worrying about dodging questions about my moli, but I can't think of what.

Mom walks past to look out the window. "Your neighbors are doing their spring planting," she says. "A bit late, but I suppose it's the right time for Toronto."

Like that, it hits me—the perfect way to spend the day. "Do you want to help me plant?" I ask.

"Plant what? Where?" She glances around my apartment.

I fold my legs under me. "I was thinking about putting in a little herb garden in the front of the store, where the broken patio stones are."

My mother purses her lips, considering. "You get a lot of sun, so it's a good place. Do you have ideas?"

"Some lavender? Rosemary? Mint?" I don't know. I've never been in a place long enough to plant a garden.

"Mint has to be in containers or it overruns everything." Mom is already on her phone. "Get ready. I'll decide the plants."

I don't mind her taking control, and by the time I come out dressed in a pair of jeans downgraded to cleaning clothes because of a stain I couldn't remove, she's listed out the herbs we can get, alongside a quick sketch of an appealing ornamental design. Luckily, it's spring, so we can pick the plants up at almost any corner store. I text Ana our plan and she replies with plant emojis, so I figure she's on board.

Mom goes to change as I drink the tea she left me. A message from Eric appears on her phone as I sit at the kitchen counter, and I read it without thinking.

> **Eric:** You missed Owen's birthday. He had a great time with
> his grandparents.

I don't need to download the photo to know it will be Owen smiling with Kelsey's parents, probably all of them at the cabin.

> **Eric:** By the way, GramGram saw the art set you sent last
> week and liked it. She bought the same one to give him
> so we're going to return yours.
> **Eric:** Kelsey says to tell Lucy thanks, by the way. After all of
> those wedding orders were canceled, they took away
> the promotion they promised her at work.

A noise comes from the bedroom, and I scramble to make it look like

I'm not an eavesdropper. Or is that term only for overhearing? Mom picks up her phone and skims through the messages, her face telling me nothing.

Why bother pretending? "I didn't mean to look, but I saw the texts from Eric," I say. "He said the ghost scent led to cancelations for the weddings Kelsey told us about."

"I saw. That makes sense."

"It does? They're in love."

"We gave them a dampener," Mom says. "If it caused them to feel a little less in love, they might be reconsidering the speed of their relationship."

"At least they still have their true love," I say, glad we haven't destroyed those hearts. They had their true loves in their lives, and that remained a gift. "That's something."

I wait for her to get on my case about understanding how my moli works, but once again, she doesn't. This freaks me out a bit.

"I'm sorry you have to be with me instead of back home," I say. "For Owen's birthday."

She gives me a dry look. "Do you think Kelsey would have welcomed me at the party?"

"I guess not. Is Eric just trying to guilt-trip you?"

Mom collects her purse and heads to the door. "One of the women in the register said trying to determine motivations is futile. I find that's as good a philosophy now as it was two hundred years ago."

"He's a dick."

Her head snaps back to me. "Luling. He is your brother."

"So?"

"So. Enough."

I know that tone. I wait until she's out the door to mumble a few choice names for my brother when she can't hear, then join her at the elevator. She's frowning at the buttons. "Mom?"

"I liked that art set."

That's all she says. We leave my building, and her mood slowly improves with the warm sun. We collect the plants and soil from the corner store, and when we get to Auntie's Closet, I find the shovel belonging to the previous owner, who for some reason left it when she sold to Ana, along with three circular saws and a welding mask. Mom has gone back to her own imperturbable self. She runs her hands over the lavender and I do the same with the rosemary, for the pleasure of releasing their oils.

The first hour is all heavy labor, as we need to pull fragments of broken patio stone from in front of the store to make the space. Mom goes to get cold drinks as I break up the dirt and turn it over. It's compacted like concrete.

"Oh, a garden!" Krystal stops on the sidewalk. "That's going to be pretty."

We chat for a minute before she tells me to hold on, she'll be right back. When she returns, it's with a few shiny rocks. "Plant them in the corners for good luck," she says.

"Thanks, Krystal."

She winks. "I know you think it's woo-woo shit, but do it anyway."

I've never had much of a community in the other places I've lived. In fact, I've been much like a bird, ready to fly at the slightest sound. Here, I'm building a nest, and I like it.

Mom comes back. "Put your hat on."

I do and we take a break, blinking in the sun. It's nice to be outside, looking at nothing much in particular. Mondays are always slow in the market; they're one of the times it becomes a place you can see as an actual neighborhood, rather than simply a destination.

"Why did you pick here?" Mom gazes at the slightly dilapidated storefronts across the street, with their tattered Tibetan prayer flags. "I would have thought your perfumes would sell better if they were stocked in higher-end locations."

I hiccup from the root beer. "I don't like those stores. They're intimidating."

"Luling, I've told you that you need to be braver and fight for what you want."

"Not that," I say. "For customers. Everyone deserves to feel they have a scent that makes them feel like themselves, or brave or attractive or seductive or handsome. The people who shop at those stores already belong to that environment; they already know perfumes have power."

"You sound like Aiai." Mom puts her can of sparkling water to the side. "She was such an egalitarian, but the money is with those other people."

"I make enough," I say.

"You could do both," Mom says. "Sell wholesale to the bigger stores and do your customizations here."

"I could, but I'm only one person."

"There's always Yixiang."

I push myself up from the creaky bench and grab my shovel without answering. By the time the garden is ready for the plants, my hands are blistering inside the cheap gloves, and my shoulders have developed a tightness that will morph into pain by tomorrow, if not tonight. Not to mention my lower back. I stand and stretch, dirt shaking off me as I move.

We decide to break for a late lunch, and by the time I return with sandwiches, Mom has set out the plants in a pattern I pause to admire. Thin rows of tarragon form a cross in the middle. In each quadrant is a little circle of lavender, rosemary, and sage. Thyme sits in each corner as a groundcover. Mom is nowhere to be found, so she must be in the store to get out of the sun, which has come out with a vengeance that I welcome after the long winter. I send a photo to Rafe, who has been asking for updates. He offered to come help, but I wanted the day with my mother, and he understood.

Rafe: Will you meet me for drinks tomorrow, though? There's
    a place I think you'll love.
Me: Yes but I might need a straw. My hands are getting too
    sore to lift anything.
Rafe: I'll hold it for you.

The bells seem to be broken since they don't ring when I open the door. I can hear Mom arguing with someone, and my greeting dies as my hand tightens on the bag of food dangling at my side. She has the phone on speaker, as usual, and I can hear my father's voice clearly from where she is in the back of the store.

"I hope you're happy," Dad says.

"This has nothing to do with me." Mom's voice is quiet.

"You're delusional. Your own son says it's your fault."

"You were the one to bring up our moli at dinner."

"Go ahead, blame it on me. I'm the worst. All my fault, as usual."

"Kevin, enough. It's not my fault Eric and his wife are separating. I only found out when you told me."

Whoa, I didn't know that. You'd think that would have been one of the texts he sent this morning.

Dad has been talking over her. "That's right, it is enough. You've never been able to compromise, Meilin. Not with your children, not with your husband."

"Because all the compromise you wanted involved my dreams," she snaps. "Never yours. You're only upset because you think everything I want steals something from you. If I want to work, it steals time from you. If I want to create, it steals attention from you. Cleaning my store was time I could have spent cleaning the house."

"You owe it to your family to be there for them," he says. "You never were."

She laughs. "Never? Tell me, Kevin. Eric was upset I wasn't at Owen's birthday. What did you get your grandson for a gift? For that matter, when have you bought any of the children gifts? Where were you in Owen's party photos? How about all those school plays and sports tournaments? How many after-school lessons did you sign the kids up for? Who stayed home when they were sick?"

One of my hands has come up to my mouth. There's a rawness in my mother's voice I don't think any child should have to hear. Moms should be calm. Moms should be strong. Moms should never sound so hurt and beaten. So human.

"I knew you never respected what I bring to this family," Dad says. "You did your best to isolate me from my children."

"I didn't have to do anything. The way you locked yourself in your office every night did that."

"You preferred it that way, so don't come across all high and mighty now," Dad says, and he doesn't sound like my father anymore. He's colder. "It gave you time to turn Lucy into a little mini-me. I thought you'd lose your mind when she left. I know it wasn't because you were worried; you were angry about the store. That's all you care about."

"You liar. I was angry because I wanted my little girl," Mom says, and this time her voice is tight. "All I wanted was my daughter in my life. I want my baby."

Tears spring up in my eyes, but I don't know if she's saying it because it's true or because she's fighting with Dad.

"You lost her because she finally understood what Eric and I have always known. You love the store, not us. Lucy only mattered because of what she could give you."

I feel sick at hearing my own thoughts, my own words, said with such contempt. Did I sound like that when we fought the other day? Shame fills me.

"That is a disgusting thing to say," Mom says. "You are a horrible man. Horrible. You twist everything in your head to make yourself a victim."

"If you don't like it, you don't have to come back."

There's a long silence. "What are you saying?" Mom asks.

"It's easy. Come home. Prove you can prioritize your family and not your precious perfumes or your little store."

"I am prioritizing my family. I'm here with Luling."

"I regret allowing you to poison Lucy with your stories. I should have put my foot down years ago."

"You never tried to understand."

"How could I?" Dad's voice crackles over the phone. "You never trusted me, right from the beginning."

"For how long will you punish me over not telling you about my moli right away?"

"It was unfair to me."

"And I apologized, but you know the moli is the heart of my family."

"I understood fine. But I'm your husband. *I'm* your heart and your family. Or I should be. This perfume stuff got out of hand, and I won't put up with it anymore."

Then there's silence. It takes me a second to realize it's because Mom has hung up on him. Just…hung up on Dad. I don't know what to do or how to process what I've heard. I wish for a moment I could talk to Eric, but I know whose side he'll take. It feels wrong to tell Rafe or Ana about this, like I would be betraying my parents.

I panic, wondering if I can sneak out without her hearing, but the store is so quiet all I can hear is her heavy breathing from the back. She's not crying, I don't think. I don't know.

Then I hear her walking, so I grab the door and open it noisily. "I've got lunch," I call as cheerily as I can.

"I'm in the back." I analyze her voice like a CIA agent looking for clues as to the identity of the mole, but she sounds fine. Almost upbeat? That can't be right.

Mom looks weirdly content as she takes the food from me while I peer at her face. "I got chickpea salad on sourdough and smoked trout on brioche."

"We can share them." She adds half of each sandwich to our plates, then checks them over before going to the fridge to get some hot sauce and chili oil. "Just in case," she says.

We eat our sandwiches in the cool semi-twilight of the store, not speaking much. I have a kind of mental nausea from the call I over-heard that's fighting with the hunger from gardening all day. It's my own fault for listening, and although I don't want to talk about it or those texts I saw this morning, I also do.

Then she says, "Your brother and his wife are separating."

"What?" I only have to fake a bit of shock, since I'm taken aback she's telling me instead of hiding important information the way she usually does. "Because of my perfume?"

"Perhaps, in part."

I wince. "Mom."

"Just because it's not the answer you want doesn't mean it's not true."

"You don't need to say it."

"Would you rather I lie? Then anytime you asked me a serious question, you'd never know if I was telling you the truth or not. I didn't say it was your fault, but what happened with the perfumes could have been the catalyst for a marriage that was already cracking."

Mom opens her sandwich to sprinkle chili oil on it.

"Right, but there's a middle way between total brutal honesty and hurting my feelings," I say, voice rising.

"I'm only trying to help, Luling."

Then it hits me. Her defensiveness isn't born out of a desire to defend herself or her worldview. She's scared. How could I have never seen this before?

I look at her across the table as if for the first time, her worn fingers digging divots into the soft bread. She's always been scared, like all those Hua women, because along with the confidence, they had fear. They were scared greedy people would come for them. They were scared the men in their lives wouldn't understand or would hurt them. That they would grow old, or ill, or something would happen to their children. Those women existed in a state of fear, and what differentiated them was how they dealt with it.

Some, like my mother, would rear up like a cobra at the first sign of dissent, unwilling to let a conflict go in case they lost everything. Others were more offensive, like Xiaoting, pushing through her life like the Ming dynasty equivalent of a bulldozer, tearing things down in the expectation they would eventually turn out and reacting with shock when they didn't. Like Aiai, I run away, dragging the fear behind me and hoping it will never catch up. Then there was Zhengyi, who faced the future head-on. That woman knew no fear. Or did she?

Then, like a bomb, it occurs to me that this is why Mom is on my case about my moli. She's frightened for me. Every Hua woman, including me, has lived in a time when men were in charge. Unlike them, I'm not property. Like them, my world hasn't been designed for my comfort or convenience. It's the opposite, in fact, and my ancestors knew it as well as I do. Dependence might have looked like safety, but the women in my family knew true safety came from independence. It came from being able to read the contracts that involved them. To make the money that would feed and shelter them, and not worry about being cast out if they were too loud or old, or on a whim. That's why Mom wants me to have my moli. So I'm not dependent on anyone but myself.

I would like to say this helps me understand my mother, but that would be untrue. Instead, I run away again. "This sandwich is good with the oil."

Weak, Lucy. Weak.

"It is."

Luckily, Ana texts to see how the garden is going and if we need help. I tell her we're fine.

"Ana is a good friend to you," Mom says.

"She is," I agree.

"You never had many friends growing up," Mom says, looking intently at her sandwich crust. "I wonder if it was because of your moli. If you felt too different or embarrassed to have them come over."

This is surprising. I never thought Mom noticed that much about me. "Not at all," I say.

"Really, Luling?"

I think back to my childhood, but although the answer could be yes, I don't want to get into it. Even if Mom is feeling introspective. "I had Rafe," I say.

"You did. He's good for you." She leaves it at that, again with a delicacy I don't remember from my youth.

We finish and go out to the potager patch, where we discover someone has come by and stolen a handful of the plants. Mom shrugs, more resigned than I would have expected. "We'll get more," is all she says.

Then we plant.

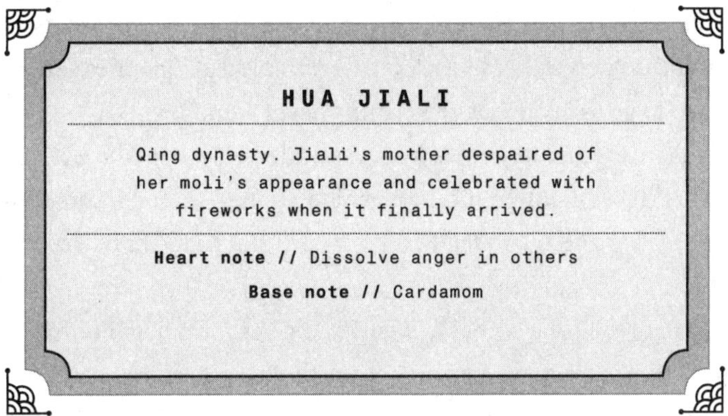

Happy birthday!" I give Ana her gift, the new custom fragrance I've made her, which is Mom-approved, albeit after a few rounds of impassioned discussion and subsequent modifications. She takes it with reverence, then laughs when she sees what I've named it. "Rainbow Sprinkles?"

"You'll see why. Oh my God, what are you doing? You don't know if you're going to like it."

Ana has already uncapped the bottle and is spraying it liberally. "Shame on you for thinking so low of both me and you." She breathes in and then sniffs her wrist, her eyes closed. "Oh, wild. I thought it would smell like a rainbow cookie—you know, the ones with the jimmies that melt into the icing and leave a little halo of color?"

"What do you smell?" I ask.

"I've been practicing," she says proudly. "Your mom was helping me. I think there's…" She sniffs again. "Coconut? Umm, yeah. It's sweet, like baking. Maybe chocolate?"

"You told me you can bake three things," I say. "Snickerdoodles, that huge cookie, and sugar pie."

She buries her face in her arm, her neatly trimmed nails a vivid green. "Cinnamon?"

I nod. "It's got notes from each of those desserts, but with some pine and some smoke, so it's like you're camping. You once said you wanted to go as a kid, but your family never went."

Ana's expression drops, and I wonder if I've made a terrible mistake. Have I gotten too personal? I wanted to make something uniquely her and try to tell her how much her friendship has meant to me.

To my relief, she comes forward and gives me a hug. For the first time, I don't strain away from her touch as the luscious scent rises, reminding me of the time she came to my apartment. I'll invite her for dinner when Mom is gone. Or maybe while she's here. Mom would love it, and it would be nice to have Ana over.

"I love this," she says. "*Love* this. I know I said I wanted it just for me, but it's a bonus that Jayne is going to faint."

"Good, because I made her one too." I pass Ana another bottle. "It complements yours, so when the two of you are together, the notes will blend."

She stares at it in astonishment. "Like when you hold all the blotters together? I've seen you do that."

"Yeah, but I've never done it with a couple's perfume, so I hope it works as planned. Hers has more of the woodiness because she loves taking Roscoe to High Park."

Ana laughs. "This is crass and capitalist of me, but holy shit, I have the best idea. We can do this for our jewelry line. Couples' jewelry, with matching or complementary scents."

"There could be a market. I did have that guy come in for matching wedding fragrances." We're looking through her designs when Jayne comes into the store to take Ana out for dinner. She sniffs the air as she comes near. "Wow, something smells good. Is that you, pretty?"

"Lucy made it for me."

Jayne dips her head down to nuzzle Ana's neck. "It's incredible. Like baking but better."

"Here's yours!" Ana holds it out, but Jayne hesitates before she takes it and gives me an uncertain glance.

"You made me one?"

We explain the concept, and although Jayne looks intrigued, she doesn't smell it. "If you don't like it, it's cool," I tell her gently. "Perfume isn't for everyone and you don't have to worry about me feeling bad."

"Actually, I've never seen you wear it before. Smelled you, I should say. Do you not like perfume?" Ana looks suddenly guilty. "Oh no, I wear it all the time."

Jayne shakes her head violently. "No, no, I do. It's just..." She sighs. "Fuck. Okay, don't laugh, but when I was younger, I loved colognes and cedars and woods and herby smells. Men's stuff. I didn't want to wear them because I didn't want people to think I was gay, so I wore the lightest of light flowers instead. It always felt wrong." She laughs, a short brittle thing. "Sounds silly when I say it out loud."

Ana wraps her arms around Jayne. "Not at all. It makes a lot of sense. I'm sorry."

Jayne shrugs and kisses her cheek. "It was a long time ago, and I'm secure in who I am."

Ana hands over the bottle. "Why don't you take a sniff? People reject Lucy's perfume all the time. She gets it."

"I mean, I prefer to call it *making modifications*, but yeah." I'm humbled by what Jayne told me, because in all my years of perfume making, and despite knowing smells bring back memory, it never occurred to me that something I loved so much could be so fraught for Jayne. I want to make her feel easy in whatever she decides. "I can always tweak it to make it what you want, or do a new one. Truly, you don't have to take it at all. I understand."

"You can change it?" Jayne's dark eyes are serious. "I never thought that was something I could do."

"You can," I assure her. "I can help you make it whatever you want."

I hand over a few blotters so she doesn't feel pressured to use it on her skin, then go to the back so she can simply experience it instead of worrying about performing a reaction in front of me.

By the time I come out, Jayne is sniffing her wrist and smiling. "It's nice," she says. "Kind of like what I used to sneak from my dad's room."

"Sit with it for a few days and see what you think," I say. "It'll change over time."

She nods, still sniffing with that little smile, and Ana drops me a wink. "It's all good," she whispers as Jayne heads for the door. "She's happy you thought of her—and holy shit, does she smell hot. Almost as good as me."

The two leave. I lock up, wincing as I struggle with the lock since my hands are aching and blistered from yesterday's planting, and head out to meet Rafe. It almost feels like a reward, to be able to sit with him again. No, *reward* is the wrong word, even though I do feel like I'm working for it. It's more of a gift. Rafe was right in that we're lucky to have a second chance. With every text he sends, I rediscover more of the yearning I thought I tucked away. It's bittersweet to have him so close, because he's shrouded with the ache of all those years apart. It doesn't tarnish what we have, but the recollection of life without him lingers like a threat.

If Ana was with me, she'd smack me for being so maudlin. I'm about to smack myself for being so maudlin. "Enjoy the moment," I say, to the astonishment of the woman passing by with a small brown dog dressed in a down cape.

"You got it," she says, stepping to the side to give me a wide berth.

The place Rafe has chosen is like an highly curated indoor campsite, and he's lounging in a double-seater ivory canvas folding chair. Behind him, the floor steps down to more folding chairs and a pebble floor. The walls look like bamboo, and the rest of the space is the epitome of lo-fi cool.

The night is chilly for spring, and Rafe wears a knit hoodie under a blazer. When he smiles as he stands to greet me, I have a strange moment. This Rafe is the teenage crush and the adult friend and potential lover all combined. My past, present, and future, where memory and reality overlap and then blur.

A woman in the corner keeps casting little glances at him, and I don't blame her. Since Rafe was reading a book while he waited, he's wearing a pair of glasses I've never seen before. It gives him a sexy librarian look I like. "Are you nervous?" he asks when I reach his table.

I am, a bit, but how does he know? I tilt my head in question and he nods to my ear. "You play with your earring when you're anxious," he says. "The right one."

I lower myself slowly into the folding chair across from Rafe. Mom and I smothered ourselves in Tiger Balm last night, and the menthol reek clings to me as a reminder of physical labor and aging.

He sees me clutch my lower back. "Aches from the planting?" he asks.

I show him my hands and he holds them, palm up, to inspect the blisters. "Damn," he says. "I could have helped."

"I know. I appreciated the offer yesterday."

He nods. "Anytime. Do you have some more photos?"

By the time we finish talking about the plants, I've calmed down enough to enjoy this time with Rafe instead of thinking about the fact I'm spending time with Rafe.

"How did you find this place?" There was no sign outside, and I had to wander around until I figured out how to get in.

"I had a few locations to look at in the neighborhood, and one of my clients mentioned it. I came for coffee and loved it."

I can see why. It's mellow, and some Japan city-sound playlist plays over the surrounding quiet conversation. Rafe has never liked loud places where he has to shout to be heard.

"Do you want a drink?"

I nod. "Surprise me." I say it automatically. It's another habit that carried over from when we were younger—for everything from choosing which movie to watch to the flavor of ice cream to buy.

He comes back with a golden-brown drink decorated with the most perfect sprig of mint I've ever seen. I sip it to savor the flavors. The leather of the whiskey, a touch of vanilla, and the mint over a bit of sugar. The ice cube is a single sphere.

"Mint julep," he says.

"It's perfect."

He looks pleased and we switch drinks without saying a word to taste the other's. I usually hate sharing food, but it's different with Rafe. It's always been different with him.

"Nice." He approves. "How was your day, apart from the muscle pain from digging?"

Although small talk can sometimes drive me out of my mind, I admit the routine of asking about someone's day, or commenting on the weather, can have its place. I give him a brief rundown on the store, and he tells me about a calico cat he saw on a leash with a diamond collar, and the backstory he made up about it. This makes me laugh, and between that and the drink, any residual tension between us diminishes.

"How's your mom?" he asks after I fetch us another round. This time I have a smoky sour, and the acrid pine around the edge of the glass mellows in the drink.

I look at my glass, where the water coming off the melting ice creates tiny eddies. "She's fine. She's trying to give me more space."

"In a good way?"

"I think so."

I don't mention the fight with Dad I overheard. I can't. Mom would legitimately prefer death over Missy Jin learning about her marital problems via Rafe.

When I tell him about Mom's slipup about me going back to Vancouver, he doesn't seem to see anything strange in it.

"It makes sense," he says as he looks at a couple passing us to sit near the stone Japanese lantern. "I think every parent wants their children home one day."

"It's not my home," I snap. While it's true he didn't direct the comment at me, I can't help but feel it was. "Not anymore."

He holds up his hands. "I was only saying."

I calm myself down, not wanting to ruin the night. "Fine."

He glances over, but instead of getting on my case and asking if it's really fine, and what do I mean by *fine*, and all the other stuff I don't want to hear when it's fine enough to not fight about it, he does me the credit of taking it at face value and saying, "Okay."

"We brainstormed a couple of perfumes together," I say. "It was fun."

"That's good." He hesitates and lowers his voice. "One of your moli perfumes? Are you closer?"

"We stopped working on what happened with me." There's a couple to the left, so I'm deliberately vague. If I can hear their conversation about the best angle to take photos of their drinks, they'll be able to hear me talk about my secret ancestral magical ability.

He waits, but that's all I give him. "Okay...?" he finally says, as if to invite me to elaborate.

"That's it." I swirl the glass in my hand like a Mob boss about to make an offer to a potentially corruptible official.

"If you want it so badly, you can't give up."

I give him a look, and he lifts his hands. "Sorry, I know. It's just this clearly makes you unhappy, and from my perspective, you've given up without trying every avenue."

This is unbelievable. My hands shake around my glass. "Why are you so invested? It's got nothing to do with you."

"Because this is a gift, Lucy, and you're tossing it away."

"It's not a gift," I say, feeling the familiar stirring of guilt that's so easy to transform into anger. What does he know? It's like he's erring on the side of overly supportive, but I can't complain that he's trying too hard to be understanding. "Even if it was, it's up to me how to use it and whether I want to. I don't owe my family anything."

"Do you think that, for real?" he asks. "We don't owe our families anything?"

"What, you disagree?"

"I want to know your explanation first."

I struggle to articulate it. "It's not that. Using the moli would help my family, and it's expected of me, but it doesn't mean I have to spend my life making my mother happy."

"Did she ask you to?"

"She didn't need to! It's what all the Huas do. They've always lived together. She doesn't have the right to expect my life to revolve around her."

He leans forward. "These are two different things. If you love someone, you do things you don't want to because it makes them happy or their life easier."

"Like a doormat."

"No," he says steadily. "Like someone who's not selfish. Like a person who wants to benefit the people they love. That's what love is. It's acting in a way that doesn't only center ourselves. Honestly, sometimes being a good person is more important than being happy."

"Let me get this straight. Are you saying I should abandon Ana and my store to go home with my mother to make her happy? To fulfill her dreams?"

"No, I'm saying you might want to keep an open mind. You were so devastated to not have the same ability as the other women in your family that you left because you couldn't handle it. That doesn't sound like a person who's happy, even if they insist they're being true to themselves."

I keep my temper. "Thank you for your concern," I say as blandly as possible.

"Don't be like that, Lucy. If you're upset, tell me."

Eavesdropping couples be damned. "All right. I'm upset because you're poking your nose in my business and calling me selfish. You don't know anything, and you think you have the right to come along and tell me how to live my life because you've transformed into this new person. I'm allowed to give up, Rafe, and to do it without guilt. I'm allowed to live without this pressure!"

He backs off instantly, although he doesn't break eye contact. "I was out of line."

I blow out a breath, wanting to fight, but it's displaced disgust at myself. He's right. Mom was right. I gave up too quickly.

I was scared.

Rafe looks at me. He's not done. "You're making the same mistakes."

"The same mistakes," I say. "What same mistakes? What?"

"When you get overwhelmed, you leave," he says simply. "You always have. When you were younger, it only meant you went home. Now it means you move across the country."

"I think this is the opposite," I say, shifting in the canvas chair as the metal support bar digs into my thighs. "I'm staying here. It's the opposite of running."

He sighs. "It's not literal running. You're avoiding your problems."

I'm done with this conversation, so I stand up, feeling dizzy. "I should get home."

Rafe pauses for a moment, looking up at me before he shakes his head. "Sure." He stands too. "Let's go."

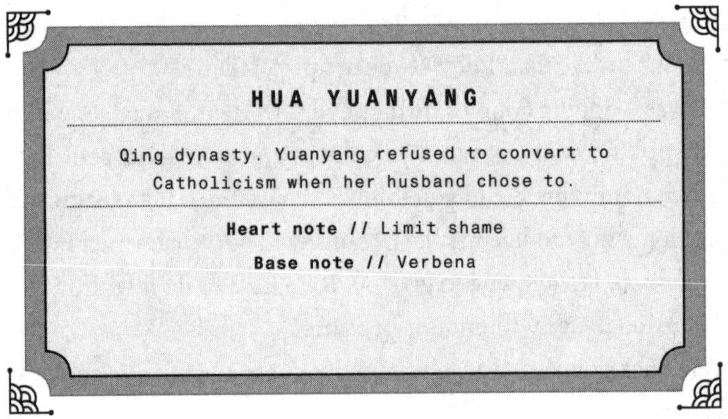

We don't talk much on the way home, and Rafe leaves me at my door with a touch on my hand. Mom is out having dinner with a vendor, and that old familiar emptiness rises from the apartment. I forgot how pleasant it was to come home to another person who could validate your existence. When I was a kid, I thought people disappeared the second a door closed on them, to the extent that I had fits if my parents tried to shut my bedroom door at night. Sometimes I wonder if a bit of this has accompanied me into adulthood. That could be why I feel faded the second I walk in.

Mom's notebook is on the counter, and I glance at it as I make some tea. There's a list of names. Evelyn Choo. Henry Lai. Xiaolan Roberts. It looks like Mom brought in some commissions for Yixiang. They must be recent, because she usually jots down a few ideas of what could work as soon as she talks to the client, but these have no details.

Mom comes in and I close the notebook, surprisingly happy to see her. "The water is still hot," I say. "Do you want some tea?"

"Lemon." She goes to change as I grab the tea bag. Like me, Mom hates wearing outdoor clothes in the house. She comes out and I bring the tea over to the couch, then give in to what I want and curl into her side. I used to sit next to her all the time at the end of the day, sometimes talking about nothing in particular, sometimes simply absorbing her presence. Perhaps it was good she came to Toronto. I got this back at least.

She lets me stay, and I listen to her breathing with my eyes closed, smelling her faint iris under a soft mix of scents, until I finally gain the comfort I've been missing for so long.

"How was your day, Cloud?" she asks. "Did Ana like her present?"

"She loved it." We sit for a while longer, chatting about what she had for dinner and the scents she tested when she passed the Holt Renfrew on the way to the restaurant. In the new ease between us, I gather my courage.

"Mom, has Dad always disliked what we do?"

Her fingers tighten on her mug before they relax. "What do you mean?"

There's no way I'm going to bring up that I overheard her conversation. "At dinner, when I was last in Vancouver."

"Ah." She shifts on the couch, but we're both looking at the wall. "That."

"I went through the register. Very few had a supportive partner."

She nods. "I noticed the same thing. Your grandfather was a wonderful man, but he died right after I was born."

"Dad knows better, though."

"He should." Mom sounds resigned. "I always thought he would get used to it. I knew it was too much to ask for us to work together like Eddie and Missy Jin, but I thought he would be proud of my work. He never was."

"Why not?" This is what I don't understand.

"Your father had an idea of what his married life would be like. He would work, and I would take care of the house and the children as well as my shop. He never understood providing for a family means more than bringing in money."

Mom is speaking to me like an adult and I'm not sure I like it, although I want to know. "What about you?"

"What about me?"

"What did you think married life would be like?"

"I don't know," she says. "I never thought about it. All the women I knew got married because that's what you did to have children and to be considered a woman. Your grandmother made sure I knew I had to have daughters, and back then, it didn't occur to me to do it without a husband."

"Do you regret it?"

"I could never regret anything that brought me you and your brother." Her answer is swift and fierce.

Despite what she said earlier, I notice she says nothing about love. I ask the question no daughter wants to ask her mother: "Why are you still with Dad?"

At first, I don't think she's going to answer. Then she says, "I stayed for you and Eric. I thought it was better for children to have both parents."

"You fight all the time."

"I didn't have a father growing up," she says.

I've never thought about how this might have affected her. Mom not having a father was simply a fact I knew without thinking too deeply about it. There's no point in telling her I would have preferred a split house than one filled with arguments or the frigid aftermath. Who's to say that would have turned out any better? Mom made the best choices she could, and it wasn't all bad. Eric and I saw flashes of what a loving marriage was like, and I choose to believe those infrequent moments were better than none.

"We're grown now," I say, eyes trained on the wall because this is my mother I'm speaking to. "You don't need to be with someone who doesn't respect what you do or who you are. You don't have to be miserable."

"Mmm." That's all she says.

Rafe was right about me running. I've held on to my hurt for too long, the way Mom held on to a marriage that didn't work. I don't want it anymore. Leaning in to Mom, I imagine the pain like a ball and mentally throw it away. A small tendril of happiness curls around my chest. It's time for a whole new me, and I know where that begins.

"I want to start working on my moli," I say.

She stills. "What changed your mind?"

I shrug and don't say anything.

"Tomorrow morning," she says. "We'll try again."

That's it—a simple acceptance of victory. I wait for the *I told you so* or *I knew you would come around*. She doesn't say any of that, and I gradually relax when I realize no fight is going to result from this. I let my shoulders drop from where they inched up, and my neck feels longer and straighter. I made the right decision. I made it for me, but I also made it for her and for my family. Duty won out, but I feel content with my choice.

The atmosphere is light enough that I start thinking about other scents and what I can make tomorrow. It occurs to me I never asked her about Luling33.

"My last birthday perfume," I say. "Did you mean for it to be blank?" I've been thinking about this since I sprayed it.

She looks confused. "Blank? It was a green citrus."

"No, it wasn't."

"I have no idea what you're talking about," she says. "It's grapefruit and tomato leaf with musk. I would never send you an empty bottle."

"I've got it here." I leave her drinking her tea to rummage through my closet for my Luling scents. Her gigantic rollie is in the way, so I yank it out to grab the plastic tub. There's a clink of bottles when I lift the suitcase, and I wonder if Mom brought some of her own fragrances. Curious, I unzip the bag and see the bottles at the bottom. Strange, those aren't the squat Yixiang bottles. They're slender glass.

Ile de Grasse bottles.

Suspicious enough to not care about Mom's privacy—and it's not like I'm going through her purse, which is completely verboten—I pick one up and see the huo symbol stuck to the side. The other has one as well. There's no question that I'm going to smell them, although I know what I'm going to find the moment my fingers lift the cap. I'm right. The first is the fragrance I brought to Vancouver as my proof, and the second, the warm incense Mom insisted I make.

Both bottles are half empty.

As if on autopilot, I walk back out to the living room holding them in my fists like dumbbells. I don't bother with unnecessarily redundant preliminary questions, like *What is this?* There's only one thing I need to know, and I cut right to it.

"What have you done?"

Mom has been sitting with her eyes closed, and she opens them to see me in front of her with the perfume bottles.

"Testing your moli." At least she doesn't bother to deflect with accusations of invading her privacy, but such a straight answer demonstrates a mind-blowing lack of shame. All the intimacy of the evening vanishes.

"What do you mean? Have you been sneaking it to my clients?" I'm not at the point where I can get angry, not yet, but I can feel the first gusts of it on the horizon. "Is that why you liked being at work with me?"

"Don't be ridiculous, Luling. Do you think I'd do that after your Kelsey debacle?"

The way she's minimizing what's going on causes those winds to strengthen enough for the clouds to come roiling in. "I'm going to ask again, what have you *done?*"

Her expression remains unruffled. "I asked some of our oldest and most loyal clients if they would test it. I told them the truth, so there's no need to accuse me of trickery or worse."

"What truth?" The wind grows to a squall, lashing the waves into small white crests.

"That we didn't know what was going on and it may or may not summon their true love. Three were willing to take the chance, and I decanted samples from your two fragrances for them to try."

I'm disgusted my first and most urgent need is to find out the result of this utter betrayal. The look on Mom's face answers the question that lies between us, and she tells me without waiting.

"None of them found their true love, Luling."

"That's impossible." The denial comes out before I can stop it. "Impossible. Kelsey's clients did. I did everything I was supposed to. Those are moli fragrances. They might need more time."

Mom only shakes her head. Her doubt has been proven. I look at her carefully. "Did you give them the samples to test? Or sell them?"

She looks insulted. "I didn't charge what I would have, if that's what you're asking."

"Did you give them away for free?" It's like all my blood has rushed to my hands, leaving them overheated and heavy, while my starved muscles shake.

Her expression, along with my knowledge of the kind of woman my mother is, answers me.

"You sold them," I say.

"Nothing comes free in this world."

She said that often when I was growing up, and it wasn't only about money. Mastery took effort. Family took proving oneself. No, nothing was ever free.

Mom took my efforts and she sold them to get the rent so she wouldn't lose her store. She never believed in me. She saw a business opportunity and she took it. Was she was going to keep having me create scents to send out as tests to old clients? Damn, at some point she'd probably cut me out completely and simply stick my huo on any old perfume. It was a test, she'd say, no guarantees, but a good price because of the risk. Caveat emptor. She would have me branded and rebranded a failure, but at least the goddamn store would survive.

"You finally got what you wanted," I say.

"What do I want?" she demands.

"Money for Yixiang."

"Not for Yixiang. For you."

She has the *nerve* to say that to me. "Stop lying! For once, admit the truth."

"What truth, Luling? I told you the truth. I sent some trusted clients your moli fragrance. You asked, and I told you."

"I told you not to do this. Would you have told me if I hadn't found the bottles?"

"No." Her eyes meet mine. "You need to keep working to understand what's happening, and I didn't want to discourage you. What happened here proves nothing."

"I hate it when you make me doubt myself."

"I don't do that."

How do you fight with someone with a different perception of reality? There's no common ground. "You do."

"I don't." No surprise that she's doubled down, and it makes me furious she won't listen. She won't see me or hear me the way I am.

"Stop it," I say. "I'm not the Lucy you wanted, okay? I'm not. I get it and I've accepted it, and you need to as well. Sorry I can't actually perform like you need so the Hua name can mean something again. At least you made some money off me. Dad is right: That's all you want from me."

Shock twists her features, so like mine, and I'm sickly thrilled to have finally said something to break through and affect her. Yet it's also scary. I want to take it all back, even as I keep going because I feel a ferocious need to push right to the limit to see what will break. "You always resented me for going my own way."

"I didn't resent you."

"You're lying."

My mother slaps her hand on the couch. "Stop saying I'm lying! You never want to see what's in front of you. I know how I feel. I was angry you gave up your potential because you refused to ask for help. I was angry because I was hanging over the edge of the well with the ladder, and you wouldn't look up. I couldn't get through to you and you twisted every word I said."

"Stop trying to put this on me."

"If I asked you how you were, you accused me of only wanting to know so I could get you working. If I didn't ask and gave you space, you were upset because you thought I didn't care, because you couldn't contribute. Nothing I did was right."

"Because you made it clear to me I had a duty!"

"You do, and I won't apologize for that. We have a duty to the women who came before us, all those Hua women."

"I don't want that responsibility."

"It doesn't matter," she says. "It's yours."

"See?" I'm drowning under the waves of my anger. "You're doing it again. Making me feel bad."

"You should feel bad," she says coolly. "I had to do what I did because one of us had to act."

"You decided, unilaterally, it had to be you. That you knew the best for me."

"You're impossible. As always. Too scared to try, too proud to ask for help. Always willing to believe the worst in people."

"Where do you think I got that from? You think you're the best role model I could have had?"

In the sudden quiet of the room, I can hear the canned laughter of my neighbor's television. He's addicted to old sitcoms, where everything is solved in less than thirty minutes. I wish I could step through the wall and into that show, because this fight has gotten to be too much and I don't know what to say or how to feel—or what happens after this because something between us has bent and changed. What we had wasn't much, but it was familiar, and whatever comes up next will be unknown.

Mom passes a hand over her eyes. "All I want is for you to be happy. I didn't want you back home because of the store. I wanted you. I wanted to be in your life, the way all the other women in our family were in each other's."

For some reason, her low, sad tone infuriates me more. It's like she refuses to understand that this is not all me or my fault, and the unfinished fury from the fight we had the other day surges back up. "Yeah, well, I wanted my mom. I wanted you to want me for who I was, not for what I could bring the family. I wanted you to love me, not what I could do for you."

"I do, Luling."

"Call me by my fucking name," I snap. This is the first time I've sworn in my mother's presence, let alone to her face. "I'm Lucy."

"You were named Luling."

"It doesn't matter what I was named, I chose something different."

Her mouth tightens. "There are some things that are chosen for you. They're gifts." She shakes her head. "I thought Rafe would convince you to come home. None of this would have happened if you stayed at Yixiang."

I knew it. I *knew* there was something with Rafe. I'd feel triumphant if I weren't so disillusioned. "I don't want to go back. And I can tell you what else I don't want. This." I point at the bottles, hand trembling until I draw it back to my side in a fist. "I don't need it. I don't need you."

I would have preferred the slap I can sense her holding back from the way her hand twitches on the couch to what happens—which is that my mother's eyes fill with tears.

Jesus. Oh my God. My mother doesn't cry. Not once. Never. Not when I failed with Ms. Kang. Not even when she broke her leg falling on the rocks near the water at dawn and had to claw her way home along the grass until her nails were broken and her fingers bloody.

A riptide of remorse joins the rage and drags me out to the open sea. I can't do this anymore. "Mom, it's time for you to go back to Vancouver."

"Luling, we can work this out." She's not pleading—Mom would never do that—but there's a softer tone. "Three people are nothing. Perhaps you're right and they only need more time. I believe in you."

"No," I say. "You never did."

Because I can't go to my room and I can't get away from her in this wretched leftover of an apartment, I put on my shoes. Then I go out and simply stand in the hallway, because despite Rafe telling me I always run away, I have nowhere to go.

33

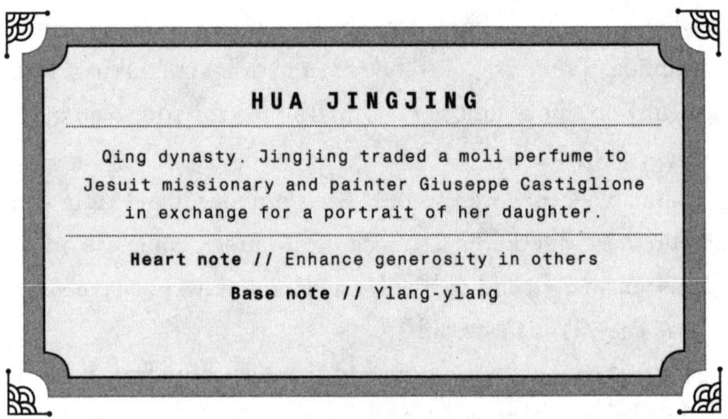

Where's your mom?" asks Ana when I come in the day after The Fight.

"She had to go back to Vancouver."

Ana frowns. "Oh, too bad. She was fun. You're lucky to have a mom who understands what you do. Every time I talk about the store, mine looks like she's sucking a lemon."

I give a noncommittal hum and go to the back room, glad my melting mascara gives me an excuse for looking terrible. It's raining today, and although I had an umbrella, my feet are soaked. I should have taken the TTC, but I couldn't deal with being crammed in with a group of damp people dripping everywhere. I was in no mood for extra aggravation after seeing Mom off in a cab this morning.

I was rethinking the fight and considering possibly apologizing for my part in it, but she came out already dressed to tell me her flight to Vancouver was leaving in four hours and there was no need for me to see her to the airport. That was all I needed to know, and it wiped out my regret instantly. It was clear that without access to my moli— officially—she was done here and ready to go back to her true love, Yixiang.

That was it. No mention of our fight. No resolution or closure. I felt as if I should say something, but I didn't know what, so I accepted her embrace and walked her out.

She didn't look back as the cab pulled away, but I didn't stop waving until it was out of sight.

That night I go to Rafe's place when I'm done working. I didn't tell him about Mom when he texted earlier, and kept the chat to small things about the day that had made me feel better, but now I want the big guns of consolation. I was the one who buried the hatchet with her right before I found out about the betrayal. I did what he'd thought I should to fix my relationship with Mom and get to the bottom of my moli. He has to be on my side. After all, she's the one who left, not me.

Rafe answers the door immediately—do men ever bother with the peephole?—and looks at me with concern. He's in comfy sweats that make him look cuddly and warm. I want to bury my face in his chest and surround myself with the tobacco smell I always associate with him.

"What's wrong?"

"Mom."

He opens the door wider and gestures me in. "What happened?"

My eyes are dry, which surprises me, and I tell him the whole story with the succinctness of an executive assistant reporting to a demanding boss. My mother's sneakiness. The nerve of her. Then the final kicker, that after all that, my moli hadn't worked. Would that scene have happened if it had? I don't know. I want it to be yesterday, when I was with Mom and felt good for once.

Rafe takes my hand. "Do you think you're being a bit hard on her?" he asks.

This is so not what I expected that I laugh. "No? She lied to get money for Yixiang when I explicitly said no."

Rafe moves a shiny black pepper shaker in the shape of a movie camera along the table, brow furrowed as he thinks. "Your mom only wants to help," he says. "She didn't go about it in the best way, but she—"

How can he say that? "Stop. Stop now. That isn't the point. She went behind my back when I told her not to do anything to test those samples."

"She shouldn't have done that, but have you considered she had no choice?"

I'm almost speechless, but not completely. "What are you saying? Of course she did."

"She came here wanting to help you because you refused to talk to her. Then you wouldn't try to get to the bottom of the problem. You knew how important it was to her and to your family."

"Rafe, *enough*. You're supposed to be on my side." I glare at him. "Remember? Supportive?"

"This is supportive, because you need to hear this. Your mother is right. She has done everything to try to reconcile with you, and you're acting like the same child you were when you left, lashing out and refusing to see how you cause most of your own problems."

I am truly and honestly shocked he's turned this on me. "What?" My hand comes up to my throat like a damsel in distress, but I shake it off as my dismay turns to betrayal for the second time in two days. I was sure Rafe would be on my team, and that finally, he was the one I could count on when nothing else went my way.

"This is your problem, Lucy. Not your mother's."

"I came here for comfort," I say, doing my best to keep calm. "Not a lecture."

"A lecture might be what you need. You have to stop pushing people away when they try to help."

"She wasn't helping! How many times do I have to tell you this? She was doing it for herself. For the money for the store. She lied to me when she said she wouldn't give people those samples. Not even give them away, but sell them."

He shakes his head slowly. "You've told yourself that story so often you believe it, and now it's like you can't see the truth. I don't know how to talk to you about this. You're being beyond stubborn."

Me. I'm stubborn. How can he say that when he's met my mother? "Sure, I'm the problem. You don't know what she's like. She deliberately put you in this apartment so we would get together. She said as much. That's how much she wants me back, that she thought you would convince me to move."

"What?" He freezes. "Lucy, you can't be serious."

"Why not? You don't think she could do that?"

"Why *would* she? That doesn't make sense. You've created this imaginary scenario to get angry about, and it has no basis in reality."

"You don't get it."

"This is the most ridiculous thing I've ever heard. I thought I was a work in progress, but you're in tinfoil-hat territory."

I want him to reassure me, to tell me that I'm being silly. But instead, he's getting angry. He takes a deep breath. "You need to grow up, Luling."

Hearing that name again spikes my rage. "I said to call me Lucy!"

My voice echoes in the room, and he shakes his head. "You don't even see how much like your mother you are."

He couldn't have thought of a worse thing to say. It was easier when I was on my own. I don't want this in my life. I don't want him. "This was a mistake, to try and be friends again."

There's a heavy silence as we both absorb what I've said. "Don't be like that," he says softly.

My fury at my mother has fully redirected toward him. It's not fair I'm the only one hurting. "No. You're using things I told you against me. I trusted you, Rafe, and here you are, trying to tell me my mother is right. That I'm in the wrong."

When he looks at me, his eyes are tired. "No, Lucy. I'm trying to tell you that you need to stop thinking of her as the enemy and making up things that let you feel like a victim. You need to think about what you want enough to fight for instead of running from the people who love you. You did it with her, and you did it with me."

"What are you even talking about?"

"When you left, when you were twenty. Sure, I was a jerk and I didn't handle what happened in the garden well. But you didn't email me, either, and when I came home, you were gone. You didn't leave me a note, like I had been nothing to you. Like I was part of your childhood you abandoned with everything else, like it was worthless." He stops talking, both hands pressed flat on the counter. "You ran."

"Maybe it's because I know I'm better off alone," I say.

"That's what you want? Me out of your life again because you had a fight with your mom?" He sounds disbelieving. "Because you've decided I'm some long-con game of hers to get you out of Toronto?"

"I want you out of my life because you haven't been in it for a decade, and since you came back, I've had nothing but problems."

He rubs his chin, then his forehead, as if warding off a headache. His face looks older, and tired. "If that's what you think."

"I do." I'm engulfed in a hurt so deep it burrows right through me.

"All right." He doesn't bother to argue. I can tell how tired he is of me. It's almost as tired as I am of myself.

That's it.

He watches me stumble out and shuts the door. It's not a slam, but it's firm enough to send its own message to confirm that whatever we had, or could have, is over.

The next few days go by as if they were copied and pasted. Each night when I get home, I look down the hall, wondering if I should knock on Rafe's door. He doesn't knock on mine, and I decide I'm not going to beg to see him.

Mom doesn't call.

"Oh, hey, Lucy!" a voice comes from behind me, and I see my film neighbor coming out of the elevator with her arms full of groceries. "It's been a while."

I hurry to help her with the bags. "You're home?" I try not to sound accusatory she's back in her own place.

"Finally. It's good to be back." She smiles at me. She's changed her hair, and it's in loose fire-red curls around her head.

"Weirdly, I knew the guy you rented to," I say as she drops her bags at her door, trying to move the conversation around to Rafe to find out what's going on.

"No way. Small world, huh? Luckily, the timing worked out for both of us. He had to leave suddenly, and my shoot ended early, so I was scrambling to find somewhere to stay."

"Well, good to have you back." My apartment has felt lonelier than ever, so I hesitate and then take the plunge. "Would you like to come over for drinks or coffee once you've settled in?"

"Love to," she says promptly. "How about Thursday?"

That was it. That's all it took to make a connection. I grab her number so we can text about details and head back home. With a long night looming, I realize I should have asked her to come back with me now. I look over to the drawer where I put the register after Mom left, but I can't bring myself to read it without feeling guilty, like I've let down not only my mother but also generations of women before us.

More days pass. It's warm and I check our new potager garden every morning and evening to see if it's thriving and to pull out the cigarette butts and weeds that accumulate. Commissions come and I do them without interest. If Maryska thought my work was soulless before, she'd consider these beyond redemption. Ana sends me worried looks but seems satisfied when I tell her the apartment feels empty with Mom gone.

"I've got something to show you," Ana says when I come in one day. She whips away the silk scarf from her table with a ta-da motion, and I notice it's one of the ones I gave her from Waipo.

I suck in my breath at what she's created. Ana's jewelry is all one of a kind, to make the pieces more covetable, and seeing them lined up on the velvet board makes me realize again how talented she is.

She points to a peony, a lovely pendant hanging off a plain chain. "This is the design your mom suggested."

I lift it up and an unfamiliar scent drifts out. "That's not one of mine," I say.

"No, sorry, your mom did that too." She looks contrite. "Did I do bad? She was excited about it and I didn't have the heart to say no."

It's a light iris, balanced with the warmth of my favorite sandalwood and a touch of lemony vanilla. "I'm going to buy this one."

Ana laughs. "You don't need to buy it, silly. Take it. It's our own collection."

"We'll make it our first sale."

"When you put it like that, how can I say no?"

I take the pendant and put it in the branded box, black with *Pulse Points* across the front in gold font with a little red heart. Ana ordered them on a high of excitement the day we decided to work together, and each box is double layered, with space for the scent refill and instructions under the jewelry. Ana watches me with a big smile. "We did it."

"We did." The satisfaction of the moment barely overcomes the edge of tears I had from smelling Mom's scent, with both of us connected in a way I briefly tasted during her visit and would never happen again.

"Are you ready to let the world see them?"

I nod and try not to ruin this for Ana with my moping. "Let's do it."

Humming a ceremonious tune, she carries the board to the little marble table and sets up the display. We decided on a soft launch so we could make tweaks if we get comments from customers, and the only thing we'll do is put them out and hand-sell them.

That's the highlight of the day, because although a few people pause, we don't make any sales. Ana is undaunted as she bends her head over her worktable to adjust the piece she's working on. "Soft launch," she reminds me. "Things that are worth it take time."

I nod.

I'm alone at the shop, sitting at my counter and thinking about everything I need to do and not wanting to do any of it, when the door opens. I stand up with my usual smile, which immediately disappears when I see who walks in.

"Ms. Kang?"

She looks around, startled. "Hua Luling? My God, what a coincidence. Is this your store?"

I come out from behind the counter. There's an Asian girl of around twelve or thirteen with Ms. Kang, dressed in baggy jeans and a big hoodie, her eyes wide as she looks around. Ms. Kang pushes her off with an indulgent smile. "Go ahead, Holly."

"Is that your daughter?" I ask.

Ms. Kang comes over to give me a light hug in greeting. "Yes, she's my wonder. I had some business in Toronto, and she's playing hooky from school for a day so we can make it a long weekend." She looks with interest at my counter. "I had no idea you were here."

I explain the store split, and we both turn to see Holly looking at a silver backpack. "This is so cool," she whispers.

"You can get one thing," Ms. Kang calls out. "Special treat."

Holly squeals and starts looking around with covetous eyes as we turn back to our conversation. Ms. Kang looks past my shoulder to my counter. "These are your fragrances?"

I move aside and watch as she begins sniffing. "I can see some of what you were doing in your youth," she says. "These are lovely. Your mother's and your grandmother's influence is here, but it's more of an homage. I'm sure they're very proud."

My face freezes and Ms. Kang looks at me curiously.

"Luling?"

"Thank you."

She doesn't move her eyes away. "I've often thought of contacting you," she says. "To thank you. I alluded to it at your grandmother's funeral, but I should have told you how much your perfume changed my life."

"What?" I stop playing with the postcards I give away as promotions to people browsing.

"It did." She lowers her voice. "It brought me my true love after all. It just wasn't in a way I was expecting."

"Mom, look!" Holly comes over with a huge smile, and Ms. Kang's face softens as she turns to her daughter. "Did you find what you wanted?"

Holly holds out one of the Pulse Points pendants, a heart on a long chain that can be turned into a choker. "Smell it."

She does, blinking. "Goodness, Luling, you've outdone yourself. I've never seen anything like this before. It's exquisite."

"Thank you." I take the pendant and show them how to replenish the scent, and after I do, Holly noses around my counter.

"Am I old enough to wear perfume?" she asks me.

I laugh. "That's a question for your mother."

"Mom?"

Ms. Kang looks at her curiously. "If you like, but why now?"

She shrugs. "I just want to."

"That's a good enough reason as any," I say. "Tell me a bit about yourself."

Ms. Kang watches indulgently as Holly talks about her hobbies—skating and reading and swimming—and what sort of smells she likes. I give her a few to try and she looks embarrassed.

"I'm not sure," she says after testing them, glancing at her mother.

"That's okay," I assure her. "You won't hurt my feelings if they don't work out for you. I can change them to something you want."

"I like this one best." She points at the pendant. "I also want it… sort of. I don't know. Different? More serious."

"Ah." I lean down and pluck a bottle out of one of my drawers. "I don't have this on sale, but it might be right for you."

She gives a sniff, then another one. It's one of the modifications for the pendant scent, but this has an emphasis on the woods aspect. "Yes," she says. "I love it."

Holly hands it to Ms. Kang, who smiles. "This smells exactly like you," she approves. "Luling, you have such a talent."

I change out the scent ball and ring her up, throwing in a few refills. Ms. Kang thanks me again, and I walk them to the door and watch them go. They stand so close together they merge into a single figure as they move away.

Then I sit back at my counter. Ms. Kang seems happy with her life and her daughter, although I failed to bring her true love. Is that right? She seemed to think it had worked for her. Did she mean *Holly* was her true love? Her daughter and not a lover? None of the other fifth daughters mentioned such a thing. I can't shake the feeling there's something in what she said. I get up to serve another customer who comes in.

Perhaps I can find it in Mom's chapter.

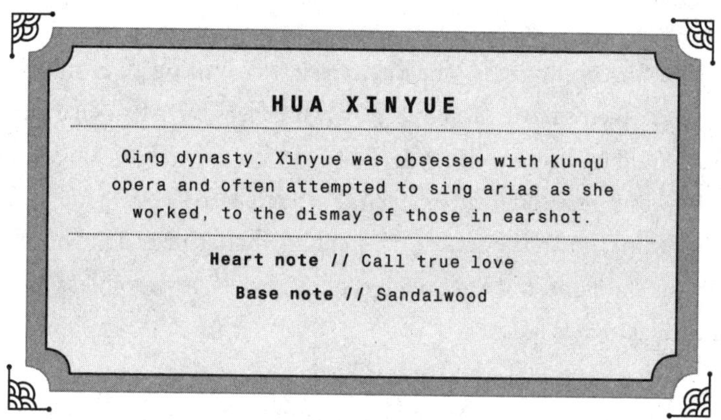

HUA XINYUE

Qing dynasty. Xinyue was obsessed with Kunqu opera and often attempted to sing arias as she worked, to the dismay of those in earshot.

Heart note // Call true love
Base note // Sandalwood

Although I spent most of the day thinking about reading Mom's chapter, once I get home, I make something to eat and take a lengthy shower before cleaning the kitchen, putting in some laundry, and tidying the place. Then and only then do I sit on the couch with the register.

It takes me a long time to open the book.

"Get it together," I say to the empty apartment.

Without letting myself think, I flip to Mom's chapter and start reading before I can find another excuse not to. I'm not sure what to expect, but the first pages follow the same general template as those of the other women. After a quick calculation, I see her first entry is a week after her twentieth birthday, and includes her birth date, place of birth, her moli, and her favored scent. Her writing is bigger than the small, tidy characters of the later pages, as if reflecting the exuberance of the younger woman.

I read each word so carefully that at first I pay more attention to the sentences than the content and have to go back. Mom's voice is in the writing, her matter-of-fact perspective visible in the bullet lists and simple language used through her chapter. Not for her was the gushing eloquence of Dongmei, whose prose was like poetry and whose poetry was like a painting. Mom's goal is to write down her life and experiences as objectively as possible.

The strange thing is, this distance in her writing gives the emotional moments more prominence. My brother's birth lists all the facts that would take up the first page of a baby book—weight, length, and so on—but she's added an exquisite sketch of him sleeping, the lashes long against his full cheeks and his chubby hands pressed to his chin. Mine is the same, but the sketch is of me awake, my toothless mouth open in a joyous laugh.

I didn't know she could draw like that.

The notes on formulae or Yixiang are interspersed with the occasional sketch of Eric or me. In one, we're in the lab, laughing over a vial. I remember that. We were competing to see who could make the nastiest scent. Eric was always good at that, and his vial smelled, somehow, like fish. I keep going until I get to the year I turned twenty, then steel myself to learn her perspective on my lack of moli. There will be anger, I'm sure, and disappointment. Instead, I find another sketch, this time of me in the robe. She's used pen to draw it, and my face is as detailed as a photo. She added the little gap in my front teeth as I smile at the perfume bottle in my hands, and the gold hoops she'd lent me for luck dangle from my ears. Every freckle is documented. There's only one line.

We must be missing something, and Luling is taking it hard.
Her greatest desire is to find her moli.

The subsequent entries make no mention of my moli. Instead,

there are quotes from reviews of my perfumes, and a list of every place I've worked and scent I had for sale. I knew she paid attention to what I did, but I always took it as monitoring my actions, judging my decisions. The register makes it so obvious she did it out of loving pride I'm ashamed to have missed it.

Then I find the list of birthday perfumes, every single one she made for me since I was five. I check Luling33—just as she said, grapefruit and tomato leaf. This doesn't make sense. Curious, I rummage through the box and find it again, sniffing it for the slightest whiff of freshness. I was right—there was nothing.

Huh. Looks like Mom can make a mistake after all.

The list of translated terms, annotated with my mother's writing, slips out, and I smooth it with my hands, frowning as I think. Mom told Ana we needed a vocabulary for what we did, a scent glossary to help us translate what we wanted to create into the world around us. The register in front of me is another translation, but it's not of words or fragrances. It's of emotions. I look at the sketch of me as a baby again. Mom had been speaking to me in her own language all this time, and I have been using the wrong dictionary. Finally, I have the correct one, and the truth of her love pours out from the page into my heart.

I was so sure my view was the true version, and now it's like I've been part of a psychological test about perspective. What else have I been wrong about in my life? What else have I misjudged or misinterpreted?

Exhausted, I put the book aside and lay my head back on the couch to think about what I read. She thought we were missing something about my moli. This confirms the strange feeling I had in the shop after Ms. Kang's visit.

Her greatest desire is to find her moli. True love. Desire. Ms. Kang's joy in life is her daughter, not romance.

I get out my laptop and settle in for some epic googling. I only have to shut my eyes to recall the three names in Mom's notebook.

Evelyn Choo. My first search ends with her obituary, which is not the start to this journey I expected. Wait, I have the wrong person. Three minutes later, I find a recent media release announcing a new collaboration between a big tech company and a climate change non-profit. There's a quote from the tech CEO, Evelyn Choo. "Syntex has been looking at partners for a while, and it's time to act. The $50 million we are contributing to help shift the trajectory of climate change is only the beginning of what we're doing to help save our world." Another more human-interest story outlines Evelyn's volunteer work with climate change boards, which she called her life's passion.

I move on to Henry Lai. According to his social media, he suddenly moved to live it up at an Italian villa he bought for a dollar. I flip through the selfies of him beaming as he holds a glass of Prosecco on the patio of his villa, which he's already renamed Sogno del Cuore and plans to turn into a bed-and-breakfast. At Waipo's funeral, he was a gray man working in advertising, who barely looked up from the floor.

The last is Xiaolan Roberts. I remember her. Her family was an old client and, like us, her family fortunes were whittled away over the years. Though she must be in her fifties, I find a photo of her standing in a plane with a parachute strapped to her back, of all things. The caption reads, "Finally had the courage to take risks. Here's to my new freedom!" All the comments are congratulating her on her new life, along with a snide note from someone who looks to be her ex-husband that simply says, "You'll be back."

None of them have found their true love.

Yet all of them have found something they *truly loved.*

I rub my thigh, thinking about this, then call Kelsey and pray she picks up instead of ignoring my call.

"Lucy?" She sounds dull. "What do you want?"

Before I get anywhere, an apology is in order. Although I still think most of what happened is partly her fault, I'm not going to get anywhere with that attitude. "I'm sorry, Kelsey. I know you've been dealing with a lot because of what happened."

"Thanks to you."

I don't remind her that I didn't want to do the perfume samples in the first place, and although I was the one to spill the beans, Eric was the one who should have pushed Mom to tell her. "I'm sorry," I repeat.

"Whatever. Tell me what the hell you want so I can get the Huas out of my life."

"It's about the samples."

"The cursed ones?"

She's hurting, so I let that go. "You said ten of the women wanted wedding and engagement bags. What about the rest?"

"Who knows?"

"Can I get their names? I'm curious."

This makes her laugh. "Hell no." She hangs up.

I call back four more times before she answers. "You don't get the hint, do you?"

She hasn't blocked me, so she's at least willing to talk, although she definitely wants me to work for it. "Kelsey, you don't owe me anything, but I really need your help."

She sighs. "I don't know. I don't care. One of them wanted a store opening bag, and one wanted a baby one, and one wanted a bon-voyage bag. Something to do with going back to school. A new dog, maybe? That's all I remember. We make luxury gift bags for all the momentous times in people's lives."

Then she's gone before I can thank her. It's what I wanted to know. There's a pattern.

The paper with Mom's translations is in front of me, and I stare at it idly as my finger taps down the characters. Then I stop. Yu. That one was of the few I looked up, and it meant greed. Mom added a few alternative meanings. Desire. Longing.

I went to a gallery in Edmonton once, a small one known for their boundary-pushing. The exhibit was a single room that forced the viewer to move through a series of digital doors and windows that led to new, bigger doors and landscapes, messing with your perception until some people got dizzy and had to sit down. I stayed for an hour, waiting to see one that repeated but never finding it. I couldn't help but feel an end was coming, a resolution, but none arrived.

Staring at that sheet, I have the same sense things are moving, but this time, the door is about to open to reveal an answer. I brace my head in my hands. Desire. Ms. Kang's Holly is her treasure. Henry, a sinking man made buoyant once he decided to become an innkeeper. I check back for his hotel's name. Sogno del Cuore. Heart's Dream. Xiaolan, who celebrated leaving her marriage and finding her new-found liberty by literally jumping into a new life.

I can feel my hand twisting the knob on that final door as my skin breaks out in goose bumps. What if we were wrong? What if the fifth daughter's power isn't to call true love? What if it's your *heart's desire*? Not a soulmate, but the thing that completes your soul? It might be a person...but could it also be breathing the fresh air of a cute villa in the Italian countryside? A collaboration with a nonprofit that helps you save the world? Freedom? The child you wanted but never thought you could have alone? A new business or education?

Ridiculous. I shake my head.

Maybe?

I scramble the book open with shaking hands, wanting to reread exactly what Aiai said about the Peony Goddess.

She wrote: *My gift was to make hearts become whole.*

I chew on this for a minute. This isn't the same as true love, is it? We've been interpreting it as romantic love and assuming that's the only thing that can make one's heart whole. But why? And why did we believe it for a millennium? It's possible I'm the only person this has happened to, and all the other fifth daughters really could call true love.

I keep reading and pull together the pieces. The first clue is from Aiai herself, and the maid they tested the moli on after Aiai's dream of the Peony Goddess. When the maid and manservant fell in love, Aiai's mother declared that to be Aiai's power. What if love was simply what that specific maid wanted? Another maid could have wanted something else, such as wealth or health or anything.

I go to the next fifth daughter's chapter, and the next, reading through all the stories. It looked like enough people truly wished for love to reinforce the assumption of the fifth daughter's power. There are other comments sprinkled through I didn't notice. One Qing dynasty woman took Xinyue's moli and thanked her "because with a husband who loved her, she could be safe."

She didn't want true love but the safety she thought it could bring her.

Of those clients who wanted true love, how many of them considered it a conduit to what they desired most? Children, or power, or wealth. For the women of the past, how much of that could have been possible without a man? Many would have been sure they needed a husband as an intermediary to achieve the things they truly wanted, and a loving husband was better than a cruel one. While I wanted my ancestors to all have been proto-modern feminists, with hidden classes to teach literacy to their girls, and earning their own money from their moli, it would be ridiculous to ignore that the environment in which they lived was one that discounted, devalued, and disrespected them. Their clients lived in the same world.

The three obediences instructed women to obey their fathers, then husbands, and for widows, their sons. Did all women follow those, or believe them? Of course not. Did enough of them? I'm sure of it. The same went for the men who went to my grandmothers for help. Many of them would also have been trapped, unable to envision their dreams outside of what had been presented to them as the life they were expected to lead. Some may have wanted love. Some may have wanted the stability that came with marriage, or children, or companionship.

I drop down on the couch and close my eyes. My heart's desire. My moli won't work on me—but as a thought experiment, what did I want more than anything?

I want my moli, but it's more than that. Oh, I do not like this poking around in the deepest recesses of my own desires. My most secret yearnings.

My moli is only my surface wish. I go a step deeper.

I want to be accepted as a Hua.

Deeper.

I want my mom.

There's more, and I reach down and yank it up.

I don't want to be alone.

This is my most secret longing, hidden beneath layers of what I told myself I wanted. It's what I was too scared to admit to myself while I was absorbed with escaping the pressure of my family.

It drops on me like a downpour. My power is not to call only one form of true love. True love, a heart's desire, comes in different shapes for all of us and might not look like what you think. Ms. Kang thought she wanted a partner, but what she really wanted was a child. Similar things probably happened for the others, including Kelsey's luxury-gift-bag clients. Maybe the woman with the new dog told herself she wanted love, but it was actually companionship and loyalty she craved. She found that through my perfume.

Kelsey's clients with canceled engagements might have found love, but once the ghost scent hit, it slowed the impact. I could only hope those couples could slowly rebuild what they thought they found, and on their own. At least they knew their love. That's more than many in the world had. On the positive side, Ms. Kang had Holly. Xiaolan had freedom. Evelyn had a way to change the world, and Henry, his villa.

I shut the book and sit there, stunned. Somehow, I know it's true.

There is nothing wrong with me. There's nothing wrong with my moli. I've had it all along. For all those years that I thought I was broken, I was complete.

I have no one to share this discovery with. Rafe isn't talking to me. Mom... I can't reach out to her. Ana doesn't know. Like always, I'm alone.

I wish more than anything that the power of the fifth daughter would work on me. I wish I could simply spray on the scent and, poof, my life would work out, like it did for Ms. Kang and Evelyn and Henry and Xiaolan.

But no Hua has been able to do that, and in this, I am the same.

35

HUA ZHENGYI

1967, LESTER B. PEARSON ERA

VANCOUVER, CANADA

Zhengyi put the pen down, wishing she could shake out her wrist but knowing the simplest gestures were fraught with risk these days. She had known age would bring frailty, but she hadn't understood the dread that came with it. She feared everything. The sounds of young people speaking loudly outside her window. The telephone ringing. The stairs that led to her room, since, despite the fear, she refused to have a bed made up for her in the living room on the main floor. That was too humiliating a display of her weakness.

She could hardly believe she'd once been young and courageous. Foolhardy at times, walking into situations with nothing but her determination to succeed.

"What are you doing?" Her great-granddaughter came in, clucking her tongue. "Ma told you she didn't want to see you writing."

Of course Lijing would say that. Her granddaughter was

sometimes too fussy over what she thought Zhengyi could manage. They spoke in their comfortable native language. Zhengyi was fairly fluent in English, but as the day slid into night, she began to tire and it was more difficult to remember the correct words.

"Your mother worries too much."

Yulan smiled at her as she fussed with the night table and its accumulation of books, knickknacks, and medicines. "She would say you don't worry enough."

Zhengyi laughed, pleased the sound didn't hurt her throat. The day she could no longer laugh would be the day she would simply give up and allow her soul to pass into God's hands. "I was adding notes to my chapter for the register," she said. "It took me so long to transcribe that beast I could barely think about my own past."

She put the heavy leather-bound book away. Unlike the previous version she had burned many years ago when she'd completed her job of transcribing it, the peony embossed on this cover retained its golden paint. Only a single scratch marred the front, which sent Zhengyi into a minor fury every time she caught sight of it. She had kept it pristine for the years she spent transcribing the fifty generations before her. Then, one careless moment with a pair of embroidery scissors later, it was ruined.

Silliness, to care about such a thing. By the time it came to the next fifth daughter—Yulan's own granddaughter—the cover would be lovingly worn once more.

"Amuse an old woman," she said. "What have you been doing?"

Her great-granddaughter served as a buffer for all those fears of the sounds outside, and the stairs, and the fruit that now passed through her like water. Yulan had come prepared with samples of what she was working on. Zhengyi sniffed with interest, grateful her nose continued to work amid the ruin of the rest of her body. The new synthetics were a boon to modern perfumers, enabling them to create the strangest, most unusual odors. What would their grandmothers have been able to create given such choice? Perhaps in the future people would wish to smell like more than flowers and spice and wood. They would smell like—she cast her mind around—like the moon, or dirt, or ink. Strange and wonderful things.

"I want to move the store one day," Yulan said as she gathered up the discarded papers and tossed them into an embroidered bin. "Ma says no, but I want to bring in more clients."

Zhengyi raised her eyebrows. "Western ones?"

"Any client who wants us." Yulan shrugged. "Also, there's a woman who would like one of your moli scents, if you have the energy."

"Of course." Zhengyi struggled to sit up straight and held her breath to force down the cough that rose to her lips. If the others thought she was too tired, they would decline on Zhengyi's behalf. It infuriated her to be treated like a child again, she who used to be the most powerful member of the family. She had been the one to insist they come to this new country after their wealth had been lost, despite her own daughter's tears and protests and her refusal to see they'd had no choice. When they were safe in Canada, Meihui had still complained about deserting China when they were needed to rebuild the country, even though the communists had outlawed bourgeois extravagances such as perfume.

She couldn't think of those times now, especially while the sun was out. The day was for living, or what passed for living in this bed. The nights were for the dead who haunted her dreams. Her son and daughter and husband. Grandson. Her mother. Her brothers. Then there was Jun, dead as well but so alive in her mind.

Yulan was chattering on about the new client, Mrs. Chen—from one of the old families who had come to Canada from Taiwan, and who had been luckier with their riches than the Huas. "I don't like her," said Yulan, frowning, her hair long and parted in the middle. So flat, although Zhengyi told her setting it would be more attractive. "She was rude to Ma, as if Ma were a servant."

"What was she wearing?"

"A summer fur. Mink, glossy and black around her shoulders. Her cigarette case was gold."

Zhengyi nodded. "Charge her double."

Yulan's narrow eyes grew wide. "Double?"

"You said she was a Chen. I know that family. They respect only two things: themselves and money. The more they pay for something, the more they will value it. Don't bargain with her. Act simply as if she would of course pay such a small amount for a treasure." She paused, thinking. "Make it triple."

Yulan looked at her with admiration. "You are a shark."

Zhengyi snorted. "I am an old woman with no time. She wishes for her true love?"

"She wore a wedding ring."

"Ah." Zhengyi adjusted the thick duvet. She loved the way it felt like being embraced by a cloud. Her great-granddaughter came up to adjust the pillows behind her, then frowned and told her to lean forward. Zhengyi did and felt the relief of Yulan drumming lightly on her back.

It was several minutes until she finished coughing, and she discreetly folded the bloodied handkerchief in her hand before Yulan took it away. "Wedding rings are no evidence of love," Zhengyi said as if their conversation had not been interrupted.

Yulan turned and arranged her face. She had looked in the handkerchief, then. Zhengyi prayed she had the sense to not worry her mother but knew it was a false hope.

"You say that with the tone of a woman who knows from personal experience," Yulan said.

Zhengyi's laugh resembled a bark, and this time it hurt. "Every fifth daughter knows this, the same way all Hua women know how difficult it is to trust people outside the family."

She said this deliberately, for Yulan had been fighting with her mother about her marriage, the same way Zhengyi had fought with her own mother. Perhaps that was another tradition of Hua women, to fight with their mothers over their husbands. Or it could be true for all women, and probably some men. Not all people make suitable spouses.

"How did you know my great-grandfather was the man for you?" Yulan asked quietly.

Zhengyi looked at the book by her side and wondered if she could tell Yulan the story she had hesitated to write down.

"I didn't want to marry your great-grandfather at first," she said. "He was an old friend, as you know. He understood what I would be doing with my life and that I could not leave my family. I had known him for years."

"You needed him to come to Canada."

"I needed a man I could rely on. You know I couldn't even open a bank account without his permission?" Zhengyi snorted. "The landlord refused to speak with me because I was a woman, so I couldn't rent the store. Hao had to sign everything."

"You must have loved him from the beginning?"

"He was good to me." She wondered how honest to be before deciding the girl was old enough to understand. "I didn't love him at first. I thought he was a bore. I was in love with a man named Jun. He was a friend of my brother's, and when he saw me on the street, he liked the look of me."

Yulan looked shocked. "He said that way back then?"

"Aiya, how old do you think I am? That I lived with dinosaurs?" Zhengyi was insulted. "It was 1900, the dawn of the new era, and I was very pretty those days. Prettier than you wearing that paint on your lips that looks like nothing. Not even pink."

"Sorry." Yulan looked appropriately penitent, so Zhengyi continued.

"I had been in Nanjing to see a client with my brothers. Jun had been there as well."

Zhengyi smiled to herself, unable to explain to Yulan the sheer excitement of being in the city. Their house in the country was large but quiet, and the sounds and movement of Nanjing kept her holding her breath to absorb everything. Jun had been so different from the other men in her life, and especially from Hao, who walked leaning forward as if he were being chased and had a permanent line of worry between his brows. Decades later, the memory of Jun's smile, slow and soft and all for her, still made her heart leap.

"My mother noticed the change in me first. I told you of the deal we had made." She looked over at Yulan, forgetting for a moment if she had.

Yulan leaned forward in the battered armchair. "That you could marry who you pleased, as long as she approved. Did she approve of Jun?"

"No." Zhengyi snorted, but delicately. "She was too smart to let me know. Back in those days I was willful and stubborn, and she knew the moment she said anything bad, I would be in his arms."

Yulan's eyebrows shot up, but she quickly schooled her expression. "You wanted to marry him?"

Matrimony had not been uppermost in her mind at the time. Zhengyi looked at her great-granddaughter, a woman in her twenties with innocent eyes and a wide brow, and judged her too young to have to imagine a wrinkled old woman panting in lust for a man who would look ridiculous by modern standards, in his long robe and queued hair. "Yes," she said.

"Yet you didn't."

"Jun courted me, but I was too blind to see his clothes were mended over and over, although he bragged about the luxuries he bought, or the secret gifts he brought were not expensive, but things he said only a woman like me could appreciate."

"He wanted your money?"

"He did, but had I been told that, I wouldn't have believed it. Or I might not have cared. My mother was sly. He came to see my brother, and she left a gold pin out as if it had dropped from her hair, and pretended not to notice when it was gone. He didn't know she had stationed me near the room. I saw him pick it up."

"He denied it when you accused him?"

Zhengyi laughed. "He didn't have to. I learned my lesson the moment the hairpin disappeared and I saw the naked greed on his face. He looked more animal than man. Mother and I both thought it money well spent to find out his true self."

Yulan stared at her in wonderment. "You weren't angry she tricked him? And you?"

"I was." Zhengyi recalled the anger and something she'd forgotten about. The relief. The knowledge she wouldn't have to try to explain her moli to Jun, and to beg to be allowed to stay with her family, and her clients, and the work that was her life. Hao—later Howard—understood and was willing to come to her. He could be trusted to support her and their children, and that stability had been worth more than anything the most exciting lover in the world could offer.

Yet she still regretted Jun. One of many regrets, to be sure, but there. She had often wondered if Hao had similar sorrows, but never had the nerve to ask.

"Then why did you not say anything?"

"My mother had told me something her mother had told her. In fact, I think all mothers have said this to their daughters in the hope that one day, we will no longer need to pass it on."

Yulan frowned. "What?"

"That we are at a disadvantage in this world." Zhengyi closed her eyes for a moment, simply to rest them. She couldn't recall the last time she felt truly refreshed, her body without aches and pain. "We women, I mean. As Huas we have been given a unique gift to help protect ourselves, and we need to be vigilant. Some would take it from us or try to control us. It's our responsibility to keep ourselves safe for our daughters, and if sometimes that means our own hearts are made heavier, that is the price we pay."

She forced her eyes open to see Yulan looking troubled. "Ma told me the same thing when I turned sixteen."

Ah. Zhengyi reached out a warped hand she no longer recognized as her own. "Perhaps you will not have to tell your own daughter. I chose wisely, in the end. Your great-grandfather respected me and our gift. He was a good man, and I loved him dearly. I miss him."

They sat in silence as Yulan came over to take Zhengyi's hand. "You're tired," she said gently. "Ma will kill me if I keep you from your rest."

She checked the water glass was full, and Zhengyi waved her away. "I'll sleep soon," she promised. "There's one last thought I need to get down."

Yulan looked like she was going to refuse, so Zhengyi summoned her old imperious look, the one that cowed rich clients and worried great-granddaughters alike. Yulan rolled her eyes, the minx. "Don't tell Ma," she said.

When she was alone again, Zhengyi took up her pen and let it drop back to the page. She was so tired, and it was late. The morning would be soon enough to write about Jun and the goodness of Hao.

With that, she let her eyes close. Morning. She would do it in the...

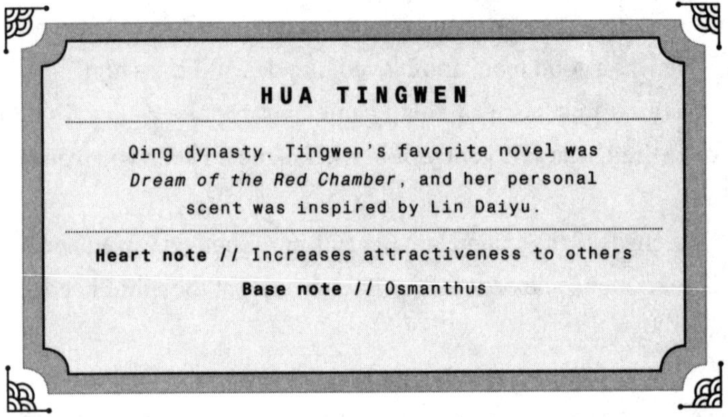

thought I would be awake through the night after my discovery, but I sleep so soundly I miss my alarm and have to run to work. It's like my body is trying to give me mental space by forcing me to physically shut down. The day helps by being shockingly busy. We're inundated with so many customers that I ask a woman as she's checking out where she heard of us.

"This place is all over social media," she says. "I'm not one to follow influencers or anything, but I saw it on the Kitty in the City blog, and it looked absolutely adorable."

When I finally get a break, I check the blog site. Ana groans and slips off her shoes to wiggle her toes and looks over my shoulder. "Hey, I remember that woman. I guess she liked what she saw. God, look at her follower count."

"Like" is an understatement. Kitty's feed is tastefully curated and she loves the scents, our aesthetic, and Ana's jewelry and vintage selection. Excellent news for us.

Ana quickly reposts Kitty's post to our social media and then DMs a thank-you to Kitty before a new wave of customers comes in. By the time we close, we have a waiting list for jewelry, I'm running low on all my scents, our online orders are swamped, and Ana and I are wiped.

Just like that, the adrenaline of working drops away and I remember all the things I've been trying not to.

"Man, all I want is to eat," Ana says, moving to the back of the room, her long red dress—vintage couture, and she had a woman try to buy it off her back—swishing as she walks. "You in?"

We go to a wine bar I haven't visited before although it's only one street over from our shop. The place is lovely, entirely staffed by beautiful women and men in toques. We sit at a high marble counter, and I let Ana decide on the wine as I unwrap copper cutlery from the thick cloth napkin. Restaurants are always a complex source of smells, and this one has an open kitchen, adding the sizzle of butter to the sharp vetiver of the man to my right, who nervously checks his phone.

Ana puts the small paper menu aside and gives me a blissful smile. "Soft launch for the win. My mother says my ideas are too out there to work, but I knew it. Dreams do come true."

Eager to forget what I was thinking about, I latch on to her words. How many hints has Ana dropped about how unsupportive her family is? She's been a good friend to me, and I only think of myself.

That can change, and this time I ask.

"What do you mean about your mom?" A bowl of fresh bread arrives with flavored sage butter.

"Nothing. There's something going on with you, though." She takes the bread and waves it at me. "Your mom isn't the type to leave without a goodbye."

She's trying to change the subject. I'm not used to pressing people, and I'm allergic to the idea of not respecting her boundaries, but I can't get over the sense she wants to talk. Thinking about it, I can see how Ana depended on a few throwaway comments to make me feel like I knew more about her than I did. "There is something with me," I say, getting an idea.

"Then spill."

"How about this." I wait until the server puts down a bowl of smoked fish dip and another of golden potato chips. "Neither of us want to talk about stuff we probably should talk about."

"I talk."

"You talk selectively."

She looks guarded, the chip hovering midair. "Okay?"

"We're going to play a game."

"I once played strip poker in university and only lost one sock while everyone else ended up naked," she says. "I'm good at games."

"That's great, but this is like emotional strip poker."

She makes a face. "That sounds less fun, but also far less awkward for tomorrow morning." She reconsiders. "Potentially less. Also, why do we need to do this?"

I look at the food because I'm not comfortable enough to make eye contact and I know I'll give up at the slightest discouragement. Being in the crowded restaurant makes this feel more intimate. "Because you say a lot of stuff that sounds like it might be good to talk about. I know you love them, but every time you say something like that about your mom or family, I haven't followed up. But I think you might want to talk about it? Maybe? Or think you should? I don't know. I'm sorry."

I shut up, already regretting this but feeling like I did a good thing. If the small decisions you make every day are what makes the kind of person you are, I made the right one this time. Ana can always say no.

"I didn't think you liked talking about stuff like this," says Ana. "It's hard for me to be open with you if you're not with me. You're not even looking at me."

I never had to open up in the way Ana is asking for. It's been a long time since I let myself be close to someone, but Ana makes it easy.

Part of me is alarmed, because I've protected myself from accidentally revealing my family secret by simply not having people to divulge it to. The rest of me almost sags in relief at having someone to talk to—really talk. Willpower gets depleted over time, and I'm as vulnerable to the idea of friendship as I am to a bag of chips after eating salad all day.

"Sorry," I say, raising my eyes.

"You don't need to be sorry," she says. "I get it. You're pretty closed off. Like, I don't want to force my friendship on you."

I've shut out Mom and Rafe. I'm not going to do that here. "I'm a witch. Kind of."

"Huh?" She blinks at me. "What did you say?"

"I left home because the women in my family are basically witches and I didn't have my power. I was ashamed. It was hammered into me that this was a huge secret, so I've never told anyone."

"Are you for real? No bullshit?"

"My magic is in my perfume. It's real."

"What about your mom?"

"Her too. All the firstborn daughters in my family."

"That's why you moved around so much?" Her eyes are huge, food forgotten. "Are you being chased by a secret society of witch-hunters that survived from the Inquisition?"

"What? No, God, why would you think that?"

"Honestly, it's the plot of a lot of books I read when I was younger," she admits. She casts a glance at my face as it to check if I'm lying. "I wasn't expecting this."

"What do you mean?"

"I thought at first you had a toxic family and went no contact," she says, fixing the pearl headband that has slipped over her forehead. "Then your mom showed up and she seemed cool. A witch was not on my bingo card. I assume it's a secret. I won't tell Jayne. What can you do?"

I might as well spill all the beans since I've already tipped the jar. "We can change emotions with our perfumes," I say.

That's it. I've said it all. I've told another person our greatest secret without my mother's approval. Yet it feels right to tell Ana in a way I could never imagine feeling with anyone else I've met. I cast a quick look around the room, half expecting the Peony Goddess to send down lightning to smite me, although that's more of a Greek god thing.

A little furrow has appeared between Ana's brows. "Not to minimize what you're saying, but I thought all scent could do that," she says. "Like how lavender is relaxing."

"That's true. My grandmother suspected our ability was related to that, but what we do is more targeted."

"Wow, cool." Ana is taking it all in stride, exactly the way I hoped. "*Wow*."

More food comes—a pasta with morels, which we share, along with tender zucchini—and we take a moment to eat.

"I hate to ask, but have you been bewitching me?" She looks uncomfortable. "That perfume you gave me?"

"No! I would never." I think about Kelsey. "Not on purpose."

"I feel there's more to that story."

"Your turn first. Put up your stakes."

"My what?"

"Stakes. Isn't that what you say in poker?"

"Have you ever played?"

I shake my head and she sighs.

"Let's put the game analogy aside, then," she suggests.

"Okay. It was more of an icebreaker thing anyway."

"It was a great idea," she says. "You don't need to try so hard. You're my friend. I'm not going to leave."

My eyes well up with tears, but I blink them back. Not fast enough, though, because Ana sees.

"Lucy?"

"It's your turn," I say, twisting my head down.

"We're going to talk about this next."

"After you go."

Ana scrunches up her nose. "It's strange, you know? When you called me out, I truly didn't remember saying anything negative about my mom."

"It's not *negative* negative." I consider. "More just not positive."

"I had no idea. Maybe it's a coping mechanism, because I can't be mad at my mom for wanting the best for me, can I?"

I shrug uncomfortably. "You're talking to someone who left home and barely talked to her mother for over a decade because she wanted the best for me."

Ana snorts. "You're such an overachiever." Then she gets serious. "I compare my family to Jayne's and I'm grateful. The only thing I wish is that Mom would let me be me instead of wanting me to be more like my sisters. I get that Fernanda is perfect. Great cook, great mom. Good housekeeper. Works full-time. Maria goes over for dinner almost every night after her amazing bank job. They're the daughters my mom wanted."

I drink my wine, letting her talk.

"The thing is, I'm happy. They think owning a store isn't a good use of my business degree, but I can't bear the thought of wasting my life on a report that's only being generated because someone up the ladder thought they might want it. They know about Jayne, but they keep mentioning my old boyfriend and wondering what he's up to these days."

She heaves a sigh that seems to have been dragged up from her toes. "Your turn."

"Shouldn't we talk about this?" I ask.

"How about we get all the sharing out of the way first?" She gives me a look. "So no one gets out of talking."

"I wasn't going to," I protest.

"Good. Then go."

I tell her about Kelsey and Mom and Rafe, and all she does is nod. Then I tell her about the register, and her eyes widen in recognition. "That's what your grandma sent."

"It's a history of my family. I found out something yesterday. About myself."

She looks sympathetic. "Whatever it is, I can say with assurance I'll still be your friend."

"I left home because I thought I didn't have my power, but I do. It's not true love I can bring. I can bring someone's heart's desire. The thing they want most in the world. It might be love or it might be something else."

"Holy shit, like a genie?" She looks impressed, and this makes me laugh.

"I guess so, but with only one wish. But I think the thing my perfume summons isn't what the person necessarily expects to happen."

"You do a bait and switch?" Her eyebrows rise in disapproval.

"Yes, but also no?" I take a sip of wine. "Like they think they want love, except what they actually want is companionship."

"They've been brainwashed into thinking they can only get that through a romantic partner," she finishes.

"I wouldn't say *brainwashed*, but basically. Or they can't admit it to themselves for some reason." I eat some of the pappardelle. "Your turn."

"Your bit was just getting good," she complains.

"So was yours."

"I don't know what to say." Ana shrugs. "It's anticlimactic, but that's family for you. I know the issues, but I'm stuck. This is why I dumped my last therapist. All she wanted to do was talk, but that didn't change anything about my situation, only how I viewed it."

She's right. "We can't leave it unresolved like this. Let's pick one thing we need to address and then tell each other what we're going to do about it."

She considers this. "Like accountability partners, but for life instead of the gym. I like it. What's your thing?"

"You go first."

"No, you."

"Fine." I think of the mess I've made of everything. It might be unfair to say, but all this started with my moli. That's where my answer will begin, although I know it won't be the end.

Aiai wrote that she'd once asked Empress Wu why only the rich should be able to afford love, and the empress had laughed and called her a village girl with a village girl mind. Aiai was the one who saw clearly, and like the interpretation of her power, her goals were warped over the years by generations of women driven by fear and perhaps greed, who limited their moli sales to those who could pay the most. I didn't like that.

"I'm going to make a perfume," I say slowly, waiting for Ana to roll her eyes and ask how that's going to solve anything.

She only nods. "I got you."

"I don't know how, but it will be a perfume to make a difference," I say.

"I know it will."

"What about you?"

She sighs. "I don't know where to start."

"Every shift starts with a small decision," I say. "It doesn't have to be big."

Ana chews her lip. "I don't like it when Mom makes fun of the store," she says. "I could tell her it hurts my feelings instead of laughing it off like it doesn't bother me. Why do I feel like a little kid saying this?"

"Maybe because moms kind of make us feel like kids no matter how old we are?" There's a reason I started with making a world-changing perfume instead of talking to my mother.

She waves her hands. "On today's episode of what I should talk about in therapy but hate to get that vulnerable about: mommy issues!"

We laugh.

"You could be right," she says. "When do you think we move past wanting our parents' approval?"

"Death?"

"That's depressing."

"Yeah. It doesn't mean we can't move on, though."

"I can do it," she says. "I can tell her how I feel."

"When are you going to do it?"

She glances at her phone. "I'm due there to pick up a package, and I've had enough liquid courage that it might be tonight."

"If you do your thing, I'll get started on mine."

She leans over to give me a hug, the scent I made for her birthday puffing out in a breath from her clothes. "I'm glad we're friends."

"Me too."

Ana thinks for a second. "Your witch thing."

"We call the power moli, but what about it?"

"What if someone's heart's desire is, like, a lifetime's supply of Caramilk bars or Jolly Ranchers or something?"

"Why would that be someone's greatest desire?"

"I don't know. People are weird."

I shrug. "Then I guess they get ready to deal with the cavities."

Ana looks awestruck. "You truly are magical."

We laugh, then pay and head out, her to her mother's and me to the lab, where I poke through my materials. I run my finger along the white label stuck to the iris accord. I need to tell Mom about what I've discovered, but much like my other moli news, it's something I need to do in person.

My hand keeps going along the vials. Tobacco Absolute 10% dil alc. After dipping in a blotter, I pull it out to sniff Rafe.

I miss him. I miss being with him. Here, alone, I can see he was right. I was acting like a child and, like a child, broke the things I cared about because I was hurt and lonely. Unlike a child, I need to find a way to fix this.

Rafe said that moment in the garden when we were twenty had helped him understand he needed to change his thinking. It's like I'm having my moment now, years later, and I have a lot of learning to do.

I put the blotter aside, then bring it back. I had a glimpse of what I wanted my new fragrance to be when Ana laughed with me. Part of what makes joy so precious is the knowledge that it's fleeting. I wonder how all those who found their heart's desire coped with it. It could never be the perfect happy ending, because there's always more work to be done and choices to be made. Yet it's the work that makes it worthwhile. I put the tobacco to the side. I'm not going to use it, but it will be my private reminder that a sacrifice can be worth the result.

Time passes. I leave the table to walk around the dark store and then outside to breathe in the night air. I've been sniffing and writing notes for at least two hours straight, and I need to rest my fatigued nose.

I pluck a few weeds out of the garden under the streetlights and listen to people walking by on their way home from dinner debating whether or not they could survive a zombie apocalypse. (Their consensus is it depends on the kind of zombie, but urban areas would be a slaughterhouse.) Then I go back into the store to assess what I have so far. The lure of working, of creating, is pulling me under, and I gratefully let it happen so I can stop thinking.

This is a gift my mother gave me.

First, gel. Then hairspray. Meilin had worked hard on the swoop of her bangs—high above her forehead, but with a thin fringe to her eyebrows—and trial and error had taught her the exact order of products required to make it perfect. She'd tried mousse, but the lack of staying power meant by the end of the day, her bangs would be a soft wave, and a total travesty.

Hopefully, Kevin would notice. She thought he would. He was the kind of person who noticed everything, and she liked that, especially when it was about her. She didn't know the last time someone looked at her and saw Meilin. Not a Chinese girl or a Hua daughter. He saw Mei, someone he liked to spend time with because he thought she was funny, and sweet. That's what he'd called her the last time they met, and he'd bought her ice cream.

"Sweet like you," he'd said as he handed the cone over, and

Meilin knew she'd gone red. She might have giggled. Kevin did that to her.

She smiled at her reflection and added some more Toast of New York to her lips before blotting it off. Kevin didn't like too much makeup. It smeared on his face while they kissed, he'd told her last time, handing her a tissue.

The butterflies that rose every time she thought of him fluttered high into her chest. They'd met through friends, at a dance club downtown, and he'd bought her a drink, then another, smiling as she tried to make him laugh by lip-synching to Roxette. He was the most handsome man she'd seen—Chinese, which was surprising since most of the people she knew were white—and from Shanghai, although his accent sounded almost British. He'd come to Canada for school. He was a few inches taller than her, and his black hair was long on the top. Sometimes it flopped over his eyes, a look she loved, although he shoved it back with an impatient hand.

He'd gotten her number from her friend, and soon they were talking on the phone every night. He wanted to be an accountant or something to do with numbers, in an established firm, the kind where he had to wear a suit. Most of her friends were working in retail, so Kevin's dream of a solid job was almost exotic. Kevin didn't seem to have many friends or go out much—he was always studying—and he'd only been at the club because one of his roommates insisted he come.

Meilin, of course, was working at Yixiang. Although she'd resented being forced to spend all her free time there in her youth, now she loved it. Knowing it would someday be hers meant each morning when she opened the door, it was like walking into her future. This location was all she'd known, although she'd seen the original storefront in Chinatown. Her mother said the old store had been too small and cluttered, although spotlessly clean. She often complained about how her own great-grandmother had made sure of that. In that store, the only customers who crossed the threshold arrived thanks to word of mouth.

The same wasn't true here. The old customers still came, but now they had people walk in off the street, intrigued by the idea of buying exclusive perfume not available anywhere else in the world. Meilin wanted to play this up further. She wanted to change the flowered wallpaper to dark green, or possibly burgundy, although that was less flattering to her skin tone. She wanted to get new floors, and beautiful wood counters and displays to showcase their fragrances. Her mother agreed, and some of Meilin's favorite days were when the two of them would make the rounds of other stores, noting what worked and, even better, gossiping cheerfully about what didn't.

When Kevin came by the store, it had been unexpected, so much so that she'd simply stared when he'd walked in, briefly unable to identify the familiar face. She'd taken the lilies he handed her, and breathed in their funeral scent as she followed his glance. In his eyes was reflected not the glimmering future but the pragmatic present. Kevin wasn't the kind to dream about what could be, and when she told him of their renovation plans, he had immediately started asking about their financing and other boring things. She tried to distract him by explaining all the perfumes to him. He'd sniffed a few, pointing out when one was too strong or too light before telling her she should close up early and come to dinner with him.

Her mother had come out from the back of the shop and stared at her, and Meilin had said no.

After Kevin left, her mother had turned to Meilin. "Is he a perfumer?"

"You know he's not." The lilies would look nice on the counter. Meilin fetched a vase.

"Take those away; they'll interfere with the scent of our perfumes," her mother commanded.

Meilin sighed and brought them to the back, and her mother followed.

"The reason I asked if he was a perfumer was because he seemed to have plenty of advice for what we should make."

"Everyone has opinions."

Her mother snorted. "Some more than others, and perhaps when they shouldn't."

"You don't need to worry about me."

"Mothers worry about daughters because we know what daughters don't."

On that note, Yulan went back to their small lab in the back of the store.

Meilin stayed in the front and stood at the glass door, looking down the street to see if Kevin was still in sight. She wished she had the nerve to do as he suggested and shut up the store so she could have fun, but she couldn't. She turned to the sketch her mother had done of how the store could be. It would be rich, sumptuous, and matching the other luxury shops downtown. Those changes would have to be saved for and planned. A new dress sacrificed here, a second pair of shoes there. It all added up, and would have to do, at least until Meilin's daughter changed things for the family and the store.

Meilin often thought of her daughter. That she would have one was a given; all Hua women did. Her daughter would be pretty, of course, and strong-willed, a trait that had run true since Aiai herself. She was proud she would be the mother of a fifth daughter, a girl who would have rosy cheeks and a strong voice.

Her name would be Luling. She'd known for years. Hua Luling.

Meilin touched her bangs to see if they were dry, then took out the clip she used to get the height she needed. Today they were going for a walk on the Seawall. It had been Kevin's idea, after she'd suggested the Sun Yat-Sen garden. "You smell flowers all day," he'd said. "It'll be a good change."

He was right, and it was thoughtful of him to get her into the sea breeze with all those new smells. He was astounded Meilin could describe her surroundings in smell rather than what she saw or heard. Kevin called her Rain Man for a while, but with a smile that told her it was meant affectionately.

"Meilin!" It was her mother, calling from the bottom of the stairs. "Are you going out?"

"I have a date with Kevin." Even saying his name caused shivers. He'd kissed her last time they'd met, under a lilac tree that had tickled her nose with its rich scent. She'd sneezed, and been worried she'd hurt his feelings until he laughed.

Her mother came up the stairs and shook her head. "You look like a rooster with your hair like that."

Her mother's hair was pulled back in a ponytail so tight it was like a cap. "It's the style."

"Huas make our own style." Her mother sat down on the bed. "You've been seeing a lot of this boy."

"Five or six dates."

"You brought him to the store."

"He came by," Meilin corrected, giving her bangs one more quick spritz.

Her mother wrinkled her nose at the smell. "Has he had any more suggestions for how we should make perfume?"

"No," snapped Meilin. "And he was only trying to make conversation."

Yulan looked at her closely. "You know we need to be careful about who we share our secret with. They must be trustworthy."

"Kevin is trustworthy." Meilin bristled. "And he wouldn't care. He has enough going on in his life that me having a job wouldn't bother him."

Her mother snorted. "You don't have a job, girl, you have a calling. Will he be able to handle being second in your life after Yixiang?"

"He's not that insecure, and it doesn't matter. He's going to Shanghai in a few months."

"Ah." Her mother relaxed instantly. "He is?"

"Yes, back home. He was only here for school."

"Good." Her mother's concern was assuaged. "Then there's no need to tell him anything."

"None at all."

Yulan paused in the door, hesitating as if she wanted to say something else.

"I have to finish getting ready," Meilin said.

Her mother nodded. "Be home in good time. You have work tomorrow."

Her mother left, and Meilin adjusted the cuffs of her knee-length jean shorts. It was nice to be able to enjoy Kevin without thinking of building a future with him. If he was staying, she would have to worry about when to tell him about her moli. She would have to negotiate with her mother over whether she could. She would need to sit him down and explain she wasn't only a perfumer, and her daughter—and his—would make him richer beyond all comprehension. But that there would be a price, and the price was that she was a Hua, and he was not, and part her life would be always closed to him.

She'd never told another person this. She'd never had to. She never wanted to. It seemed almost sacrilegious to have to tell a man about her ability, as if she was sharing something more intimate than even her body. If she could guarantee how someone would react, that would be better. If only they had a moli to control unpredictability.

But they didn't.

Almost time to go. She remembered Kevin had been off last time, upset about something or other. She glanced at the vial on her nightstand. She'd made him a moli perfume last night, similar to the fougère of the Calvin Klein Eternity For Men he usually wore. She lifted it up, then put it back down.

It would be nice if he was in a good mood. She tucked it in her pocket, pulled on her rhinestone-studded sandals, and left.

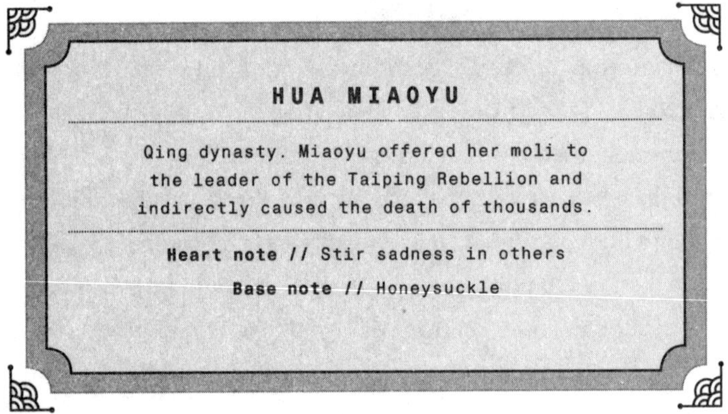

The slamming of a door rouses me from sleep. As a person with terrible sight, the first few moments of every morning are experienced as a haze of amorphous shapes, but today they're not as blurry as they should be. I must have left in my contacts. I blink and the back room comes into focus through my morning fog and sticky eyelids. Ana appears at the door, bleached hair in a high smooth puff that matches her Mondrian minidress and white vinyl go-go boots.

"Did you sleep here last night?" she says.

I sit up, feeling grubby and gross. "I guess so? I only meant to rest my eyes for a second. What time is it?"

"Nine." She looks at me with sympathy and hands over her coffee. "Here, I haven't touched it yet."

I take it gratefully, and the first sip—almost syrupy with sugar—is heavenly. I cross my legs on the couch and lean forward to stretch what I think are my hip flexors but might be some other muscle. Ana checks my worktable, which is messy and not like me. "How'd it go?"

I stand beside her. "Perfect."

"You sound sure. Normally, you say it needs some work, but you suppose you're happy with it, although it could probably be better."

It gives me an intense flash of joy that she knows this about me.

"Not this time." I reach down and dip a blotter in. "Want to smell it?"

Ana steps back and waves me off. "No, thanks. I want to get my heart's desire for myself. Actually, I don't need it. I already have Jayne." Her voice is nasal from holding her nose.

"Understood, and that's very sweet, but this is only the scent. I haven't done anything to it."

"Oh, gotcha." She leans forward and sniffs, then grabs it out of my hand. "Wow, Lucy. This is incredible."

I drip some into a spray bottle and she holds out her wrist. "What do you smell?" I ask curiously.

"Freedom. Joy." She sniffs again. "Are you sure you didn't do anything?"

"Honest."

"There's citrus. I think yuzu? A flower or sorts." She shakes her head. "I can't tell anymore."

"The flower is ylang-ylang." I put the bottle back on the desk, satisfied. "There's some patchouli and sandalwood too." It's not a unique mix but is deeply satisfying.

"Why haven't you magicked it up?" she asks. Ana is so casual about this, like of course me having this power is cool with her. Mom was wrong about that, at least. There are people who don't simply want to use us for what we can give.

"I wanted to sleep on it to make sure I didn't have to change it," I say.

"Look, I don't know squat about scent, but this is a winner." She can't get her nose off her wrist. I knew last night that I had it, but having Ana's opinion is a nice confirmation. "What's it called?"

"Aiai." It had come to me in the daze before sleep claimed me, clicking like a sprocket into a chain. "It was the name of the first Hua with our power and 'ai' means love. Also, Aiai hated that she was forced by the empress to work for her and her only."

"Sidebar," says Ana. "I can't believe your family was buddies with an empress from a thousand years ago."

"Tell me about it, but from what Aiai said, they were far from buds. A patron at best, a jailer at worst. The point is, why do only the powerful deserve to get what they want?"

"That's my good anti-capitalist," she approves, taking my used blotters and tossing them in the trash.

"Well, I'm still going to sell it for a significant price," I say.

"That's okay, we can work on beating the system from within," she assures me. She smells it again. "This is so good, Lucy."

"Thanks." I know it is, but her enthusiasm makes me happy. "How about your night?"

"It started off fantastic, with Mom saying at least Ferd had steady work where she was respected instead of only being a shopkeeper."

I wince and she keeps going.

"I had already made it to the kitchen before I realized what she'd said, because I've heard versions of it for so long I didn't notice. So, not proud of this, but I took a couple shots of the booze she keeps in the kitchen. That gave me the guts to go talk to her."

"What did you say?"

Ana pokes at a pile of rhinestone bracelets. "I said I was sorry she thought so little of my shop and what I do because I work hard. I said if they were going to be unkind, I would prefer they not talk about it at all." She frowns. "It was hard. I felt like I was being stripped."

"Then what?"

"Oh, the excuses. They didn't mean it. I was being oversensitive. How could I think so poorly of them and be so rude."

"No."

"Yeah, it was demoralizing, and it occurred to me they cared more about protecting their self-image than apologizing for hurting me. It sucked. I didn't know what to say, but then my older sister, Maria, stepped in and said I was right and they were being mean. That shut them up because Maria is Maria and you don't mess with her, not even Mom."

"Not to sound like a therapist, but how do you feel?"

"Sad I had to say it. Glad I did. Jayne reminded me it's possible to hold both feelings at once." She shrugged. "We'll see what changes. We can talk more after you freshen up, though. You're a mess."

I hold the bottle in my hand. "I'm going back to Vancouver," I say.

"Forever?" Ana's voice goes high.

"No, for a visit. I'll be back in a few days."

"Talking to your mom?" She sees my face. "And Rafe? I'm rooting for you."

"Thanks."

"Not looking forward to it?"

"It has to be done."

She nods. "You know, the thing about joy is there's always the moment when the fear comes. It happens the other way around too."

I must look unconvinced because she laughs.

"Eventually. So I'm told."

This time I tell Mom I'm coming to Vancouver and what flight I'm arriving on. I do it via text, however, and right before I get on the plane, so I don't applaud my courage too much. To my shock, I hear my name as I'm coming out of arrivals. It's Mom. She looks calm, but when I smile at her, I can see her chest rise as she takes a deep breath.

"Hello, Luling," she says. "Good flight? How is Ana?"

Thank God for Ana, who from the other side of the country can provide enough conversational fodder to get us to the car and about halfway home. Updates about Jayne take another few minutes, and then Mom says in a careful tone, "I was surprised when you said you were coming back."

Talking in the car is less stressful than at a table. It could be because we're facing the road instead of each other. "I want to talk to you," I say.

"Then we should wait until we're home," she says firmly. "So I can focus on the conversation and not the drive."

Damn, there goes that. "How's Dad?"

"On a work trip. He'll be sorry to have missed you."

It's quiet until we pull into the driveway and I take my suitcase into my old room, which smells fresh and clean. The bed is smooth and newly made, and I want to burrow inside instead of talking to Mom, who is making tea in the kitchen. I linger over washing my hands and undoing my suitcase, but then tell myself to stop being a wuss and to go out there and say the things I came to say.

In the kitchen, I put down the bottle of Aiai, this one "magicked up," as Ana would say. Mom looks at it but waits for me to talk.

"How's Eric?" I ask instead, catching sight of a photo of Sophie and Owen on the fridge.

"I don't know. He's not talking to me."

"Oh. I talked to Kelsey."

"Is she well?"

"She blamed me for her marriage ending."

Mom sighs. "You were right. I should have kept quiet. I should have been more welcoming to her."

"I'm not the one who has to hear that," I point out, although I'm surprised to hear Mom admit she was wrong. She's never wrong. About anything. Apart from sending me a bottle of perfume for my birthday with no actual scent, but I keep that to myself.

Mom doesn't say anything, but looks at the bottle. "What's this?"

"I made a perfume."

She gives me a questioning look and reaches for it when I nod. "This is good, Luling." She smells it again. "Very good. Extraordinary in its simplicity. I'm impressed. Did you come all this way for me to smell it?"

"No." I take the bottle back. It's cool in my hand. "I call it Aiai."

"I saw the label."

"It's for you."

Now her thin eyebrows rise high. She plucked them out when she was younger and they never grew back. She had them tattooed back on when I was eleven. "For me?"

"For Yixiang. It's a moli scent, and I'm certain of it."

Her hands jerk enough that she nearly drops the bottle. "What are you saying, Luling?"

"I'm saying you don't have to write my chapter for me anymore." I hand her the register and flip to the very last pages. *Hua Luling*, it reads, in both English and Chinese. Her eyes widen as she scans what I wrote about my discovery before I passed out in the store last night.

"Talk to me about this," she says when she puts the book down.

"I know why my moli wasn't working the way we expected. I'm not sure if it's only me or if this is true for all the fifth daughters, but my gift isn't to call true love at all."

She glances at the bottle. "You wrote that it calls your heart's desire? What does that mean?"

"It's what you want most in the world."

Mom taps the register with her finger. "You thought this after talking to Ms. Kang?"

I nod. "She came by the shop with her daughter. Then I looked up the three clients you gave the test samples to. I thought about Kelsey's gift bags, and all twenty of the recipients had some kind of new beginning or change in their lives afterward."

I pull back the register and point to Aiai's chapter, telling Mom my thoughts about the maid and love, and what I learned from the people she gave the testers to. She listens without interrupting until I finish.

"I had my moli all along," I say. "It wasn't what we expected, but it was there."

"I don't understand why other fifth daughters didn't have this problem."

"Maybe many of their clients did want true love. Or the old client families believed the fifth daughters could call love, so that would be what they went for. Or maybe I'm wrong and it's only me who's different. Or we have more options to dream about these days. I don't know. What I do know is that this is *my* moli. This is the purpose of my power."

I wait for her to question me, but she looks fascinated. I nod at the bottle in her hand.

"I know it's not what you expected. I'm not going to be the daughter you wanted, Mom, the one who works by your side day after day, or who rebuilds the family the way you wanted."

She shakes her head. "That's not true."

"Mom, come on." After the flight and the exhaustion of creating Aiai, plus, honestly, a shitload of emotional highs and lows, I don't have the patience for this. "You've made it clear my role is here at home, doing my part with Yixiang."

"No, and I'm sorry I made you think that. You don't need your moli to be a Hua. The reason I wanted you home was because I love you. I wanted to help you when you were hurting, and I didn't know how to do it from the other side of the country. How could I hold you when you were thousands of kilometers away? How could I calm you when you refused to pick up my calls? Support you when you closed off your life from me?"

She looks steadily at me, the years and griefs she's endured patterned on her face.

"I'm sorry I made you believe you needed your moli to be loved," she says. "You were always loved, Lucy."

The words hang in the air, and I pull out a chair and sit down heavily, not sure what to do. Mom said I didn't know what she wanted, and it seems she was right. I let my assumptions run my life. No, add another *i* into one of those words. I let my assumptions *ruin* my life.

I say, "I'm sorry I left instead of asking for help."

Mom swallows hard and looks at the bottle. "This is a moli scent?"

"A diluted one. It's only a breath of what it could be, but it's enough to have an effect. This Aiai can help you identify what you want rather than simply delivering your heart's desire. Like a direction sign, instead of teleporting you right there." I pass her the blurb I scrawled in a notepad on the plane.

Aiai, named after an adviser to the Tang Empress Wu. For those who wish to uncover the layers of their heart's desire.

"I see."

"No one will believe it because they'll think it's marketing. It's what I can give you so you can finally have what *you* want most."

Higher go the eyebrows. "What do I want most?"

"For the store to survive. Maybe not here, but in a new place. For the Hua name to mean something again. The money and the power. That's why you sold those three moli samples. You can have this. I'm giving it to you."

She looks at me, wry amusement twisting her features. "That's not why I sold the decants. The store is done, Lucy. I can't afford the rent. This is the last month of the lease."

"What?" I stare at her. "Then what happened to the money? Is it paying the mortgage?"

Her eyes drift to the corner of the room, and for the first time I see luggage piled up. "Mom? What's going on?"

"I meant to tell you in a different way, but your father and I are getting a divorce." She rushes over the word a bit.

I wait for the shock to subside and the hurt to take its place, but none does. "What happened?"

She turns to pour more tea. "I always hated being in this kitchen," she muses. "I hated cooking. Cleaning. All the work I was expected to do and did out of love. Then you and Eric left, and I was only doing it because I was supposed to."

"Did you realize that recently?"

"In a way. Missy had me over for dinner, and after, she and I went to the garden while Eddie cleaned up. He wasn't irritable or making it clear he was doing her a favor. He joined us, and when Missy spoke, he listened instead of speaking over her or telling her she was wrong no matter what she said. He forgot to make a medical appointment and didn't blame her for not reminding him."

"You've known them for years, though."

"True, but I had never noticed the way I did that night. Then I came home to a table full of dirty dishes to clear and wash. Your father greeted me with complaints about the money I spent on the store and told me the toilet roll was empty in his bathroom."

"He always does that."

"This time I thought of the rest of my life refilling another adult's toilet roll because they'd decided their time and energy were more important and better spent elsewhere." She gives me a faint smile. "You said in Toronto that I didn't have to be miserable."

My heart is pounding. "Mom, you smelled my perfume. The moli perfume. Is this my fault?"

"You know it doesn't work on us."

"But..." I'm still uncertain. "What if it's different for me?"

She comes to hug me, grabbing me tightly. "Never. Never think that for a moment. I made this choice, Luling. I don't know what my heart's desire is yet. I do know I'm free to find it."

With one arm around my shoulders as if she doesn't want to let me go, she reaches out the other to take the bottle. "This perfume you made, this Aiai," she says. "It will be legendary."

I laugh. "How do you know?"

"Because this has heart in it. I can smell it. This is what you're meant to do, whether here or back in Toronto."

"Well, it's yours."

"You don't need to do this," she says.

"I want the store to survive too."

She sighs and reaches into her bag, then slides a check over to me. It has a lot of zeros on it and is dated from two weeks ago. "What's this?" I ask.

"It's the money from the moli testers I sold." She gives me a faint smile. "As you know, the fifth daughter scents are by far the most lucrative, even if there's only a chance they'll work."

"Why are you giving it to me?" She sold them for Yixiang. Didn't she?

"Ana is lovely, but I wanted you to have the opportunity to get your own space if that was what you wanted. That's what I was asking Rafe about. I wanted to know if there was a good place for Ile de Grasse."

"Mom." I don't know what to say, but I do know I can't accept it. Another one of my assumptions has been utterly demolished. Nor was she using him to get me back home. "I'm happy where I am with Ana right now. I like having a friend to work with."

"I would like that too," she says. "Missy knows a fashion designer looking for space, if we can find a place to share."

I push the check back along the table. "Then take this and extend the lease on the Yixiang store. I want you to have it."

"It's your money."

I point to Aiai. "I'll make more."

She laughs, then reaches across the table and I put my hand on hers. "Thank you, Lucy." She wipes at her eyes and smiles at me.

"Perhaps I'll reach out to Kelsey and ask her to do the gift bags for the reopening."

We laugh, and then we sit there, drained, as the sun goes down.

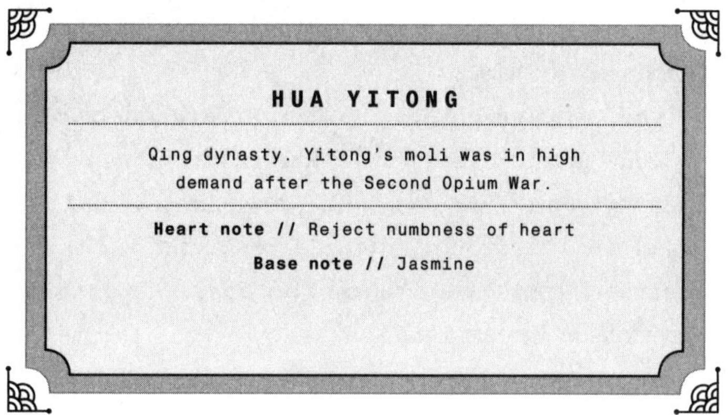

The next morning, high off my successful talk with my mother, I text Eric to tell him I'm in town and want to see him.

Eric: Did you know Mom and Dad are splitting up? Was
that you too?

I stare at the phone, already having second thoughts because Eric remains Eric. I keep going because it's the right thing to do, not because it will irritate him more if I'm being the better person. That's a bonus.

Me: She told me last night. I want to talk.
Eric: Whatever. Fine. Kelsey is only letting me stay in the
guest room for the sake of the kids, so you can't make
things any worse.

I'm a little nervous by the time I arrive, but when Kelsey opens the door, the smell of cookies drifts out. "The kids wanted to bake you something," she says by way of greeting.

I hold out two gift bags. "These are for them."

Kelsey's expression becomes slightly less cold. "Thank you," she says.

I follow her in and greet the kids. Not with hugs—I'm still me—but they seem content to look up from their devices long enough to wave hi, then rip into the bags.

"I love it," says Sophie, holding up a hat from Ana's side of the shop. Owen seems equally pleased with his wacky socks.

"Nothing for me?" Eric asks, coming down the hall.

I hand over a bag of his favorite childhood gummy worms, which he takes with surprise. "Oh. Thanks." Then he grins despite himself. "I'll have to hide these from the kids."

Kelsey gets one of the Pulse Points earring sets, and she looks taken aback. "These are gorgeous," she says, examining the small filigree silver cubes on threaders. Given our history, I felt it prudent to take out the scent disks.

The kids are already back to their screens. "Can we go somewhere to talk?" I ask.

The two of them seem to have put aside their animosity to unite against me, because they share a look before Kelsey leads the way to the kitchen. The buzzer goes as we step in. She pulls out a delicious-smelling tray of oatmeal cookies and swats Eric's hands away. "You know they're too hot," she says.

Leaving the cookies on the range to cool, she pours coffee and waits until Eric goes to the fridge to get the milk. "Well, what do you want?" he asks as he comes back to the table and pours some in her cup.

"To talk about us. The family."

"What's the point, Lucy?" He looks tired. "We know you're Mom's favorite. Did you come to rub it in and remind me I'll never be as good as you?"

"That's for you and Mom to figure out," I say. "There's enough I can reasonably take blame for, and I'm not taking on extra."

"She's right," Kelsey says. "This is Meilin's fault."

"She was in the wrong to keep you at a distance," I say. "That's for you to figure out as well."

"Then why are you here?" Eric asks. "If everything is up to Mom to fix."

I pull out a bottle of Aiai. "I made a perfume."

The two of them eye it like a bomb. "Thanks, but no thanks," says Kelsey. "I'm done being your guinea pig."

"Hear me out, okay?"

Again, that exchange of glances, and I wonder if distrusting me is what will heal their marriage. Nice to know I'm bringing good into the world. Not all heroes wear capes. "Five minutes," Kelsey says. "Don't think of opening that thing up, though."

"It's new. It's a moli scent," I say. "Diluted, so it won't cause the kind of havoc it did before. I'm truly sorry about that, Kelsey."

"I probably shouldn't have nagged you into it in the first place," she says grudgingly, and I know that's as good as it's going to get. For the sake of family harmony, I'll take it.

Eric rolls the bottle in his hand. "Aiai. That's the first Hua woman."

"Yes, the one who worked for Empress Wu."

"Okay, Lucy." He puts it down on the table and crosses his arms. "Get to the point. I have to take Owen to soccer soon."

"It's a moli scent, but not strong. It will help you discover your heart's desire, but it won't deposit it in your lap like it would at full strength. You still have to work for it, but at least you'll know what it is instead of only assuming you know what you want and going down a false path."

Kelsey looks skeptical, but Eric frowns. "The fifth daughter's power is true love."

"I don't think it is," I say. "It's just that in the past, some women couldn't see a way to get their heart's desires except through men, and they were dissuaded from thinking they wanted anything besides children and marriage."

On my sister-in-law's face is a dawning understanding, but Eric shakes his head. "That's bullshit," he says. "Women weren't the only people who bought those perfumes."

"No," I agree. "The same goes for men. They want love, too, and they want children and marriage."

He looks frustrated. "You just said no one wanted true love."

"She's not saying that love was never someone's greatest desire," Kelsey says. "It probably was, for a lot of people. I bet a lot of the men who could afford those perfumes were men who had other opportunities to get what they wanted in life. Love was the last thing they had left to acquire."

"Why are you giving this to us?" asks Eric.

"In case you wanted some help in getting your dreams," I say. "Not a lot. It's more like starting you on the path than anything else." I don't want to oversell the impact. "I can make you a full-strength one as well."

He and Kelsey stare at the little bottle standing on the counter. Eric frowns. "Did Mom smell this before she decided to leave Dad?"

"No. You know why she's leaving." Eric lived the same childhood as I did.

He's quiet for a second. "Yeah. It's just..." His voice trails off and Kelsey hesitates, then touches his hand.

"Hard." I finish his sentence. We might be adults, but a fracture like this is destabilizing at any age.

"I know it's for the best," he says.

"They should have done it years ago." We look across the counter at each other. Is he wondering the same thing as me? Whether our relationship would be different if theirs had been?

In the front room, Sophie and Owen are playing a game together with excited yells, the same way we used to when we were kids. My brother and Kelsey look over to the noise, and I look at them. There are heavy bags under Kelsey's eyes and her face is bloated and pale, while Eric's sparse stubble doesn't cover the jowls that are coming with age and good eating. His hair reveals a new bald spot on his crown. What do they want? How many of us can even recognize what we desire most?

Kelsey takes the bottle from Eric, then glances up as hysterical laughter comes from the other room. "Not for me," she says firmly. "I know what I want."

Her words break through Eric's reverie. "I agree," he says.

The two of them look at each other tentatively as the game ends and the kids burst into the kitchen, oblivious to the relaxing tension between their parents. "Are the cookies ready yet?" asks Sophie, hauling herself onto the stool next to me.

"They are," Eric says. He puts them on a plate as Sophie and Owen tell me about why they decided on chocolate chips instead of raisins or, worse, cranberries. I rise in their esteem when I agree it was the correct choice, unlike the other adults in the house, who were apparently Team Raisin. Out of the corner of my eye, I see Eric hesitantly take Kelsey's hand, and although she freezes, she doesn't shake him off. This seems like a good start.

I put away the perfume before the kids can get hold of it and bring my attention back to my family.

When I get home, Mom is surprised Eric and Kelsey didn't take the Aiai I offered them, and sighs. "I miss the children," she says.

"You know what you need to do."

"I do."

I leave it at that, knowing it will take her time to apologize to Kelsey.

They might never be close—I know I'll never see Kelsey as a friend—but perhaps they can find their way to a respectful relationship.

I pull out my phone, wondering if I should visit Rafe as the next stop on my British Columbia apology tour, when Mom casually mentions that he and Eddie Jin are in Ottawa. "Missy is looking forward to this expansion," she says. "It's been good to talk to her about the new direction for Yixiang as well."

I take the plate of pineapple she gives me. "I always thought she was your competition."

Mom laughs. "Nothing wrong with a little competition to keep you on your toes." She checks the mirror complacently. "Plus, Missy's had work done. I'm winning there. Look at this bone structure."

"Mom!"

"I'm kidding, Lucy." She brushes my hair with her hand. "You have no humor. Missy loved that joke. Then she asked me if I needed a ride in her new car."

"So it was a draw?"

"Of course not. I won that round." She takes some of the pineapple, then breathes it in. "I think I'll make a scent with fruit for winter."

"That would be good."

We spend the rest of the night working on the pineapple scent, and it's perfect. I don't think about Rafe at all.

Except once, when I slide out of bed and find the vial of the tobacco and bergamot scent I brought for him as an apology.

I'll put it in the mail tomorrow.

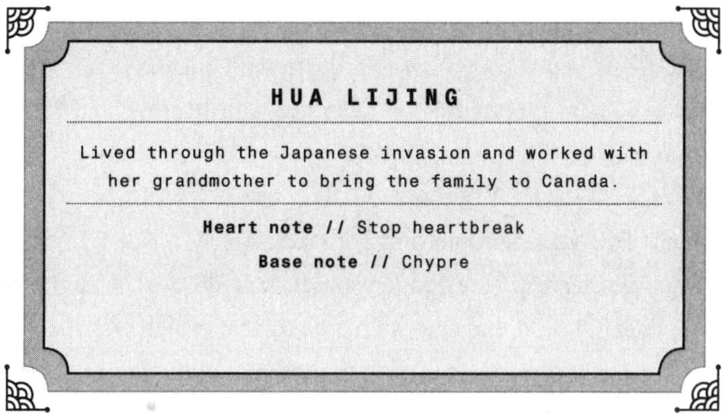

This time when I get home, I'm not surprised to see Ana sitting out front of my apartment building in the fading evening sun, waiting for me.

"I brought snacks," she says.

I grin at her and hold up a bag from the corner store. "I bought ice cream."

We go up, chatting about nothing in particular, just enjoying the conversation. In the kitchen, Ana uncovers a monster of a cookie.

"I made one for my mother too," she says. "She said it was better than she could make."

"Really?"

"I nearly passed out. Maria had to pinch me, and she told Fernanda to shut up when Ferd said it would be better with nuts, like how she makes cookies."

"Nuts are gross."

"That's what I said, and then she sulked until Mom told her to grow up." Ana beams. "It was a great moment in my life. Tell me about your trip. All fixed?"

Since we kept in touch while I was gone, there isn't much to update her on. I relay the latest discussion with my mother and then sit back.

She looks at me expectantly. "And?"

"And what? I don't know how it's going to work out, but I think it will."

Ana looks exasperated. "You talked to your brother and Kelsey. Your mom."

"I did."

"Aren't you missing something? Someone."

"Dad was on a trip." I texted him and he said although he and Mom were splitting, I would always be his daughter. Which was nice, but a little concerning since I hadn't thought that would change. I sent it to Eric, and he replied with a screenshot of Dad's text to him, which replaced son for daughter, and we exchanged a series of laughing emojis.

"That's too bad, but not who I meant."

"I know what you're going to say. I didn't talk to Rafe."

"Why not?"

"You know why. He was away."

She goes to my cupboard to take out the dulce de leche. "Did you text him?"

"No."

"So you didn't talk. After being childhood friends, having a misunderstanding, deciding you wanted to work through it, accusing him of being your mom's pawn to get you home—which is weird, by the way—you did nothing. You are the queen of self-sabotage."

I grew up knowing emotions could be influenced, and the last decade of being on my own shows that if there's an attachment style past avoidant, that's probably where I sit. Escapist? Disappearing? I crumble the suddenly tasteless cookie in my fingers. "I sent him some perfume."

"So he thinks you're trying to enchant him."

"No!" I sit bolt upright, horrified. "Do you think he will?"

"What did the note say?"

"I didn't add one."

She stares at me and shakes her head.

I groan. "I screwed up, okay? There was so much history, and I don't think I was in the right headspace."

"Clearly not."

"I wanted him to know I was sorry."

"Still could have put that on a note."

"I want to say it in person."

"I just had a thought." Ana licks her spoon thoughtfully. "Have you dated much in general?"

I shake my head.

"You could broaden your horizons," she says. "You've been fixated on this guy for years. You might benefit from seeing the rest of the dating pool." She looks suddenly grim. "Or not, actually. It's a pool with a lot of sharks."

It's an idea. "But I miss Rafe."

"Do you miss him or just want to be with someone?"

"Him?" I hadn't thought about it like that.

"I know a cool guy," she says hesitantly. "If you want to try? He's Jayne's cousin, so it's close enough that you have some external validation he's not horrible, but it's not so close you have to see him all the time if it's a bust."

"What's he like?"

"Cute. Funny. Has a cat he got from me, a job he likes, and he talks to his exes but not in a creepy way."

"Why's he single?" I drop some caramel on my shirt and smear it away. No big deal.

"I dunno, he didn't smell your desire perfume? Why is anyone these days?"

It almost kills me to say yes, but she's right. How do I really know what I felt for Rafe? What if it was only the weight of memory and nostalgia that linked us?

"Okay," I say.

"Nothing like enthusiasm!" She nudges me. "You don't have to, you know."

"I want to try."

She looks at me carefully. "It's only coffee or a drink," she reminds me. "You can end it anytime. You might realize you would work as friends. What ruins these things is the fantasy of a potential future and what a person could be in your life, rather than experiencing it for what it is in the moment."

"Poetic."

"I got it from Jayne. She's seen a lot of dates at the bar."

"Does she have any other advice?"

Ana nods. "Say no to something at least once to see how they respond. If they keep pressuring you to change your mind, nope on out."

"Jayne should write a dating-advice book." I think for a beat and then brighten up. "Or an advice column! She'd be great."

Ana sighs. "Yeah. She would be. She's so smart."

We finish up the cookie, and I wrap up a huge chunk of the leftovers to give to my new friend down the hall as a neighborly gesture. I've only emptied half of my suitcase when a text comes from Ana. It's a phone number.

Ana: His name is Matt and he's waiting for you to text him.
   When you want. If you want.

I stare at the number as another message comes through.

Ana: No pressure, honest.

Me: Thanks.

I toss the phone onto my bed and keep unpacking, thinking back to all the pivotal moments in my life when I acted to make things worse instead of better. Because at a certain point, I could absolve myself of any responsibility to fix it. Things would simply be unfixable.

Is Rafe unfixable? Am I self-sabotaging right now by agreeing to go on a date with this guy?

The question haunts me as I go to sleep, wishing, yet again, that my own moli worked on me.

The next day, I talk myself out of texting Matt until the evening. I don't want to look too eager, after all, or disturb him at work. It makes sense to hold off for a bit. Plus, I need to decide what to say.

The day goes by quickly enough. The Pulse Points have become bestsellers and have started making more influencer and blog lists, so I fix up the front window to prominently display our new jewelry. "Here," says Ana, handing me a vase. "Tie one of the necklaces around the neck of this. It'll look cool."

It's pure white with little knobs, and a chip out of the base makes me shudder. I twist it around and put it—with the necklace—in the window. Ana likes it, so I let it be.

"What do you think about having your mom sell Pulse Points in Vancouver?" Ana asks during a lull. "Broaden our market."

"I'll ask her." I talked to her earlier, and she was full of plans after a conversation with Missy's fashion designer friend, who sounded like a perfect match for my mother's style. She sent me his lookbook, and Ana and I gasped at his designs: gorgeously constructed modern interpretations of old Shanghai. They've decided to give up the Burrard store and open up in a hipper part of town. Mom's already hired someone to put a vault for the Hua perfume collection in the house, which she's going to keep after apparently much negotiation with Dad.

"Do it now." She looks back out the window. "Oh, Priscilla and Elvis are holding hands and looking at your garden. That's sweet."

Elvis bends down to pluck a sprig of lavender, which he tucks behind Priscilla's ear. It's surprisingly chaste for the two of them, and she looks thrilled.

"Good for them," approves Ana.

The message comes back from Mom, and I turn to Ana. "She's happy to be a distributor," I say. "She also has some ideas about what would work well in the market there. We could do limited editions."

"Love it." She looks over fondly at the table display. "Have you thought about contacting Matt?"

"I'm going to do it after work today."

"Whenever you want," she says softly. "It's totally up to you. You might want to…"

Her voice trails off as she glances out the window. "Oh, that is a *man*. You should forget Matt and go for that guy."

"What?" I turn around, then stop, because at the door stands a gorgeous man dressed in a black T-shirt and jeans. "Rafe?"

We all stand there for a moment, and then Ana clears her throat. "Uh, welcome."

"Oh. Ana, this is Rafe. Rafe, Ana."

"Hi? Nice to meet you." She gives me a look.

He nods to show he heard her. I haven't moved because I know there's no way I want to text Matt or any other man. Rafe has always been mine.

Ana waits but senses I don't know what to do. "Why don't you show Rafe the garden?" she finally suggests, like a chaperone looking for an acceptable activity. "Or go for a walk?"

"Ah, excuse me?" a woman's voice comes from behind Rafe. "Are you going in?"

That breaks the spell, and he mumbles an excuse as he steps aside, eyes not leaving me. Two women come in and head straight for the Pulse Points display. Ana gives me a little shove, and I know I can't avoid this talk anymore.

I don't want to. Avoidance hasn't worked out so well for me after all. As I approach him, the smell of tobacco and bergamot draws me in. "It came in the mail," he says.

He follows me out to the garden, where Jayne has added a little bench that's become a beacon for social media influencers. Ana and I don't mind, although it would be great if more of them bought something from us instead of using it to document hauls from other shops. On this cool afternoon, it's only Rafe and me.

"My mother said you were in Vancouver," he says.

"I was." We sit down and I don't wait. "I'm sorry," I say. "Our fight was my fault. I was angry, and I took it out on you. I was a complete asshole. I got a whole lot of things in my head, and everything rolled into this tsunami of wrongness. I was wrong about everything."

"Do you still think I had some nefarious deal with your mother?"

I do my best not to cringe. "I do not—although to be clear, I thought she was using you and you had no idea."

"Lucy. That's not much better."

"I know, and I am sorry that I completely, totally got in my own head and severely overreacted. It was not my best moment."

He leans forward and breaks off some rosemary. The herbaceous smell rises from where he rolls the slender green leaves in his hands. "I wasn't at my best either," he said. "You were hurting, and I added to it instead of listening. I apologize too."

We sit in silence. "Good talk," I say to try to break the tension.

Rafe's lips quirk up in a little smile. "I've been thinking about how we never decided the path we wanted to pursue. You and I, friends or more."

"Okay." Here it comes again, the sting of rejection that seems to be the calling card of any talk with Rafe.

"I should have said what I wanted at the beginning," he said. "To me, we were never only friends. I was in love with you long before you were doing your magical perfumes. From that first day we went to the beach, it's been all you and me, but I didn't understand."

I take some lavender for myself. "Can you tell me what you're saying, exactly? What do you want from me?"

"We're making the same mistake we did before," he says.

"How so?" I add some tarragon to the mix, the licorice scent mixing with the floral of the lavender. A group of women walk by, laughing at the shirt one of them has bought, which is covered with cowgirls wearing bikini tops.

"We weren't honest with each other from the beginning, and that's why neither of us fully trusted the other. We said we were friends, best friends." He clenches his hands. "The thing is, I always wanted more."

"Always?"

"Yes." He releases the rosemary and runs his hands over his thighs. "I was worried you were going to find a boyfriend. Do you remember Logan?"

I think back. "Logan?"

"Logan."

"Logan," I repeat. "Yes, from our grade 11 math class. With the hair." Logan had long bangs styled in his face that, in retrospect, made him look like a gale-force wind was blowing at him from behind.

"With the hair." Rafe's mouth twists. "One day after class, I saw the two of you talking. That's when I knew for certain I was in love."

"You were jealous?" I ask, a deep sense of pleasure unfurling that he had been thinking about me as his. The way I'd always considered him mine.

"I wasn't jealous you were talking to him." He shakes his head. "I think it was dread, that if you got a boyfriend, you'd be gone from my life. I didn't know what I'd do without you. Then I didn't have a choice. You were gone and it was worse than I feared. You left me and I felt empty."

It's time for the question that's haunted me. "Did you want me to kiss you? That time in the garden?"

He nods. "It was literally one of the best moments of my life, before I fucked it up. Lucy, here's the truth. I want to date you. I want the relationship we might have had if we hadn't blown it when we were young."

"What if there's no way to get around our history?"

"I don't believe that." His confidence takes me aback.

"What do you mean, you don't believe it?"

He waves his wrist so I can smell the perfume. "This could be the most moli perfume you ever create, and it wouldn't matter. It would have no effect on me, because I already found my true love."

I melt to hear him say it, but... "It's not true love. That's not what my moli brings."

"Sorry. What?"

"It's your deepest desire. Your heart's desire." I explain my discovery.

Rafe's eyebrows are high. "So you're telling me true love...doesn't... exist?"

"It still exists," I assure him. Then I frown. "Doesn't it? I mean, if you want love as your heart's desire, doesn't that still make it true love?"

He laughs. "For the sake of argument, let's say yes so it doesn't blow my big romantic speech." Rafe reaches across but doesn't touch me. Instead, he waits.

I'm the one to take his hand. My heart beats so hard I can barely make out my own thoughts.

"I want to try again, with you, the way we were meant to be," he says. "I love you, Luling. I always have. No matter what happens after this conversation, I probably always will. The thing is, you leave when things get hard, and I can't deal with that. Not anymore. Not when I want you in my life forever."

I don't answer him with words. Instead, I lean in. When my lips touch his, it feels right. More right than anything I've ever felt. I shut my eyes and let that feeling take me over.

When we finally break apart, Rafe gives me a smile so shy it makes me laugh, given his usual confidence. "I want you in my life as well," I say. "You said you talked to someone, and therapy seems like a good plan for me as well."

Rafe looks at me, and I have to admit, I'm impressed with my emotional maturity and openness. Ana is good for me. "Are you going to get a dog as well?" he teases.

"Since I'm in Toronto, it might be a cat. Cats and therapy seem to be de rigueur here."

Rafe laughs and leans in to kiss me again.

"Worth waiting thirteen years?" I ask.

"Worth waiting fifty years," he says. "Swear on Stevie. As long as you stop running."

"I don't have anything to run from now," I say. "Not if you're with me."

He looks at me searchingly and I tell him again, and again, until his eyes soften and I can tell he believes me. Then Rafe leans in, wrapping me up in the scent that's always been his, and I finally get my heart's desire.

And I didn't even have to pay fifth-daughter prices.

DAUGHTERS OF THE HOUSE OF HUA

DYNASTY	NAME	MOLI
Tang dynasty (618–907 CE)	**Aiai**	**Call true love**
Tang dynasty (618–907 CE)	Mingyue	Reduce timidity
Tang dynasty (618–907 CE)	Baochai	Increase niceness
Tang dynasty (618–907 CE)	Caihong	Increase daring
Tang dynasty (618–907 CE)	Dachung	Heighten charm
Tang dynasty (618–907 CE)	**Fangsu**	**Call true love**
Tang dynasty (618–907 CE)	Chaoxing	Reduce annoyance
Tang dynasty (618–907 CE)	Miaoling	Stop nervousness
Tang dynasty (618–907 CE)	Huiying	Improve tranquility
Tang dynasty (618–907 CE)	Haifen	Cause debilitating fear
Tang dynasty (618–907 CE)	**Lanying**	**Call true love**
Five Dynasties (907–979 CE)	Liwei	Lessen grief

DYNASTY	NAME	MOLI
Five Dynasties (907–979 CE)	Ruoxuan	Strengthen confidence
Five Dynasties (907–979 CE)	Lihua	Increase loving feelings
Northern Song dynasty (960–1127)	Peizhi	Increase trust
Northern Song dynasty (960–1127)	**Xiaodan**	**Call true love**
Northern Song dynasty (960–1127)	Qingyang	Higher tolerance for daily irritations
Northern Song dynasty (960–1127)	Meixing	Induce caution
Northern Song dynasty (960–1127)	Yuming	Boost wonder
Northern Song dynasty (960–1127)	Yanya	Crave freedom
Northern Song dynasty (960–1127)	**Suyin**	**Call true love**
Southern Song dynasty (1127–1279)	Siyu	Halt embarrassment
Southern Song dynasty (1127–1279)	Pixin	Ghost dampener
Southern Song dynasty (1127–1279)	Feili	Reduce surprise
Southern Song dynasty (1127–1279)	Zhilan	Lessen disappointment
Southern Song dynasty (1127–1279)	Liqiu	Lift gloominess
Southern Song dynasty (1127–1279)	**Mingxia**	**Call true love**
Yuan dynasty, early (1279–1368)	Yanlin	Intensify gratitude

DYNASTY	NAME	MOLI
Yuan dynasty (1279–1368)	Jing	Block insecurity
Yuan dynasty (1279–1368)	Hao	Increase affection
Yuan dynasty (1279–1368)	An	Reinforce bravery
Ming dynasty, early (1368–1644)	Xiaoting	Call true love
Ming dynasty (1368–1644)	Guilan	Suppress jealousy
Ming dynasty (1368–1644)	Yingling	Increase eagerness
Ming dynasty (1368–1644)	Changchang	Boost hope
Ming dynasty (1368–1644)	Dongmei	Diminish yearning
Ming dynasty (1368–1644)	Qiaohui	Call true love
Ming dynasty (1368–1644)	Shihong	End weepiness
Ming dynasty (1368–1644)	Ninghong	Reduce frustration
Ming dynasty (1368–1644)	Chuhua	Cause quietness of soul
Ming dynasty (1368–1644)	Guoli	Lift enthusiasm
Ming dynasty (1368–1644)	Mingzhu	Call true love
Qing dynasty (result of Manchu conquering Ming empire) (1644–1911)	Liling	Boost eloquence
Qing dynasty (1644–1911)	Jiali	Dissolve anger in others
Qing dynasty (1644–1911)	Yuanyang	Limit shame

DYNASTY	NAME	MOLI
Qing dynasty (1644–1911)	Jingjing	Enhance generosity in others
Qing dynasty (1644–1911)	**Xinyue**	**Call true love**
Qing dynasty (1644–1911)	Kexin	Increase respect from others
Qing dynasty (1644–1911)	Tingwen	Increases attractiveness to others
Qing dynasty (1644–1911)	Miaoyu	Stir sadness in others
Qing dynasty (1644–1911)	Yitong	Reject numbness of heart
Qing dynasty (1644–1911)	**Zhengyi**	**Call true love**
Republic of China (1912–1949) to Vancouver	Meihui	Boost confidence
Republic of China (1912–1949) to Vancouver	Lijing	Stop heartbreak
Republic of China (1912–1949) to Vancouver	Yulan	Keep bad tempers in check
1960s–present Vancouver	Meilin	Lift moods
1960s–present Vancouver	**Luling**	**Call true love**

THE LANGUAGE OF PERFUME

A

ABSOLUTE: A highly concentrated form of a fragrance extracted from plants or flowers.

ACCORD: A combination of notes blended together to create a new, distinct fragrance. Often used to create scents that can't be distilled from nature, such as amber.

B

BASE NOTE: If pictured as a pyramid, base notes are at the bottom. They are heavy, so they will be the notes that linger the longest on the wearer.

BLOTTERS: Another term for test strips, scent strips (or if one is fancy, mouillettes). Thin strips of paper used as an alternative to skin to test a fragrance.

D

DECANT: Moving perfume from a larger to a smaller container.

DILUTION: Mixing concentrated ingredients with a solvent such as alcohol to change the intensity of the scent.

DUPE: A perfume "clone," created as a more affordable alternative to an expensive fragrance.

F

FLANKER: A variation of a perfume (like a spin-off) that will often use similar packaging or notes, and builds on the branding of the original.

FORMULA: The "recipe" of a fragrance, laying out how much of each ingredient is in the scent.

FRAGRANCE FAMILY: A category of scents that share common elements or characteristics.

G

GOURMAND: Fragrance category featuring sweet and delicious edible scents such as vanilla, caramel, and chocolate.

H

HEART NOTE: Middle notes of the fragrance that linger after the top notes evaporate and transition into the longer-lasting base notes. These shape the core of the fragrance.

I

INDOLE: Chemical compound found in redolent white flowers such as jasmine, with an animalic quality.

J

JUICE: The liquid in the perfume bottle.

M

MARINE: Often created with synthetics, they evoke fresh scents such as sea breezes and the ocean.

MOD, MODIFICATION: Trial versions of a fragrance that a perfumer tests and compares as they try to achieve their vision.

N

NOSE: The perfumer, an expert who uses their nose to compose olfactory art.

NOTE: A single individual scent in a fragrance.

O

OLFACTORY FATIGUE: Sometimes called nose blindness, when the sense of smell becomes temporarily insensitive to certain odors.

OVERDOSE: Use of a material in a higher-than-expected amount in a fragrance.

P

PERFUMER'S ORGAN: A perfumer's workspace; traditionally this was a semicircular desk with bottles of ingredients arranged for easy access so the perfumers could compose the notes of the fragrance.

PIPETTES: A hollow tube used to measure and dispense small amounts of liquid.

S

SACHET: A small bag that contains fragrant ingredients.

SILLAGE: The trail of scent that remains after the wearer passes by; from the French for "wake."

SYNTHETICS: Ingredients developed in the lab to replicate or create scents, rather than extracted from natural materials.

T

TOP NOTE: First notes smelled in a fragrance. Tend to be lighter molecules, and because they evaporate more quickly, they will disappear first to reveal the heart notes. The pointed top of the pyramid.

V

VOLATILITY: The speed at which molecules evaporate after application. Lighter molecules are more volatile.

READING GROUP GUIDE

1. When the family register arrives, it's a weight on Lucy. When do family mementos or traditions become more of a curse than a gift?

2. Why did Meilin agree with Lucy's waipo that it was Lucy's responsibility to take care of the register instead of taking it back (as per the family tradition)? Why did Waipo send Lucy the register in the first place?

3. Lucy is shattered when she believes she can't access her moli. Do you think her relationship with Rafe might been mended earlier if that had not been the case?

4. Lucy's father says the Huas are "an average family dying to make themselves feel important and preying on the hopes of others." What are the kinds of stories families tell about themselves, and why?

5. Ana says, "What I need is a magical potion to make her fall in love with me so I wouldn't have any doubt. I'd give

anything for that." Would you take such a potion if you had the opportunity?

6. Do you wear perfume? Do you have a signature scent?

7. When smelling her mother's creations, Lucy is stunned at the realization of how good a perfumer her mother is. Have you had a moment where you've seen a friend or family member in a new light?

8. Eric says, "What do you think it's like, not knowing if your own wife is using it to control you? Your own daughter?" Is this a reasonable concern for men related to Hua women? What does it say about the foundations of those relationships?

9. Lucy's mother says, "We are disadvantaged in a world that wasn't made for our safety. Look around and show me a powerful woman who doesn't have a sea of people trying to drag her down. Show me any woman who doesn't have that." Is Meilin overly suspicious or realistic? What might have shaped her perspective?

10. What do Aiai, Xiaoting, and Zhengyi, the women featured in the historical chapters, have in common?

11. Does the register force the Hua women to live in the past, or does it prepare them for the future?

12. Meilin taught Luling to connect smells to memories. What smells do you have a strong association with?

13. Lucy journeys from loneliness to community. Why do you think it took her so long to be able to reach out?

14. Does Kelsey have a point? Do you think the Huas' use of their moli is moral?

15. Do you have a written family history? Would you consider starting one?

A CONVERSATION WITH THE AUTHOR

What was your fragrance journey?

I've worn perfume for most of my life, simply because I like good—or at least interesting—smells. It could also be because my mother wore perfume and burned incense constantly. I simply assumed fragrance was something one just did.

The first perfume I bought for myself was Colors by Benetton. In my memory, it smells like watermelon, and I'm fairly sure a whiff of it today would instantly transport me back to the days of bad perms and popped collars. My mother, on the other hand, was a sandalwood diehard for years, which eventually became my own scent and the one I reach for more often than not. I think by this point I must have tried at least a dozen to find the perfect sandalwood. In general, I tend to like heavier scents rather than light ones. A good sillage is key.

You're normally a romance writer. What made you want to write this story?

I love writing romance, but I also wanted to explore a character's relationship with her family and her past more intensely. With romance, the central relationship and the story is between the love interests. *The Library of Flowers* gave me more scope to write about Lucy's journey. I also finally got to put my Chinese history degree to work.

Do you see yourself or any of your relationships in Lucy and her experiences?

I think all my characters have an element of me in them. I remember periods of my life when I was very lonely, and I wanted to incorporate those moments and the relief of finding someone you could rely on. However, I need to stress that Lucy's relationship with her mother is much more fraught than mine. Love you, Mom!

What resources did you use to research *The Library of Flowers*?

This book required a ton of research for the historical chapters, as well as for the perfumery. I've included some of the perfume resources here.

Chandler Burr, *The Perfect Scent: A Year Inside the Perfume Industry in Paris and New York*

Luca Turin, *The Secret of Scent: Adventures in Perfume and the Science of Smell*

Luca Turin and Tania Sanchez: *Perfumes: The A–Z Guide*

Jean-Claude Ellena: *Perfume: The Alchemy of Scent*

The Institute for Art and Olfaction: artandolfaction.com

Bois de Jasmin: boisdejasmin.com

Smell Ya Later podcast: smellyalater.live/about

Fragrantica: fragrantica.com

ONE

Valerie Peng needed it to be a good day.

A few things were trending in her favor. The June sun hung bright in the turquoise sky, and the lack of humidity meant her hair looked fantastic and would stay that way. The never-ending Toronto road construction outside of her apartment had slowed. Her breakfast banana, so often a hit-or-miss fruit, had been at the perfect ripeness, that sweet spot between mushy or so green it made her teeth chalky.

It was *going* to be a good day, she decided as she locked the door. It *was*.

She was halfway down the street when the phone rang with a call from a potential client. "I'm still not sure about this celebration-of-life thing," Mike said.

Valerie ducked into an alley to focus on the discussion. "Let's talk about your concerns." She hoped he didn't hear the horns blaring in the background.

"Well, the main one is Mom's not here to appreciate it."

This was a common reaction. Ad Astra was the only company in the city to focus on planning memorials and celebrations of life, and people were often unsure about what Valerie could do, or even what they wanted.

"I find it helpful to remember that while the celebration is to honor your mother, the true value is for her friends and family," Valerie said. "It's a way to gather and share stories and memories after you've had some time to process."

"The funeral was so depressing," he said morosely. "I can't deal with that again. Mom loved light, you know? She took down the curtains in her room so she could see the dawn."

Valerie considered this. "We could have her celebration in the morning. I know a gorgeous garden with a gazebo."

"We could?" His voice became more hopeful.

"Absolutely," she assured him. "There are no rules for a celebration of life. I did one at night in an observatory for an amateur astronomer."

"Mom always wanted flowers in the house but the cats ate them, so she was stuck with fake ones." Mike laughed. "Yeah. A garden. I'd like to have something truer to how she was, not all solemn and serious."

Valerie confirmed a few details before leaving the alley with a bounce in her step, pleased that she'd come up with something for Mike. She'd worked hard to get Ad Astra on the road to success, although her old wedding planner boss, Ruth, had wrinkled her impeccable nose when Valerie told her why she was leaving.

"Isn't that morbid?" Ruth considered death a disreputable act and not to be discussed at full voice or in groups of more than three.

"It's uplifting." Valerie didn't often disagree with her boss—she hated contradicting anyone, let alone the person who signed her paychecks—but this was important. "People who are grieving deserve the same consideration and attention as those experiencing joy."

"Very altruistic of you, although I'd argue weddings are hardly a time of unmitigated bliss." Ruth swung her low ponytail over her shoulder. Multiple brides, and some grooms, had seen that sleek blond tail, wrapped in a silk bow that matched Ruth's outfits, and insisted on the same look for their special days. "You certainly won't have competition from me."

Yet Ruth had been good about mentioning Ad Astra when she heard someone had, as she delicately put it, passed. Over the last two years, it had become more acceptable to hire Valerie to plan a memorial or to book her in advance of one's own death in an attempt to maintain control over life's most uncontrollable situation. Business was growing slowly, but definitely steadily.

And it might explode if today went as well as she hoped. Three weeks ago, Roger Badgerton hired Ad Astra to plan his father's celebration of life. This could change everything for Valerie. Not to be crass, but Malcolm Badgerton had been a pillar among a certain set of wealthy Torontonians, and the event would be packed with people whose last names were prominently emblazoned on hospital wings, university faculties, and art gallery learning centers. When she helped the Badgertons remember their father in the way he deserved, the city's movers and shakers would see what Valerie Peng could do—and why they should hire her themselves.

That's why the day had to be good, and *would* be. She squared her shoulders and strode into the venue, ready to wow the Badgertons. Respectfully, of course.

"Ricky," she called as she pulled the door shut. "Your favorite event planner has arrived."

"So she has, bright and early." The manager came out from the back, a tiny espresso in hand. He turned on the music and Mariah filled the room. "You ready to work?"

"Let's do it." They had five hours until the event began, but she wanted to make sure everything was in apple-pie order.

An hour later, they were debating whether the welcome table should be moved to the left of the door when a loud squeal came from the entry. "Valerie, did you dress like the catering staff on purpose?"

Valerie turned to see her assistant, Alexis, late but holding her usual caramel ice coffee.

"The caterers wear aprons," Valerie said, looking down at her black pants and white shirt and trying to make it into a joke. "I brought my gray suit for later."

"Right, the one you wear all the time." Alexis sipped her coffee. "Don't you think it's a bit dowdy?"

"No?" She'd always considered it professionally chic.

"Really? I thought you'd want to represent your brand a bit better." Alexis rolled her eyes at whatever expression had appeared on Valerie's face. "Don't be like that. You know me—I'm brutally honest, but you do you."

Valerie wasn't sure if, like many of Alexis's comments, this was genuine advice, a veiled insult, or a murky combination of the two, but it was better for their working relationship to assume the first. They'd known each other for more than a decade through their mutual friend group, and when Alexis had lost her job as an office manager, everyone assumed the assistant role Valerie had just posted would be hers. Backed into a corner since she didn't want to rock the boat or feel responsible for Alexis not being able to pay her rent, Valerie had agreed.

Alexis herself had been more than confident she could handle the work. "I did my wedding all by myself, and the planner was only there for emergencies or when I was too busy," she'd said. "Memorials can't be harder than that."

Two months later, Valerie was kicking herself for saying yes. She watched Alexis lift a pile of tablecloths off a chair and drop them to the floor so she could sit and decided it was time for a talk. Not an official reprimand between a boss and employee, which would make Alexis more defensive than usual, but a chat between friends about expectations. That was reasonable. She'd do it tomorrow.

"Did you get your hair done?" Alexis asked. "It's too red."

It was, and when the stylist had asked, Valerie had lied and said she loved it before forking over a hundred bucks, plus tip. However, she had zero desire to go into this with Alexis and murmured something noncommittal.

"By the way, Margaret Roberts called yesterday," continued Alexis. "Something about the time needing to change."

The celebration for Margaret's husband was next week, so this was important information. "What exactly?"

"I told you. Something about the time." Alexis yawned and checked her phone.

Valerie set a reminder to call Margaret later. "Did you go by the office and get the boxes I stacked by the door?"

Alexis gazed up at the latticed smoked glass of the high ceiling. "I can get them now."

"You were supposed to bring them with you so we can set up before Nico Hever arrives." Nico was Roger Badgerton's executive assistant and had been her primary contact. He was also curiously intriguing for a guy she'd had limited interactions with, and entirely by phone, thanks to a work trip that had taken Nico and Roger out of town. Despite focusing solely on Malcolm's memorial, their initial conversations had been enough for her imagination, always in overdrive, to create a vision of him in her mind.

She had decided Nico Hever would be pale, with short dark hair, a long nose, and a prominent widow's peak—an expectation she suspected was influenced by his name and a picture she once saw of Niccolo Machiavelli. This wasn't fair to poor Nico, who had not once discussed the cunning ruthlessness needed to acquire and keep a city-state during their conversations about dates, venues, and guest lists. She'd also decided his shirt would be ironed and tucked in, because no one who took a sincere interest in napkin thread counts would neglect his own creases.

He would not only possess his own lint brush, but also use it regularly.

Some of these expectations had been laid to rest when Nico agreed to a video call to view the event space before booking. On the screen had been an attractive white guy with dark hair. Then he met her gaze and Valerie had been momentarily and unusually stunned into silence. It took a moment for her to place why he was familiar. Nico resembled a World War II squadron leader portrait she'd recently spotted in a museum display, with the same disciplined expression, strong bone structure, and spare features. His slate-gray eyes gave him a brooding expression, as if he was full of secrets he had no problem keeping.

She was looking forward to seeing him in person today, and not only because of those eyes. His serious attitude and clear competence were instant draws, making him not only physically appealing but also good to work with. It was a rare combination.

"Right, the tight-ass." Alexis didn't look up from her phone. "Tell him we have it under control. That's what I would say if this was my business."

But Ad Astra was not Alexis's business. Nor would Valerie say anything of the sort to Nico, since she had the impression he was under a lot of stress. He'd subtly let Valerie know that Malcolm Badgerton had been almost fanatically concerned with his reputation and status and reminded her this was the family's final farewell. Valerie understood and was ready for the challenge. She'd considered every angle. There were spreadsheets and checklists out the wazoo. She had paper trails and approvals and had accounted for every what-if she could think of.

The Malcolm Badgerton Celebration of Life was going to be perfect.

As she was thinking of a diplomatic way to ask Alexis to please not insult their bread and butter, the phone rang. It was her mother, and since her mother rarely called, she picked up immediately.

"Oh, Val, I have the most amazing news," her mother said. "Erica is getting married!"

Figures it would be about her stepsister. Valerie's free hand shook with the sudden force of the resentment she thought she'd put to rest years ago, and she clenched her fist to make it stop.

"That's wonderful!" She made sure to smile as she spoke—Ruth's trick to radiate authenticity during difficult calls. After all, love was good and weddings were great. Her older stepsister was nice enough, and almost as perfect as Valerie's mother believed.

"It's why I'm calling. She needs a wedding planner."

Because why else would Mom call? Certainly not to wish Valerie luck on today's career-defining event, which she'd probably forgotten about. The resentment swelled sluggishly, too weary to do more, and she tamped it down with her sneakered foot.

"Oh?" Ruth had made Valerie swear on a pile of vintage bridal magazines never to do an event for family, but she knew herself. If her mother wanted help, she would plan a thousand weddings. She opened her mouth to offer, but her mother kept speaking.

"Can you recommend someone?"

Valerie's gut lurched, although it was ridiculous to be hurt that she wasn't asked to do something she didn't want to do in the first place. "I have a big event starting in a few hours, but I can get her some names later this week."

Her mother sighed. "Val, you know your sister likes to plan ahead. Surely you can spare ten minutes from Aurora and get it to us today."

"Ad Astra." Her mother always got it wrong, and Erica wasn't her sister. Mom got that wrong too.

"How long has it been since you've been doing that?"

"Two years." Was she not going to pick up Valerie's comment about the event?

"Right, it was the same time Justin moved to Halifax. It's good to see you finally sticking with something. Remember when you quit that cooking class after two weeks?"

"I quit because I needed to work nights for a special event series."

"Mmm. Get Erica those names, will you? She's depending on you."

When she disconnected, Valerie inhaled so deeply it oxygenated her toes. Her mother's interest in all things Erica and, to a lesser degree, Erica's brother, Justin, and no things Valerie was nothing new. When her parents remarried, Valerie became an afterthought on both sides. She supposed it was understandable. Her mother's new husband had two children of his own who lived with them full-time. Valerie's father was busy with his second wife, and when their twins were born, Valerie had made herself useful as a babysitter and collected compliments on what a good girl she was as if they were Pokémon.

Unable to help herself, she hid in the corner to compile a list of names for Erica, then hurried to place the Badgerton family photos on the tables. Valerie lingered on one of the siblings in their twenties, a candid shot as they laughed on a dock. They looked like they belonged together and she fought off a quick pulse of envy at their easy comfort. She put the photo down as Ricky came over.

"We've got the tea bar, coffee bar, and whiskey bar here, there, and there." Ricky pointed at various spots in the room and raised an eyebrow. "I still can't believe you're having a whiskey bar at a memorial."

"Malcolm loved a good smoky single malt," said Valerie. "As for the quartet…"

"Over in that corner." Alexis jabbed a confident finger and Valerie stifled a sigh. It was supposed to be under the big window, but Alexis feeling validated would make things easier in the long run.

"Sure."

"The guest register should be near the door," said Alexis. "That's what I'd do if I were you."

The register for people to leave their memories had been hand-bound by an artisan who lived near the family cottage in the Mariposas. After signing, guests would collect booklets detailing Malcolm's founding of the Bread Company, a beloved local bakery before it became a multimillion-dollar enterprise. Valerie had to put her foot down. "It'll interfere with the flow if guests line up and block the entrance."

"Oh, look at *that*." Alexis looked over Valerie's shoulder, register forgotten, then pulled her hair up before letting it drop with a shake of her head. "Yummy. I hope he's included in the event fee."

"Don't talk about people like…" Valerie's reprimand died as she turned around. Standing in the doorway was a man backlit like a god from the heavens, so perfectly proportioned he could have stepped down from a pedestal at the Louvre.

Okay. Valerie didn't entirely blame Alexis for her inappropriate reaction, although she hoped the poor guy hadn't heard.

"Hi there," called Alexis, giving a little wave. "And you are?"

"Nico Hever," said the man—Nico—as he walked into the room. Also, there it was. Nico's voice was the outlier that made her wonder if she was wrong about him and his lint brush. It was low and he spoke slowly, as if fully confident whatever he said was worth listening to. It was the opposite of Valerie, who rushed through her sentences to outrun the inevitable interruption. Yet there was a roughness to the edges, like he could get sort of growly if he wanted, although she couldn't see him getting worked up over anything except a misplaced table setting.

She squinted to see him better and immediately decided the video call had not done him justice. Nor had it given her an immunity to those eyes, which held her gaze as if he was seeing only her. She bet he smelled good, but it wasn't until he was close enough to shake her hand that she caught the faintest whiff of citrus.

"I'm pleased to meet you in person," he said. Was he holding on a moment longer than necessary? It was probably wishful thinking.

She put herself back in professional mode, which did not involve drooling over her client's intermediary. "I'm glad you're here. Everything is under control, garbage cans and all." She couldn't help but tease him about his recent call to check the number of waste receptacles (his words).

"Good," he said. "Guests will need a place to dispose of their debris after indulging at the high-protein, gluten-free, preservative-free, organic tapas table."

"It's also locally sourced."

"I recall. Within fifty kilometers?"

"Twenty-five."

This made him laugh for the first time ever, and she was astonished that all it took was a weak joke about hors d'oeuvres. She quickly introduced Ricky, then turned to Alexis. "This is my assistant."

Alexis pushed forward to stand between them. "I'm more of a deputy. You can ask me for whatever assistance you require."

Valerie was grateful that Nico didn't react to the low purr in Alexis's voice. He merely nodded and took the event folder Valerie handed to him.

The next hour went quickly as Valerie walked Nico through the space, Alexis hovering behind. He paused to examine the display of Malcolm's museum-quality Malacca walking sticks.

"They'll make an awesome photo op for guests," enthused Alexis. "Even better than the flower wall at the nail studio."

That was about all Valerie could take. "Alexis, would you mind grabbing some sandwiches for lunch?"

"Take some from the catering platters like I did."

Why did Nico have to witness this? She shut her eyes. "Please."

"Fine, I need a break anyway. Give me the credit card."

With Alexis out of the way, Valerie was able to focus. Normally she might stress at being in such close proximity to a man who made her skin tingle, but she'd worked hard on this event and refused to be derailed by the dopamine flood that occurred when they made eye contact.

Or so she thought, until he smiled at her. It was incredible what it did to his face, transforming its cold perfection into a surprisingly intimate warmth, and satisfying because she had a sense that Nico wasn't someone who smiled often. It felt special, just for her. She took a step back and lifted the folder filled with print copies of the event plan to her chest as if that would hide the sudden pounding of her heart.

Work. It was time for work. "Shall we move to the coat check?"

Nico listened attentively and Valerie let the folder drop to her side as she relaxed into the rhythm of her tasks. It was pleasant to be with

Nico. It gave her intense satisfaction to go over everything, in part to show him she knew what she was doing, but mostly because it was gratifying to have someone appreciate the small details that made an event appear seamless. Nico cared about the importance of specifics, such as the number of roses in the arrangements (six in the small, twenty in the large), and the greenery used for filler (fern, not baby's breath).

Alexis arrived with lunch just as they finished, and haphazardly set out the food on an empty table. Valerie examined the trays, which did not hold the sandwiches she requested.

"I felt like sushi," Alexis said breezily, taking the California and kappa rolls for herself. Valerie and Ricky split the spicy salmon and tuna, while Nico politely refused. He went off to examine the selection of whiskeys Valerie had stocked on the advice of a master distiller Ruth recommended.

Alexis checked her phone. "I'm leaving at six to meet the girls," she said. "Are you coming by later?"

"I'm not sure I'll be done here." No one in their shared friend group had told her there were plans, and Valerie's last message dangled at the bottom of the group chat like a hook filled with uneaten bait. It would have been nice to be invited instead of being an afterthought. Or maybe they'd simply assumed she'd be there. She cheered and took another salmon roll. That made more sense, and she could think about whether to go later.

Right now, she had an event to run and a name to make for herself.

TWO

Nico Hever turned from the whiskey display and again surveyed the room with approval. The somewhat generic event space had been transformed into a sophisticated Pall Mall club reading room, ideal for a man who took pride in his old-fashioned outlook. Malcolm's oil portrait, a traditional sitting in the style of van Dyck, dominated the area from its place of honor near the front. The deep-red roses were decorative but acceptably masculine.

He examined the photos on the tables, set out in matching frames. It was a big day for Roger Badgerton, the Badgerton family, the Bread Company corporate entity, and by extension of all that, Nico himself. Luckily, thanks to Valerie's mix of creativity, pragmatism, and attention to detail, he was convinced the memorial would unfold without issue. The Badgertons would be able to see off their patriarch with the dutiful reverence Malcolm would have demanded and the respect for the Badgerton name he held dear.

Laughter came from the lunch table. It couldn't be easy to run a business like Ad Astra and work with people coping with the valleys rather than the peaks of life, but Valerie had surpassed his expectations. She'd dealt with Roger, and then Nico, with a compassionate sensitivity complemented by her superb knowledge and experience.

"People should leave uplifted," she'd told him in one of their early conversations. *Rather than depressed by thoughts of their own mortality* had been left unsaid, but he'd filled it in. It had been a treat to watch Valerie tie in elements of Malcolm's life. Take the heavyweight LL Bean–style canvas bags, filled with a fresh loaf of Malcolm's favorite Bread Company sourdough rye, which would be provided to guests as they left. They were the perfect memento of Malcolm, who had prided himself on his generosity (admittedly, only at a personal level and limited to his peers, since he'd fought viciously against increasing minimum wage and corporate taxes). The bags had been silk-screened with a commissioned pen-and-ink sketch, an idyllic scene of a lakeside dock with a steaming coffee cup and one of the Bread Company's distinctive honey buns balanced on the arm of a Mariposa chair. It radiated an exclusive *if-you-know-you-know* allure the guests would appreciate.

Nico adjusted his green tie in the window reflection. A woman once said he looked good in green, a casual compliment he'd hung on to for years. He'd taken more care than usual over his appearance, telling himself it was to honor Malcolm and not to impress Valerie. It was curious that a woman so filled with life had picked such a grim focus for her business. His due diligence research had uncovered Valerie's background in weddings and galas: high stress but without the added weight of heartache and bereavement.

He'd spent a lot of time over the last three weeks wondering why Valerie had chosen to embrace the worst moments of people's lives, which meant he'd spent a lot of time thinking about Valerie herself. It made him a little uncomfortable, like a kid with a crush, but he suspected this would soon fade. Work would rush back in to fill the space where Valerie had taken up more of his thoughts than seemed reasonable for a woman he barely knew.

He listened to her chat with Ricky over the sushi. The serious expression and primly clasped hands of her online corporate head-shot barely resembled the real-life woman. He didn't know if it was her personality that animated her face, or if she simply photographed terribly, but in person she dazzled in a way the camera didn't come close to capturing. Her features were fascinatingly narrow—long eyes, a thin nose, and a mouth with delicate lips he found sexier than a magazine-perfect pout—but it was her presence that caused him to stumble over his polite greeting. A light shone from her, and when he'd reached out to shake her hand earlier, part of him wondered if it would linger on his skin like bioluminescence on a night beach. Her black pants clung to generous curves and the white shirt made her skin glow.

She glanced over Ricky's shoulder and smiled at him, instantly decimating any idea of his crush fading. Confirmed: He would ask her for coffee when this was all done. Or drinks. Dinner. Anything. All of it.

Hoping he was staying professional—although he was already calculating if it was inappropriate to ask her out right after the event, or if he should at least wait for tomorrow—he was about to join them at the table when his phone rang. Expecting it to be Roger, who had an allergy to texting, Nico was surprised to see it was his middle sister. Kimmy rarely called, as she preferred to communicate via memes that he often found incomprehensible. He moved to the corner and answered.

"Stefanie and I have been talking," she said.

Those six words were enough to ruin his day although Kimmy and Stefanie left him out of conversations all the time. While he disliked talk simply for the sake of it, he'd felt empty when he'd heard them giggling behind Kimmy's door as a kid or seen them leaving to go somewhere without him. As an adult, the only thing that had changed was that he'd gotten better at hiding his feelings.

Which meant he did not say, *What else is new*, but instead acted like a grown man and said, "Talking about what?"

"Mom and Dad. Their fortieth wedding anniversary is coming and we need to mark the occasion."

"Okay." He wasn't sure why she was calling. His two older sisters—mostly Stefanie, to be fair—rarely listened to him.

"Stef says she's tired of being the one to plan family stuff and wants you to step up." Kimmy's tone said, *Don't shoot the messenger.*

"I'm working on a project with a tight deadline." He wasn't, no more than usual, but he resented Stefanie acting as if he was the one slacking when she refused to listen to any idea he ever had to offer. What was the point of contributing if he was only going to get shot down?

"You always have work."

"My job is busy."

"Mom gets upset when you miss the biweekly family dinner. Dad does, too, but he won't say anything because he's a human clam." Kimmy sounded serious, which was not her usual default setting.

"You know I was out of town, and before that I was sick."

"Before that, you were at an event and before that, blah blah. That's a pattern of avoidance, in case you didn't notice."

This was true enough. He was tired of feeling like he didn't belong, while forcing a smile through Stefanie's endless teasing. The relief when he'd missed the first dinner, and then the second, and so on, had been enough to overwhelm the guilt he felt from staying away.

"I'm worried about you," Kimmy said. "You don't have any life." At least she'd let the family thing go, although he wasn't sure this was an improvement.

He was going to say he had Roger, but decided that didn't negate her point.

"You haven't gone on vacation in years," she added.

"I was in Edmonton last week."

"Did you see anything besides the inside of a conference room?"

"I drove by the legislature building."

"Wow, living life to its fullest."

"It's *work.*" He ran his finger along his collar, not liking this discussion and itching to join Valerie as she debated some point with Ricky.

"Correct, you're an employee. For money. Not a friend, or a member of the family. It's like you forget there's a difference."

That stung, but he rallied. "I have a job I like, with a boss who appreciates me. I also get paid well. It's natural to put more into what I do."

"Just because you've basically hit the golden trifecta of employment doesn't make it impervious to critique," she said.

His phone beeped with another call. "I have to go. Bye, Kimmy."

"The anniversary, Nico. It's important."

"I'll send some ideas." There, he could contribute but keep his distance from Stefanie's digs.

"Send them to both of us. Me and Steffy."

"Fine." At least if he kept it to email he could delete the messages when Stefanie started inevitably being Stefanie. The phone beeped again.

"Thank you." She paused. "Hey."

"What?"

"Like it or not, a good job is only a job, but we'll always be your family. I love you."

She disconnected. Kimmy had no patience for the drawn-out farewells that their mother and Stefanie deemed necessary, a trait Nico appreciated, especially with Penny Badgerton-Willis waiting on the other line.

"Where are you?" she demanded when he picked up. Roger's sister was Malcolm's only daughter and eldest child, the self-proclaimed matriarch of the family, and a woman unused to hearing the word *no*.

"Helping set up for today." Roger frequently told him it wasn't his job to deal with Penny, but Nico considered protecting Roger's peace of mind as part of his role. Sometimes, that meant from his own family.

"Is the planner there? I want to talk to her."

"I can pass on a message." Running interference from Penny was the least he could do as Valerie finished setting up.

"Never mind. I still can't believe we're doing this gauche pass-around thing, like some low-rent suburban Christmas office party," Penny said. "A formal meal is the correct way to honor my father."

Nico had heard this complaint several times since the decision had been made two weeks ago, and he stuck to the party line. "Roger agreed this was more suited to Malcolm's personality," he said as he watched Alexis berate a member of the catering staff for apparently asking a question. "He hated rubber chicken dinners."

"As if I would allow chicken at Dad's memorial when capon and pheasant exist. A quail would do. Duck at a stretch, although the quality has plummeted since every taco restaurant in the city put it on their menu."

"There's a smoked duck canapé on the grazing board," he said to be difficult.

"Grazing boards, my God."

Nico fell back on his usual method of dealing with Penny: agreeing she was right. "I understand," he said as he watched Alexis move a table away from its proper spot to where it would block access to the entrance. It hadn't taken Nico long to realize she was the embodiment of the Dunning-Krueger effect and would require monitoring.

"You might as well serve those jalapeño poppers from the grocery store."

"I hear you." There was no point telling Penny it was too late to make changes. She had the rich woman's belief that anything was possible, given enough money.

"This is an important day and I should have known better than to trust Roger with it. I would have planned this properly myself if my gallery hadn't been launching a new artist. And of course I had to get the dogs settled on their diets. I'll be there in an hour to check on things." She hung up.

Nico wasn't worried about Penny's arrival. Valerie had it all together. He glanced down at the plan she'd given him, labeled neatly with his name, and went to move the table back to where it should be. As Valerie joined him to check through the final details, he relaxed. For the first time in his career, he didn't need to worry about an event.

And he would definitely ask her out before he left today.

THREE

Showtime was in fifty-six minutes, and Valerie, in her gray suit, had decided to stop worrying if she was in fact looking dowdy. Her goal was not to win the best-dressed award at her client's celebration of life, and her outfit was perfectly suitable, if dull.

Was it dull? Too late now.

She turned her attention to more pertinent topics, like whether the room was in complete readiness, which it was. The string quartet was tuning up in the corner, preparing to play an inoffensive selection of Mozart's greatest hits. The catering staff had finished knotting their ties. She checked the signing pen for the register, then the backup pen, and the *backup* backup pen to make sure all three worked. They did. Her stomach was starting to get the flutters that normally preceded a big event. She'd had enough of these feelings over the years to know they would fade once people started arriving and her anticipation shifted to participation.

Valerie looked around for Nico. She'd been doing that all day, searching for him and feeling an intense satisfaction to find that often he'd been doing the same to her. This time, though, he was standing in the corner frowning at his phone, which cause a small beat of disappointment.

She glanced up at the ceiling fans as sweat beaded on her forehead.

"It's getting hot in here," she said to Ricky, waiting for him to finish humming the expected follow-up song line before she continued. "Can we turn those fans on?"

"Good idea. I'm overheating."

"Are you kidding?" demanded Alexis. "It's freezing."

Ricky studied Valerie as he wiped his face. "You don't look so good."

"She's always that color," Alexis said.

The honor table caught Valerie's attention. "Alexis, did you secure that portrait like I asked you?"

"I'm not sure how. You'd do it so much better." Alexis left to busy herself organizing the Bread Company booklets.

There were fifty minutes left, but Valerie knew from experience that the first guests would start to arrive in twenty, and the Badgertons even earlier. She turned on the slideshow of Malcolm's triumphs to play in the background and was about to fix the portrait when the door opened to reveal Roger Badgerton in a navy suit and crisp white shirt. He paused and looked around as Valerie watched, stomach getting tighter, until he finally nodded, his gaze lingering on the painting of his father. Behind him was an older blond woman, Roger's sister, Penny Badgerton-Willis. Valerie hung back, not wanting to disturb the family as they prepared themselves for the celebration of life. She'd learned it was best to give people some space before greeting them.

Nico joined Valerie and looked at her closely. "Are you okay?" he asked.

She wasn't, now that he mentioned it. The room was still too warm, and the butterflies in her stomach had spread, along with a faint nausea when she caught a whiff of the food. Nico didn't need to hear that, though. "All good," she said. "Feeling one hundred percent."

"Nico, come," called Penny.

He crossed the room to where Penny was waiting. Valerie's wellness percentage might be closer to fifty than a hundred, but she could muscle through for the next few hours. She had to. Planning only went so far in determining an event's success, and managing all of the last-minute issues that inevitably popped up could make or break the experience. At one of Ruth's weddings, a guest had inadvertently stepped on a wasps' nest, which could have been a disaster had Ruth not trotted across the lawn in her stilettos with a huge plastic tub to cover the nest without batting an eye. Luckily, due to the advanced age of many guests, Ruth also had a St. John Ambulance crew stationed discreetly in one of the upper bedrooms who could take care of any stings.

Valerie wasn't worried about wasps, but she suddenly had grave doubts about the freshness of the sushi Alexis had fetched for lunch. Her stomach lurched thinking about it.

Oh no.

No. No, no, no.

"Valerie?" asked Ricky, coming up. His face was sweaty. "It's like a sauna here."

She didn't have time to answer. She clamped her hand over her mouth and ran to the staff washroom. This couldn't be happening. Not today.

A few minutes later, the door swung open behind her. "Eww," said Alexis. "Gross. At least pull your hair back. People are arriving. What should I do?"

"Can you deal with it?" Valerie managed to gasp.

Alexis disappeared, then came back. "I can't find Ricky."

"Please," begged Valerie, now on her knees. "You have the plan. Figure it out."

This time it was five minutes. "This is revolting," Alexis observed. "I can hear you in the hall."

Valerie struggled to her feet. "You can do it," she whispered to her red-faced and wild-eyed reflection in the mirror. "You have an event to run. You have clients to impress. Presentations to queue up."

"Are you coming or what?"

She had... Valerie slumped against the sink as waves of nausea and realization hit her.

She had to get home.

She couldn't run an event feeling like this, let alone deal with the ick factor of being ill around a crowd of people. At least it was obviously food poisoning and nothing contagious. Ricky and Alexis would have to keep the event on track. Although she hated the idea of it, she could ask Nico to help out as well. She suspected he'd rather step in to make the event a success than stay in his lane.

The door flew open. It was Ricky, looking green and clutching his stomach. "Fuck," he said before she heard him run toward the stairs.

Excellent. Just fantastic. Ricky had eaten the same thing as her. She listened to a door slam and it felt like the shutting down of her career.

No. She was being ridiculous and melodramatic. Nico and Alexis remained functional. She could work with that. Valerie did a body scan and decided she had about ninety seconds to safely get to Nico before she escaped home. After scrubbing her hands, mouth and face, and then her mouth again, she straightened her clothes and went out to the main room, doing her best to walk normally. A quick chat with Nico, another with Alexis, and she would be out in the fresh air. She could do it.

The room was filling up, and while the planner in her was pleased at the turnout, that meant it was harder to find Nico. Finally, she caught sight of him but had to take a break to sit down and get herself under control. She cringed back as Penny strode by, looking at her phone. There was no way she could deal with one of the Badgertons in her current state. Penny looked right past her to Nico.

"Nico, whatever you're doing can wait. The dog sitter just called. She can't bring Julius and Augustus to the vet, so you have to take them. I had to wait a week for this appointment, if you can believe it."

"I'm needed here," said Nico. Valerie leaned forward and tried to think about anything besides food.

"What did we pay the event planner for if not to run the event?" Penny examined the room with grudging respect. "I must say though, this is better than I expected."

Valerie had done adequately well. High praise, indeed.

Roger joined them and Penny turned, her hair swinging in an elegant arc. None of them noticed Valerie and she was pitifully grateful because she didn't trust what would happen if she had to open her mouth. "Roger, I need Nico to take the dogs to the vet. This is important to me, and it's not like I can send John."

"Pen, seriously?"

"Nico's not part of the family. He doesn't need to be here."

"I'd be happy to go," said Nico. Go? He couldn't leave. Valerie needed him. She looked around, frantic, as her stomach tensed again. If Nico left and Ricky was out…she'd have to stay here to support Alexis.

Penny gave a brisk nod as if this resolution was never in doubt. "Lina will text you the information. Oh, there's Tracey Jefferies. I'm surprised she bothered to come."

Then she was gone. Roger sighed. "I'm sorry, Nico, but I need her off my case about the damn dogs so I can pay attention to Dad's friends."

"It's not a problem."

Valerie sat bolt upright, hand on her stomach. She'd run out of time and dashed up to Ricky's private office, where Ricky himself was grabbing his bag.

"I'm sick," he said, face pale. "Like, bad. I gotta go."

"Me too," said Valerie, trying not to sound pathetic.

"Hot take, but maybe you should also leave. I called Josette. She's my assistant manager and she'll be here in less than an hour."

"I can't. I have to run this event."

"Let your assistant take care of it," he advised. Then he closed his eyes and held onto the desk, swaying. "Sorry."

He was gone before she could speak, but that was fine. She needed a moment of privacy and was happy to not fight Ricky for the use of his washroom. After rinsing out her mouth again, she checked her phone to see a text from Nico, apologizing for having to leave "due to an urgent matter." *I have no concerns about how well Malcolm's event will run without me,* he'd added.

She relaxed slightly. He was right. She'd done a lot of work to make sure this would go smoothly. She would stay here in Ricky's office and run interference. It would basically be like being downstairs in the heart of the event herself. Everything was going to be fine.

She leaned over again. Or not. At least this time, she managed to pull back her hair.

ACKNOWLEDGMENTS

This book had its genesis on a hot, dusty day in August 2015. I was in Beauville, in Paris, and talking on the phone to my agent, Carrie Pestritto, about perfume. It all sounds far more sophisticated and fancy than it was, and why we were talking about work while I was *on vacation in Paris*, I have no idea. We agreed a book about perfume sounded fun, and I went away and wrote a historical romance about an alchemist in the time of Anne Boleyn. That book didn't get past my laptop and was resurrected years later through its own particular alchemy to become *The Library of Flowers*.

But the book would not be here without that conversation and the help of many people.

To my agent, Carrie Pestritto: Thank you for believing in me all those years ago and your occasional gentle and then not-so-gentle reminders that we should do something with the perfume book I refused to show you.

To my fabulous Sourcebooks editor, Mary Altman: Thank you for loving this story and working tirelessly to make it the best we could. And, as a fellow perfume lover, for your recommendations on the fragrance front!

Thank you to the Sourcebooks team: Cristina Arreola, Molly

Waxman, Jessica Thelander, Erin Fitzsimmons, Laura Boren, Tara Jaggers, Stephanie Rocha, and so many more.

Thank you to Sija Hong: Your beautiful artwork made me gasp out loud.

Thank you to my parents, Brian and Sharon: for showing me what a partnership of equals should look like.

Thank you to Nyla: always and forever.

And finally, the most heartfelt there-is-no-way-to-repay-you thank-you to my husband, Elliott, who picked up the slack when I was writing, who only complained a bit when my perfume collection filled up the shelves, and for being the first man to tell me the scent of my perfume always reminded him of me.

ABOUT THE AUTHOR

L. C. Chu, who also writes romance as Lily Chu, is the critically acclaimed author of eight books, including titles in women's fiction, romance, and young adult. Her romance books have been released in audio as Audible Originals, performed by Phillipa Soo, and translation rights have been sold in nine languages.

She lives in Toronto, Canada, with her family, two cats, and far too many (yet not enough) books.

Website: lilychuauthor.com
Instagram: @lilychuauthor